THE HERODIAN
TRILOGY

The Herodian Trilogy covers the years 35 BCE to 73
CE. the most eventful and tragic period in the history
of the Jews, which affected not only the Jews but had
a tremendous impact on Western Civilization.

by David Mandel

Published by Damkor Books
Gan Hashikmim 11, Savyon 5690500, Israel
Telephone + 972 54 229 0204
Fax + 972 3 534 3270
E-mail enfoque@netvision.net.il

Copyright @ David Mandel, 2021
ISBN: 9798719853055

To Ruth

always in my heart

Contents

Introduction..1

In King Herod's Court
1. Tutor to Cleopatra's children......................... 7
2. A visit to the Museum................................. 13
3. In the Serapeum.......................................21
4. The Lighthouse of Alexandria.........................27
5. Mark Antony's announcement..........................33
6. From Alexandria to Ostia............................. 39
7. From Ostia to Rome..................................47
8. In Octavius' house..................................51
9. Lucius the butcher.................................. 55
10. The scroll with Cicero's speeches.................... 59
11. In a Roman public bath............................. 63
12. In Suburra..69
13. Choosing candidates for consul...................... 71
14. The latrine near the Forum..........................73
15. Election of the consuls............................. 77
16. In the Roman Senate................................ 81
17. Secretary to Mark Antony........................... 85
18. In Alexandria's Jewish Quarter...................... 89
19. Octavius defeats Mark Antony........................ 93
20. From Alexandria to Ptolemais........................ 101
21. In Ptolemais.. 105
22. King Herod... 109
23. Rabi Hillel... 113
24. The three Jewish philosophies.......................117
25. A tour to Herod's palaces........................... 121
26. Herod's autobiography – First Part...................127
27. Herod's autobiography – Second Part................. 131
28. Herod's autobiography – Third Part..................135
29. Herod's autobiography – Fourth Part.................139
30. The execution of Hyrcanus...........................143
31. Herod's autobiography – Fifth Part..................147
32. Herod's autobiography – Sixth Part................. 151

I

Contents

33. The meeting of Herod with Octavius................... 155
34. Family problems................................159
35. The deaths of Alexandra and Costobarus.................163
36. Herod marries the second Mariamne.................... 167
37. The construction of the Temple.......................171
38. Alexander and Aristobulus go to Rome..................175
39. Alexander and Aristobulus return from Rome...........179
40. Herod's friendship with Agrippa.........................181
41. Antipater returns to the palace..........................183
42. Salome makes trouble...................................187
43. The visit of Archelaus, king of Cappadocia............. 191
44. The two brothers are sent to prison.....................193
45. The execution of the two brothers...................... 199
46. The death of Pheroras.................................203
47. Antipater is sent to prison............................207
48. Herod's death.. 211
49. The massacre in the Temple...........................215
50. Archelaus and Antipas dispute the throne............... 217
51. Augustus' decision,,,,,,,,,,,............................ 221
52. A visit to Augustus' house............................. 225
53. An evening in Augustus' house......................... 229
54. In Antioch..233
55. The death of Augustus' grandsons...................... 237
56. Augustus' testimony................................... 239
57. Livia's testimony...................................... 241
58. Julia's testimony......................................245
59. Tiberius' testimony....................................247
60. The death of Augustus.................................249
    Epilogue...253

The memoirs of King Agrippa the Great

1. I am Agrippa, Herod's grandson...................... 257
2. We move to Rome.....................................261
3. A walk in Rome.......................................267
4. A visit to Lady Livia................................. 271
5. My friends in Rome................................... 277
6. My school education in Rome........................281

Contents

7. The Jewish Community of Rome........................283
8. A lecture about the Jews.............................. 285
9. Germanicus' triumphs................................ 289
10. A visit to my friend Claudius....................... 291
11. Tiberius and his son Drusus.........................297
12. Germanicus' tragic end.............................. 301
13. Marriages...303
14. My friend Drusus' death.............................307
15. Antipas celebrates his birthday.....................311
16. Antipas gives me a job...............................317
17. The carpenter's son..................................319
18. I am a market inspector............................. 321
19. In Antioch... 325
20. An overnight stay in prison......................... 329
21. In Alexandria.. 335
22. My new best friend: Caligula........................ 341
23. A stopover in Alexandria.............................353
24. Herodias pays for her envy..........................355
25. Caligula's madness...................................359
26. Apion incites hatred against the Jews...............363
27. The assassination of Caligula...................... 367
28. Claudius is proclaimed Emperor......................371
29. I am the king of Judea..............................377
30. My problems with Vibius Marcus..................... 381
    Epilogue – Letter from Vibius Marcus to Claudius... 383

The War of the Jews against Rome

    Preface...387
1. A short autobiography............................... 389
2. A description of the Temple.........................393
3. My visit to Rome..................................... 397
4. Back in Judea.. 409
5. The beginning of the rebellion......................413
6. Agrippa tries to appease the people.................415
7. The rebels massacre the Roman garrison..............419
8. The rebels defeat a Roman army..................... 421
9. Commander of Galilee.................................423

Contents

10. I organize the defense of Galilee............................ 425
11. Oposition and revolts....................................... 427
12. About the Roman army...................................... 433
13. The siege of Yodfat... 435
14. I surrender to the Romans.................................. 443
15. My prophecy to Vespasian................................. 449
16. Vespasian... 453
17. The Battle of the Lake...................................... 457
18. The siege of Gamla... 461
19. The conquest of Giscala.................................... 465
20. Anarchy in Jerusalem...................................... 467
21. The Idumeans come to Jerusalem.......................... 469
22. The Zealots' reign of terror............................... 473
23. Vespasian postpones the attack on Jerusalem............. 475
24. The rise of John of Giscala................................ 477
25. Simon bar Giora arrives in Jerusalem..................... 479
26. My prophecy to Vespasian comes true..................... 481
27. Eleazar ben Simeon forms a third faction................. 485
28. Description of Jerusalem................................... 487
29. The Romans surround Jerusalem........................... 491
30. The siege of Jerusalem 495
31. The Romans capture the Third Wall....................... 499
32. The Romans capture the Second Wall..................... 503
33. My speech to the defenders of Jerusalem................. 505
34. The famine in Jerusalem................................... 509
35. Titus crucifies thousands of Jews......................... 511
36. The rebels destroy the Roman ramps...................... 513
37. The Romans surround Jerusalem with a wall.............. 515
38. Jerusalem becomes hell.................................... 517
39. The Romans conquer the Antonia fortress................ 519
40. The rebels refuse to surrender............................ 523
41. The rebels set a trap....................................... 529
42. The horrors of the famine................................. 531
43. The 9th of Av.. 533
44. Titus' speech to the crowd................................ 537
45. The Romans conquer the Upper City...................... 539
46. The Romans complete the conquest of Jerusalem........ 541

Contents

47. The Romans dispose of the survivors.....................543
48. Titus awards prizes to the soldiers.........................545
49. John of Giscala and Simon bar Giora captured...........547
50. Anti-Jewish riots in Antioch.............................549
51. Celebrations of triumph............................,........551
52. The conquest of Masada.................................553
    Epilogue...559
    A note to the reader..563
    Bibliography..564

Books by David Mandel

Long was the road..565
The Saga of the Jews 567
The Secret of the Santamaria family.......................569
Joseph's Version..570
The Lyre and the Sword...................................572
The Art and Life of Ruth Mandel..........................573
The Ultimate Who's Who in the Bible....................575
Goliath's mother...577
Family matters...578
Adventures and misadventures of Luis Cabrejos.........579
Three Peruvian stories....................................580
Doña Maria and the School Inspector....................581
The autobiography of Moses..............................582
Operation Balaam's mule..................................583
The Book of Job modernized: a parody..................584

Contents

Introduction

The Herodian Trilogy covers the years 35 BCE to 73 CE. the most eventful and tragic period in the history of the Jews, which affected not only the Jews but had a tremendous influence on Western Civilization. Never again, until the 20th century, did the Jews experience such traumatic and pivotal events.

The first book, *In the court of King Herod,* relates the history of Herod, the greatest builder in antiquity, the constructor of the Temple in Jerusalem, which, according to the chroniclers, was one of the largest, most magnificent, and most beautiful buildings in the Roman world. The Western Wall, today's most sacred place for the Jews, is what remains of the retaining walls that increased the area at the top of the Mount.

Its narrator, Nicholas of Damascus, a historian, diplomat, orator, statesman, and philosopher, was, like other people mentioned in this Trilogy, a real person. He was born in Damascus in 64 BCE and died in Rome in 16 CE at the age of eighty.

Nicholas was the son of a renowned orator and lawyer, a member of one of Damascus' most prominent families. He received a thorough education in Greek schools in Syria. From an early age, Nicholas wrote tragedies and comedies. He also studied philosophy and wrote a treatise on Aristotle.

During his youth, he was the tutor of Mark Antony and Cleopatra's children. After the couple's death, he went to Jerusalem, where he became a personal friend and adviser of King Herod and shared the king's interest in rhetoric, philosophy, and politics. He also carried out important diplomatic missions. He spent his last years in Rome, where he became a close friend of Emperor Augustus.

His works have come down to us only in fragments. They include a universal history of the world in 144 volumes, Herod's biography, Augustus' biography, comedies, tragedies, autobiography, and philosophical treatises. His history books served as a source and inspiration to the historian Josephus Flavius.

The second book, *Memoirs of Agrippa,* is told by Marcus Julius Agrippa (born 11 BCE, died 44 CE, at the age of 54), Herod's grandson, better known as Agrippa the Great. He was educated in Rome alongside Drusus, the son of Emperor Tiberius.

On the death of Drusus, Agrippa, who had been recklessly extravagant and was deeply in debt, was obliged to leave Rome, fleeing to the fortress of Malatha, south of the Dead Sea. There, it was said, he contemplated suicide. His uncle and brother-in-law Herod Antipas, tetrarch of Galilee and Perea, put him in charge of the market of Tiberias with a small yearly income. But after quarreling with Antipas, he fled to Lucius Pomponius Flaccus, Governor of Syria.

Soon afterward, through information provided by his brother Aristobulus he was convicted, of having received a bribe from some people who wished to purchase his influence with the proconsul, and chose to flee. As he was about to sail for Italy, he was arrested in connection with a debt he owed to Caesar's treasury but made his escape and reached Alexandria, where his wife succeeded in receiving a loan from a prominent Jew.

Agrippa returned to Italy and became friends with Caligula. A "freedman", a slave that he had freed, denounced him for expressing a wish for Tiberius' death. The Emperor sent Agrippa to prison, but Caligula set him free after Tiberius' death and made him king of the Golan Heights and other territories. Caligula also allowed Agrippa to use the title "Friend of Caesar", that many years before had been given to his grandfather, Herod.

After Caligula was assassinated, Agrippa convinced the Roman Senate to name his friend Claudius, Caligula's uncle, as Emperor. Claudius rewarded him with more territories, which made Agrippa one of the East's most powerful kings. His domain was as extensive as Herod the Great's kingdom, but in contrast to his hated grandfather, Agrippa was loved by his people for his piety and generosity.

2

He began building a third wall around Jerusalem, which Emperor Claudius prevented him from completing.

He was being acclaimed by the people in the Caesarea stadium when he was suddenly overcome with violent pains and died after five days.

The narrator of the third book, *The War of the Jews against the Roman Empire,* is Josephus Flavius (Joseph ben Matityahu), who was born in Jerusalem in 37 CE and died in Rome in 100 CE). He participated in the Jewish war against the mighty Roman Empire's army, led by General Vespasian. The defeat was one of the most traumatic events in the Jewish people's history.

Josephus belonged to the priestly caste and claimed that he descended from the royal family of the Hasmoneans on his mother's side. He initially fought against the Romans in Galilee, but he became their interpreter and advisor after he was captured. After Vespasian became Emperor in 69 CE, he granted Josephus his freedom, at which time Josephus assumed the Emperor's family name of Flavius. He settled in Rome and devoted his time to writing the history of the Jewish people and the war of the Jews against Rome.

The outcome of the war changed the history of the Jews and transformed their religion. It also converted Christianity from a Jewish sect to a separate religion.

The destruction of the Temple meant a complete change in the Jewish religion. Until then, the cult was based on animal sacrifices performed by a priestly caste. When the Temple was burned down by the Romans, the Jewish religion could have disappeared, but, instead, it had a remarkable transformation. Synagogues that were built in all the localities where Jews lived replaced the destroyed Temple of Jerusalem. The fulfillment of the Written Law's commandments (the Torah) and the Oral Law (later compiled in the Talmud) replaced the animal sacrifices performed by the priests in the Temple.

Today's Judaism (which historians call "Rabbinic Judaism"), is different from the Judaism that existed until the

Second Temple's destruction. It can be said, in our current terms, that the Jewish religion became democratic.

Before the destruction of the Temple, the only participation of a Jew, who did not belong to the priestly caste, (apart from the pilgrimages to Jerusalem during the religious festivals) in religious worship and ritual was to bring a bird or animal to the Temple for a priest to sacrifice it.

After the destruction of the Temple, any Jew over the age of 13 may lead the community's prayer and read the Torah. The priestly caste lost its importance by losing its function and was replaced by rabbis (the literal translation of rabbi is "teacher," a scholar in Jewish law, who is usually chosen by his community to lead the synagogue),

The defeat of the Jews and the destruction of Jerusalem and the Temple facilitated the spread of Christianity, initially just a small Jewish sect whose base was in Jerusalem before the destruction of the Temple.

The following effects contributed to converting a Jewish sect into Christianity:

- The fact that the Christians did not participate in the war against Rome caused a separation between traditional Jews and believers in Jesus.
- The destruction of the Temple made unnecessary the participation of Christians in the Temple's cult and the subsequent religious rites of the Jews.
- The fact that the followers of Jesus stopped considering Jerusalem as its religious center allowed it to spread and become universal.
- The destruction of Jerusalem and the Temple gave Christianity powerful propaganda arguments in favor of their beliefs and against the traditional Jewish religion.

The destruction of the Temple was attributed by the Christians to God's punishment of the Jews for not having accepted Jesus. This assumption was one of the foundations of the anti-Semitism prejudice that exists till this day, mutated in diverse expressions, racist, economic, and political.

In the Court of King Herod: The Memoirs of Nicholas of Damascus

The events related in this book took place between 35 BCE and 14 CE

Chapter 1
Tutor to Cleopatra's children

Caesar Augustus died yesterday, and already there are whispered rumors in Rome that his wife Livia poisoned him. He was the last to part of the three great men who honored me with the title of friend, General Mark Antony, King Herod, and Emperor Augustus.

Today, when, pen in hand, I write down these memoirs, my greatest pride is to have been the advisor and confidant of King Herod.

Many ask me if it is true that Herod killed his favorite wife and three of his children. Of course, it is true! But, ask yourself honestly, are we all perfect? He did kill them, but he had his reasons. If you agree or disagree with them, that is something else.

Rumors circulate in some circles that Herod killed the children of the city of Bethlehem. Before I proceed, I wish to clarify this matter. Did Herod kill many people? Yes! Did he kill members of his family? Again, yes! But, he never killed the children of Bethlehem. I am the author of the king's official biography, and I can attest that these rumors have no historical basis.

My name is Nicholas. I am a descendant of Greeks who settled in Damascus after the death of Alexander the Great. Seventy-eight years ago, one month before I was born, General Pompey conquered Syria, my native country, and annexed it to Rome. Thus I was born with the best gift that any person can hope to receive: Roman citizenship.

I never married, nor did I have children. I have been a historian, philosopher, orator, dramatist, and diplomat during my long life. I speak Greek, Latin, Aramaic, Arabic, Egyptian, and Hebrew. I am the author of a universal history of the world consisting of one hundred and forty-four volumes. My biography of Herod pleased Emperor Augustus so much that he gave me a generous gift, the house where I live now, in District XIV of Rome, across the Tiber River.

My father belonged to one of the most distinguished and wealthy families in Damascus. He wanted me to have the best education. To this end, he went to Athens and brought back with him Philip the Macedonian, the leading Greek philosopher, and teacher at that time.

I showed an amazing aptitude for learning. When I was not yet thirty years old, my fame as a philosopher, historian, and writer had spread throughout the civilized world, from Egypt to Rome. Several of my works, especially my *Commentaries on Aristotle,* are considered essential reading in the most prestigious academies of the Empire.

Imagine my pride when I received an invitation from General Mark Antony to come to Alexandria, Egypt's capital, and be the tutor of the children he had with Queen Cleopatra. I accepted immediately.

Two weeks later, I boarded a ship in Beirut and, a few days later, I arrived in Alexandria.

An escort of Roman soldiers met me at the port with trumpets and unsheathed swords and took me to the Royal Palace, Mark Antony, and Cleopatra's residence.

Cleopatra received me in the Throne Room and greeted me in Greek. This did not surprise me, as I knew that Egypt's royal family descended from Ptolemy, one of Alexander the Great's Greek generals. What did strike me was that Cleopatra spoke to her maid in Egyptian, a language that her predecessors had always refused to speak due to their feelings of superiority over the native inhabitants. The maid bowed to the Queen and left the room.

I looked at Cleopatra to determine if the fame of her allure was justified. She was of medium height. Her hair was black, her face oval-shaped, and her eyes blue like a cloudless summer sky. Her voice was sweet and musical. I guessed she was about thirty-five years old. I knew that many people considered her beautiful, but my first impression was that her nose was too prominent and her breasts too big. Naturally, all

8

this is a matter of personal taste. The fact is that both Julius Caesar and Mark Antony, men who had well-deserved reputations for womanizing, fell in love with Cleopatra, probably more because of her character and intelligence than for her physical beauty. As time went by, I came to feel a great admiration for her brilliant intellect, erudition, and administrative and political skills that allowed her to prolong Egypt's independence for a few years more.

During the following weeks, I learned that Cleopatra had become Queen when she was a teenager, seventeen years old, and had married her brother, Ptolemy, according to the ancient tradition. The marriage lasted until Cleopatra overthrew her brother and had him killed. She then had a love affair with Julius Caesar that resulted in a son named Caesarion. After Caesar's murder in Rome, Cleopatra fell in love with Mark Antony, the great love of her life.

But, back to my story. The maid returned with a teenager and three small children.

"Nicholas, these are my children. The oldest is Caesarion, the twins are Selene, the girl, and Helios, the boy, and this cute one is Philadelphus, my youngest, who is two years old," said Cleopatra. Turning to the children, she said to them, "Meet Nicholas of Damascus, who will be your tutor. I want you to treat him with the respect that he deserves. Say welcome to him and then return to your rooms."

The children bowed to me, kissed their mother, and left the room accompanied by their maid.

"Nicholas, my soldiers will escort you to the house that I have assigned to you. Rest for a few hours, and come tonight to the palace to dine with us", Cleopatra said with a smile.

Ten soldiers armed with spears awaited outside the palace gate and took me to my new abode. Five soldiers marched ahead of me and five behind. They led me to the Greek district (Alexandria is divided into three districts: Greek, Jewish, and Egyptian), to a beautiful house set amidst a large garden. Servants and slaves welcomed me at the front door and showed me to my room. I read for a while and then rested in the softest bed I ever had. When it became dark, I returned to the palace.

The guards at the entrance had orders to receive me. They led me to a room where maidens stripped me naked and rubbed my body with oil. Then, they dressed me in a luxurious robe and took me to the palace's dining room. It was a vast room illuminated by great chandeliers lit with perfumed candles. Frescoes showing scenes of the Nile River adorned the walls. On one side of the room, a band of musicians played the harp, lyre, cymbal, flute, and tambourine.

It seemed to me that there were more than one hundred guests crowded in the dining room. The numerous servants who carried trays laden with food and wine jars made it awkward to move around. There was a bronze sculpture in the middle of the room. It represented an ass carrying two baskets; one contained green olives, and the other black olives.

Along the walls were couches where the guests reclined and ate. On the tables were milk jugs, pitchers of wine, and dishes of pork meat fried in olive oil and seasoned with fragrant blends of herbs, pepper, and nuts. Other plates contained sauces of vinegar, honey, pepper, herbs, and spices. The pungent odor of *garum*, a dish considered a delicacy in Egypt, filled the air. It consisted of an intensely flavored sauce made with fish waste left to soak in saltwater for several weeks.

Cleopatra was reclining on one of the couches. A man at her side sat a man who was caressing her while drinking a glass of *mulsum*, an intoxicating mixture of boiled wine and honey. It was Mark Antony, the most famous general of Rome.

Cleopatra saw me and whispered something in Mark Antony's ear. The general looked at me with curiosity and made me a sign to approach.

"Welcome, Nicholas. I want you to meet Mark Antony, my husband and father of your pupils", said Cleopatra.

"So, you are Nicholas of Damascus. You are younger than I imagined, but I hope you will justify your fame, and my children will benefit from your teachings", exclaimed Mark Antony.

"I will do everything that I can to satisfy Your Majesty and Your Excellency," I answered.

"I am sure of that," said Cleopatra, "but now I want you to enjoy the evening. Enjoy the music, try the delicious dishes that my cooks have prepared, and mingle with my guests. I expect you to be tomorrow at noon to teach your pupils."

"With your permission, Your Majesty." I bowed to them and went in search of an unoccupied couch.

I found an empty couch near the royal couple; I lied on it and ate the food that the servants brought while I listened to the songs played by the musicians. I could not take my eyes off the Egyptian Queen and her husband, the Roman general.

Mark Antony was a stocky man, about fifty years of age, with curly brown hair, cut in the Roman style. His handsome masculine features explained his success with women. He had been married five times, including his current wife, Cleopatra, whom he had married without bothering to divorce Octavia, his fourth wife, thus violating the Roman law that forbids bigamy.

I had heard so much about Mark Antony that, before I met him, I almost felt as if I knew him personally. It was different seeing him in front of me. I knew that he had been a close friend of Julius Caesar, and now, after defeating the conspirators who killed Caesar, he shared the government of the Roman domains with Octavius, the adopted son of the slain dictator. Seeing him in Egypt, so far from the Senate in Rome, the center of world power, made me think that if one day there would be a conflict between the two leaders, the fact that Octavius was in Rome would give him a decisive advantage over Mark Antony.

As one of the guests explained to me, the dinner was to celebrate the successful military campaign of Mark Antony that had culminated in the conquest of the kingdom of Armenia. In another week or two, the traditional victory procession with which the Romans celebrated the victories of their generals would take place in the main avenue of Alexandria,

That night, I confess, I consumed more wine than food. It was already dawn when I left the palace and went home. On the way, I bumped into a boy and talked to him. He agreed to accompany me to my house for a few hours to share my bed and my solitude in exchange for a few coins.

Chapter 2
A visit to the Museum

Sunlight illuminated the room when I opened my eyes. The boy that I had brought to my house was at my side, sleeping. I still did not know his name, I had not asked him, and he did not tell me. I shook him gently until he woke up.

"Get up! It's time for you to go," I said.

Silently, the boy dressed. I gave him the promised coins. He thanked me, kissed me on the cheek, and left. I got up and called one of the servants to bring me breakfast.

I left my house at noon and headed for the palace. Daylight allowed me to see what I couldn't see in the darkness of the night. White marble covered the outer walls of the royal compound. I entered through an unguarded open gate and crossed a beautiful garden adorned with statues of gods, fountains, and ponds where colorful fish swam. The palace itself stood at the end of the park. Its shape was rectangular with Greek-style columns around it on all four sides.

"Are you Nicholas, the tutor of the princes?" the commander of the soldiers guarding the palace entrance asked me.

"Yes, officer," I replied.

"I have been instructed to inform you that the children went to bed late and are still sleeping. Today, you are not needed. You can go home and return tomorrow at this same time."

The truth is that I was glad to have the day off. I would enjoy walking in the city. It was summer, but a breeze blowing from the sea cooled the air.

Since my childhood, I had always dreamed of visiting Alexandria. Damascus, my hometown, had beautiful temples and monuments, but many travelers had informed me that it did not compare to Alexandria, the second-largest city in the civilized world. Although Rome, with over one million inhabitants, had twice the Alexandria population, the Egyptian capital exceeded it in beauty and culture. On the Mediterranean Sea coast, its location had made Alexandria the

13

most important port in the known world, and its active trade conferred untold wealth to its fortunate inhabitants.

Since the royal palace was in the Greek district, I decided to use the remainder of the day to visit that section of the city, leaving the Jewish and Egyptian neighborhoods for another time. Instead of returning along the path I had entered the palace, I crossed the garden and went out of the compound from a gate on the opposite side. I found myself facing an imposing building that had the word 'MUSEUM' engraved over its entrance.

"Pardon me," I said to a man standing near the entrance to the building. "I am a foreigner, a newcomer to the city. Is this a Temple"?

"Indeed, it is a Temple, but a unique Temple. It is called the Museum because it is consecrated to the Muses, the goddesses of the arts and sciences," he replied.

I thanked him and started to walk away, but the man stopped me.

"Excuse my curiosity. Who are you, and where are you from?" he asked me.

"My name is Nicholas. I am from Damascus and have come to this city to be the tutor of the Queen's children," I answered.

"I have heard your name and know your reputation. It's a pleasure to meet you, Master Nicholas. My name is Strabo."

I looked at him thoroughly. He was a tall, thin, bald man dressed in an elegant white gown.

I had a feeling that I had seen him before. Suddenly I remembered who he was.

"You are Strabo, the historian and geographer!" I exclaimed. "Two years ago, I was present at a lecture that you gave in Damascus and even asked you a couple of questions. There were so many people there that you probably don't remember me. I have read your books with great delight and can claim that I know a lot about you. Your family is originally from Crete, but you were born in Amaseia, on the Black Sea coast.

Am I right? Never mind, Tell me, what are you doing in Alexandria"?

"I am writing an account of my travels around the world and preparing to participate in an expedition that will try to find the source of the Nile River. I have thousands of scrolls at my disposal in the Museum's library that I can consult, but why are we still standing in the street? Come in, and I will be very pleased to explain to you what we do here," Strabo suggested.

"With pleasure," I answered.

Of all my visits to the Museum during my stay in Alexandria, the first one was unforgettable. Even if the gods would allow me to enter the palace of Zeus on Mount Olympus, it couldn't be a more sublime experience. The melodies that the god Apollo plays on his lyre could not be sweeter to my ears than the arguments expressed by the Museum philosophers in their discussions.

There were many portraits of distinguished-looking men on the walls of the first room that we entered. I stopped to examine them, and Strabo explained to me who they were.

"We are in the Hall of Philosophers whose knowledge and wisdom include all branches of philosophy, science, physics, engineering, biology, medicine, astronomy, geography, mathematics, and literature. The painting in front of us depicts Archimedes, the famous mathematician. The one to its left is the portrait of Euclid, who developed here his theories of geometry. Further on, you can see Hipparchus, who explained trigonometry; Aristarchus of Samos, a controversial geographer who proclaims, against all visual evidence, that the Earth revolves around the Sun; Eratosthenes, who determined the size of the Earth; Herophilus, a physiologist who concluded that intelligence is not in the heart but the brain; and finally, the man surrounded by stars in that painting, is Timocharis, the astronomer."

Strabo led me around the Museum. There were so many people in the corridors that it was difficult for us to make our way through the crowd.

"What are all these people doing here?" I asked Strabo.

"They are teachers and students. The Museum is an academy with five thousand students taught by more than one hundred poets and philosophers. They all come to the library daily to read, research, and learn," he answered.

Before going into the Museum, I felt that it was a single building, but now I saw that I had been mistaken. The Museum was a complex of buildings in the middle of a park with a zoological garden with animals that I had never seen before. Next to it was a botanical garden with plants brought from all over the world. A net under which multicolored birds chirped and fluttered covered an area of the park.

The Royal Library of Alexandria occupied the largest building. It was the largest in the world, according to Strabo. It had thirteen conference rooms and ten halls, each of them dedicated to researching a different discipline.

A fire started by the soldiers of Julius Caesar years before had damaged a section of the Museum. Fortunately, the library was not affected, and the damaged buildings had been rebuilt. The walls of the rooms were covered with shelves from floor to ceiling, all full of scrolls.

"How many scrolls does the library have?" I asked, amazed.

"The Library has more than nine hundred thousand scrolls, including the two hundred thousand that Mark Antony took from the library at Pergamum and brought to Alexandria. Most scrolls are the writings of Greek philosophers and playwrights, but we also have works from Persia, India, Armenia, Parthia, Judea, and Africa," he answered.

We entered a room where about fifty people were writing. They looked and smiled at us, but none of them spoke. I understood their silence when I saw a sign on a wall that read, "It is forbidden to talk."

"This is the room where the scribes copy the original works, either on scrolls of parchment or on papyrus. The Royal Guard searches all the ships that arrive in Alexandria. They bring to the library all the scrolls that they find. The scribes copy them, and afterward, they return the original scrolls to their owners. The library also sends representatives to foreign countries to

16

buy whole libraries or to receive scrolls on loan to be copied," Strabo whispered in my ear.

Several clerks heard us speak, raised their heads, and looked at us disapprovingly. We rushed out and entered the building next door.

"This is the building where the scholars, grammarians, philosophers, and doctors live. Queen Cleopatra pays their expenses. She often comes to dine with them because she enjoys their conversation and their company," Strabo explained. "Come, I want you to meet some of them."

Strabo introduced me to several grammarians whose names are known and respected throughout the Roman world. During my stay at Alexandria, I struck up a lasting friendship with some of them.

The scholars lived on the lower floor. An astronomical observatory occupied the top floor. I visited the building many times during the following months to participate in debates where we discussed whether the sun revolves around the Earth or the Earth around the sun. We never reached a unanimous conclusion.

The building that impressed me the most was the School of Medicine, not because of its architecture, although it was impressive, but for the study of the human body that took place there. The city authorities sent them the bodies of executed criminals, which the researchers cut open and dismembered. When I first saw arms and legs thrown on the floor and the tables and severed heads, whose features had ghoulish smiles, I had to cover my mouth with my hand and run out of the room, unable to suppress my nausea.

The alchemy building was the last one that we visited that day. Alchemy is a new science developed by philosophers who are trying to turn lead into gold, with promising results, or so they assured me.

Strabo led me back to the entrance of the Museum. We parted with mutual promises to meet again soon.

I decided to go home via a broad avenue lined with porticoes. It was four miles long, started at the Sun Gate and ended at the Moon Gate.

I walked at a slow leisurely pace gazing with admiration at the many temples and palaces. On one side of the avenue, I saw a cube-shaped building surrounded by columns and golden bars. About a hundred people, standing in a row, were waiting patiently to go in. Curiosity made me join the line. Minutes later, more than twenty people were already in the queue behind me. Nobody spoke, so I also kept silent, overcoming my desire to ask what was in that building. The line moved slowly, but eventually, it was my turn to enter.

The candlelight that illuminated the enclosure allowed me to see an open coffin in the center of the room. I looked inside and saw a mummified body. The luxurious garments that adorned the mummy made me think that it must have been a person of great importance, perhaps a king.

The visitors looked at it with reverence and stood in front of it in complete silence for several minutes before leaving. I went out of the building without finding out whose body it was.

While I looked around to decide where to go, a man spoke to me.

"Excuse me, Your Excellency. Am I right in assuming that you are a stranger in this city?" he asked.

The man was short, unshaven and his hair was disheveled. His age was difficult to determine. He could have been a young man that looked old because of a dissipated life or an old man whose boyish features were due to a healthy lifestyle. He wore a tattered yellow robe that was not clean.

"Yes, you are right. I arrived a few days ago, but how did you guess"?

"Most people who visit Alexander the Great's tomb are newcomers to our city," he answered with a toothless smile, which gave his face an odd appearance.

"Alexander the Great!" I exclaimed in disbelief.

"That's right, sir. If you wish, we could have a glass of wine in that tavern across the street. For just a copper coin, I, Jason, the best guide in Alexandria, will relate to you the history of the tomb of the great king."

"My friend, I accept your proposal willingly. My curiosity is as great as my thirst.

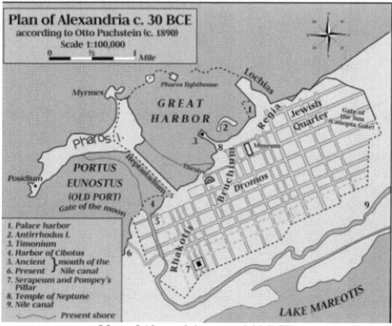

Map of Alexandria around 30 BCE

A visit to the Museum

Chapter 3
In the Serapeum

I hesitated to cross the street and looked apprehensively at the swift carriages pulled by horses and at the riders galloping on spirited steeds. None of them showed a willingness to stop or even to slow down. The responsibility to avoid getting killed or maimed by the carriages and riders rested solely with the pedestrian who tried to cross the street.

It seemed to me that if I attempted to do it, I would be risking my life, or at least my physical integrity. Jason noticed my fear and, without a moment's hesitation, grabbed my arm and, with skill and agility, took us to the other side without incident.

The tavern where Jason had taken me was a room with a dirt floor. It was furnished with some chipped tables and several fragile-looking chairs. Several clay jars that exuded the fragrance of cooked meat were simmering on top of the brick counter. Amphorae and wine barrels leaned against the walls painted with frescoes showing Bacchus wrapped in bunches of grapes.

"I beg your pardon, Your Excellency, for having brought you to such a humble place but, believe me, it has the best selection of wines in the whole of Alexandria. The owner brings them from Italy, Greece, Gaul, and Judea," Jason told me. Turning his face toward the counter, he shouted pompously, "Bartender, bring us your best wine!"

An obese man, wearing an apron stained with grease and wine bent behind the counter, grabbed a jar and brought it to our table. His short stature, combined with his waist's large diameter, gave him the appearance of a human sphere.

Jason tasted the wine, grimaced, and spat it on the floor.

"Are you stupid, or are you deliberately insulting us? I told you to bring us your best wine, and you bring us crappy Egyptian wine that tastes like vinegar and not even good

21

vinegar. Bring us two bottles of Greek wine or, by Jove, I will break your head!"

The bartender apologized profusely and, after a moment, returned with two dusty bottles. Jason tested the wine and smiled approvingly.

"Now, this is what I call wine! Listen carefully," he said to the bartender, "as soon as you see that the bottles are empty, bring us two more bottles immediately, without waiting for me to call you. Do you understand?"

"Yes sir," replied the bartender and went to attend on other tables.

I looked around and saw that the other customers were dressed in simple clothing. I assumed, and afterward, several people confirmed this, the clientele of this establishment were poor people who could not afford a private kitchen and that the absence of people of a higher class was because they disdained to eat at taverns like this one.

Jason filled his glass with wine, drank all of it (a procedure that he repeated numerous times while he related the story of the tomb of the great conqueror), and began to tell the life of Alexander the Great, starting with its birth. I interrupted him impatiently.

"I am not interested in stories about the life of Alexander, which I know quite well. Tell me what happened to his body after his death."

"Alexander died of malaria in Babylon when he was only thirty-three years old. His body was mummified and placed in a golden coffin. The coffin, in turn, was placed inside a casket of gold. A magnificent funeral car was built to take the body to Macedonia. Alexander had left instructions to be buried in his native country next to his father's grave. One of his generals, Ptolemy, who had made himself king of Egypt, attacked the funeral procession, took possession of the coffin, and carried it with him to Egypt.

"Why did Ptolemy do that?" I asked Jason.

"A seer told him that the country where Alexander would be buried would become the most prosperous country in the world. Years later, Ptolemy's son and successor, Ptolemy II, moved the body from Memphis to Alexandria and built the mausoleum that you visited today. Two centuries later, king Ptolemy IX, who needed money, seized the golden sarcophagus and replaced it with the current coffin. The citizens of Alexandria, outraged by the sacrilege, killed him." Jason paused to drink a cup of wine.

Jason could not resume his story because two men, who had been sitting at a table near ours, stood up, threw aside their chairs, shouted insults, and rushed against each other. They rolled on the ground, punching, kicking, and strangling each other. When one of them pulled out a knife and tried to stab the other, the bartender grabbed a heavy stick that was behind the counter and, without showing preference, hit both men with all his might. After he managed to separate them, he threw them out into the street.

"What caused the fight?" I asked Jason, who hadn't paid any attention to the brawl, busy drinking the wine.

"It was nothing," said Jason. "Ignore it. It happens all the time. It is enough for a Jew and a Greek to drink some wine, and then they insult and try to kill each other. Most of the time, the fight ends with the two in the dust, sleeping it off."

I called the innkeeper, paid him for the bottles of wine that Jason drank, gave Jason the copper coin that I had promised him, and said goodbye.

Years later, I included the information Jason gave me about Alexander's corpse in my History of the World. The five silver coins that I paid to the bartender for the bottles of wine that Jason drank that evening were worth it.

Outside, in the street, near the entrance to the tavern, I found Jason's description was accurate; the two opponents were lying on the ground, embracing each other, sound asleep.

Jason ran after me, reluctant to lose the source of easy income that he thought he had found in me.

"Please wait, Your Excellency."

I stopped and asked him what he wanted.

"There are still several hours before nightfall. If you give me one silver coin, I will take you to the Serapeum, the Temple of the god Serapis," offered Jason.

I smiled to myself, noticing that his fee had jumped from a copper coin to a silver coin, probably because he had seen that I did not argue with the bartender over the bill.

"All right, Jason," I replied.

"Your Excellency will not regret it. The Serapeum is only a few minutes away. While we walk, I will tell you who Serapis is."

To my relief, we did not need to cross to the other side of the avenue. We strolled towards the west of the city while Jason explained to me what we were seeing.

"General Ptolemy, a Greek by birth, after he proclaimed himself king of Egypt, concluded that a new god was necessary to unite the Greeks and Egyptians in his kingdom. He ordered his sculptors to make a statue of a god in the Greek style, but with traditional Egyptian motifs.

When the sculpture was ready, Ptolemy proclaimed it to be a new god who united in a single divinity the gods Osiris and Apis." Jason paused for a moment and then said in a solemn voice, "We have arrived. Before us is the Serapeum, the Temple of the god Serapis, Creator of the World, Sovereign of the Universe, God of Alexandria, Egypt's Protector."

It was the largest and most beautiful Temple that I had yet seen. (Years later, when King Herod built the Jewish Temple in Jerusalem, I had to admit that the Serapeum of Alexandria could not compete with Herod's Temple, not in size and not in beauty).

"The Serapeum Temple is five hundred feet long and ninety feet wide. Its door is made of solid brass. The facade, which we will see in a moment, is decorated with hieroglyphic inscriptions in low relief. There are two obelisks, one on each side of the door of the sanctuary," Jason informed me.

"What is inside the sanctuary?" I asked him.

"There are two sculptures. One is the god Serapis. His head carries a grain basket, the symbol of the land of the dead. In his right hand, he holds a scepter to indicate his majesty. At the base of the statue, there is an engraving of a serpent, the symbol of Egyptian royalty. The other sculpture, which is at the feet of the god, is the dog Cerberus, guardian of the underworld."

We entered through a gate in the wall that surrounded the Temple and walked along a path lined with sphinxes that had lion faces. On one side of the path, halfway between the wall and the shrine, we saw a huge bull made of black basalt.

The sanctuary door was extremely heavy, but the two of us managed to open with great effort. I could make out in the dim light of the room the statue of the god Serapis.

I was lost in the contemplation of the sculpture when suddenly, two soldiers grabbed me by my arms.

"Sacrilege!" shouted a furious priest. "This is the palace of the God, his holy dwelling. The entrance to the shrine is permitted only to the king, the priests, and people of the nobility."

I heard a noise, turned my head, and saw that Jason had pushed one of the soldiers and ran out of the sanctuary. The soldier, who had fallen to the ground, got up and ran after him, sword in hand.

"I am a foreigner and have come to sacrifice to the god Serapis," I told the priest, giving him the first excuse that occurred to me.

"This is not a suitable hour for sacrifices," replied the priest.

"I belong to a noble family in Damascus. Queen Cleopatra asked me to come to Alexandria to be the tutor of her children," I explained.

"Let his Excellency go." ordered the priest to the soldiers. "I am sorry for the misunderstanding, but you must leave. It is almost night, and the god does not receive visitors when it is dark."

I left the Temple escorted by a soldier. Once outside, I looked at both sides of the avenue and, seeing no sign of Jason, decided to return directly to my house. The next day was my first day with my pupils, and I wanted to be rested and ready for them.

Chapter 4
The Lighthouse of Alexandria

Early the next morning, I went to the palace. One of the soldiers who were on duty at the entrance escorted me to the room where my three pupils were waiting. I found them sitting in front of a couch, which, if I guessed correctly, had been reserved for me. At the back of the room, standing against the wall, were the nannies of each child.

The older boy, son of Julius Caesar and Cleopatra, was twelve years old. His name was Philometor Caesar, but people called him by his nickname Caesarion (little Caesar), a name given to him by the Alexandrians. He was a tall boy for his age, had a willful character, and showed, by his actions, that he was too conscious that his mother was the Queen of Egypt and his father, the Divine Julius. (The Roman Senate had proclaimed Julius Caesar a Roman god on the anniversary of his assassination).

Caesarion demanded that I address him as "His Majesty," a formal greeting to which he was entitled because his mother had named him king when he was seven years old. Cleopatra gave him the proper title of Ptolemy XV, the successor to the previous king, her brother, Ptolemy XIV, whom she had slain.

The twins Selene and Helios, children of Cleopatra and Mark Antony, were five years old. Their mother adored them, and they were her whole world, as implied by the names that she had given them, Selene which means the Moon in Greek, and Helios, which means the Sun.

I did not doubt that the girl would be as beautiful as her mother one day, with the same black hair and blue eyes. The brown hair of the boy made him look a lot like his father, Mark Antony.

I sat on the couch and realized that I had a problem: the large age difference between the twins and Caesarion.

It was impossible to teach a twelve-year-old boy and the five-year-old children at the same time. I had to perform two completely different functions that I could not exercise simultaneously. I had to be their *Magister* [master] for the younger children and teach them to read, write, and mathematics. Regarding the older child, my obligation, as *Grammaticus*, was to teach him Greek and Latin grammar, literature, rhetoric, oratory, geography, history, and mathematics.

I asked the maids to approach.

"I have decided to teach the children separately. In the mornings, I will teach only His Majesty Ptolemy and the prince Helios and the princess Selene in the afternoons. The maids who attend the prince and the princess can now take the twins to their rooms and bring them back to me after midday."

Two of the maids took Helios and Selene by their hands and withdrew. The third maid remained in the back of the room, ready for any service that Caesarion might need.

"Your Majesty, we will start by reading the *Iliad*. I have brought two copies, one for me and one for Your Majesty. I will read a page aloud, and then you will give me your comments."

I was surprised by the sharpness and depth of Caesarion's questions and comments. He even analyzed some points that I had not noticed. The morning passed quickly for both of us. The same happened on the following days, weeks, and months during the five years that I had the privilege of having Caesarion as a student.

At noon, a Greek slave brought me a bottle of wine, bread, and cheese.

"Your Majesty," I said to Caesarion," we will continue tomorrow. I would like you to continue reading the *Iliad* by yourself and write down your observations, which we will analyze together during our next lesson."

"*Grammaticus* Nicholas," he answered in a warm tone, without the arrogance that he had shown at the beginning of the lesson; "I want to thank you for your wise and entertaining explanation of Homer's book. I hope my brother and sister will enjoy their lesson as much as I have enjoyed mine. I look forward to tomorrow's lessons."

Caesarion left the room, followed by his maid. Minutes later, two nannies came in with Selene and Helios.

"Good afternoon, children. My name is Nicholas, but you must call me *Magister*. I will teach you to read and write and also to do arithmetic. We will start by playing with these letters cut in wood and ivory that I have brought."

During the following hours, the children played with the cutout letters. I told them the name of each letter and showed them how they could combine them to form words. I was impressed and enchanted by the speed and intelligence with which the two children understood my explanations and their excitement when they formed words.

It did not take me long to realize that the girl had a habit of speaking on behalf of her brother. She had more poise than the boy and showed more initiative and curiosity. She rarely allowed her twin brother to answer my questions, but this did not seem to bother Helios, who was a quiet and shy child.

After the lesson, the maids took the children back to their rooms, and I went home.

The next day was very similar to the previous. In the morning, Caesarion was already waiting for me in the classroom. Complying with my request, he had read several chapters of the *Iliad* and written down his comments. I was amazed again by his insights. In the afternoon, Helios and Selene continued combining letters and giving shrieks of joy when they could detect a word in the combination.

"Children," I said to them. "I have brought you waxed tablets and puncheons. You will notice that one end of the puncheon is pointed, and the other end is shaped like a spatula. You will use the pointed end to draw letters on the waxed tablet. The spatula at the other end you will use to smooth the wax to erase what you have written so that you can write on it again."

I stayed five years in Alexandria, a period of intense professional satisfaction that I remember with pleasure and longing. My three students were respectful and intelligent. The lessons usually ended at a time that allowed me to visit the Museum in the evenings, read scrolls, and enjoy the conversation of the most brilliant philosophers of the world. Every nine days, I had a free day, which I would spend by wandering around Alexandria or staying at home writing letters and books. At night, from time to time, I allowed myself a few hours of love and cuddling with the boy that I had met on my first night in Alexandria.

"What is your name?" I asked him the second time that I brought him to my house.

"Aristotle," he replied.

I smiled because his name was the only thing that the boy had in common with the famous philosopher. He did not know how to read or write, and I failed to teach him despite all my efforts. But, I confess, this failure did not bother me. His tenderness was ample compensation.

One day, after I had finished teaching my pupils, I went again to visit Alexander the Great's tomb. Jason was standing near the entrance speaking to a passerby, who ignored him and walked away. I approached, and he immediately recognized me.

"Your Excellency! What a pleasure to see you again. The day we visited the Serapeum, and you stayed talking to the priest, I waited for you outside. Since you did not come out, I went home. Would you like to see other monuments?"

Jason stopped talking for a moment to catch his breath, and I took advantage of his brief silence to ask him a question.

"Can you take me to see the lighthouse on Pharos Island? In Damascus, they told me that it is one of the wonders of the universe."

"It certainly is, Your Excellency. And, seeing that you are one of my oldest and most valued customers, I will only charge you a silver coin to take you there."

"You mean a copper coin," I said, smiling.

"You cannot imagine Your Excellency how expensive life has become in Alexandria. But, because it is you, I agree to receive a copper coin."

We walked on one of the streets that started from the city's main avenue and ended at the seashore. A short distance from us was a causeway, about a quarter of a mile long. It connected the city with Pharos Island.

There it was! The famous lighthouse of Alexandria! It was by far the tallest building that I had ever seen.

"If we walk a little further, we will reach a place from where you can appreciate the height of the tower much better," said Jason.

I followed him and was not surprised when we arrived at a tavern, and Jason invited me to enter.

"Your Excellency, I suggest, for your convenience, that we sit in this establishment and drink a glass of wine while I explain to you all about the lighthouse."

I remembered that, in our previous encounter, Jason's insatiable thirst had cost me several silver coins, but, as I was also thirsty, I disregarded the memory and entered the tavern.

We sat next to a window from which we could see the lighthouse. Jason asked the waiter to bring us two bottles of wine and began to explain.

"The Pharos Island Lighthouse in front of us is the pride of Alexandria. The first king Ptolemy built it two hundred years ago. Its height, four hundred and fifty feet, is greater than any other building in the world. The tower was built on a platform made of marble assembled with molten lead. Thick glass blocks line the foundations to protect the building from the erosion caused by the constant hammering of the waves of the sea."

Jason gave his explanations in a monotonous tone of voice and accompanied them with exaggerated hand gestures. He gave me the impression that he had memorized a few facts but did not know what he was describing. I could not help but smile, imagining him as a human parrot.

31

The waiter brought the wine bottles, and Jason interrupted his explanation to pour himself a full glass, which he drank with much pleasure. He emptied the glass and poured another.

"What is the purpose of the Tower?" I asked him impatiently when I saw that he was filling his third glass.

"Its function is to allow the ships to arrive faster and safer to Alexandria. To achieve this purpose, the builders installed on top of the tower a mirror made of polished metal that reflects the sunlight during the day. At night they light a fire that ships see from fifty miles away."

That night I dreamed that I climbed a stairway that had countless steps and reached the top of a huge tower. From there, I could see the whole world. Far away, across the sea, a small black spot in the sky was approaching and becoming bigger. When it was quite close to me, I saw that it was an eagle. Its feathers were made of gold and its beak and claws of iron. Suddenly, the eagle attacked the tower. The building crumbled and fell to the ground with a terrible noise. I woke up shivering. It was a dream with an evil omen.

The Lighthouse in Pharos Island, Alexandria, Egypt

Chapter 5
Mark Antony's announcement

The next morning, I left my house, worried and distracted by the mysterious dream that I had during the night, and walked aimlessly toward the city's center. When I was near the Temple of the god Serapis, I noticed that thousands of people crowded the avenue, and the buildings were festooned with flags. Bands of musicians played martial music at major intersections. A familiar voice shouted a greeting.

"Good morning, Your Excellency."

It was Jason (who else could it be?). He was leaning against the Temple wall just fifteen or twenty feet away from me.

"Sorry, my apologies, sorry, my apologies." Ruthlessly, Jason pushed aside several men and women while making his way to me. The angry looks he received made no impression on him.

"What is going on?" I asked him.

"It is a triumphal procession in honor of General Mark Antony's victory over the Armenians. More than that, I cannot tell you because there has never been such a celebration in Alexandria. Until now, triumphal processions took place only in Rome."

The loud sound of martial music and enthusiastic applause interrupted him. A band of soldiers playing trumpets and drums came parading down the avenue, followed by men in chains. The king of Armenia and his defeated generals walked stumbling in the chains that bound them. Then came wagons pulled by mules, loaded with weapons, gold, silver, and other valuables captured in the war. The Senators and magistrates of Alexandria walked behind the wagons, followed by beautiful women who threw flower petals to the crowd.

A sumptuous chariot, drawn by white horses, appeared. The applause grew louder. Amulets against the evil eye covered the sides of the chariot. The face of the driver was painted red to resemble the god, Jupiter. It was Mark Antony! He wore a

33

purple toga embroidered with gold, and on his head was a crown of laurels. His three children, Selene, Helios, and Philadelphus, stood with him on the chariot. Behind them rode Caesarion on a black stallion, followed by the army commanders, mounted on white steeds.

A group of priests rode on a wagon pulled by two white oxen. Garlands adorned the heads of the animals, and their gold-plated horns shone like the sun. Row after row of soldiers, dressed in gala uniforms, marched behind them, shouting, "Victory! Victory!"

Mark Antony stopped his chariot in front of the entrance to the Temple of Serapis. He alighted from the carriage and entered through the gate that remained open, allowing the people, including Jason and myself, to see the ceremony inside the Temple compound. The general walked down the garden path, which ended in a platform with a ramp erected in front of the bull's basalt statue. The priests brought the two white oxen and made them climb up to the platform.

"I dedicate this sacrifice to the god Serapis, in humble gratitude for the victory that he has granted me," shouted Mark Antony with a stentorian voice that, despite the loud noise of the crowd and the music of the bands, was heard by the cluster of people at the gate.

A priest gave him the sacrificial knife. Mark Antony approached one of the oxen and cut its neck. The animal fell heavily to the ground. Its blood spurted over the boots of the general, staining them red. Mark Antony repeated his thankful phrase to the god and slew the second ox.

"This afternoon at the theater, I will inform the people of momentous decisions that I have made regarding the dominions of Rome. Afterward, we will have public games and entertainment," Mark Antony declared from the platform.

The crowd began to disperse, and I decided to go home. I wanted to rest for a while before going to the theater in the afternoon. On the way, I saw people on the streets eating and drinking, sitting around tables heaped with food and wine. I had the impression that the entire city was celebrating a feast.

I met an acquaintance who told me with great excitement that the king and Queen of Armenia had been brought to the palace and asked to kneel at the feet of Cleopatra. However, when they were in front of her, they refused to do so. Cleopatra was furious and ordered the soldiers to flog them to teach them good manners.

I was already halfway to my house when I changed my mind and decided to go straight to the theater to secure a good seat. I had been in the theater of Alexandria on a previous occasion to listen to a poetry reading, and I knew (because of that frustrating experience when I arrived late and almost was not allowed to enter) that the thirty rows of marble seats could only accommodate a limited number of viewers. At the entrance, I received a small ceramic plaque on which the row's letter and my seat number were engraved. I congratulated myself when I saw that I had done well to come early. My seat was in the center of the front row. The box seats in the highest section of the auditorium were reserved for important people. City dignitaries were already sitting there.

Spectators gradually filled the theater until not one empty seat remained. Two golden thrones had been placed on the stage. A constant murmur of voices was heard from people in the auditorium, asking each other if they knew what Mark Antony would announce. The musicians played a fanfare with their trumpets to announce the arrival of Mark Antony and Cleopatra.

Mark Antony came dressed as the pharaohs that are depicted in the frescoes of ancient tombs. He had a leopard skin over his shoulders, and a lion's tail hanged from his belt. Cleopatra, adorned with earrings, bracelets, rings, and necklaces, wore a semi-transparent linen gown. On her head, she wore a crown with the solar disk of the goddess Isis. Behind them came Cleopatra's children: Caesarion, Selene, Helios, and Philadelphus, all four dressed in purple robes, with crowns on their heads. The royal couple sat on the golden thrones, and the children stood next to them. Again the trumpet blasts were heard. The entire audience stood and applauded until Mark Antony, with a gesture, indicated that we should sit down.

Mark Antony stood up and walked to the front of the stage.

"Citizens of Alexandria! I have invited you to come today to this theater to hear important policy decisions. Rome is no longer the capital of our Empire. As of today, Alexandria has that honor."

A deafening roar of the crowd interrupted his words.

"I have ended my alliance with Octavius, and today I have assumed all the roles, responsibilities, and honors that were his." He looked at Caesarion and gestured for him to come closer. "This young man, Ptolemy XV, is the son and the true legitimate heir of Julius Caesar. Today I name him king of Egypt. He will rule together with his mother Cleopatra, Queen of Egypt."

Caesarion kissed Mark Antony's hand and took several steps backward respectfully to avoid showing his back to the general.

"Helios, come to me." The boy, who had celebrated his sixth birthday a few days before, timidly approached his father. Mark Antony embraced him and kissed him. "You are the new king of Armenia, and when we conquer the Parthians, I promise that you will also be the king of Parthia. This is my gift for your birthday."

Looking at the girl, he exclaimed, "Selene, you are now the Queen of Cyrenaica and Libya." The girl ran to her father and kissed him.

"Bring me Philadelphus," ordered Mark Antony to the maid standing next to the child. He lifted the little boy and said, "Philadelphus is the king of Syria and Cilicia."

Mark Antony returned the child to the maid. He looked at the audience in silence for a minute and then made the Roman salute (the right arm raised in an angle, the palm down, the fingers together). The audience stood up and replied with the same arm salute. Mark Antony, Cleopatra, and her children left the stage amidst applause and cheers.

I could not believe what I had seen and heard! Octavius' spies in Alexandria would not lose a minute to inform him that Mark Antony had distributed Asia and Africa's Roman territories to his young children. In my opinion, which I kept to myself, Mark Antony was reckless. Octavius would never allow a child of Cleopatra to be considered the true heir of Julius Caesar.

How accurate is that old phrase that says: "The gods first make mad those whom they want to destroy." 7

Mark Antony's words amounted to a declaration of war against Octavius, but they also meant death sentences, not only for Mark Antony but also for Cleopatra and Caesarion. The other children would probably also die. The family's days were numbered.

When I left the theater, the sun had not yet set. I looked up and, for a moment, I thought I saw an eagle with feathers of gold and talons of iron flying threateningly over Alexandria.

Mark Antony's announcement

Chapter 6
From Alexandria to Ostia

One day, after I had finished teaching the children of Cleopatra, an official of the palace told me that Mark Antony wanted to see me. I followed him through several corridors to the room from which Mark Antony ruled Egypt. The general was sitting behind a table covered with scrolls and maps. I bowed to him. He got up and shook my hand.

"Good afternoon, Nicholas," he greeted me.

"Good afternoon, My Lord," I replied, flattered that he called me by my name.

'Sit down," he said, pointing to a chair opposite his desk. I sat, ready to listen most carefully to what the general would say to me.

"I don't know if you are aware that in the theater yesterday, I announced that I had ended my alliance with Octavius."

"I was in the theater...."

Mark Antony ignored my disrespectful interruption and continued. "I need to inform the Roman Senate about the decisions that I have made, and I want you to help me prepare the text of my letter."

"It will be a privilege."

"Very well then. Let's start."

Mark Antony dictated a letter to me in which he asked the Roman Senate to confirm the gift of kingdoms and crowns that he had bestowed on his children. In my opinion, (which I took great care not to express either in words or gestures), Mark Antony's request evidenced an excessive optimism that bordered on self-delusion.

I corrected his text by substituting some phrases that were offensive with more diplomatic expressions. I gave my version of the letter to the general. He read it, approved it, and signed it. After sealing the scroll with wax, he looked at me thoughtfully for a while. Then he gave me an order so unexpected and so surprising, I could never have imagined it.

"You will go to Rome and will carry these three letters. This one you will deliver to the Senate. The other two are for my wife Octavia and her brother Octavius. You must deliver all three of them personally. Tomorrow morning I will send one of my officers with an escort to take you to the ship. You will remain in Rome until you receive an answer from the Senate. During your stay in Rome, I want you to try to ingratiate yourself with Octavius and find out his plans. Understood?"

"My Lord, I am honored, but I am just the tutor of your children; I am not worthy of such trust and responsibility."

"Nicholas, You are under the impression that I brought you to Alexandria only to be the tutor of my children. That was not the main reason. You are here because I knew of your talents as a historian and philosopher. I need your gifts now for a diplomatic mission that is crucial to my future and the future of Rome. No one in Alexandria can match you in intelligence and ability."

Overcome with emotion, I couldn't speak and just nodded to accept the mission. Mark Antony handed me three letters and a generous sum of money to cover my expenses in Rome. I bowed and withdrew from the room.

I could not sleep that night. It was an honor to go to Rome as Mark Antony's ambassador, but it was also a severe risk to me. I feared the Senators' possible reaction when they learned that Mark Antony had given Roman territories to the children of Cleopatra. It is not unheard of for rulers to kill the messenger that brings them the bad news.

Just before dawn, a vigorous pounding on the door told me that my armed escort had arrived. I had been awake for several hours waiting for them. I opened the door and went out. The commander saluted and informed me that a ship was waiting for me in the Large Harbor (the causeway that linked the island Pharos to the city divided the bay into two harbors, Large and Small). Half of the armed escort marched ahead of me and the other half behind me.

Ships and boats of all sizes filled the harbor. I saw fishing boats, warships, and commercial vessels. The commander told me to get into a boat. It took me to one of the largest ships, which had the name *Fortune* written on its side. The size of the vessel impressed me. It measured from bow to stern almost one hundred and twenty feet. I had never seen a ship so big.

Fortune was a merchant ship with a large storage capacity below deck. One of its sailors informed me that it had arrived from Hispania two weeks before with a cargo of ten thousand amphorae full of the Iberian Peninsula's excellent oil. Now it was being loaded with wheat destined for Rome. I cut short my conversation with the sailor when a uniformed man approached me.

"Your Excellency, my name is Licinius. I am the Captain of this ship. General Mark Antony has given me orders to take you to Ostia. I have prepared the best cabin on the ship for you. It is next to mine."

"Thank you, Captain. I hope that I will not be an inconvenience to you during the trip. Please inform me as to when we will set sail and how long you estimate will take our voyage to Ostia"

"We sail at noon today. Concerning the duration of the journey, taking into account the sixteen hundred nautical miles that we will sail and the stops we must make in Utica, Malta, and Marsala, I hope to arrive at Ostia in a fortnight, if the gods send us favorable winds," he answered.

We set sail at noon, just as the Captain had told me. We sailed westward along the coast toward Utica, the capital of the Roman province of Africa. Five days later, we arrived in Utica, where we stayed for one day to stock up on food and water. I took the opportunity to visit the city. I saw the thermal baths, the warehouses, and the docks. What struck me the most was an amphitheater with a seating capacity for over twenty thousand spectators. I returned to the ship, and an hour later, we departed. We sailed north for three days until we reached the island of Malta.

I had brought some scrolls with me that I finished reading during the first few days of the trip. After that, I spent most of my time watching the sailors at work. A sailor pulling a log that was tied to a rope caught my eye. Another sailor was beside him with an hourglass in his hand. I approached them and asked them to please explain what they were doing.

"We measure the speed at which the ship moves. First, we throw the log into the sea. We wait for it to be afloat and steady in the water. Then, we release the rope, which has knots tied at fixed distances, and we measure with the hourglass how much time elapses until the next knot gets away from the boat. Thus, we can calculate the speed of the ship with the hourglass."

The sailors also engaged in another practice that piqued my curiosity. One or two days before our arrival at the next port, the sailors let loose some of the birds kept in cages. The birds flew away, and the Captain and the sailors stared at them until they disappeared into the horizon. I thought this was a religious ritual to persuade the gods to allow them to arrive safely to port, but the explanation I received was completely different. The direction to which the birds flew revealed to the sailors where was the nearest shore.

The Captain guided the ship at night by the brightest star in the constellation Ursa Major. He called it the Phoenician Star.

Three days after leaving Utica, we arrived at the island of Malta, where we spent five hours stocking up. I went ashore and was amazed to see the large number of establishments selling honey. I entered one of them. The owner invited me to taste his goods.

"This honey is exquisite! I have never tasted anything so delicious." I exclaimed.

"That is why the island is called Malta. The name comes from the word *Melite*, which in Greek means' sweet as honey';" he said proudly. "The quality and the quantity of honey produced by the bees of this island has no equal in the whole world."

I was standing behind another customer who had purchased a jar, waiting for my turn to pay. The man looked at me, smiled when he heard the owner's explanation, and shook his head in a negative gesture without saying a word.

When both of us left the establishment, my curiosity prompted me to ask the reason for his gesture.

"It is true that the honey of this island is excellent, but the name *Malta* does not come from the Greek language. Its origin is much older. It derives from the Phoenician word *Maleth* which means 'shelter' because of the numerous bays and inlets found on the coast of the island," he answered.

To this day, I do not know which of the two explanations is the correct one, but, what I do know, and have no doubts about it whatsoever, is that the honey from Malta is the best in the world.

Three days after leaving Malta, we reached Marsala, a port on the west side of the island of Sicily. We stayed there for a few hours, during which I remained in the boat watching the sailors loading water barrels and large pieces of salted beef.

Four days later, we reached our final destination, Ostia, a port located at Tiber's mouth. Because of the river's narrowness and shallowness, the Captain anchored his ship in the sea some distance from the coast and transferred his cargo to small boats that unloaded at the port.

I took leave from Captain Licinius, whom I had befriended during the fifteen days that the trip lasted. He was Greek, born in Crete, and educated in Rome. During the following years, I met him again several times and renewed our friendship.

I loved Ostia from the moment we landed. It is one of the most flourishing Roman towns and a major commercial center and port because it is located only thirty miles from Rome. It is a bustling city. The inhabitants work in the port or engage in the sale of the products brought from overseas. Unlike Damascus or Alexandria, where the homes have only one floor, in Ostia, most people live in apartments in brick buildings that are five or six stories high. In most of its eight hundred taverns, the second floor serves as a brothel to cater to the thousands of seamen who arrive from all countries. Besides its numerous temples dedicated to the Roman gods,

Ostia also has about twenty sanctuaries where people worship the Persian god Mithras. There are at least a dozen synagogues in its populous Jewish neighborhood.

I found an inn in which to spend the night before proceeding to Rome the next day. In the dining room of the inn, I fell into conversation with a Greek from Athens. I asked him if he knew of any brothel of ephebes in the neighborhood. He answered that there was one within walking distance of the inn and intended to go there after dinner. I told him that I would be pleased to go with him.

We had an enjoyable dinner together, joking and exchanging funny stories of our experiences in brothels in various cities.

It took us less than ten minutes of leisurely walking to arrive at the brothel. The young men there bowed and greeted us. They undressed us and anointed scented oil all over our bodies. Then, wrapped only in short towels, they took us to another room where murals of men in all conceivable combinations of erotic poses covered the walls. It was full of customers seated at tables, drinking, laughing, and loudly singing obscene songs.

We sat at a table, and two young men sat beside us. A slave brought us a jar filled with a liquid called *satirion*, made from a plant whose root, mixed with wine, produces an aphrodisiac that increases sexual enjoyment. We drank almost the whole jar while telling jokes and sharing stories. After some amorous dalliances, my friend and one of the boys got up from the table and, holding hands, went to a room. I continued drinking, and when I emptied the jar, my lad got up and led me down a corridor to his room.

Walking through the corridor, I had a disappointing and unpleasant surprise. The door of the room occupied by my friend and his young man was open, which allowed me to see something I could have never imagined. My friend was the passive partner!

When the Greek and I left the brothel, I looked at him with contempt and refused to respond to his conversation attempts.

44

That night, although I was exhausted by my sexual activity, I found it hard to fall asleep, afraid of what might happen to me in Rome.

From Alexandria to Ostia

Chapter 7
From Ostia to Rome

At dawn, to replenish my strength, I ate a hearty breakfast of eggs, ham, bread, and milk. I paid the owner of the inn and went out. Standing near the entrance was the Greek that I had met the night before. He greeted me in a friendly manner, but I pretended that I did not see him and did not return his greeting.

I went to the city market to rent a carriage to take me to Rome. There were carriages of different sizes, for one, two, or three persons, and entire families, apart from vehicles used to carry goods. Some of the carriages were drawn by horses and others by mules,

After inspecting several vehicles, I approached the driver of a four-wheeler whose horses seemed strong and fast.

"Good morning. I have a few questions, my friend. How far are we from Rome? How long will it take to get there? And, most important, how much will you charge to take me there?"

"Rome is thirty miles away, and the trip usually takes three to four hours. Regarding the price, because it is you, Your Excellency, I will only charge you ten silver coins."

"I am indeed a newcomer, but that is not a good enough reason to pay you such an exorbitant sum," I told him.

We had a polite discussion about the price. Finally, I agreed to pay him six silver coins.

Carriages, wagons, and people on foot congested the road from Ostia to Rome, but the driver's estimation of the time had been correct, and we reached the capital before noon.

"Sir, we have arrived. This is the Trigemina Gate, one of the twelve gates of Rome. I cannot enter the city because the Senate has forbidden the circulation of animal-drawn vehicles during the daytime. Cross the gate and, just next to it, you will find carts and litters for hire that can take you to the Forum," the driver told me.

I paid him the agreed price and went through the gate to the other side of the wall. I was in Rome, the world's largest and most important city! I made my way through a multitude of vendors of loaves of bread, fruits, fish, vegetables, all of them shouting and proclaiming the excellent qualities of their goods. A short distance from the city gate, I saw litters offered for hire, surrounded by slaves and mules.

After arranging the price with the owner of a litter, I climbed in. I was used to the Alexandrian litters carried by two mules, one in the front and the other in the rear. This one was different. It was an enclosed litter, mounted on shafts and could only hold a single passenger.

Four stout slaves carried the litter on their shoulders. Two slaves ran ahead of us shouting, 'Make way for our master.' When their shouts were not enough to drive the crowd aside, they cleared our way by shoving, kicking and punching left and right the people that were too slow to move.

We passed the Aventine neighborhood. Then we skirted Palatine Hill and arrived at the Via Sacra, the main avenue of the capital lined with numerous temples and basilicas.

I got off at the Forum, the open space at the end of the Via Sacra. I approached a passerby. His fine robe gave me the impression that the gentleman belonged to the nobility.

"Excuse me, Your Excellency. I am a newcomer to your beautiful city. I must deliver some documents to the Senate and would appreciate if you would tell me which of these buildings is the Senate," I said to him.

"Gladly. The Senate meets there," he said, pointing to a building with a bronze door reached by a flight of stairs in the middle of its austere façade. "But it is now closed and will remain closed for several weeks. The Senate will meet again as soon as the Assembly of the Centuries elects two new consuls to replace the previous two consuls. One of them died a few days ago, and the other has resigned."

"I need to deliver some documents urgently. What can I do?"

"If it is so urgent, I advise you to deliver the documents directly to the triumvir Octavius, the man who rules Rome. Whenever the Senate is in recess, Octavius attends to government affairs at his home, on Palatine Hill, not far from here. Walk down the Via Sacra to its beginning and then turn right. You cannot miss it."

When I arrived at Palatine Hill, I asked some people on the street, and they pointed to the house of Octavius.

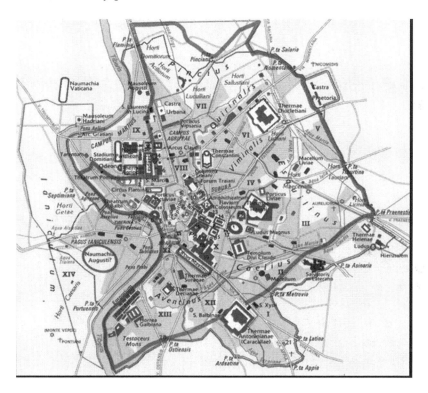

Rome during the reign of Augustus

From Ostia to Rome

Chapter 8
In Octavius' house

Palatine Hill is the most prestigious residential neighborhood in Rome. It has the largest and most beautiful mansions in the city. I was surprised to notice that Octavius' house was modest, unadorned, and relatively small compared to the imposing neighboring villas richly decorated with pillars and statues. A squad of armed soldiers stood in front of his house.

"My name is Nicholas of Damascus. I have come from Alexandria bringing letters from General Mark Antony that I must deliver to the Triumvir Octavius," I said to the commander of the guards.

"Give them to me. I will hand the letters to his Excellency."

"I am very sorry, but General Mark Antony has given me strict instructions to deliver the letters to Octavius personally."

"Wait here!" he ordered and went inside. He returned a few minutes later.

"The triumvir Octavius will receive you."

One of the soldiers guarding the house entrance frisked me carefully to make sure that I was not carrying concealed knives, and, once satisfied that I was unarmed, I opened the door and let me in, accompanied by the commander. I found myself in a rectangular courtyard that had a decorative pool in its center. An opening in the roof allowed the rainwater to fall directly into the pool. On the sides of the courtyard, there were doors to, what I assumed, were bedrooms. I walked to the end of the courtyard and entered a living room through an open curtain. The room had an open window, from which I could see a garden with flowers and shrubs.

Two men, about thirty years old, were in the room sitting on stools and talking to each other. Two children, a boy of about eight and a two-year-old girl, were playing on the floor. The two men stopped talking when they saw me.

"Triumvir! Nicholas of Damascus brings letters from General Mark Antony," announced the commander. He clicked his boots, gave the Roman salute, turned, and left the room.

One of the men, who had the muscles of a gladiator and the coarse features of a street fighter, greeted me with a nod.

The other man got up from his stool and shook my hand. He had a dark complexion and curly hair of a color between brown and blond. His gaze was penetrating, his nose was aquiline, and his teeth were small, clear, and well preserved. He compensated for his less than average height by wearing sandals with thick soles.

"Welcome to Rome, Nicholas. Sit on that stool while I read the letters of Mark Antony that you've brought me." Turning to the children, he said, "Tiberius, Vipsania, go and play in another room."

Octavius broke the seals of the letters and began to read the first one. After a while, he smiled and then laughed.

"Agrippa, you must hear this. Mark Antony writes that my paternal grandfather was a freedman. My grandmother was of the African race; my maternal grandfather had a bakery, and my father was a corrupt buyer of votes. And, if that is not enough, he says that I allowed Julius Caesar, my uncle, to have sex with me in exchange for naming me his heir. Cleopatra not only has obsessed the loins of the poor man, but she also has affected his brains."

"Give me the letter, Octavius. I want to see it," said Agrippa.

Octavius handed him the letter. Agrippa read it quickly and also could not control his mirth. The two men could not stop laughing.

As soon as he regained his composure, Octavius broke the second letter's seal and read it.

"This is a letter from Mark Antony to Octavia informing my sister that he has divorced her."

I would have thought that this news would make Octavius angry, but his reaction was completely different.

"Great news! It means that there is no longer a family relationship that binds me to Mark Antony. This leaves me free to act in the way that best suits me," said Octavius with a wide smile.

Octavius opened the third letter, which was addressed to the Senate. When he finished reading it, he crumpled it and threw it to the ground. His face expressed anger.

"The bastard insults the Senate by handing our territories to his children as if they were his personal property," Octavius shouted.

Agrippa picked up the letter from the floor and read it. He could not suppress his fury and burst into insults and threats against Mark Antony.

"Calm down, Agrippa. Emotions will not dictate to us what to do." Octavius said, putting a hand on his friend's shoulder.

Addressing me, he said, "Nicholas, I thank you for bringing me the letters. The Senate will give you its answer after the Assembly of the Centuries elects two new consuls, which could take a few weeks. Where are you staying in Rome?"

"I do not have any accommodations yet, My Lord. I came directly from Ostia to Rome to deliver the letters as soon as possible."

"I will give you a note for my freedman Lucius. He owns a building on Aventine Hill, where he runs his butcher shop on the ground floor and rents the upper floors' apartments. You will find him easily. Everyone knows him. I will contact you as soon as the Senate reconvenes and decides on an answer for Mark Antony."

In Octavius's house

Chapter 9
Lucius the butcher

As Aventine Hill was not too far away, I decided to walk to Lucius' butcher shop. It wouldn't take me more than an hour.

The contrast between Palatine Hill, Rome's most beautiful neighborhood, and the Aventine was as day to night.

There were no parks or gardens in Aventine Hill. Its streets, narrow and malodorous, were full of people and stray dogs. In some of its alleys, there were stinking holes where it was easy to trip and fall. Manholes were usually clogged with dead animals and filth of all kinds.

Buildings five or six stories high, built of wood and bricks made of clay and straw, lined the streets. Commercial establishments, such as vegetable markets, bakeries, butcher shops, and taverns, used the buildings' ground floors.

Two hours later, I was still walking, lost in the alleys of Aventine Hill, unable to find Lucius' butcher shop. I approached a man who was leaning idly against a wall.

"Excuse me, sir. I am looking for Lucius' butcher shop. Could you please tell me how to get there?" I asked him.

"With pleasure, sir. Walk down this street until you see a grocery store. Turn left there. Advance two streets, make a right turn, and you will see a butcher shop a block away. It is Lucius'. Impossible to get lost," he answered.

An hour later, I concluded that the man had been wrong. It was far from being impossible to get lost on Aventine Hill. On the contrary, it was easy as the streets had no names, were not straight, and the buildings had no numbers. It was enough for me to walk a few minutes to get lost again. I spoke to another stranger, who alas was not the last one to tell me how to reach Lucius' butcher shop. Again and again, I received detailed instructions. Again and again, I got lost.

After a couple of bad experiences, I chose to walk in the center of the streets to avoid the impact of garbage and worse things that the upper floors' residents constantly threw from their windows. So, walking and asking, asking and walking, I finally reached my destination.

Upon entering the butcher shop, I understood why every person I had spoken to in Aventine Hill knew Lucius. The large size of his shop, the number of slaves who worked there, and the many customers waiting to buy were evidence that Lucius, the owner of the biggest butcher shop in the neighborhood, was a very wealthy, important, and respected person.

A tall fat man, wearing an apron stained with blood and grease, was attending to the customers. He stood behind a counter on which there were all kinds of meat. He managed to wait on two or three clients with amazing skill while simultaneously giving orders to the slaves.

Carcasses of pigs, sheep, and goats hung from hooks secured to the ceiling. The customers indicated to the slaves what they wanted. The slaves cut the meat and passed it to the man behind the counter, who weighed it, gave it to the customer, and received the payment. I assumed correctly that the man was Lucius.

Cages holding chickens, ducks, and geese, constantly clucking and quacking, were on one side of the shop. On the other side, there were pots full of water in which live fish swam. A customer would choose a fish, and a slave would pull it out of the water and kill it by hitting its head with a mallet. Another slave killed the birds by twisting their necks.

The only decoration in the shop was a fresco on the wall behind the counter, which showed Mercury, the god of merchants.

"Friend," Lucius said to me when he saw me standing patiently next to the counter. "What kind of meat do you want? We have the best meat in Rome. Fillet at the best price you can find, steaks, loin, shoulder for a rich stew, and tail for a tasty broth. Believe me, people come even from as far away as Trastevere and even further to buy my meat."

"Thank you, but I have not come to buy meat. I bring you a note from Octavius," I answered.

Lucius looked at me with newfound respect, wiped his hands on his apron, and received the note. He read it, took off his apron, instructed one of the slaves to replace him behind the counter, and asked me to come with him. He walked towards a door at the back of the shop, and I followed him.

We climbed a staircase to the next floor, where there was only one door. Lucius tapped, and a middle-aged, plump woman opened. A smile lighted her pleasant features when she saw us. She wore a long, loose, cream-colored embroidered tunic. Her brown hair, which showed some grey streaks, was covered with a bonnet.

"Master Nicholas, please meet my wife Fausta," said Lucius. "Fausta, meet Master Nicholas of Damascus. He will be dining with us, and tonight he will rest in the empty apartment on the sixth floor. Tomorrow I will search the neighborhood for an apartment that befits him better, one that has a latrine."

We entered a room lighted with oil lamps hanging from the ceiling. Frescoes decorated the walls. A mosaic of birds and animals covered the floor. Thick curtains hung on the windows. The room was furnished with stools and a table in the center with three couches around it. A lit bronze stove kept away the winter cold.

. "Master Nicholas, please excuse me. I must leave you for a few minutes while I wash and change my clothes," said Lucius.

Lucius went to his room, and Fausta returned to the kitchen. I was left alone in the room. I sat on one of the stools. Tired from walking, I closed my eyes. I awoke to the aroma of the stew that Fausta brought from the kitchen. Moments later, Lucius returned, smartly dressed in a robe of silk imported from China, further evidence of his prosperity.

The food cooked and served by Fausta was delicious and proved that the lady of the house had great culinary talents. The entrée was an excellent vegetable salad. The next dishes were meat and fish. I had to acknowledge that Lucius had not exaggerated when he praised the meat sold in his shop. Beans, cabbage, and asparagus accompanied the grilled meat. Herbs and spices covered the fish. Fausta served us grapes, apples, and pears for dessert, and, to top a wonderful dinner, Lucius filled our glasses with excellent Greek wine.

Both Lucius and Fausta were discreet people who refrained from asking me personal questions. Our conversation was limited to commenting on the weather and my first impressions of the city of Rome. Lucius told me that he was the owner of the building. Downstairs was the butcher shop; the apartment on the first floor was the family residence, and he rented out the apartments on the upper floors.

After the meal, Lucius said that he would take me upstairs to the sixth floor to the apartment where I would spend my first night in Rome.

"Mrs. Fausta, I thank you for such a delicious dinner," I said to her.

"Wait a moment, Master Nicholas," replied Fausta. She left the room and returned with a blanket. "Take this blanket with you. The nights are cold, and this will keep you warm."

Chapter 10
The scroll with Cicero's speeches

Lucius lit a torch to illuminate our way down the staircase. Once downstairs, we crossed the butcher shop, still full of customers, and went outside. Right next to the door of the shop was the entrance to the upper stories of the building. Lucius opened a door, and we climbed a steep staircase.

"Fortunately, one of the apartments on the sixth floor became vacant a few days ago, and you can sleep there tonight. Tomorrow I will find an apartment with running water, heating, and a latrine in one of the neighboring buildings. My apartments lack these amenities."

When we reached the sixth floor, Lucius pulled a bunch of keys out of his pocket and opened one of the corridor doors. My first impression of the one-room apartment was not favorable, and a subsequent more detailed inspection did nothing to change my mind.

"The bed is there," said Lucius pointing to a wooden board that rested on loose bricks, covered by a thin mattress splattered with stains about whose origin I had no wish to ask or speculate. A chamber pot on the floor near the bed and a bucket full of water completed the furnishings.

"Master Nicholas, please be very careful with the torch. This building has more wood than bricks, and fires are common in the neighborhood. If anything happens, use the bucket of water that is next to the bed. Rest, and tomorrow I will find a more suitable apartment for you."

Lucius left, closing the door behind him, and I went to sleep on what Lucius euphemistically had called "a bed."

The next morning, upon waking, I felt a call of nature and used the chamber pot. The previous day, while walking through the streets of Aventine Hill, I had seen that it was a custom in the neighborhood to throw the contents of the chamber pot out the window. I was going to do the same because, as the saying goes, when in Rome, do as the Romans do. Then I remembered that I had seen a barrel, which gave off a foul odor, full of overflowing excrement on the first floor under the stairs. I went downstairs and emptied the chamber pot into the barrel.

During the day, I walked around the city and visited various temples and basilicas. At noon I had lunch in a tavern. It was late in the afternoon when I returned to Aventine Hill. This time I did not need to ask how to get to Lucius' butcher shop.

The shop was as full of customers as the day before. Lucius greeted me warmly, ordered one of the slaves to stand behind the counter, and told me to follow him.

We went outside, and after walking a hundred yards, we came to a building whose facade looked much better than Lucius' building. We went up to the first floor and entered a tastefully furnished apartment.

"This apartment belongs to a friend of mine who is spending a few months at his villa in Pompeii. He owes me a few favors, so I do not think that he will mind that Mark Antony's ambassador will stay in his apartment.

Lucius went back to his shop and left me to explore the apartment before going to sleep. Frescoes of hunting scenes decorated the main room. A multicolored mosaic that pictured peacocks covered the floor. There were three bedrooms, a bathroom, and a kitchen. In the kitchen, there was a bronze furnace and a cupboard containing a jar of olive oil, a jar of honey, a bottle of vinegar, several bottles of wine, and four or five bags with walnuts and almonds.

In one of the bedrooms, I found several scrolls. I examined them. Some of them were excellent, including a translation of the Odyssey into Latin and Julius Caesar's report about his Gaul campaign. Other scrolls were mediocre, for example, a philosophical study by Callistratus, a sophist whom I detested because his style was dry and affected.

I was excited to discover that one of the scrolls included the four speeches that Senator Cicero had pronounced against Catilina thirty years before. Until then, I had not read them because the Library of Alexandria did not have a copy.

I immediately resolved to hire a scribe to make me a copy. I would take it back to Alexandria and donate it to the Library in gratitude for the many hours of happy reading that I enjoyed there.

I poured myself a glass of wine, lit an oil lamp, rested on the bed in one of the bedrooms, and read the four speeches.

Ah, Cicero! His eloquence had no rivals! His talent allowed him to express abstract and complex thoughts so clearly! I will never forget the first sentence in the scroll: "How long, Catilina, will you abuse our patience?"

Unfortunately, Cicero's life ended tragically. He and Mark Antony hated each other. When Cicero gave a series of speeches in the Senate against Mark Antony, the General response was to send murderers who killed Cicero, cut his head and hands, and nailed them to a platform in the Forum.

Fulvia, who, at that time, was Mark Antony's wife, grabbed the head of the murdered man, forced open the mouth, pulled out the tongue, and pierced it repeatedly with a hook from her hair, thus taking revenge for Cicero's speeches against her husband.

The scroll with Cicero's speeches

Chapter 11
In a Roman public bath

The next morning I went to the Forum and saw that the Senate's door was still closed. I approached a slave who was sweeping the steps and asked him if he knew when the elections would take place. He looked at me insolently and did not answer.

"When will the elections take place?" I asked him again, less politely the second time.

"Three weeks from now. The judge will interview tomorrow those who want to be candidates," he answered reluctantly and continued sweeping.

From his horrendous accent, I deduced that he was a foreigner, probably born in Gaul. He must have been one of the slaves that Julius Caesar brought back with him on his return from the lands that he had conquered.

It was still early, and, as I had no desire to return to the apartment, I walked for a while on the Forum. I went to two or three temples, and then I entered the Basilica Julia, built recently. I found myself in a large rectangular space with a wide central nave and two aisles separated by rows of columns. Inside the Basilica, many people walked around or bought in the shops that were along the walls. Some of them gambled with dice or played some game in diagrams marked on the floor.

I heard someone shout my name. I looked around and saw a familiar face. It was Lucius, the butcher. He made quite an impressive figure, carefully combed, closely shaved, and elegantly dressed with a robe of fine wool. He greeted me with a smile.

"Nicholas, what a pleasure to see you. What are you doing here?"

"Nothing really. Just walking and exploring the city," I replied.

"I have an appointment here in the basilica with one of my suppliers. He is the one standing there next to the wall wearing a red robe. The scoundrel wants to raise his prices, but I will force him to lower them, or I am not called Lucius. It might take me an hour to convince him, but afterward, I will be completely free, and, if you like, we can spend the rest of the day together. I promise that I will take you to sites that visitors never see and cannot even imagine exist. Can we meet at the door of the basilica in an hour?"

"With pleasure!" I answered.

He said goodbye and went to talk with his supplier. Minutes later, I saw them arguing heatedly. At times it seemed as if they were going to hit each other but soon after, they laughed and hugged.

One of the shops in the basilica sold parchments, feathers for writing, and ink. I went in and asked the owner if he could recommend a scribe. One customer turned to me.

"Excuse me, sir, but I overheard your question. I am a scribe. How can I help you?" he asked me.

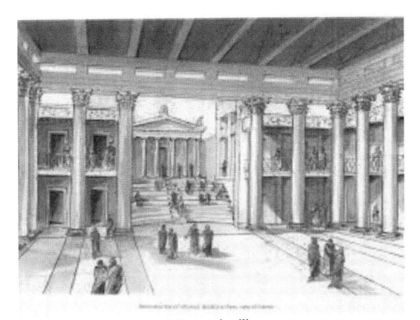

A Roman basilica

I explained that I wanted to copy the speeches of Cicero. The payment he wanted for his work was so outrageous that I decided to copy myself. I would save money and put to good use the weeks that I had free until the Senate elected new consuls.

At the back of the basilica, there was a podium where a judge was holding court. Legal procedures fascinate me, so I went to listen and stood as close as possible. It was an interesting case. The plaintiff had sold the defendant a mare that was pregnant and had charged his customer a price that included the foal that was born after the sale. To the surprise of both parties, the mare gave birth to twins, and now the seller wanted the buyer to pay him an additional sum of money because he had received two foals instead of one. The defendant refused to pay, arguing that the two parties had agreed upon the price. The judge ruled in favor of the seller. The buyer had to pay the additional amount requested by the plaintiff, based on the principle *expressio unius est exclusion alterius* (The express mention of something does not include what is not mentioned). The judge explained that when a seller (as in this case) specifies exactly what he is selling, what is not specified is not included in the transaction. Therefore the request for payment for the second foal was justified.

Marveled at the judge's impeccable logic and impressed by how quickly he had rendered a just decision, I wanted to stay and listen to more trials, but an hour had already passed. Without much enthusiasm, I went to the basilica entrance, where Lucius was already waiting for me.

"Nicholas, my friend, we have to celebrate. I convinced my supplier to include ten more cows at the same price in the next shipment. And now, to celebrate, we will go to the best public bath in Rome. It is very close to this basilica. Don't worry about the expense. You are my guest."

A short walk took us to the public bath chosen by Lucius. On the way, we passed other public baths, but Lucius insisted that the one he was taking me was the best.

I wanted to enter by the nearest door, but Lucius pulled me back.

"Nicholas, what are you doing? That's the entrance for the slaves who come to assist their masters. Our entrance is that one, by the statue," he said, pointing to a gate that was next to a sculpture of a naked woman.

Lucius paid the doorman, and we walked in. A slave came and helped us remove our clothes. Nude, we went to a huge room where there were three pools. We first dove into the pool of cold water, then into the warm water pool, and finally, we entered the hot water pool, from which arose clouds of vapor.

Several people were bathing in that pool.

"Lucius, there are naked women in the pool!" I exclaimed, amazed.

"That's right. I did not mention it before because I wanted it to be a surprise. This is one of the few public baths in Rome where men and women bathe together," he replied, laughing.

Lucius approached the women and tried to start a conversation with one of them. I noticed that she was the one with the biggest breasts. She ignored him, and he, without being discouraged and always with a smile, approached another woman.

The men in the pool were not young enough to attract my attention, so I did not speak to them. I preferred to enjoy the hot water temperature and admire the beauty of the room. Frescoes of trees, birds, and pastoral scenes decorated the walls. The domed ceiling was painted blue with white clouds and golden stars. The floor was paved with polished slabs of marble of different colors. Along the walls were benches, fountains, and statues.

Lucius and a woman came out of the pool holding hands. I followed them. The three of us entered a room in which eunuchs were giving massages. I asked one of them for a massage and then slept for a while. When I woke up, I did not see Lucius or the woman. I wrapped myself with a towel and decided to explore the various facilities of the place.

This public bath had facilities that I had not imagined. There was even an infirmary in which a physician attended people complaining of rheumatism and arthritis. In another room, slaves served meals and drinks. Next to it was a shop that sold exotic perfumes from different countries, some as far away as China and India. But what impressed me the most was the well-stocked library room which had couches for comfortable reading. That's where an hour later, Lucius found me laughing aloud while reading Plautus' comedy *The Braggart*. I do not doubt that Plautus, although he is justly criticized for being obscene and rude, had a comic talent unrivaled to this day.

"Are you ready? There are more places that I want us to visit tonight," Lucius said." I am ready," I replied.

In a Roman public bath

Chapter 12
In Suburra

I do not remember how many dissolute young men, courtesans, pimps, musicians, dirty old men, and drunken soldiers I met that night in the places I visited with Lucius. What I do remember, though vaguely, is that, after drinking many cups of wine and glasses of beer in several taverns, we went to a theater. We arrived before the show had begun, but people were already pushing each other to be the first in getting in. The plot, a comedy about adultery, was only a pretext to present erotic scenes between combinations of both sexes. The dialogues, songs, and dances were all obscene. At the end of the play, the actors, men, and women bowed while the audience applauded and shouted in chorus, "Take off your clothes!" "Take off your clothes!" The actors complied willingly and soon were standing naked on the proscenium.

"Nicholas, do you see the actress who is standing next to the dwarf? I know her and would like to greet her," Lucius said.

We went to the dressing room. Lucius knocked. The woman who opened the door gave a cry of joy when she recognized Lucius, embraced, and kissed him. Lucius winked at me.

"Nicholas, I want to congratulate this wonderful actress. Could you wait for me outside? It will take me perhaps half an hour to tell her how wonderful she was in the play."

"Of course. I'll wait outside the room," I replied.

It took Lucius a lot more than half an hour to congratulate the actress on her performance. I waited outside the dressing room for more than an hour. Finally, the door opened, Lucius kissed the actress goodbye, and we left the theater.

"No woman can compare to an actress. Even when they do not feel passion, they know how to pretend," he said, patting me on the shoulder. "And now, to end the night, we will go to Suburra. It is the best!"

I had heard a lot about the Suburra neighborhood, and none of it was praise. People told me that Suburra was worse than

Aventine Hill, a description that I had found difficult to believe, but realized that it was accurate after that night. I also heard that Suburra had more taverns and brothels than all the other Rome neighborhoods put together. I found out that this was true. Totally true!

The local people, proud that the great Julius Caesar was born there, had turned the house of his birth into a pilgrimage center. But that evening, neither Lucius nor I had the slightest interest in visiting Julius Caesar's home. We could not take one step in the streets without prostitutes or painted adolescents offering us their services.

"Ignore them, Nicholas," Lucius warned me. "Wait a while because I am taking you to the best brothel in Rome."

Lucius had not exaggerated. He brought me to a brothel, a multistory house with the most beautiful women and the most beautiful young men I had ever seen in my life. Some sat on couches, and others danced among themselves or with their clients. The musicians were excellent, and the wine was abundant and heady. That night I spent most of the money that Mark Antony had given me for my expenses. Even if I had spent twice as much, it would have been worth it. The youth that I chose that night gave me the most thrilling, the most daring, and the most varied sexual experience that I ever had since my first visit to a Damascus brothel.

Upon leaving, as we walked toward the Aventine, my curiosity prompted me to ask Lucius a question.

"Why are you willing to pay prostitutes when you have such a lovely, loving wife as Fausta and such a beautiful mistress as the actress?"

"Neither wives nor mistresses have the sexual skill of a first-class prostitute. Only prostitutes know the frenzy of pleasure. Only prostitutes know how to kiss with an open mouth. Only prostitutes wallow in bed like crazy women. Only prostitutes make me burn with desire. By Jove, my wife does not even pant when we engage in the love act!"

The memory of the two hours that I spent with my young man was fresh in my mind. I smiled and said nothing.

Chapter 13
Choosing candidates for consul

Despite having returned very late the night before to my apartment, I got up early and went to the Forum to witness the public interviews by which a judge would choose the candidates for the post of Consul.

Thirty hopefuls were patiently waiting their turn, standing in a row in their order of arrival at the Forum. Someone mentioned that several of them had arrived at midnight to be among the first to be interviewed.

It was easy to identify by their clothing who belonged to the patrician class and who were plebeians. The nobles wore a white and purple toga fastened with a gold buckle, while the commoners wore dark clothing.

The judge's first interview was at ten o'clock in the morning, and the last one was at two o'clock in the afternoon. The judge always asked the same questions:

How old are you? (If the applicant was less than forty-five years old, the judge disqualified him on the spot).

Did you register at the last census? (Those who were not registered could not be candidates).

In how many annual military campaigns have you participated? (The minimum was ten).

The interviews were usually solemn affairs, but an incident occurred that the public celebrated with laughter and the judge with a slight smile.

An applicant, thin and small in stature, with a long white beard and white hair, took the stand. A group of teenagers celebrated his mocking answers to the judge's questions with laughter and applause.

I found it odd that this white-bearded person's voice sounded too youthful for such an old man. The judge nodded to one of the officers of the guard. The officer approached the applicant and unceremoniously pulled off his beard and wig.

The boy jumped off the platform and ran away laughing, followed by his friends.

The judge restored order and resumed the interviews. Fourteen candidates were finally approved. The magistrate gave orders to list the candidates' names on a scroll, which an officer nailed to the Senate's door.

The three weeks before the elections passed quickly. During the first days, I stayed in the apartment, copying Cicero's speeches on a parchment. For breakfast, I ate bread smeared with garlic, accompanied by a piece of cheese. At noon I had lunch at one of the taverns in the neighborhood, always eating bread, cold meat, vegetables, fruit, and a glass of wine. In the evenings, I usually dined with Lucius and his wife, enjoying the delicious food prepared by Fausta while listening to Lucius boasting about the excellent business deals that he had made that day, was making or planned to make.

I went on two more occasions to the brothels in Suburra, the first time alone and the second time with Lucius. Both times I enjoyed myself as much as I did on my first visit.

Chapter 14
The latrine near the Forum

When I felt nature calling me urgently and was away from my apartment, I had no choice but to use the local public latrine., which was a very unpleasant experience because the place stank and was dirty. The queue to get in was always very long, and more than once, I witnessed fights for the few seats that were available inside.

I mentioned this to Lucius, and he recommended that I go to a latrine near the Forum. "It is, by far, the best latrine in Rome," he told me and added that, although the entrance fee was much higher than what the Aventine latrine charged, it was worth it. Members of the highest social class in Rome, Senators, tribunes, and judges patronized it.

When I went to that famous latrine, I saw that Lucius had not exaggerated when he called it the best in Rome.

The white Carrara marble slab, which was along the wall, had round openings on which people sat next to each other to fulfill their physiological needs. Below the marble, there was a channel through which flowed water carrying the feces. The long handles with sponges on their end that the customers used to clean themselves were scrupulously scrubbed and washed by slaves after each use.

The man sitting on my left must have been the champion of all the gossips of Rome. He told me stories about the most prominent people of Rome in a mincing voice without any prompting. As I did not know those people, I did not pay any attention until he mentioned the name of Octavius.

"You've probably heard the rumors about Octavius. You haven't? Well," he lowered his voice. "Mark Antony's friends say that Octavius had an unnatural relationship with Julius Caesar, which Caesar rewarded by naming his heir. But I do not believe them. Octavius, although he has just turned thirty, has been married three times. He sent his first wife, Claudia, back to her mother with a note saying that he had not consummated the marriage and returned her 'intact.' He divorced Scribonia, his second wife, the same day she gave birth to his daughter Julia. Do you know why? Don't you? To marry Livia! He had fallen in love with her when Lidia was six months pregnant and still Tiberius Claudius Nero's wife. Nobody knows how Octavius forced her husband to divorce her. Did he persuade the poor man with arguments, threats, or bribes? The fact is that Tiberius Claudius had to play the bride's father's role and give Livia away to Octavius. The wedding ceremony took place only three days after Livia gave birth to her son! It was the scandal of the month," he said, laughing the whole time.

The man finally left my side, and a distinguished-looking elderly woman sat on the place that he had vacated. She extended her full gown to cover her legs and greeted me with the utmost courtesy. I returned her greeting.

"Excuse me for asking, but I cannot help being curious. It seems to me, judging by your accent, that you are not from here. Are you a visitor?" she asked me.

Illustration of a latrine in ancient Rome

"I was born in Damascus, and yes indeed, I am visiting Rome," I answered.

We struck up a lively conversation. I mentioned that I was making a copy of Cicero's speeches. She told me that she had known the Senator very well, and it had been a horrible shock for her to see his decapitated head stuck in the Forum. Before she left, she made me promise to visit her house before I would go back to Alexandria.

During the following week, I went to the Forum every day to hear the candidates' speeches, which, boringly, were all the same. Each candidate declared, without false modesty, that he was the ideal person to lead the destiny of Rome during the following year: "I am the most capable, the most intelligent, and the most honorable of all the candidates, and all the others are a pack of scoundrels, crooks and liars, who belong in jail."

The latrine near the Forum

Chapter 15
Election of the consuls

Election Day finally arrived. I left my apartment hurriedly without having breakfast to arrive at the Forum before the beginning of the Ceremony of the Auspices. The fourteen candidates, dressed in white robes, were already on the platform surrounded by cages filled with birds.

Romulus, the founder of Rome, established the Ceremony of the Auspices by a law that permitted holding an election only when the omens were favorable.

The augur—a religious official who foretold events by observing and interpreting signs, omens, and flight of birds—, his head adorned with a wreath of laurel leaves, opened the cages allowing the birds to fly away. He observed their flight to determine if the omens were favorable or unfavorable.

We all sighed with relief when the augur decreed that all the signs were favorable and that the elections could take place.

The judge stood up, and we heard a drum roll. The crowd became quiet, and there was complete silence in the Forum square.

"Roman citizens! We have gathered today to fulfill the sacred function of electing two consuls who will govern our republic for the next twelve months. First, I must make an important announcement: Roman law allows an absent candidate to participate in the elections. Therefore, in addition to the fourteen candidates present here on the platform, we have also accepted Octavius, the deified Julius Caesar's son, as a candidate. Although he is younger than the minimum age, we have decided to waive that requirement in his case." Loud cheers and enthusiastic applause interrupted the magistrate.

The judge waited until silence prevailed again in the Forum, and then he continued speaking.

"The citizens will gather themselves into centuries, groups of one hundred persons. Each century will vote for the candidate of its choice. Here on the platform, there are fifteen jars, each with the name of a candidate. Three hours from now, a representative of each century will come to the platform. He will deposit a pebble in the jar that bears the candidate's name chosen by his century. Let the gods illuminate your minds." The judge finished speaking and sat down.

The men who had Roman citizenship gathered in groups of one hundred at various locations around the Forum. Some groups held their meetings in the temples, others in basilicas. The only people who remained in the Forum had no right to vote because they did not have Roman citizenship. They were freedmen, slaves, or foreigners, like myself, or were not registered in the city census.

Three hours later, we heard a drum roll again. Representatives of the centuries approached the dais and put their pebbles in the jars of their chosen candidates.

The magistrate's assistants emptied the jars, counted the pebbles, and recorded the numbers on parchment under the candidates' watchful eyes.

After the count, we heard a drum roll for the third time. The judge stood up to announce the result.

"Romans! In their wisdom, the citizens have elected two consuls who will chair the Senate and command the army during the next year." The judge paused. Absolute silence reigned in the square. "The candidate who received the most votes is Octavius."

The loud chants of the public drowned his voice. The people repeatedly shouted, "Long live, Octavius Caesar." Many began to sing patriotic songs. People embraced each other, and tears of joy ran down many faces. I was impressed by this evidence of Octavius' popularity and the affection that the people felt for him. This was not a good omen for Mark Antony.

It took quite a while for the judge to succeed in quieting the crowd.

"Gentlemen, gentlemen! Quiet, please. This is not a market, and you are not in an amphitheater. It is my duty to conclude this ceremony by announcing the name of the second Consul that you have elected. He is Volcacius Tullus. I ask for a round of applause."

A few people clapped, and then the crowd dispersed, still cheering Octavius.

I decided to go to Octavius' house to congratulate him and try to find out what he intended to do about Mark Antony.

The commander of the patrol that guarded the house was the same officer as the last time. He recognized me, and after a soldier frisked me to search for hidden weapons, he let me in. The house was full of Senators, magistrates, sycophants, and well-wishers who had come, like me, to congratulate Octavius on his election.

Octavius stood at the center of the room, surrounded by admirers and friends. A beautiful woman at his side greeted everybody with a smile and talked animatedly.

Octavius saw me and beckoned me to come close.

"Welcome, Nicholas. I am pleased to introduce you to Livia, my dear wife and my best counselor." Looking at the lady, he added, "Livia, this is Nicholas, the ambassador sent by Mark Antony."

"It is an honor to meet you, My Lady," I said, bowing to her. She smiled at me but did not return the greeting.

"I am glad that you came," Octavius continued. "I have news for you. Tomorrow the Senate meets, and I will preside. The letter sent by Mark Antony will be the main issue to be addressed. I would like you to be present and hear the debate. At the end of the session, the Senate will give you a written answer for Mark Antony.

I thought to myself that Octavius had already written the Senate's answer, and it only lacked a small formality, the Senate's seal.

"At what time do you want me to come to the Senate, My Lord?" I asked him.

"Come at noon. But let's now forget these boring political matters. Livia has asked Fausta, the wife of my freedman Lucius, whom I believe you have met, to prepare some of her excellent dishes for us. I also have a superb Greek wine that I am sure you will enjoy."

Chapter 16
In the Roman Senate

I had timed it well. I entered the Senate only a few minutes before Octavius started his speech. He was dressed, like all the other Senators, in a white toga made of wool. To prevent it from sliding down, he held it close to his body with his left arm.

I was amazed when I heard him speak to the Senators. He looked completely different from the friendly and informal host that I had seen the night before. His speech was full of fire and passion. Despite his youth (he had just turned thirty), he exuded authority and showed immense self-confidence. Most of them twice his age, the Senators listened in silence to his every word, captivated by his eloquence.

"Your Excellencies! It is my patriotic duty to denounce a traitor. I do it with sorrow and shame because this traitor's actions against our Republic also affect me personally. This man, this traitor, is married to my sister Octavia. Yes, gentlemen, he is no other than Mark Antony."

Several Senators stood up and protested loudly.

"It is a vile slander," exclaimed one of them.

"It cannot be," cried another.

Pandemonium broke loose. Senators argued with each other, and there were threats of violence. Octavius waited until the tempers calmed down and then continued.

"I have a letter here from Mark Antony, in which he informs the Senate that he has distributed Roman provinces to his children and given them royal titles. And not only to his children but also to the son of Cleopatra, a foreign Queen, thus violating all the norms of our Republic."

A group of Senators stood up angrily and left the building. Other Senators ran after them and tried to hold them back by force.

"Let them go. We will punish them in due time. But now I ask to approve a resolution declaring Mark Antony a traitor."

There was no debate. The Senators who remained in the hall unanimously declared Mark Antony a traitor.

"War against the traitor!" cried one of the Senators. Other Senators shouted, "War against Mark Antony!"

Octavius spoke again.

"No, gentlemen. I understand and sympathize wholeheartedly with your righteous indignation, but Romans have shed too much Roman blood in too many civil wars. We will go to war, not against Mark Antony, but against the foreign Queen, Cleopatra."

The Senators applauded, and Octavius ended the session. He saw me standing near the entrance, called me with a gesture of his hand, and handed me a scroll. There was no doubt in my mind that he had written and sealed the letter before the meeting of the Senate.

"Nicholas, this letter is a response from the Senate to Mark Antony, in which we inform him that we have revoked all his privileges and order him to return immediately to Rome to be tried for treason."

"My Lord, I will return immediately to Alexandria and personally deliver the letter to General Mark Antony," I replied.

"Have a good trip," and, without saying another word, he turned aside and started talking to Agrippa, who was looking at me with a wry smile.

I went directly to Aventine Hill, said goodbye to Lucius and Fausta, and picked up the parchment where I had copied

Cicero's speeches. A litter took me directly to the Trigemina Gate. There, I hired a four-horse carriage, and in the evening, I found myself in Ostia.

It took me three days to find a ship that traveled directly to Alexandria. It was a small vessel with a mast in its center. Its main sail was square and, above it, were two small triangular sails. The day we sailed, I paid my fare to the captain without haggling with him. The captain, pleased to have received a much higher payment than usual, gave me the ship's best cabin.

The journey lasted fourteen days without any incident. The captain was a man of about sixty years, which he carried well. He was muscular, his skin tanned from the sun. He was always in good spirits and loved to tell stories of his life at sea.

Of all the stories that he told me, the one I remember best was about an event that had taken place nearly forty years before when the captain had been a young man.

"Julius Caesar was captured by pirates while sailing in the Aegean Sea. The criminals demanded a ransom of twenty talents to let him go free. Caesar mocked them for their lack of greed and told them to ask for at least fifty talents. Caesar's friends paid the ransom. The pirates released him, and Caesar, when parting from the pirates, said to them, 'I promise that I will crucify you'. The pirates laughed, believing that Caesar was joking."

The captain drank a glass of beer, wiped his mouth with the back of his hand, and continued with his story.

"Caesar organized a flotilla of boats, pursued the pirates, and captured them. They begged him to treat them with compassion. Caesar answered, 'I will be merciful with you. I will not crucify you. I will only cut your throats'. And so he did."

The captain stopped talking due to a prolonged and uncontrollable fit of laughter.

In the Roman Senate

Chapter 17
Secretary to Mark Antony

As soon as I disembarked from the ship in Alexandria, I went to the Museum Library and handed the librarian the parchment where I had copied Cicero's speeches. He was thrilled to receive the scroll and did not cease to thank me. After greeting some of my friends, I went to the royal palace to deliver the Senate's letter to Mark Antony.

The commander of the palace guard personally escorted me to the office of the general.

"My Lord, I have brought a letter sent to you by the Roman Senate."

"A letter from the Roman Senate? You mean a letter from the boy Octavius. Give it to me," he ordered.

I handed him the sealed scroll. Mark Antony broke the seal and read the letter. His face reddened, and the veins of his forehead swelled.

"That upstart, that usurper, that forger of adoption papers, accuses me, Mark Antony, to be an individual of low morale, who has abandoned his faithful wife and children to sleep with a promiscuous Egyptian whore. He says that I have forgotten our dignified Roman customs and adopted the degenerate Oriental tastes. How dare he!" bellowed Mark Antony. He crumpled the scroll and threw it to the ground.

Cleopatra heard the shouts of Mark Antony and came running into the room.

"What is it, my love?" she asked, alarmed when she saw Mark Antony kicking the furniture, throwing the flower vases against the walls, expressing his fury with inarticulate mumblings and extraordinary violence.

Mark Antony did not answer. He just pointed a finger to the scroll lying crumpled on the floor. I picked it up and gave it to Cleopatra.

The Queen sat on a stool and read the scroll. Mark Antony sat beside her, his eyes closed, holding his head with both hands.

"The Senate has stripped you of your powers and declared war on me," said Cleopatra with an incredulous voice.

"They have declared war on us, not just on you," replied Mark Antony. If the boy wants war, he will have it. I will give him a thousand reasons to curse the day he was born.

****

The war did not begin immediately. During the next two years, the popularity of Octavius continued to grow in all the territories controlled by Rome, while Mark Antony's gradually diminished.

One day Mark Antony called me to his office.

"Sit down, Nicholas. From today on, you will no longer be the tutor of my children," he said to my surprise and disappointment.

"Why, My Lord? My pupils have made great progress, and Queen Cleopatra, on more than one occasion, has congratulated me and told me how happy she is with my work," I protested and made an effort to hold back my tears.

"Calm down, Nicholas. I am also very pleased with the work that you've done. I called you to inform you that from now on you will be my secretary. I need intelligent and capable people like you to help me govern my territories in Africa and Asia. You will notice that I have said 'my territories.' They do not belong to Rome. They do not belong to the Senate and even less to the boy. They are mine. I conquered them, and I can do with them what I want."

"My Lord, words fail me to thank you for the honor that you have conferred on me. I promise that I will do my best and will not disappoint you."

From that day on, I served as Mark Antony's secretary, but, in my spare time, I continued to oversee the education of his children.

Secretary to Mark Antony

I got to know Mark Antony quite well. He was brave, generous, frank, and honest, but he had several shortcomings. The most serious of them was his recklessness, which ultimately caused his defeat and death.

Mark Antony was carried away by his emotions, especially by his passionate love for Cleopatra. He acted too often without considering the possible consequences of his actions. Octavius was the opposite, a cold-blooded man, patient and calculating, who planned everything in detail and considered every possible eventuality that might happen.

Another of Mark Antony's shortcomings was his inability to discipline his children, especially Antilus, a fifteen-year-old boy, who had been left motherless at the age of seven. His mother Fulvia had been the third wife of the five women that Mark Antony had married through the years.

Years before, Octavius had proposed to Mark Antony that his daughter Julia become engaged to Mark Antony's son Antilus and marry the boy as soon she reached marriageable age. Mark Antony agreed, but when Octavius became his enemy, he called off the engagement. Antilus left Rome and went to Alexandria to live with his father.

Antilus had never been my student, unlike the children that Mark Antony had with Cleopatra. His tutor, a Greek named Theodore, always flattered him, which turned Antilus into an arrogant and conceited teenager, an idler, and a wastrel.

Antilus had a habit of hosting ostentatious banquets every night for his friends and flatterers. He once invited me to dinner. There were only six guests, his tutor Theodore, four young men of Antilus' age, and me. The food on the table included eight roasted wild boars that could easily have fed fifty people and dozens of wine bottles.

We had an enjoyable after-dinner conversation. I related the story that the ship's captain had told me about Julius Caesar and the pirates. Inspired by the many glasses of wine that I had drunk, I added juicy details that were products of my imagination.

Antilus, laughing, stood up and raised his cup.

"Nicholas, I loved your story. As a token of my appreciation, I am giving you this cup," Antilus said.

I thought that he was joking because the cup was of pure gold inlaid with precious stones. I could not believe that a boy of fifteen was allowed to give away such valuable gifts. I decided to leave the cup on the table when I went home.

The next day, Antilus' slaves came to my house, bringing with them the gold cup wrapped in a silk cloth.

"Tell your master that I am very grateful, but I cannot accept such a valuable gift," I told him.

"Excuse me, sir. Don't you know that the son of Mark Antony has the right to give any gift to whomever he wishes?" he said to me.

I accepted the cup, and, when the slave retired, I examined it with great admiration. It was a work of art made hundreds of years ago by the ancient Egyptians. It probably was stolen from some royal tomb by grave robbers. I still have it with me.

Chapter 18
In Alexandria's Jewish Quarter

It was about that time that I met and became friends with Nicanor, a Jew born in Jerusalem who had settled in Alexandria. Through him, I met many other Alexandrian Jews.

The Jews of Alexandria were proud that their community had resided in the city since Alexander the Great had founded it three hundred years before. Despite having lived in the city from the start, the Jews were not given citizenship because they refused to worship the local gods, arguing that they were followers of an invisible God, the only true God. They said that all the other gods were false. Of course, this arrogant affirmation upset and offended the Greeks of Alexandria and was the cause of frequent violent fights between Jews and Greeks.

The first time that I saw Nicanor was during one of my walks around the city. When I entered the Jewish quarter for the first time, I saw a majestic building surrounded by two rows of columns. The doors were open, and my curiosity prompted me to go in. It was a large hall, empty, except for the stools lined up along the walls. The absence of sculptures and the fact that the walls did not have any frescoes were glaring. A man dressed in a white robe adorned with black stripes and tassels on the corners approached and spoke to me.

"You are in a synagogue. Please cover your head. This is our custom in this sacred place," he told me in a firm but friendly tone.

"Excuse me, I was not aware of the custom," I said as I covered my head with my hood.

"Are you a proselyte?" the man asked me.

"No. I was just walking by and saw that the doors of this beautiful building were open. I came in to see it from the inside. I hope that I have not offended."

"It is not offensive to come in peace to our synagogue. Our doors are always open for all those who want to know the truth about the Lord of the Universe," he replied.

"Do you have many proselytes?" I asked him.

"We have many, thank God. They come on Saturdays to hear the reading of our divine Law, the Torah, and the explanations. We encourage those interested in becoming Jews and fulfilling the six hundred and thirteen commandments specified in the Torah for Jews. Come this Saturday and listen for yourself," he said.

"Thanks, maybe I will," I answered.

I did not go to the synagogue that Saturday. I preferred to take a walk in a part of town that I had never seen before, the neighborhood where the ancient Egyptians' descendants lived.

Unlike the Greek District and the Jewish District, the Egyptian neighborhood was impoverished. The dwellings were huts made of mud and straw. The streets were unpaved. In the rainy season, thick mud covered them, and in the summer, the constant traffic of donkeys and mules raised clouds of dust.

Some half-nude children threw stones at me, and I hastened to leave. I never went to the Egyptian neighborhood again.

On Saturday, two or three weeks later, I did go to the synagogue. Outside in the street, a crowd of men and women listened with respectful silence to the prayers read aloud inside the synagogue. Judging by their appearance and clothing, I had the impression that they were not Jews.

I covered my head and entered the synagogue. It was full of men, all dressed in long white shawls that had black stripes. One of them gave me a shawl and told me in a low voice to puts it over my tunic. There were women behind a curtain that separated them from the men.

A man was reading with a loud voice a scroll that lay on a table. I could hear him clearly, but the language was incomprehensible to me. (I did not know then that the language was Hebrew and that one day I would speak it fluently). The reader was the man who had spoken to me in the synagogue two weeks before.

"Who is the reader," I asked the man next to me.

"He is Nicanor, one of the wealthiest and most important Jews in the city," he answered.

Nicanor finished reading and translated what he had read into Greek.

"I am the Lord your God. You shall have no other gods before me. Do not make idols. Do not use the name of the Lord your God in vain. Observe the Sabbath day and dedicate it to the Lord your God. Honor your father and your mother, and you will enjoy a long life. Do not kill. Do not commit adultery. Do not steal. Do not bear false witness. Do not covet your neighbor's wife."

The ceremony ended with a prayer of praise to the Lord of the Universe, which was repeated by the people who were outside. The crowd dispersed, and I approached Nicanor. He recognized me and greeted me warmly.

"I found it very interesting that you translated the text into Greek. I'd like to hear more about it," I said.

"I'll be delighted to explain our Torah to you. Come tonight to my house for dinner, and we will talk. I live in this street, opposite the synagogue."

"I accept with pleasure," I answered.

I went to Nicanor's house that evening. It was a two-story mansion. I knocked on the door, and while waiting for a servant to open it, I noticed on the door's right jamb a small receptacle made of wrought silver. It was about ten inches long and was set diagonally.

Nicanor greeted me warmly and introduced me to his wife, Miriam. We sat at the table, and slaves brought us plates of food and a pitcher of water. I thought the water was for drinking, but Nicanor poured it into his hands and asked me to do the same. Before we started to eat, my host filled two glasses with wine, gave me one, and indicated that we should stand.

"Blessed are Thou, Lord our God, Ruler of the Universe, Creator of the fruit of the vineyard."

After we both drank, Nicanor gave his cup to Miriam, who also drank from it.

Nicanor recited another blessing.

"Blessed are Thou, God, our Lord, Sovereign of the Universe, who extracts bread from the earth." Nicanor broke the bread into three pieces; he gave one piece to his wife, gave another to me, and ate the third.

The dinner was as delicious as the meals I enjoyed in Lucius and Fausta's apartment during my stay in Rome.

After dinner, Miriam retired to her quarters.

"I have a question, Nicanor," I said. "I have noticed that there are small receptacles fixed on the doorposts. When she went out of this room, your wife, Miriam, put her hand on the receptacle and then kissed her fingers. Could you please explain this custom?" I asked.

"The receptacle is called *a mezuzah*. It contains a small scroll of parchment with two verses from our holy book, the Torah. The first says, 'Hear O Israel, the Lord our God is the only God.' The other says, 'If you listen to My commands, it will rain, and the grass will grow in the fields for your cattle.' Whenever a Jew enters or leaves his home or any room in the house, he always kisses the *mezuzah* to remember that there is only one God."

That night I asked him many questions about his beliefs. The hours passed quickly, and, without realizing it, it was midnight. I thanked Nicanor and bid him farewell. I was surprised when he gave me a scroll wrapped in a linen cloth.

"This is a gift for you. Open it in your home, read it and, if you have any more questions, please visit me at any time," said Nicanor.

As soon as I got home, I opened the package impatiently. The scroll was written in Greek. I started reading it immediately. *'In the beginning, God created heaven and earth....'*

Chapter 19
Octavius defeats Mark Antony

The two consuls who had been elected after Octavius' term ended fled to Alexandria. They were supporters of Mark Antony and were afraid that the Senate would put them in prison. Upon their arrival, they asked to see Mark Antony. They told him that Octavius had recently given an impassioned speech in the Senate, accusing Cleopatra of being a threat to Rome and denouncing Mark Antony as a traitor easily manipulated by a corrupt and depraved woman. The response of the Senate was a unanimous vote for war.

Octavius appointed Agrippa, his loyal friend and companion since childhood, as head of the army. It was a wise decision because Agrippa proved to be a military genius.

Agrippa's first success was the capture of the important Greek port of Modona, located in the southwest of the Peloponnesus, which, until then, had been in the hands of Mark Antony's supporters.

Mark Antony ordered his army, which was stationed in Armenia, to go to Greece immediately. He instructed his commanders to meet him in the Bay of Actium, where he would wait for them with a fleet of warships, most of them contributed by Cleopatra.

The senior aides of Mark Antony traveled with him on his flagship. Cleopatra traveled separately on her royal ship.

When we arrived at Actium, we saw that our army was already camped in the field. Octavius' army was also there, a couple of miles away. A few days later, Agrippa's fleet appeared and blocked the bay.

Mark Antony had two alternatives. One was to leave his ships and fight on land against Octavius' troops. The other option was to try to defeat Agrippa at sea.

Mark Antony and Cleopatra summoned their commanders to discuss the situation. There was a bitter exchange of arguments. Mark Antony wanted to fight Octavius on land.

Cleopatra argued that it would be better to fight at sea. The long march from Armenia to Greece had exhausted our soldiers. They were weak, hungry, and sick and would find it difficult to fight a land battle against Octavius' army.

Seeing that they could not agree, I decided that the time had come to give my opinion.

"Your Majesty and Your Excellency, allow me to propose a third alternative. Instead of confronting the forces of Octavius onshore or Agrippa's fleet at sea, we should escape to Egypt with our fleet taking with us most of our soldiers. Then, we would have enough forces in Egypt, and Octavius would think twice before invading."

"Our fleet consists of five hundred ships, but we do not have enough men to handle them," Mark Antony interrupted me.

"I suggest that we use only our fast boats. We must burn the heavy ships and the small ships that are too slow. Otherwise, they will fall into the hands of Agrippa," I said.

My plan was adopted unanimously. Mark Antony burned the heavy and slow ships. We were left with only two hundred and forty ships against the four hundred that we estimated that Agrippa had in his fleet.

We could not leave immediately due to a violent storm that lasted four days. On the fifth day, the strong wind died down, and a gentle breeze replaced it. Finally, we set sail. Mark Antony and I were in the same ship, in the middle of the fleet.

Agrippa's fleet consisted of triremes equipped with spurs in the bow and catapults. Mark Antony's quinqueremes were floating fortresses with towers for archers on the bow and stern and room for hundreds of soldiers in their spacious decks. In addition to the warships, Mark Antony had boats that carried the chests with the treasures he had accumulated from war spoils. A squadron of Egyptian warships protected these vessels and Cleopatra's flagship.

Agrippa's ships blocked the bay. We planned to escape and head for Egypt. At first, we sailed in serried ranks to force our way out. When we did not achieve this goal, Mark Antony ordered the ships on his right and left flanks to sail away from the center, forcing the enemy to move with them.

The maneuver was successful. An opening appeared in the center of Agrippa's formation, and the Egyptian fleet, including Cleopatra's flagship, took advantage of it and escaped to the open sea.

We saw with joy that Agrippa's ships had retreated, but, unfortunately, at this moment, Mark Antony made the biggest mistake of his life. Instead of following our original plan to escape, he ordered the pursuit of the enemy ships.

It was a ruse, and he fell into the trap. Agrippa's ships turned around unexpectedly, attacked our flanks, and dispersed our vessels. Then they attacked our center. Mark Antony's flagship was caught in the middle of the fighting.

Mark Antony at the Battle of Actium

95

Agrippa's ships came so close that there was no space between us and an enemy ship. The enemy soldiers boarded our vessel, intending to capture Mark Antony. There was hand-to-hand fighting. The fencing lessons that I had taken during my adolescence in Damascus were only a faded memory, but as Plato said, necessity is the mother of invention. A wounded soldier dropped his sword. I picked it up and ran to where Mark Antony was fighting against two enemy soldiers. I plunged my sword in one of them, and Mark Antony killed the other. We managed to make our way to the edge of the deck, where we saw that one of our ships was quite close. We jumped to the sea, swam to our ship under a rain of arrows, and climbed aboard, grabbing the ropes that the sailors threw to us. As soon as we were aboard, Mark Antony gave the order to escape as fast as possible.

Agrippa's ships pursued us, but our ship was faster. Before they could catch us, we were at the side of Cleopatra's flagship. We estimated that at least one hundred of our ships had managed to escape.

Mark Antony stayed in the bow without talking to anyone, his head resting in his hands. Two days later, we arrived at Cape Taenarus, one of the three capes in the southern Peloponnesus. There, we dropped anchor and waited for our other ships to join us.

In Taenarus, we learned the extent of our defeat. Agrippa had captured the hundred ships that we thought had escaped, and the garrison that we left in Greece had surrendered to Octavius.

Mark Antony gave orders to depart immediately for Alexandria to take charge of the four legions stationed in Cyrenaica. When we arrived in Alexandria, we were informed that those troops had sworn loyalty to Octavius.

In desperation, Mark Antony and Cleopatra tried to bribe Octavius to persuade him not to attack Egypt. Cleopatra sent him a message, accompanied by the gift of a golden crown, offering to abdicate in favor of Caesarion. Mark Antony, meanwhile, sent his son Antilus to Octavius with a large sum of money and a letter promising to renounce all political positions and retire to live in Athens as an ordinary citizen.

Octavius rejected both proposals and landed in Egypt with his army shortly after that. Mark Antony, with the few troops he had left, bravely confronted him but was badly defeated. He managed to escape from the battlefield and came to the palace where his children and I had taken refuge. Cleopatra, in the meantime, had locked herself in a nearby mausoleum.

Mark Antony saw his children crying, and he hugged them.

"Dear children, do not cry. Look at me. I am smiling. That's how I want you to remember me. But for now, let me have a moment alone with Nicholas."

Still crying, his children kissed him and left the room.

"Nicholas, all is lost. I want you to promise me that you will take care of my children. I hope that Antilus will bring honor to my name, Selene will be as beautiful as her mother, Helios will be a better politician and a better warrior than his poor father, and Philadelphus, Oh, Philadelphus!", he sobbed.

"I promise, My Lord," I said, crying too.

Mark Antony drew his sword and fell upon it. Mortally wounded, he spoke weakly.

"Nicholas, I beg of you. Take me to the mausoleum where Cleopatra is hiding. I want to see her before I die."

I ordered two slaves to carry him to the mausoleum on a litter soaked with his blood. I walked along, accompanying Mark Antony on his last trip, and witnessed his death in the arms of Cleopatra.

Octavius entered Alexandria at the head of his victorious army. His commanders waved flags with Octavius' emblem: an eagle with golden feathers, with iron beaks and claws.

Octavius entered the palace and sat on the throne.

"Egypt is now my property," he declared.

I lack the courage to write what happened later, but I must, though tears wet my cheeks at the memory.

Octavius ordered that Cleopatra be brought to the Throne Room. The soldiers brought the Queen, and Octavius informed her that he intended to take her to Rome to walk in chains in his triumphal procession, after which she would be executed.

That evening, to avoid dishonor, Cleopatra committed suicide by having a poisonous snake bite her.

I was unable to fulfill the promise that I gave to Mark Antony of caring for his children. Octavius ordered the death of Caesarion so as not to leave any doubt that the sole heir of Julius Caesar was he and not an alleged bastard son. The children, Selene, Helios, and Philadelphus, were sent to Rome and given to Octavia, the woman whom Mark Antony had abandoned for Cleopatra.

Octavia, a noble-hearted woman, received them with love. Unfortunately, Helios and Philadelphus fell ill and died soon after. Selene was the only child of Mark Antony, who grew up to have a happy life. As beautiful as her mother, she married the king of Mauritania and became the current king's mother. I am flattered to say that she is still in contact with me and, to this day, we write to each other.

The end of Antilus, the son that Mark Antony had with Fulvia, was tragic. When the young man learned that Octavius had killed Caesarion, he escaped from the palace and hid in the house of his tutor, Theodore. The tutor told him that he knew the captain of a ship that would sail that night. He would arrange with the captain for Antilus' immediate departure from Alexandria. Antilus thanked him profusely. Theodore, instead of going to the port, went to the royal palace where he betrayed Antilus to Octavius.

The soldiers that Octavius sent to Theodore's home dragged Antilus back with them. Antilus begged for mercy, but Octavius ordered the soldiers to cut off his head.

Theodore, who was present at the beheading, knelt beside the body shedding false tears. Believing that no one was watching him, he grabbed the collar of precious stones that Antilus always wore around his neck. A soldier saw the theft and informed Octavius.

Theodore denied stealing the necklace, but the soldiers searched him and found the jewel hidden in his belt. Octavius immediately ordered his soldiers to crucify him.

Fearful that a similar fate might befall me, I left my house secretly and asked my Jewish friend Nicanor to let me stay with him for a while. He generously agreed, although he knew that his kind action put him at enormous personal risk.

I hid in Nicanor's house until, two months later, Octavius, now absolute master of the nation, returned to Rome. Three years later, the Senate appointed him Emperor giving him the title of Augustus.

Octavius defeats Mark Antony

Chapter 20
From Alexandria to Ptolemais

One night after dinner, I informed Nicanor that I had decided to leave Alexandria.

"Mark Antony and Cleopatra are dead, and their surviving children are in Rome. Nothing holds me in Alexandria. I want to go away to try to forget the tragedies that I have witnessed," I told him.

"Where do you want to go, my friend?" Nicanor asked me.

"I will return to Damascus, my hometown," I replied.

"I wish to propose something. I must travel to Judea soon and have chartered a boat to take me to the port of Ptolemais, and from there, I will go to Jerusalem. Come with me, stay for a while in the Holy City, and then, whenever you decide, you can proceed with your journey to Damascus," he offered.

He saw a look of doubt on my face and added, "I will introduce you to King Herod. As a historian, you cannot miss the opportunity to meet the king of the Jews."

The possibility to meet Herod tempted me. I had heard much about the Jewish king, a descendant of converted Edomites. I knew he had usurped the throne displacing the Hasmonean royal family, but I did not know the details. My indecisiveness disappeared, and I accepted Nicanor's invitation with gratitude.

"You will not regret it," said Nicanor. "Jerusalem is a beautiful city, and Herod is an exceptional person. Tomorrow I will take you to my foundry and explain the reason for my journey to Judea."

Nicanor took me to his foundry the next day. It was one of his many properties. He told me that he also owned land where he grew wheat and raised cattle, besides importing and exporting merchandise.

Nicanor was not only the richest man in the Jewish community of Alexandria but also the most generous. He donated dowries to poor brides and maintained at his expense

101

the synagogue, an orphanage, a school, and the cemetery of the Jewish community.

There were two gigantic doors on the floor of the foundry. They were made of polished bronze that shone like gold.

"Do you have any idea where these doors will be installed?" he asked me with a mischievous smile.

"No," I replied.

"These doors are my contribution to the Temple of Jerusalem that King Herod intends to rebuild. On my last visit to Jerusalem, I learned that the king is planning to replace the current modest Temple, which is several centuries old and is crumbling, with a building that will be the most beautiful Temple in the world. The idea seemed wonderful to me, and I decided to donate the doors. For over a year, I have spent all my days and nights working on this project. I hired the best craftsmen and bronze workers from other countries. I told them not to rush but to work as perfectly as possible. At last, the doors are ready, and I can take them to Jerusalem."

The following day Nicanor hired a team of carpenters to build a cart to transport the enormous doors from the foundry to the port.

On the day the carpenters finished building a massive wagon, Nicanor's workers yoked twenty mules to the cart, loaded the doors on it, and transported them to the port. The people in the streets commented with wonder and awe that they had never seen such a large wagon in Alexandria.

In the harbor, fifty longshoremen lifted the doors and placed them on the deck of the ship. Nicanor said goodbye to his wife Miriam and boarded the ship. I followed him.

The early days of sailing were uneventful, but we encountered a terrible storm with powerful winds when we approached Gaza's coast. Large waves hit the sides of the ship and, at times, flooded the deck. Nicanor and I, not used to traveling by sea, became violently ill. The captain ordered the crew to tie us to the mast to avoid us being dragged by the waves into the sea.

The storm became even more potent. Huge waves raised our ship on their crests and then threw us down violently. The timbers of the hull creaked, and we felt that any minute would be our last.

Desperately, the captain approached us and talked to Nicanor.

"Sir, we must throw the doors into the sea. They are too heavy for the ship and, in this storm, they could cause the ship to sink. Our only chance to survive is to throw them into the sea. Please, Sir," begged the captain.

Nicanor asked one of the sailors to untie the ropes that bound him to the mast. When he was free, he threw himself over the doors, holding on to them.

"If you throw these doors to the sea, you must throw me also," shouted Nicanor.

The captain couldn't decide what to do. He knew that to save the ship and his sailors, he had to throw the heavy doors to the depths of the sea, but that would mean the death of Nicanor.

"Only a miracle can save us," the captain groaned.

At that moment, over the awful noise of the storm, we heard Nicanor's voice, loud and clear, praying to his god.

"God of Israel, Lord of the Universe, blessed is your name. If I offended you in any way, forgive your servant, and allow these doors, made with love for you, to adorn your home in Jerusalem. Amen."

I am not a believer. I consider the Greek gods to be myths and legends. I cannot believe in the invisible Jewish god because my philosophy requires me to see to believe. It must have been a coincidence. There is no other possible explanation. As soon as Nicanor finished his prayer, the sea calmed, the clouds cleared, and a rainbow appeared in the bright blue sky.

The sailors shouted for joy, Nicanor rose, and the captain kissed his hand. I stared at him, stunned, unable to believe what I had seen.

Two days later, we reached the port of Ptolemais (the Jews call it Acre), situated in a bay between the territory of Judea and ancient Phoenicia.

Chapter 21
In Ptolemais

The Greek citizens of Ptolemais, a majority of the city's population, took justified pride in their splendid temples dedicated to Zeus, Aphrodite, Athena, Apollo, and other gods. The largest Temple of all was consecrated to Poseidon, the god of the sea and chief deity of the city. Ornaments of coral and gems decorated it and made it look like a palace on the bottom of the ocean. On the main square in front of the Temple, the city erected a statue of Poseidon holding a scepter in the form of a three-pronged spear while driving a chariot which rode on the waves of the sea, pulled by horses.

Nicanor had several acquaintances among the Jewish community in the city, and through them, we found accommodation at an inn. The meals were entirely satisfactory, and the rooms were spacious, comfortable, and reasonably clean.

During the weeks that followed, Nicanor hired carpenters and oversaw the construction of a wagon bigger and stronger than the one he made in Alexandria.

This time, it was not a matter of merely transporting the bronze doors on Alexandria's paved streets. We needed to climb mountains, cross valleys, and wade through rivers on our way from Ptolemais to Jerusalem.

Nicanor was busy, working day and night, eager to finish the wagon and depart for Jerusalem as soon as possible. I had a lot of free time in my hands and decided, as a historian, to go to the schools, speak with the teachers and learn the history of the city from them.

Ptolemais, formerly called Acre, had been conquered in antiquity by the Pharaohs of Egypt. The Israelites could not conquer Acre, and it continued to be part of Phoenicia for many centuries until the Greeks arrived with Alexander. The Roman general Pompey conquered the city three decades before I visited it, and, since that time, Ptolemais and the rest of Phoenicia were a Roman province.

In addition to my historical research, I also explored the city. I found that Ptolemais had an institution of great importance to the Greek population. This institution, called "gymnasium," was a place dedicated to both physical and intellectual activities. People interested in sharing and discussing ideas came to hear lectures from visiting philosophers. Young men came to train in sports and to receive lessons in morals and ethics.

The gymnasium institution never took root in Rome because the Romans thought that such training for children leads to idleness and immorality.

The Ptolemais gymnasium was a set of buildings built in the style of the Acropolis of Athens. It was located on the outskirts of the city next to a forest. Paintings of beautiful landscapes covered its doors and walls. It had conference rooms, pools, and public restrooms. Outside there was a huge lawn where the young men practiced sports, including running, jumping, boxing, and throwing the discus.

What most attracted me to the gymnasium, apart from the well-attended lectures, was that the athletes practiced their sports completely naked, smeared with oil. I never saw such beautiful young men.

I became friends with the gymnasium director and took advantage of many opportunities to ask him questions about his institution. He always answered with kindness and patience.

He told me that the oil used to anoint the young athletes was bought with money provided by public funds and private donations, and it was the most costly gymnasium expense.

He also told me something that caught my attention. Many parents sent their children to the gymnasium to attract the attention of older and influential men who could serve their sons as mentors and who were able to help them forge important social positions in the future. The relationship between a mentor and a youth was usually platonic, but it could also be passionate in some cases.

To be an object of desire, a boy needed certain qualities: attractiveness, kindness, bravery, and modesty. He should also be demure and not be easily seduced.

I regretted that my stay in Ptolemais was too short to permit a close relationship with one of these beautiful athletes. Still, I consoled myself by frequenting several of the many brothels that were in the city.

The day came when Nicanor announced that the wagon was ready for the journey to Jerusalem. I was amazed when I saw it. It was so big that it needed thirty mules, managed by the same number of mule drivers, to pull it. It had six enormous wheels on each side. This allowed its platform to be much higher than was usual, an indispensable necessity because it was the rainy season, and most of the route would be through mud and over rocks.

The wagon had two rooms on its platform, one at each end. Nicanor told me that one was for me and the other for him. I went to my designated room and saw it had a bed, a stool, and a small table with a candle-holder for reading at night.

The next day we departed for Jerusalem. The distance was about ninety miles, and the trip lasted a week. On the last day of the journey, Nicanor ordered the mule drivers to stop the cart at the bottom of a hill and asked me to climb to the summit with him to visit the prophet Samuel's tomb.

While Nicanor prayed, I looked east and saw in the distance the walls of Jerusalem. The bright sunlight gave them a golden hue and, for a moment, I thought I saw a city of gold.

I had intended to remain in Jerusalem no more than two or three weeks, but I stayed there for the following twenty-five years. They were the best and most exciting years of my life.

In Ptolemais

Chapter 22
King Herod

In Jerusalem, we stayed in the house of one of Nicanor's cousins. Three days later, King Herod granted us an audience.

"Your Majesty," said Nicanor, "during my visit to Jerusalem last year, the priests of the Temple told me that you intend to replace the current Temple with a large modern Temple, more beautiful than any other in the world. As soon as I returned to my hometown of Alexandria, I hired the best craftsmen to make two bronze doors that I have brought with me. I beg Your Majesty to accept these doors as my contribution to the new Temple."

"I have seen the doors, and I appreciate your valuable donation. If this project comes through, I will order that the doors be officially called 'The Gates of Nicanor.' Your name will be linked to the Temple for all eternity," replied the king.

"Your Majesty, I am grateful and honored. Please permit me to introduce my friend Nicholas of Damascus. He was the tutor of Queen Cleopatra's children and the counselor of Mark Antony," said Nicanor.

"My children already have a tutor, but I have heard about your friend, and I would like to have a conversation with him," said the king. Addressing me, he added, "Come to the palace tomorrow at this time."

During our meeting the next day, King Herod asked me many questions regarding my experience as Mark Antony's counselor, my diplomatic mission in Rome, and my personal opinion about Octavius' victory's impact on Rome's relations with Judea. He expressed great interest when I informed him that I was a historian and philosopher and told me that these arts fascinated him. However, Herod added, he regretted that so far he had not found a single person in Jerusalem who could share those interests with him or had as much knowledge on these subjects as he had".

"Nicholas," he said in a friendly voice, "get used to the idea that I will not allow you to leave. You will stay here and do for me what you did for Mark Antony."

"I will be honored, Your Majesty," I answered, flattered.

It became a habit for King Herod and me to have long conversations every night after dinner, in which I argued with the king as an equal and expressed my opinions frankly. Unlike the other palace officers, I was not afraid to give my opinion to the king even if it contradicted his. I can say without exaggeration that I was the only person that Herod allowed to disagree with him.

The king took a liking to me and expressed his concern about my physical condition more than once. He told me that being obese was shortening my life and was why I walked with difficulty and breathed heavily. He went so far as to say that I looked ten years older than him though I was ten years his junior.

It is true that I never exercised, rode a horse, or swam in the palace pool. On the other hand, Herod was an excellent athlete, a great rider, a nimble fencer, and an experienced hunter. His height was less than average, but he was well proportioned. His features were manly and attractive, although a scar on his left cheek, which ran from the side of his mouth to his forehead, disfigured his face. It resulted from a wound received in one of the many skirmishes and battles in which he had taken part. His cropped black hair and his brown skin revealed his Idumean ancestry.

"You must believe me, friend Nicholas," he once said to me, "the best guarantee for a long life is a healthy body, accompanied, of course, by a good daily dose of paranoia."

"Your Majesty..." I started to say, but he interrupted me.

"I have told you before, and I don't like to repeat myself. When we are alone, there is no 'Your Majesty.' My name is Herod, and that is how I want you to call me."

"Your Majes.... Sorry, Herod, permit me to ask a question. How can one live with constant paranoia?"

"It is better to live with paranoia than to die because of excessive trust. Being paranoid has saved my life on many occasions and has taught me how prudent it is to be wary of everyone, including my wives and children. Perhaps the only exception is to trust God."

"I feel the opposite," I said with a smile. "I trust men, or, at least, some men, but I have no trust in gods, whether Greek or Jewish. If I may say so, my human God is the philosopher Aristotle, and I believe only in him, his philosophy, and his teachings. To indulge my intellectual curiosity, I visited last week the two most famous rabbis of Jerusalem, Shammai and Hillel. I asked each one of them, separately, to teach me the essence of Judaism in the time I could stand leaning on one foot."

"What answers did you receive?" asked Herod.

"Shammai told me in an angry voice that if I did not leave instantly, he would tell his students to kick me out of his house. Hillel's reaction was very different. He smiled and said, 'the essence of Judaism is not to do to another person what you do not want to be done to yourself.'

"What you are telling me doesn't surprise me at all. Both men have been here in the palace several times debating their views in my presence. I am aware of their beliefs and opinions. For example, Shammai believes that only outstanding students should study the Torah, while Hillel says that the Torah should be taught to all. On one occasion, I asked them if one should say to an ugly bride that she is pretty. Shammai answered that one should never lie, but Hillel said that all brides are beautiful on their wedding day.

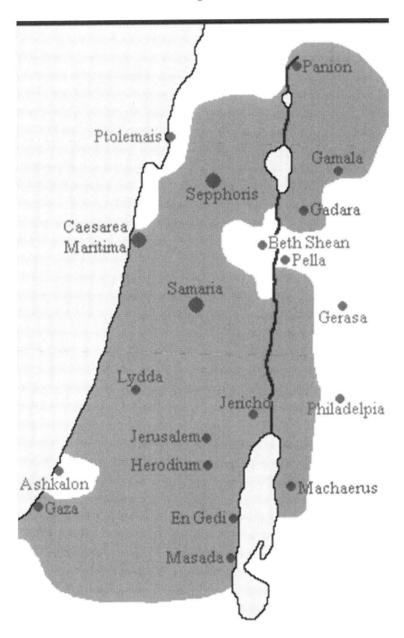

King Herod's kingdom

Chapter 23
Rabbi Hillel

When I first met Rabbi Hillel, he was already in his eighties, and I was not yet thirty-five. Despite the significant difference in our ages, we became close friends.

He was bald, thin, and tall, although he was beginning to stoop due to his advanced age. His forehead was broad, his eyes shined with intelligence, and his constant smile revealed his joy of living. Despite the many years, he had lived in Judea, he had not lost his characteristic Babylonian accent when speaking Hebrew, Aramaic, Latin, or Greek.

Rabbi Hillel was born in Babylon and lived there until he immigrated to Jerusalem at the age of forty. For several years he lived in extreme hardship, earning his living as a lumberjack. At night Hillel studied the writings of Moses. Gradually he became a famous scholar and founded an Academy of Jewish Philosophy, or, as he called it, a *Yeshiva*.

Over time, his intelligence, wisdom, and knowledge were recognized, appreciated, and admired, and his academy became the most prestigious institute of learning in Jerusalem. When I met him, he was the president of the Sanhedrín, the Jewish Senate of Elders.

During my frequent visits to his school, we had many conversations, which I would like to believe he enjoyed as much as I did.

Our philosophies had different sources. Mine was based on the writings of the Greek philosophers Socrates, Plato, and Aristotle, and his on the teachings of Moses, the Jewish lawgiver. But most of the time, we arrived at the same conclusions.

I have read the writings of Moses, but I do not consider myself an expert on them. Despite this limitation, I once helped Hillel solve a problem that eluded a solution for the 1500 years that have elapsed since Moses' time.

The problem was that a law promulgated by Moses required creditors to forgive their debtors and cancel their debts in the last year of each seven-year cycle.

As is also the case with other legislators, Moses did not consider all the possible ramifications of the law. Without a doubt, it was a generous law, praised and appreciated by the debtor, but it was unfair and highly prejudicial to the creditors. To cancel the debts owed to them meant a significant loss of money.

What happened in the real world was that people refused to lend money when there were only one or two years left until the end of the seven-year cycle established by Moses. They preferred to keep the money in their own pockets instead of lending it and running the risk of not getting it back.

One day I was visiting Hillel when his maid interrupted our conversation, saying that a man was at the door with an urgent query.

"May I let him in?" she asked.

"Yes, of course," Hillel replied.

The maid brought a man whose modest clothing, stained with mud and dust, showed that he was a farmer.

"Welcome, my son. How can I help you?" asked Hillel.

"Rabbi, I urgently need money to buy seeds to plant. If I don't plant them right away, I will not be able to harvest this year."

"Please explain your problem," said Hillel.

"I don't have the money to buy seeds, and no one is willing to lend it to me because they say the seven-year period will end in a few months, and, according to the law, I will not be obligated to return them the loan," the visitor complained.

"That's the law," confirmed Hillel.

"Is there any way to force somebody to lend me the money I need?" the man asked in a desperate tone.

"I am very sorry. No law can obligate a person to lend money to another person," said Hillel. The man left heartbroken.

I thought of a possible solution.

"Hillel, I understand that the law obligates creditors to forgive their debtors and cancel their debts in the last year of each cycle of seven years. But, here is my question: does this law also apply to loans made by public institutions?"

"No, it doesn't", Hillel answered. "The law applies only to loans made by private persons. Public institutions are exempt."

"That's the solution to the problem! The creditor should transfer to a court of law the documents of the loan. The debtor would be required to pay the money that he owed to the court, which the court would then deliver to the creditor."

Hillel was thoughtful. Then, after a while, he smiled.

"It is a wonderful solution! I will present the motion to the Sanhedrin and request its approval," Hillel said to me.

As the matter interested me very much, I asked Hillel for permission to be present during the debate.

It was an intense, heated discussion. I wish that I could have given my opinion, but I did not have the right to speak or vote because I was not a Sanhedrin member. The elders who opposed the motion said that Hillel's proposal was a legal fiction and declared they would never repeal or modify Moses' law. Some of them accused Hillel of proposing an unprecedented and controversial rule which bordered on heresy. Others demanded, shouting angrily, that Hillel should resign from his position as president of the Sanhedrin.

I am glad to say that, in the final vote, the Sanhedrin approved Hillel's proposal by a large majority to the benefit of both creditors and debtors.

Rabbi Hillel

Chapter 24
The three Jewish philosophies

In Alexandria, I had acquired the habit of walking around the city, exploring its neighborhoods, and, once I had settled in Jerusalem, I continued doing the same. The distances that I covered in my walks were short because the capital of Judea, although very beautiful, is a small city. When I lived there, Jerusalem had about sixty thousand inhabitants, which increased to several hundred thousand during the religious festivals, when Jews came in pilgrimage from all over the civilized world.

Herod's palace, located in the northwest corner of the city, was three hundred feet long by about one hundred feet wide. It consisted of two main buildings, separated by gardens, canals, and water fountains. Each building included banquet halls, bathrooms, and bedrooms for hundreds of guests.

Select soldiers were garrisoned in three tall towers that guarded the royal palace. The king called the first tower Phasael in honor of his late brother. He gave the name Hipicus to the second tower in memory of a childhood friend. He named the third tower, which was the most beautiful, Mariamne, to honor the wife he loved the most.

The king gave me a house and five slaves (three males and two females). The house was located near the palace in the area called "The Upper City." Wealthy and influential people lived there in luxurious mansions whose exterior walls, covered with a white stone, gave the impression of being magically constructed of snow. A deep valley, with a bridge over it, separated the Upper City from the Temple Mount.

The poor people lived south of the Temple Mount in a neighborhood called "Lower City." Their houses were built of mud and limestone yellowed by the sun and the wind. The streets of the Lower City were narrow, unpaved alleys.

Surrounding the city was a high wall that had in it several gates. Herod's officials were stationed at the gates collecting the taxes for the goods that entered or left the city.

My walks usually took me from my house to the amphitheater built by Herod, from there to the Hasmonean kings' former palace, and finally to the Temple Mount. Sometimes, I would enter the Temple, but I could go in only as far as the square called the 'Court of the Gentiles', the only place where non-Jews, such as I, were allowed. There I could find people from all over the world, Greeks, Armenians, Ethiopians, and Arabs, with whom I struck up conversations that were very useful for the book of World History that I was writing at that time.

Compared to living in Alexandria, Rome, Ptolemais, or other cities of the Empire, the only disadvantage of living in Jerusalem was that the Jewish capital had no brothels because of the Jewish religious laws. I solved this inconvenience by traveling to Ptolemais whenever I had the urge, which would happen from time to time.

Before coming to Jerusalem, I knew very little about Judaism, except that Jerusalem was a religious center visited annually by hundreds of thousands of Jewish pilgrims from all over the Empire. Being in the city sparked my interest in learning about this strange religion that, unlike all the other religions that I know, is satisfied with one God which no one can see.

My inquiries gave me two surprises. The first was discovering that the Jews weren't unanimous in their beliefs. They were divided into three sects, each with its own theology: Sadducees, Pharisees, and Essenes.

The second surprise was that these sects didn't only have philosophical and theological differences, but they also behaved like political parties trying to influence the government.

My interest in learning about Judaism led me to converse with people from the different sects to know their beliefs. One day I went to see my neighbor Nathan ben Asher, a prominent

Sadducee who held a high position in the Temple's priestly hierarchy. He prided himself on being a direct descendant of king Solomon's High Priest.

"Nathan," I told him, "I am not Jewish, but I would like you to explain to me the beliefs of the Sadducees. Who knows, maybe you will convince me to convert," I said smiling.

"Dear Nicholas," he answered, "I will explain our beliefs gladly. We believe in the one and only God but deny the immortality of the soul and the resurrection. Nor do we believe in the existence of angels. We do not accept predestination. We believe that God has given human beings free will to choose between good and evil. For us, the only holy books are Moses' five books, and we obey only the laws on these books and not the laws and customs derived from the oral tradition. Because we deny that there is life after death, we believe that God rewards the good men while they live, giving them wealth and high social positions. Genealogy is of vital importance to us. A priest must be the son of a priest. The most important place in the world is the Temple, and only priests may enter its holy sanctuaries."

A few days later, I went to a synagogue of Pharisees in the Lower City. There I spoke to one of the rabbis (a word which means 'master' or 'teacher'), who was willing to explain his beliefs to me.

"We believe that God gave his laws to Moses in both written and oral forms, and both are equally important. We believe in the resurrection of the dead and the reward and punishment that the individual will receive after his death. God controls everything, but individual decisions can also influence the destiny of a person. For us, the Temple is the House of God, but the synagogue is where we gather to pray and study the holy books. The rabbi is not a priest but a teacher. Any man with learning and understanding of the written and oral laws may be appointed as a rabbi by his congregation," he explained.

To complete my inquiries, I needed to talk with an Essene. To my frustration, when I tried to locate one in Jerusalem, I discovered that the members of this sect lived isolated in a separate neighborhood, were convinced that their version of Judaism was the only true one, and despised people who belonged to the other sects. I had no choice but to visit my neighbor, the priest Nathan ben Asher, again and ask him to explain the Essenes' theology.

"That sect is not for you, Nicholas," he said, laughing. "To be accepted as an Essene, the candidate must undergo instructions on the beliefs of the sect and then spend two years being closely watched by the elders of the sect before they accept him. Your assets become community property when you join them. Those whom we welcome into the community must dedicate their life to the study of the sacred laws, as interpreted by the founder of the sect, a mysterious character called "the Teacher of Righteousness."

I never converted to Judaism, and despite what I had said to my neighbor, I never intended to do so. Herod, who, I suspect, shared my indifference to religion, did not demand that I convert. But if I had been forced to become a Jew, I would have chosen to be a Sadducee. They were aristocrats, educated, and spoke Greek (although I learned to speak Hebrew fluently, I still preferred to speak Greek, my native language). The Sadducees sympathized with Rome and used their power, influence, and wealth to maintain peace and order.

Chapter 25
A tour to Herod's palaces

"Nicholas, you will come with me on an inspection tour of the palaces and forts that I am building," said Herod to me one day. "The leading architects and engineers of Judea will accompany us. I hope that when you see the buildings and appreciate their size, you will be able to give me suggestions on how to raise funds to finance their construction."

From the first day that I spoke with him, I realized that architecture was Herod's main interest, but, during that tour, I found that this was not just an interest but also his passion. His obsession (that's the only word for it), to build beautiful palaces, strong forts, and entire cities, defined his personality as much as his need to hold absolute power in Judea.

Thirty people accompanied Herod. Some of us rode on horseback, and others on mules. The cooks, servants, and porters traveled on carts pulled by donkeys. A detachment of soldiers in charge of our safety followed us.

The king told me that our first stop would be Jericho. From there, we would go to Masada, a fortress-palace situated on top of an isolated rock plateau, on the eastern edge of the Judean desert, overlooking the Sea of Salt. The tour would end at Herodion, a palace that Herod was building on a mountain near Bethlehem.

In all the years that I lived in Judea, I never saw Herod so happy, so joyful, so at peace with himself, as he was when inspecting his palaces on that tour.

Early in the afternoon, we arrived at Jericho, a city a distance of about fifteen miles east of Jerusalem. Unlike Jerusalem, a city located in hilly terrain, Jericho is in a fertile valley watered by freshwater springs. Local farmers used the water to irrigate plantations of spices, especially balsam, whose export was one of the primary sources of Herod's income. Some years later, I bought land in the valley of Jericho, where I planted date palms.

121

We stayed that night at the former residence of the Hasmonean kings. The next day we went to see the palace that Herod was building. It consisted of two buildings, located on both sides of a narrow and deep valley, linked together by a bridge over the deep gorge. Although the palace was unfinished, I could already see that it would be much larger and more luxurious than the old Hasmonean palace. A profusion of shrubs, planted in pots that gardeners could move from place to place, surrounded a hundred feet long pool. One of Herod's innovations in this palace was a Roman bath whose floor was laid on ceramic supports, leaving a gap through which hot air circulated, thus warming the room.

The construction workers greeted the king in Latin. I was stunned. How could workers in such a distant place from Rome speak such perfect Latin?

Herod saw the expression of surprise on my face and explained what seemed a mystery to me.

"The foremen and the masons that I have contracted for this project are all Romans. They use technologies that are unknown in this country. Look at the walls, for example. They are built of concrete covered with small stones cut into squares. The Romans are the only ones who know how to do this type of work," explained Herod.

It was noon when we left Jericho for the oasis of Ein Gedi. We traveled forty miles along the shores of the Sea of Salt. The ground was wild, and we found it difficult to move. We arrived at Ein Gedi after midnight. I was exhausted because I was not used to riding a mule for so many hours. As soon as our servants set up camp, I fell asleep in my tent. I woke up on the afternoon of the next day.

I noticed that the camp was empty except for the servants who were busy lighting a fire to cook the meal they would serve us that night.

"Where is the king? Where is everybody?" I asked them.

"The king is hunting the wild goats that abound in this region. Some of his friends went with him. Others are bathing in the springs, and a third group went down the hill to bathe in the Sea of Salt," they answered.

I had heard much about the Sea of Salt but had never seen it up close. The king had told me that it was impossible to sink in its waters and that these had healing properties, especially for skin diseases.

I had been suffering for a long time from an annoying, sometimes painful, skin itch. The doctors that I had consulted in Alexandria and Jerusalem had prescribed ointments that had three things in common: they were expensive, they gave off a foul smell, and they proved to be a total failure.

I told myself that if I was so close to the Sea of Salt, it was worth a try to bathe in its waters. I went down the hill to the shore and saw that many of my companions were floating on the water. They invited me to join them, but I only entered the water for a few minutes. It felt oily. When I came out, I smeared myself with the black mud that covered the beach and lay on the sand letting the hot sun dry me. Almost instantly, the itching disappeared, never to return.

When my companions came out of the water, we went to a nearby freshwater spring and washed away the salt and the mud from our skin. Then we climbed the hill back to our camp.

In the meantime, the king had returned to the camp with the carcasses of several wild goats, which he gave to the cooks.

That night we sat around the campfire and ate delicious roasted meat seasoned with spices that grew in the oasis. The king was in an excellent mood; I was happy to be finally rid of the itch, and all the others were in high spirits, having a great time singing and telling jokes.

In the morning, we continued south toward Masada. We covered the distance of ten miles in five hours.

Masada is a plateau whose height is about four hundred feet. It is six hundred feet long and three hundred wide. Its cliffs are steep, almost impossible to climb.

The king dismounted from his horse and gestured for us to follow him. He stopped beside a narrow path that went up the mountain.

"This trail leads to the summit. It's called 'The Way of the Snake' because it is narrow and winding. It is half a mile long, and it will take us about one hour to climb up. We'd better start at once because the intense heat of the sun will soon make it impossible," said Herod.

Without waiting for our reply, the king began climbing with enviable agility. We had no choice but to follow him. The trail was narrow, only two feet wide in some sections. A misstep meant falling off the cliff to certain death. The climb was challenging, and I found that the effort was too much for me not being used to physical exercise. I could not breathe; I was sweating profusely and my heartbeat so violently that it seemed that it wanted to escape from my chest. As soon as I arrived at the top, I threw myself on the ground and did not move for a long time. The king came to me and made me drink from a waterskin that he had brought with him. Little by little, I began to feel better. After a while, I was able to sit up.

I looked around and could not believe my eyes. Herod had built two exquisite palaces, gardens, swimming pools, and a fully-equipped Roman bath at the plateau's summit. A wall bordered the plateau.

"Herod, Masada is a fortress impossible to conquer." I cried. "Any enemy soldiers who would be foolish enough to try to climb the path will be easily shot down by the defenders' arrows."

"It is indeed impossible for an army to climb up by the Way of the Snake, but it is possible from the other side by building a ramp. I calculate that it would take twenty thousand men, working day and night for several months, to finish the ramp. It is fortunate for us that none of our enemies has that capability. So, you're right. Masada is impregnable, at least for now", said the king.

We spent the next few hours visiting the palaces and gardens of Masada.

"Herod, this is the most impressive site that I have seen in my life. I have a question regarding the water needed for everyday use, to irrigate the gardens and to fill the swimming pools. Where does it come from?"

"The water supply was our main problem, and it was not easy to solve, but my engineers succeeded. This area gets very little rain, but when it rains, the desert hollows fill with water that channels conduce to the cisterns that we have built," explained Herod.

That night we slept in Masada. We woke up before sunrise and watched the sky turning pink on Moab's mountains across the Sea of Salt. I cannot remember ever seeing a more beautiful dawn.

We returned to Ein Gedi, where we stayed a few days because Herod wanted to hunt more goats and deer. Then we crossed the desert towards the west to visit Herodion.

In contrast to other sovereigns, Herod didn't like to give his name to his buildings, with one exception. Herodion is the only building in Judea that Herod called by his name. It is situated on top of the highest mountain that lies between Jerusalem and the Sea of Salt. I was amazed to learn that the truncated cone of the mountain was not natural. Hundreds of workers added height to the mountain and gave it the shape of a woman's breast.

We ascended a wide staircase that led us to the summit. Herod stopped halfway and pointed to a tower that was still unfinished.

"That tower will be my mausoleum. There, when the time comes, I will be buried for all eternity," Herod told us proudly.

The palace on the hill's summit consisted of four towers, seven stories high, each one with bathrooms, banquet halls, and luxurious rooms decorated with Roman-style frescoes on the walls. There was also a theater in the compound.

Although the king had planned to stay for a week at Herodion, officials that arrived from Jerusalem asked the king to return to the capital immediately to attend to some urgent issues. Herod ended his inspection tour, and we returned to Jerusalem.

The palace at Masada

Chapter 26
Herod's autobiography – First Part

Herod was eagerly interested in the history of his own country and that of the neighboring nations. He was conscious that whatever he did was historical and wanted posterity to remember his feats.

When I told him that I had recently embarked on the ambitious project of writing the history of the world, he asked me if I might agree to write his biography.

"It would be a great honor!" I exclaimed. "The world must know the story of your life and admire your achievements."

"Fine! We will meet daily after dinner, and I will tell you my life story. If something is not clear, you can ask me any questions that you wish," he said.

"When do you want to start?" I asked him.

"Right now," he replied and ordered his servants to bring two bottles of wine, a parchment, pen, and ink.

"I understand that you descend from a noble family of Jews who returned from the Babylonian exile with Ezra the scribe four hundred years ago," I said.

He laughed and said, "That's a false rumor that I have circulated for political reasons. The truth is that I am an Edomite. My ancestors lived in Edom, a region in the south of the Sea of Salt. One hundred years ago, the Jews, under king John Hyrcanus, conquered us and forced us to convert to Judaism."

"Continue, please. I will try not to interrupt you," I said, ready to write what Herod would tell me.

****

Herod's story

My father, Antipater, was a great man, a brave warrior, and a brilliant politician. All I am I owe to him. My mother, Cypros, was of noble descent, related to the royal family of the Arab kingdom of Petra.

The Queen of Judea, Salome Alexandra, impressed by my father, brought him to her court and appointed him Royal Counselor. A short time later, she died, leaving two sons: Hyrcanus and Aristobulus.

Hyrcanus, the firstborn son, ascended the throne. One of his first acts as king was to confirm my father's appointment.

Aristobulus, the younger son of the late Queen, conspired against his brother, ousted him, and proclaimed himself king. That night, my father and Hyrcanus escaped from Jerusalem and took refuge in Petra. A few days later, my father persuaded the city's king to go against Jerusalem and surround it with his army.

Aristobulus sent a messenger to Damascus with a gift of 400 talents for the Roman general in charge of the garrison, along with a letter asking him to come to Jerusalem and save him from the siege. The general came to Jerusalem immediately. The presence of the Roman army was enough to convince the king of Petra to withdraw its troops.

Shortly after that, Pompey, Rome's most powerful man, arrived in Syria. The two rival Hasmonean brothers went to Damascus to inform Pompey of their complaints and demands.

Hyrcanus, who was not a self-confident man, asked my father Antipater to speak to Pompey for him.

"Your Excellency, it is a universal law of nature that the firstborn son is the successor of the late king and assumes the throne. Hyrcanus is the rightful king of Judea. His brother Aristobulus is a vile usurper," argued my father.

When it was his turn to speak, Aristobulus spoke with contempt of his brother and accused him of not having the

128

ability and the temperament to govern the country. He boasted that he possessed those attributes in abundance. He spoke eloquently but made a serious tactical error. He mentioned that he had bribed a Roman general to persuade him to save him from the king of Petra's siege.

The Romans like to receive bribes, but they intensely dislike anyone mentioning this fact in public. Pompey looked coldly at Aristobulus but merely said that he intended to go to Jerusalem, and there he would listen to both sides again and come to a decision. Meanwhile, the two brothers should stay in Damascus until he would permit them to return to Jerusalem. Aristobulus ignored the request of Pompey and returned to Judea immediately.

Pompey was offended by this gross lack of courtesy. He invaded Judea with his army and entered Jerusalem with Hyrcanus, treating him with the highest honors. Pompey appointed Hyrcanus High Priest but did not give him the title of king.

Aristobulus and his family were taken prisoner and sent to Rome, where Pompey forced him to walk in chains in his triumphal procession. Months later, Aristobulus escaped from prison and returned to Judea. He was recaptured and, shortly afterward, died, poisoned by Pompey's officers.

****

Herod yawned, finished drinking his cup of wine, and rose from the table.

"Enough for today," he said.

Herod's autobiography — First Part

Chapter 27
Herod's autobiography – Second Part

The next night I showed Herod what I had written so far, based on our previous night's conversation. He read it, made some minor corrections, and approved it. The servant brought us two bottles of wine, and Herod continued to tell me his story.

****

My parents, Antipater and Cypros, had four children. Phasael was the oldest. I was next, followed by Joseph, Pheroras, and my sister Salome.

When I was still a child, my father helped Julius Caesar conquer Egypt. Pelusium, a city located on the border between the Sinai and the Nile delta, opposed the Romans. With three thousand Jewish soldiers under his command, my father attacked the city, destroyed its wall, and captured it. He was also victorious in other battles, but his most outstanding contribution to the Romans was to persuade the Jews of Egypt to support Caesar.

To show his gratitude and appreciation to my father, Caesar granted him Roman citizenship, a privilege the Romans don't give too often. Caesar freed my father from the obligation of paying taxes and, most important, appointed him Governor of Judea. Caesar, at the request of my father, confirmed Hyrcanus as High Priest.

My father named me Governor of Galilee when I was twenty-five years old and appointed my brother Phasael to be the Governor of Jerusalem. When I arrived in Galilee, I found that thieves and robbers, who made life miserable for honest people, infested the region. I captured the bandits and hung them on the gallows. This act caused envious people to accuse me of murder. The widows and the children of the evildoers also complained to the Sanhedrin about me.

131

By law, only the Sanhedrin could decree the death penalty. I had assumed powers that were not mine when I hanged the bandits. Technically, I had committed murder. Hyrcanus, who presided over the Sanhedrin, ordered me to come to Jerusalem to respond to the allegations.

My father advised me to appear before the Sanhedrin accompanied by my soldiers. At the same time, my father requested the Roman Governor of Syria to order Hyrcanus to declare me innocent or face the consequences.

I entered the Sanhedrin surrounded by armed soldiers. Not one of my accusers dared to open his mouth. Hyrcanus declared me innocent and ended the trial.

A man named Malicus, jealous of my father's high position, bribed a steward to put poison into my father's cup during an official reception. Thus died a man so distinguished by his intelligence, his honesty, and his administrative talent.

Malicus denied all responsibility for the death of my father. Knowing that I did not doubt his guilt, he fled to Tyre in Phoenicia. I sent a message to Tire's Roman commander asking him to kill Malicus as soon as he entered his city. The commander received the bastard with a friendly welcome and killed him with his knife.

Once, while I was visiting Hyrcanus in his palace, I saw his granddaughter, a beautiful teenager named Mariamne, bathing in the swimming pool. I was impressed by the girl's beauty and that she was a princess of royal blood. Becoming an in-law of the royal family would help my future.

I called Hyrcanus aside and asked for Mariamne's hand in marriage.

"The girl is too young to get married," he replied

"Yes, she is. So, for now, it would be enough for us to be engaged. I am willing to wait three or four years until we get married," I said to Hyrcanus.

"But, you are already married and have a son." he protested.

"That's true," I said. "Four years ago, I married an Idumean woman named Doris. She gave birth to a son, whom I named Antipater in honor of my father's memory. But, that's not a problem. I will divorce her tomorrow, and I will send both away, the woman and the boy."

So I did. Hyrcanus, with some reluctance, agreed to promise me his granddaughter in marriage. We signed the *ketubah* [pre nuptial agreement] and decided to hold the *chuppah* [wedding canopy] four years later.

A group of my opponents traveled to Syria to talk with the Roman general Mark Antony, who was visiting Damascus on his way to Egypt. My enemies complained that Phasael and I had usurped power in Judea and that Hyrcanus had become a mere figurehead. Mark Antony, to whom I had previously sent a generous gift, refused to receive them.

Shortly after that, Hyrcanus and I went to Damascus. Hyrcanus assured Mark Antony that I ruled with his consent and that he and the nation were pleased with me. Mark Antony threw my opponents in jail and sentenced them to death. Then he continued his journey to Egypt, where he met Cleopatra and fell in love with her.

A new problem arose. Antigonus, son of the late Aristobulus and nephew of Hyrcanus, escaped from his prison in Rome. He took refuge in the Parthians' country and promised the king of that nation one thousand talents and five hundred virgins if he would overthrow Hyrcanus, kill me, and make him king of Judea.

The Parthian king, leading an army, came to Judea and invited my brother Phasael and Hyrcanus to his camp to discuss the demands of Antigonus. Phasael accepted the invitation, even though I warned him that it was a trap meant to capture him. I begged him not to go, but Phasael, although he was usually very prudent and cautious, would not listen to my pleadings. He went to see the king of the Parthians accompanied by Hyrcanus.

What I feared happened. It was a trap, a betrayal. As soon as Phasael and Hyrcanus arrived at the Parthian camp, the Parthians king ordered his men to tie their hands and put them in prison.

Fearing that the Parthian army would attack Jerusalem and take me also prisoner, I decided to escape from the city, taking my mother, my sister, Mariamne, and her mother with me, accompanied by a troop. I left the women at Masada under the protection of eight hundred soldiers.

From there, I went on to Petra. A messenger brought me terrible news, the Parthians had captured Jerusalem and had proclaimed Antigonus king of Judea. Even worse, Phasael, my brother, whom I had loved, admired, and emulated all my life, had committed suicide by hitting his head against the stone walls of his prison cell.

Antigonus did not kill his uncle Hyrcanus but instead cut off his ears because, according to Moses' Law, a mutilated person cannot be a High Priest. The Parthians kept Hyrcanus in prison for several years.

Chapter 28
Herod's autobiography – Third Part

"Where were we?" asked Herod in our following meeting

"You mentioned that you left the women of your family at Masada and that you continued to Petra," I answered after consulting my notes.

I asked the king of Petra for a loan of one hundred talents to recruit soldiers for my army. I offered to leave with him as collateral my late brother Phasael's son, who was seven years old at the time. The king refused to grant me the loan. I continued my journey and arrived at Alexandria.

Queen Cleopatra offered me the post of commander of her army. This employment was not in my plans, and I did not accept it. The next day I embarked on a ship that sailed to Rome.

A terrible storm caused the boat to sink near the island of Rhodes. I swam for hours until fishermen rescued me from the sea and brought me to the island. A few days later, I boarded another ship that took me to Ostia.

In Rome, I met Mark Antony and told him everything that had happened in Judea, the Parthians' invasion, the proclamation of Antigonus as king, the death of my brother, and the captivity and mutilation of Hyrcanus.

Mark Antony invited me to speak to the Senate and repeat everything that I had told him. The Senate's reaction was better than I expected. Antigonus was declared an enemy of Rome because of his alliance with the Parthians, Rome's most feared enemies.

Mark Antony took the floor and proposed that the Senate name me king of Judea. The Senators voted unanimously in my favor. I had not expected this because I was not a member of the royal dynasty. When I arrived in Rome, I had intended to propose that the Senate name Aristobulus, the younger brother of my fiancée Mariamne, as king of Judea.

At the end of the Senate's session, I went out arm and arm with Mark Antony on one side and Octavius on the other. Of course, that happened many years ago, before they became enemies. That evening, Mark Antony hosted a banquet and gave a toast in my honor, calling me by my new title, King Herod.

I remained in Rome for only one week, and then I embarked on a Roman military ship that took me to Ptolemais. A Roman army was waiting there for me, and the officers placed themselves under my command. We marched southward, and, along the way, more men joined our ranks. We had some skirmishes with the troops of Antigonus, but we trounced them. I sent my mother and the other women I had left in Masada to Samaria for their protection. I continued with the army to Jerusalem.

Outside the city walls, I proclaimed loudly that I only wanted the welfare of the city and its inhabitants. I offered amnesty to all who had been my opponents.

Antigonus sent me his reply with a messenger: "I do not recognize you as king and will not surrender."

I decided not to attack Jerusalem immediately. Instead, I adopted a different tactic. I left my brother Joseph in charge of the troops besieging the city and went to Galilee with a regiment. There, I systematically destroyed the garrisons of Antigonus, village after village.

The people of the region informed me that some criminals were active in the area and that a gang was hiding in caves on Mount Arbel, near the Sea of Galilee.

It was impossible to climb to the caves because Mount Arbel's cliff on that side is vertical. We climbed the mountain from the opposite side. We built wooden platforms, which we lowered with chains from the summit until they were in front of the caves. There were soldiers on every platform, equipped with long hooks to pull the bandits out of their caves and throw them into the abyss. After doing this, the soldiers threw burning straws inside the caves. The fire and the smoke killed the bandits who remained there.

Hearing that Mark Antony was besieging a city in Syria, I went with my troops to help him. Mark Antony's enemies ambushed us during the journey when we were crossing a narrow pass, but we defeated them.

Mark Antony hugged me affectionately when he saw me. With the help of my troops, he conquered the besieged city and then left for Egypt. I returned to Judea.

On the road, I dreamed that my brother Joseph had died. A few days later, a messenger brought me the sad news.

Joseph, whom I had left in charge of besieging Jerusalem, went to Jericho with a group of soldiers to buy wheat for his army. The soldiers of Antigonus suddenly attacked them, and, although my brother fought bravely, they captured him. Antigonus ordered his commander to kill Joseph, cut off his head, and send it to Jerusalem.

I hurried to Jericho with my army to avenge the death of my brother. One night, after dining with my commanders in one of the village dwellings, I returned to the camp. Later that evening, the roof of the house where we had dined collapsed. If this had happened an hour before, I would have died. This incident was twice lucky for me. Not only didn't I die, but I made sure to circulate a rumor that God protected me, and my popularity grew.

The next day six thousand soldiers of Antigonus' army came down from the mountains and attacked us. We defeated them. We did not leave even one of them alive.

An incident that happened that night confirmed that God protected me. After the battle, I was tired and sweaty and decided to take a bath. I went to one of the abandoned houses in the town, undressed, and began to wash when several enemy soldiers, swords in hand, came from the other room. I don't know who was more surprised, they or I. The fact is that the soldiers rushed out of the house and fled instead of killing me with their swords, despite seeing me naked and unarmed.

I should mention that we captured the enemy commander who had killed Joseph. I cut off his head myself while he was still alive and sent it to Antigonus with my compliments.

Herod's autobiography — Third Part

Chapter 29
Herod's autobiography – Fourth Part

"There are things in life besides war. Let's now talk about love," Herod said, laughing when we met again. He drank a cup of wine and started.

I went to Samaria, where Mariamne, her mother Alexandra, my mother Cypros, and my sister Salome stayed in a fortress protected by my soldiers. Four years had passed since I had signed the *ketubah* with Hyrcanus, Mariamne's grandfather. The pretty adolescent girl had turned into a young woman of astounding beauty. There was no need to wait anymore. The time had come to stand in the *chuppah* with my fiancée and consummate the marriage.

I will not go into details, but no woman beats a princess of royal blood when it comes to love. During the early years of our marriage, Mariamne and I loved each other passionately. I had four children with her: two boys, Alexander and Aristobulus, and two girls, Cypros and Salampsio.

A week after our wedding, I returned to Jerusalem, leaving Mariamne in Samaria under my mother and sister's care.

During my absence, my soldiers had cut all the trees in Jerusalem's forests and used the wood to build ramps and attack towers.

The Roman Governor of Syria sent an infantry legion and six thousand cavalry soldiers to help me conquer Jerusalem. I had over thirty thousand Jewish and Roman soldiers under my command.

The population of Jerusalem defended their city courageously. Antigonus' soldiers would come out through tunnels almost every night to try to burn our attack towers. It took us forty days to conquer the first wall surrounding the city and fifteen days to take the second. Antigonus' soldiers fought against us in the narrow streets of the Lower City. The Roman soldiers, furious at the defenders' unexpected resistance, massacred all they could find, including women and children. Seeing that all was lost, Antigonus appeared before the Roman commander and threw himself at his feet. The Roman treated him mercilessly, mocked him, calling him "Antigone" as if he were a woman, and put him in prison.

The Romans sacked the city and continued to kill the people. I spoke to the Roman commander and made him an offer. If he would end the looting and the massacres, I would personally reward him and every single Roman soldier with my own money. He accepted, and a few days later, the Roman army left the city, taking the gold and silver that I had given to the commander and the soldiers. The Romans took Antigonus with them in chains.

I worried that if Antigonus would be sent to Rome, the Senate might appoint him king of Judea because he was of royal blood, and I was not. I sent a significant amount of silver to Mark Antony, who was in Syria and asked him to kill Antigonus. He did as I asked, thus showing me his friendship and his gratitude for my gift.

Finally, three years after being appointed king of Judea by the Roman Senate, I assumed power in Jerusalem and throughout the country. My first action was to kill the supporters of Antigonus and appropriate their land. I also forced the rich people of the city to give me part of their wealth. This way, I gathered a large fortune, a portion of which I sent to Mark Antony.

The High Priest's position was too important and influential to be occupied by a person who could constitute a danger to me. My solution was to bring from Babylon an obscure priest called Hananel, whom nobody knew in Jerusalem, and appointed him High Priest.

This appointment outraged Alexandra, Mariamne's mother. Since her ancestors, the Maccabees, had fought against the Greeks, one hundred and thirty years before, and liberated Judea, the High Priest's position had always belonged to a member of her family. My mother-in-law wanted Aristobulus, her seventeen-year-old son, to be appointed High Priest.

Alexandra, a woman experienced in intrigues, sent a note to her friend Cleopatra, the Queen of Egypt, asking her to persuade Mark Antony to order me to name the young Aristobulus as High Priest. When several weeks passed without receiving an answer from Mark Antony, Alexandra sent him a portrait of her son Aristobulus. The adolescent was reputed to be the most handsome young man in the kingdom of Judea.

Mark Antony received the Aristobulus portrait and sent a message to Alexandra asking her to send her son to Alexandria. That message somehow fell into my hands. I was acquainted with the virtues and vices of Mark Antony. I also knew that Cleopatra was jealous only when her lover showed interest in other women, but not when Mark Antony found a beautiful boy attractive.

I was sure that if Mark Antony had an intimate relationship with Aristobulus, he would reward the boy by naming him king of Judea. I couldn't take that risk. I wrote to Mark Antony saying that Aristobulus could not travel to Alexandria because that would cause great turmoil in Jerusalem.

Mariamne and her mother Alexandra pestered me day and night, begging me to name Aristobulus High Priest. Eventually, I accepted, not because of the two women's insistence, but because I had learned that religious law and custom forbid the High Priest to leave the country.

I called Alexandra and informed her that she and her daughter Mariamne had convinced me that Aristobulus deserved to be appointed High Priest.

My mother-in-law wept with happiness and told me how proud and happy she was that her son would be the High Priest. She swore that neither she nor her son had any claims regarding the throne, and, in the unlikely case that the Romans would offer the crown to her son, she would force him to refuse it. Alexandra said that she greatly admired my talent to govern the country and that she was grateful for the honor given to her son. Last but not least, she begged me to forgive her for having written to Cleopatra.

That same day, I dismissed Hananel, sent him back to Babylon, and replaced him as High Priest with young Aristobulus.

In the meantime, the Parthians had released Hyrcanus. My wife's grandfather settled in Babylon, where the Jewish community treated him with all the honors he deserved for having been High Priest and king of Judea. I sent him a letter inviting him to return to Jerusalem. I mentioned that he being Mariamne's grandfather, was also my grandfather. I ended the letter saying that I could not forget the debt that I owed him for having declared me innocent when the Sanhedrin accused me of murder.

The Jews of Babylon took up a collection to pay for Hyrcanus' travel expenses to Jerusalem. I welcomed him warmly and gave him a palace in the Upper City, close to mine. I made sure that everybody treated him with respect and honor in all the official and public functions.

****

"Have you written down all that I have told you?" Herod asked me.

"I have done so," I replied.

"Bring me your notes tomorrow. I want to review them."

Chapter 30
The execution of Hyrcanus

The next morning I arrived at the palace later than I usually did. I saw the officers and courtiers gathered in small groups whispering with each other and looking over their shoulders, afraid of being heard.

"What happened? Why is everybody whispering?" I asked one of my subordinates.

"Hyrcanus has been arrested, accused of treason," he replied, visibly disturbed.

If this was a joke, I failed to find it funny. It was hard to believe. Hyrcanus was a sick old man, eighty years old, who took no part in the country's government. Since his return from captivity in Parthia and exile in Babylon, he rarely left his house. He avoided being seen in public, embarrassed by the mutilation that he had suffered when the Parthians cut off his ears.

I decided to talk to Herod to find out the reason for the arrest. It had to be a mistake. Probably.

I found the king in the Throne Room, surrounded by various officials. He saw me and called me to his side.

"I want to speak with Nicholas alone. All others leave this room." the king ordered.

I expected to see him worried and sad, but it surprised me to find him in an excellent mood. He greeted me with a big smile.

"Nicholas, my dear friend, you cannot imagine how long I have waited for this moment."

"Herod, please explain what is happening," I said.

"Hyrcanus is the last of the royal family. The sooner he is gone, the sooner my throne and my dynasty will be safe forever. I have accused him of treason and will make sure that he is found guilty and sentenced to death."

"I cannot believe it! You have charged Hyrcanus with treason, a man who lacks initiative, a man whose ambition died years ago?"

"The old bastard is not ambitious, but his daughter Alexandra, my mother-in-law, certainly is. I discovered that she convinced Hyrcanus that, while I was alive, he was in danger and that he should not forgive me for having, in her words, usurped his throne. At first, Hyrcanus rejected her arguments. Nevertheless, the woman repeated the same argument day and night. Finally, she convinced Hyrcanus to write a letter to the king of Petra in which he requested asylum and asked for help to overthrow my government. His messenger, rather than take the letter to Petra, brought it to me. Here it is," said the king smirking.

He went to the door and ordered, "Bring Hyrcanus!"

Two soldiers dragged the aged Hyrcanus into the room.

"Hyrcanus, at your age, why are you conspiring against me?" the king asked him.

"I do not know what you are talking about, Herod," answered Hyrcanus.

"You will call me 'Your Majesty,' you old fool! On your knees immediately!" yelled Herod.

The soldiers forced Hyrcanus to kneel before the king. It broke my heart to see the old man humiliated in that way. I could not forget that the pathetic figure before us had once been the king of Judea and the High Priest.

"I want you to look at this note and tell me whether or not it is your handwriting," said Herod.

"Your Majesty, I beg you to be merciful! Please remember that when the Sanhedrin accused you of murder, I declared you innocent," pleaded Hyrcanus.

"Did you receive a letter from the king of Petra?" Herod asked.

"Yes, Your Majesty, but it was just a greeting."

"Have you received a gift from the king of Petra?" Herod asked again.

144

"Yes, Your Majesty. The king of Petra sent me four fine horses for my stable," answered Hyrcanus.

"I am glad that you confessed. We will add the charge of bribery to the betrayal. The trial will take place today. Take the traitor away." ordered the king to the soldiers.

I was present at the trial of Hyrcanus and must say that the old man behaved calmly and with dignity. He denied all charges, and when the judges pronounced him guilty, he declared that he accepted the court's decision with the same serenity with which he, many years before, had agreed to be High Priest and king.

The soldiers took Hyrcanus to the courtyard of the palace. The executioner forced him to kneel and then cut off his head with an ax. The blood of the slain man gushed out and dyed a brilliant red his white beard.

His daughter Alexandra and granddaughter Mariamne witnessed the death of Hyrcanus from a window on the upper floor of the palace.

Herod and I also watched the execution from another room. Tears of pity ran down my cheeks. I looked at Herod and saw that his face was impassive.

"Tomorrow night, we will resume my biography," said Herod and went out of the room.

The execution of Hyrcanus

Chapter 31
Herod's autobiography – Fifth Part

At our next meeting, Herod carefully read all the notes that I had written so far, made a few corrections, and continued with his story.

****

The letters that Alexandra had sent to Cleopatra and Mark Antony increased my distrust of my mother-in-law. I ordered her to be brought to the royal palace and forbade her to intervene in state affairs. I instructed the guards to watch her, report back to me in detail everything that she said, and write down the names of every person she met. They had to bring me any letter that she would write or receive. All these precautions turned Alexandra's aversion to me into profound hatred.

Alexandra wrote to Cleopatra a long letter (which, of course, I read). She complained to the Egyptian woman about the way I treated her and asked for help. Cleopatra answered, advising her to escape immediately with her son Aristobulus to Egypt, where they would be safe, and the Queen would protect them.

Alexandra ordered her servants to make two coffins with holes for breathing. She hid in one of them, and her son hid in the other. The 'funeral' procession left Jerusalem furtively during the night and made its way to the port of Jaffa. There, an Egyptian ship waited to take them to Alexandria.

Naturally, I was aware of Alexandra's plans and intentions from the outset. I let the procession advance undisturbed until it came to a place in the road where I was waiting with a battalion of soldiers.

I ordered the 'mourners' to stop and open the coffins.

"It would be a desecration, Your Majesty, and a lack of respect for the dead," said the one who seemed to be in charge

147

"Please do not worry. If that's a sin, my soul will pay for it. Now, open the caskets before I run you through with my sword, in which case your funeral procession would need a third coffin," I warned him.

My argument convinced him. He opened the coffins, and, big surprise, the "corpses" inside arose from the dead.

"Dear mother-in-law." I greeted her. "You cannot imagine how glad I am that the rumors of your death turned out to be exaggerated and that I find you in good health."

I ordered the soldiers to take Alexandra and Aristobulus back to the palace and place them under guard. I sent their companions to prison.

I doubled the guard that watched Alexandra, but I refrained from taking other measures against her for fear of an adverse reaction from her friend Cleopatra who had too much influence over Mark Antony.

Young Aristobulus was a tall, handsome boy, loved by the common people. The crowd's enthusiasm bordered on hysteria when he, dressed in his priestly garb, performed the duties of his office publicly. They cheered and chanted his name. His popularity worried me, and it was clear to me that this situation could not continue. I had to do something about it. I decided not to take any action for the time being, but I instructed my guards to watch him day and night.

I invited the whole family to spend the seven days of the Feast of Tabernacles with me at my palace in Jericho. One day when it was hotter than usual, I suggested to Aristobulus that he refresh himself in the pool where several of my servants and officials were bathing. Aristobulus played with them, and without anyone noticing until it was too late, he drowned. What a tragic and unfortunate accident!

Alexandra was very much agitated. She questioned the men who had been with her son in the pool. They were unable to explain how the young man could have drowned. Maybe he had had a cramp, or perhaps he did not know how to swim. Alexandra assured them that her son was an excellent swimmer and had never suffered from cramps. When no other explanation came forth, she went away crying without asking further questions.

I ordered three days of national mourning for this tragedy and organized a magnificent funeral for our late High Priest Aristobulus. I hoped that this would be a comfort and consolation to Alexandra and Mariamne.

Alexandra succeeded in secretly sending, without my knowledge, a letter to Cleopatra, who was in Syria with Mark Antony. In that letter, Alexandra accused me of having murdered her son. Cleopatra showed the letter to Mark Antony and demanded that he punish me. Mark Antony ordered me to come to Damascus to explain the death of Aristobulus.

That was an invitation that I could not refuse. I left immediately, bringing with me precious gifts to Mark Antony to allay his anger.

Mark Antony received affectionately as always and listened with great sympathy to my explanations. He told me that he would have done the same and would speak to Cleopatra about it.

"I forbid you to meddle again in the actions that a king must do when he needs to bring order to his country," Mark Antony admonished Cleopatra in my presence.

I knew that Cleopatra hated me and, on more than one occasion, she had asked Mark Antony to depose me and annex Judea to Egypt. Mark Antony swore to me that this would never happen.

I returned to Jerusalem, pleased that my position was as safe as before.

Regarding my mother-in-law, I placed armed guards outside her rooms in the palace and forbade her to go out.

Herod's autobiography — Fifth Part

Chapter 32
Herod's autobiography – Sixth Part

Mark Antony marched to Armenia with his army, and Cleopatra returned to Egypt by land, crossing Judea. During her Judea journey, she sent me a messenger informing me that she wanted to meet me in Jericho. I went there and waited for the arrival of the Egyptian Queen. Mariamne preferred to stay in Jerusalem and did not come with me.

Mark Antony had given the valley of Jericho to Cleopatra as a personal gift. She leased it to me in exchange for an annual income equivalent to fifty percent of the money that I received from the sale of balsam and dates. Balsam is an exquisite perfume that comes from an aromatic resin of a plant that only grows in this area, and the sweetness of the dates of Jericho is unmatched and world-famous.

Cleopatra arrived and told me that the first thing she wanted to do was to see my accounts of income and expenses. We sat in my office, and I showed her all the documents. She reviewed them thoroughly, asked many tricky questions, and when she was

satisfied that everything was in order, I gave her the money.

To be polite, I invited her to dine with me. I was amazed when Cleopatra made clear her wish to have intimacies with me at the end of the meal. At first, I thought she was joking, but I realized that she meant it when her behavior became obvious.

My vanity and my paranoia fought with each other. My vanity made me think that Cleopatra had succumbed to my manly attractions. My paranoia argued that Cleopatra was setting me up to destroy my friendship with Mark Antony. Of course, my paranoia prevailed, as it always does.

I needed to consult with the palace officials who were in the next room. I asked Cleopatra to excuse for a moment, giving her some pretext, and left the room.

"I hate that woman! Her visit is an excellent opportunity to kill her and rid the world of her overwhelming presence. I am sure that Mark Antony, free from her spell, will thank me. What do you think? How shall I do it?" I asked my officials, speaking quietly.

"Your Majesty, please don't do anything rash! Mark Antony loves that woman more than you can imagine. You would be signing your death warrant and also the end of Judea. Besides, she is your guest, and the whole world would condemn you," they said to me.

They were right. It was not the time or the place to kill Cleopatra. I returned to the dining room where I had left Cleopatra and asked her to excuse me.

"I have just been told that there is an urgent problem which requires my immediate attention. I have to work the rest of the night with my officials. I wish you good night."

The next day Cleopatra announced that she had to leave. I escorted her to the Egyptian border, treating her with the utmost kindness and courtesy. I was sure that one day she would ruin Mark Antony's life and congratulated myself that I hadn't allowed her to destroy mine.

Some weeks later, I received a note from Mark Antony. He thanked me for the attention that I had shown Cleopatra during her stay in Judea and reiterated his eternal friendship.

I never saw Mark Antony or Cleopatra again. Octavius defeated Mark Antony at the naval battle of Actium. Mark Antony and Cleopatra committed suicide. I still think that if I had killed Cleopatra that time in Jericho, Mark Antony would be alive today.

On the same day that I learned of Mark Antony's death, a terrible earthquake shook Judea. The destruction was unprecedented. Whole villages were destroyed, and more than ten thousand people died. My army was not affected because the soldiers slept in tents in open fields.

I sent ambassadors to the neighboring countries asking for help. The Arabs of Petra reacted with an evil and uncivilized act. They killed my ambassadors! All countries condemn such a crime because the person of an ambassador is sacred and inviolable. I could not allow this crime to go unpunished.

I crossed the Jordan River and defeated the Arab army. We killed more than five thousand Arabs and took four thousand prisoners. The king of Petra surrendered, and since then, he pays me tribute.

****

"Nicholas, you arrived in Jerusalem soon after my victory over the Arabs. Since then, you have been a witness to everything that has happened to Judea and me. Therefore, you may continue writing my biography by yourself without my help. I have to solve a severe problem. My friend and protector, Mark Antony, is dead. His enemy Octavius is now the indisputable ruler of the world. I don't know what may happen to me."

Herod's autobiography — Sixth Part

Chapter 33
The meeting of Herod with Octavius

Herod had been Mark Antony's loyal friend, and if the general had asked him, he would have fought at his side against Octavius. Now that Mark Antony was dead, Octavius guided Rome's destinies, and Herod's future as king of Judea was in danger.

As he demonstrated throughout his life, Herod was not a person who passively waited to see what might happen to him. He always took the initiative, and this time it was no different. He summoned his advisors and the senior officials of the kingdom and informed us what he had decided.

"Octavius is on the island of Rhodes. I will go and talk to him. Nicholas will come with me. It is possible that while I am away, somebody might take advantage of my absence and rebel. Therefore, I leave my brother Pheroras in charge of the kingdom. My mother Cypros and my sister Salome will stay in Masada. Unfortunately, Mariamne does not get along with them, So, I will send her and her mother Alexandra to the Alexandrium fortress in the Jordan Valley. Sohemus, a man who has always been loyal to me, will look after them."

He asked me to remain after all the others had left the room. When we were alone, Herod, in a low voice, told me that he had given Sohemus secret instructions to kill Mariamne if he did not return. He added a phrase that shocked me, "I love her so much that I do not want her to survive me."

A few days later, we boarded a ship that took us to Rhodes. A Roman officer greeted us upon our arrival.

"Octavius has ordered that Herod be brought to him immediately," the officer informed us.

I noticed that the Roman had said 'Herod' and not 'King Herod.' I whispered to the king to take off his royal diadem and advised him not to speak to Octavius pleadingly nor ask him for forgiveness as if he had committed an offense. Herod nodded in agreement.

155

Octavius greeted us coldly, but I was flattered that he called me by my name. Herod asked permission to speak to him.

"My Lord, I must tell you frankly that I was a true friend to Mark Antony and always helped him with everything that I could. If he had asked me to fight against you, I would gladly have done so. I sent him money for his army and grain for his soldiers, but that is nothing compared to what I should have done for him. On more than one occasion, I advised him to leave Cleopatra, the woman who caused his downfall. I regret that he did not listen to me. I do not deny my friendship with him, and I am not ashamed of it. This is the kind of friend I am, and that is how I behave with my benefactors."

"Herod, I respect and appreciate your honesty. I want you to be the kind of friend for me that you were for Mark Antony," said Octavius.

That night Octavius gave a banquet in honor of Herod and insisted that he should wear the royal crown on his head.

Herod sent a messenger in a fast ship to Pheroras to tell him the good news and instructed him to bring back the women of the royal family to Jerusalem.

We returned to Judea, pleased that Herod's throne was safer than before and that the most powerful man in the world considered him his friend.

As soon as he entered the palace, Herod went to Mariamne's quarters to tell her the good news. She reacted with hatred and said that she would have preferred hearing that Octavius had killed him.

Bewildered, Herod wanted to punish Mariamne for her insolence. However, he loved her too much to do anything at that moment.

Months later, we learned that Sohemus, Mariamne's bodyguard, had confessed to the Queen that Herod had given him instructions to kill her if the king did not return from Rhodes. At first, Mariamne did not believe him. When Sohemus insisted that he was telling her the truth, she felt an uncontrollable rage and lost all the love she had previously felt for Herod.

The two persons whom Herod loved most in the world were his mother, Cypros, and his sister Salome. The two women hated and envied Mariamne because of her royal blood. They took advantage of every opportunity to slander her and invent gossip that made the king angry and jealous. However, Herod had other things in his mind. He heard that Octavius was in Egypt and decided to see him there.

He went to say goodbye to Mariamne, whom he found in her room accompanied by Sohemus.

"Herod, we owe thanks to Sohemus for having taken such good care of me while you were away in Rhodes. I want you to reward him with a promotion," Mariamne said to him.

Herod granted her request and traveled to Egypt. Octavius received him with great honors and proclaimed publicly that Herod was his best friend. As a token of his friendship, he transferred to Herod the valley of Jericho that Mark Antony had detached from Judea and given to Cleopatra. Octavius also gave Herod the four hundred soldiers who had been Cleopatra's chosen guard.

In Jerusalem, Herod treated Mariamne with love and tenderness, even when she told him that she hated him. He reacted with good humor when his wife insulted him, hoping that her aversion to him was temporary and would end soon.

The meeting of Herod with Octavius

Chapter 34
Family problems

Herod's family split into two factions that hated each other. On one side were Mariamne and her mother, Alexandra. On the other were Cypros, the mother of Herod, and Salome, the king's sister.

It was very unpleasant for me to witness how Mariamne treated Cypros and Salome. Her arrogance and disdain would cause the two women to break into tears and leave the room. I felt that it was my duty to Mariamne to mention my concern about what could happen to her if she continued treating so badly Herod's closest relatives, the two women that he loved the most in his life.

"Your Majesty, please pardon me if I am overstepping my bounds, but I feel obliged to say that nothing good will come of the way you treat the mother and sister of the king," I said to her one day after she had grievously insulted the two women again.

"I cannot tolerate that these common women, of such low birth, consider themselves to be my equals. I am a descendant of kings," she answered.

"Please remember Your Majesty that while a wife is replaceable, a mother is not," I warned her.

For a while, Mariamne followed my advice. She refrained from insulting Cypros and Salome, but she treated them again with unbearable contempt and superiority after some time.

It all culminated one night when Herod wanted to sleep with Mariamne. The king sent for her, but she refused to leave her room. The king himself came to fetch his wife, knocked on her closed door, and called her name in a loud voice heard by everybody in the palace. Mariamne spurned his demand.

While this was going on, I was in the room next door chatting with Salome, Herod's sister. I saw that Salome made an almost imperceptible signal to the butler. He placed a cup

159

filled with a greenish liquid on a tray and entered the king's room. I stood by the door to hear the conversation.

"Your Majesty," said the butler, "Queen Mariamne ordered me to bring this cup to Your Majesty. It contains, so she says, an elixir of love. As I am not aware of the ingredients of this elixir and do not know its effects, I felt that it was best if I informed Your Majesty about it."

Herod ordered his guards to immediately arrest Mariamne's faithful eunuch and torture him until he would reveal the ingredients in the greenish liquid and its real purpose. The eunuch said that he did not know anything about a green drink, but he knew that the Queen hated the king because of some secret that Sohemus, Mariamne's bodyguard, had revealed to the Queen.

"Sohemus betrayed me by revealing to Mariamne my secret instructions to kill her if I did not come back from my meeting with Octavius in Rhodes," cried Herod. "The only possible explanation for his treason is that he has been intimate with her. Kill him immediately! Then arrest and try Mariamne in a court of law."

I was one of the three judges appointed by the king to decide Mariamne's fate.

"The court calls the defendant, Queen Mariamne, to explain her actions," I announced aloud during her trial.

"I am innocent and have nothing to declare," said the Queen.

The king was the next witness. We heard his testimony regarding the elixir, and we took due note of the anger and intensity with which he accused his wife.

After consulting with the other judges, we decided that it was not necessary to call more witnesses. It took us only a few minutes to reach the unanimous decision that the Queen was guilty of adultery and of attempting to kill the king by poisoning him. We condemned her to die.

Alexandra, Mariamne's mother, was present during the trial. When she heard the judges dictate the death sentence, she chose to save herself. She stood up from her seat and rebuked Mariamne.

"You are a bad woman. An ungrateful wife. The death sentence is what you deserve," said Alexandra sobbing and tearing her hair.

Mariamne looked at her mother with compassion and did not answer.

Salome, the king's sister, saw that the king was unwilling to kill a woman that he still loved and hesitated to give the order to execute Mariamne. She requested to speak privately with Herod and told him more tales about Mariamne's alleged infidelities. The next day, the executioner cut off the unfortunate Queen's head.

After his wife's death, Herod's melancholy was so extreme that it made me fear for his mental health. More than once, I heard the king walking through the corridors of the palace moaning and screaming, "Mariamne. Mariamne." Once, when I was dining with him, I was shocked to hear him ordering his servants to invite the Queen to join us.

"Herod," I said one day, "you must try to forget Mariamne. Perhaps a change of environment might help you."

Herod took my advice and went to one of his fortresses in the desert. During his stay, he suffered from terrible headaches that his doctors could not cure or alleviate.

Family problems

Chapter 35
The deaths of Alexandra and Costobarus

Herod left me in charge of the government during his absence. Fortunately, the issues that I had to deal with were simple, mainly routine matters, easy to solve. The situation changed when a guard informed me that Alexandra, Mariamne's mother, was outside my office demanding to speak with me.

"Let her come in," I ordered the commander of my guard.

I stood when Alexandra entered the room. After all, she was of royal blood, the daughter of Hyrcanus, a man who had been king.

"Nicholas, I have heard that Herod is very ill and may not survive. Therefore, I have decided to assume power," she said with arrogance.

I immediately sent a message to Herod informing him of Alexandra's intentions. The messenger returned with a document signed by the king, ordering me to execute Alexandra. I complied with his order, although the pitiful pleas of the woman moved me.

My spies discovered that Costobarus, the husband of Salome, the king's sister, was plotting to overthrow Herod. I gave orders to arrest him.

The king, as soon as he recovered from his illness, returned to Jerusalem. The first thing he did when he entered the palace was to order his officials to kill Costobarus. However, he relented when Salome begged him to forgive her husband.

Sometime later, Salome found that Costobarus had been unfaithful to her, and she divorced him. Assuming that Salome no longer cared for her former husband, Herod gave orders to execute him.

Herod was in a good mood. He had recovered from his illness, and Costobarus, whom he had always detested, was dead. I suggested that he organize games in honor of Octavius in Jerusalem, similar to those in Rome.

Herod liked the idea and invited athletes from many different countries to participate and compete for awards. He also organized horse and chariot races and imported lions and other wild animals from Africa to fight each other, as well as men who had been sentenced to death.

These activities, especially the fights of men with wild animals, transgressed the religion of the Jews and caused Herod to lose his popularity.

On the last day of the competitions, Herod gave trophies to the winners. The public thought that the awards were statuettes, which would violate the Torah law that forbids images. An angry crowd gathered outside the palace, screaming 'sacrilege' and 'death to Herod.'

When the mob tried to assault the palace, the guards' commander ordered his soldiers to push back the unruly crowd even if it meant killing some of the rowdier protesters.

It would have been a massacre if I hadn't intervened. I solved the crisis without any bloodshed because I was the person who had designed the trophies.

"Let the leaders of the mob enter the palace and examine the trophies," I ordered the commander.

A group of men entered the palace. I received them and showed them a trophy.

"Look at this and tell me what it is," I said.

"A blasphemous image!" one of them answered and spat on the statuette that I was holding in my hand.

I took off the trophy's external ornaments and showed them that it was a formless piece of wood. Everybody laughed and apologized. They left the palace and told the crowd what they had seen. And so, tempers became calm again.

Religious fanatics could not forgive Herod for organizing games that offended Jewish traditions. Ten people, whose chief was a blind man, outraged by what had happened, vowed to assassinate the king. They went to the theater, where

Herod would attend that night. They had daggers hidden under their clothing.

The conspirators did not know that Herod had an army of spies and secret police, and one of them had infiltrated the group. He revealed the plot to me, and I told Herod about it when the king was still outside the theater. The king returned to the palace immediately, and the conspirators were caught red-handed with their weapons. Herod had them tortured and killed.

The friends of the executed conspirators suspected that our spy had betrayed them. They stabbed him over fifty times, dismembered his body, and threw it to the dogs, who devoured it. The murderers committed their crime in broad daylight on a crowded street in the presence of many witnesses. All of them, when interrogated, swore that they had seen nothing.

The king's men apprehended several people who lived on the street where the man had been assassinated and questioned them. After undergoing torture, they revealed what they had seen and named those responsible for the murder. The king seized the murderers and their families' properties and ordered his soldiers to cut off their heads.

The deaths of Alexandra and Costobarus

Chapter 36
Herod marries the second Mariamne

The country suffered an epidemic that killed more than ten thousand people. This unfortunate event coincided with a severe drought that caused the loss of the harvest. As a result, there was no food in the kingdom, and people died of hunger. Religious fanatics immediately said that this was divine punishment for the games that Herod had organized in Jerusalem.

The king summoned his advisors to an emergency meeting and asked my opinion.

"Your Majesty, we need drastic solutions. Although there is no money in the government coffers, gold, silver, and precious stones adorn the furnishings of your palace. The palace cutlery is gold and silver. I suggest that we take all these items, send them to Egypt, and sell them in Alexandria. With the money that we will receive for them, we should buy flour, which we will deliver to Jerusalem bakers. They will distribute the bread to the needy without charge," I proposed at the meeting.

The reaction of the other advisors was absolute silence. Everyone looked to the king, hoping that he would punish me for my bold and, in their eyes, disrespectful suggestion. However, I was not worried. I knew Herod to be a shrewd politician that knew how to deal with the populace. I was sure that he would see my point and would accept my proposal. So, I was not surprised when his answer was what I had expected, although, of course, I was delighted.

"Nicholas is right. There is no other way to save our people," said the king, to the astonishment of all the others who were present.

Everything was done according to my advice. The king ordered the palace servants to remove the gold and silver ornaments from the luxurious furniture, and together with the vessels made of precious metals, he sent them to Egypt to be exchanged for wheat flour. The flour was brought to

167

Jerusalem and delivered to the bakers who distributed the bread among the poor people.

When we learned that the drought had not affected our neighboring country, Syria, I suggested to the king that we should send seeds to Syria to plant there. Months later, the Syrians repaid us by sending us part of their crop.

That winter was freezing. Thousands of people would have died if Herod had not bought them warm clothing paying with his own money.

It was at this time that Herod fell in love with a beautiful green-eyed girl, a tall blonde, who, by coincidence, not only looked like his late wife, Mariamne but also had the same name.

"Nicholas, I want to marry this girl, but there is a problem. Her father, Simon, is a minor priest in the Temple and therefore lacks the necessary social position to be my in-law," the king told me confidentially.

"Herod, the solution to the problem is in your hands. Don't you, as king, have the right to choose the High Priest?"

"You are right! I will depose the current High Priest and will appoint Simon in his place. It will be an honor for me to marry the daughter of the High Priest," he laughed and clapped me on the shoulder.

He, eager to marry the girl, dismissed the High Priest and awarded Simon the position. A few days later, I accompanied the king to the house of the new High Priest. The king asked Simon for his daughter's hand, and the High Priest was pleased to grant it. Both men signed the *ketubah* and agreed that the *chuppah* would take place the following week.

Until then, I had never been that close to a High Priest, and Simon's appearance impressed me. He wore a white robe embroidered with a gold and silver thread with a linen girdle at his waist. He wore a leather breastplate, adorned with embroidered crimson threads, over his tunic. Two straps hanging from it held two onyx stones engraved with the names of the twelve tribes of Israel. He had a gold necklace around his neck with a square plate of silver embedded with four rows of precious stones. Over his robe, he wore a purple mantle with small golden bells that jingled when he walked. On his head was a miter adorned with a golden crown.

On the day of the *chuppah*, Herod and his friends walked from the palace to the High priest's house. The bride and her maids were waiting at the entrance.

The High Priest blessed the couple. After the ceremony, Herod and his new wife entered a room where they consummated their marriage, while we, the guests, celebrated in the next room, drinking and toasting the couple's health and happiness.

The king came out of the bridal room and handed the bloody sheet, proof of his bride's virginity, to the girl's parents, who in turn gave it to the bride to keep.

Then, the newly married couple, their relatives, friends, and guests walked in a procession to the royal palace, where we enjoyed a sumptuous wedding banquet.

During the following years, Herod married more women. One was a Samaritan girl called Malthace. Another was the daughter of a noble family of Jerusalem who had the same name, Cleopatra, as Egypt's dead Queen.

Herod's wives usually got along quite well among themselves. They always remembered the tragic end of the first Mariamne and made every effort not to give Herod any reason to be angry with them.

In my opinion, the only woman that Herod loved, and that he continued to love to the end of his days, was the first Mariamne, the beautiful and unhappy Queen.

Herod marries the second Mariamne

Chapter 37
The construction of the Temple

On my daily walks through Jerusalem, I could not help but notice the great contrast between Herod's palace, beautiful and modern, and the Temple of the god of the Jews, a modest and humble building built four centuries before. The Temple's front was crumbling, and some walls were in imminent danger of falling and crushing the priests.

Large amounts of building materials had been placed on the side of the Temple, including the bronze doors donated by my friend Nicanor, but there was not even one single mason working.

This situation bothered me, especially when I remembered my friend Nicanor's love and dedication when preparing the bronze doors. It now seemed to me that the doors had been forgotten. In one of the conversations that I had with Herod, I spoke frankly about this matter.

"Hundreds of thousands of pilgrims come to the city annually to visit the Temple, but when they see it, they cannot hide their disappointment. Who can blame them? The current building is old, shabby, and in poor condition. It does not do justice to the spiritual feelings of millions of people worldwide."

"It is true," he replied. "The current Temple was built by the Jews who returned, centuries ago, from the Babylonian exile. Their poverty did not allow them to make it as beautiful and grand as Solomon's Temple that the Babylonians had destroyed centuries ago."

"I know that for many years you have had in mind a project to rebuild the Temple of God, but so far, you have done nothing about it. The bronze doors donated by my friend Nicanor are still lying around. My advice is that the time has come for you to rebuild the Temple. This sacred building will make your name immortal."

"You're right, Nicholas," cried Herod excitedly. "I will build the most beautiful temple in the world in Jerusalem."

The king sent a delegation to Rome that returned with the famous Roman engineer, Emilio Cornelius. On the day of the engineer's arrival, Herod took him personally to inspect the Temple Mount. I accompanied them. The engineer took notes and measurements. Back at the palace, the king showed Cornelius the architectural plans that he had drawn. Herod was a most accomplished amateur architect and a good draft artist as well. The engineer scrutinized the drawings, looked over his notes, checked the measurements that we had taken on the Mount, and shook his head.

"Your Majesty," he said, "there is a problem. The buildings and open courts that you have designed with rows of columns on all four sides need an area much larger than the small flat top of the Mount. The only solution is to modify your plans and reduce the number of buildings that will occupy the existing area."

"Cornelius, there is another alternative. Instead of reducing the number of buildings and courts, I will enlarge the flat area at the summit of the Mount," said Herod.

"How could we accomplish that, Your Majesty?" Cornelius asked the king. I noticed a condescending smile on the engineer's face, which he quickly hid when he saw that I was looking at him.

"You are the engineer, not I. I give you three days to find the solution. If you do not find it, I will conclude that you lied when you told my men that you are the best engineer in Rome. If that would be the case, I will have to cut off your head, which hopefully will not be a great loss for the guild of engineers."

The engineer's smile faded.

Three days later, Cornelius came to the palace with scrolls of drawings. Nervously, he spread them on the table.

"Your Majesty, I think I have found the solution. We can extend the summit of the Mount by building underground vaults upon which the Temple would be built, surrounded by a ninety-foot high wall of cut and carved stones," said Cornelius drying the sweat from his brow with a handkerchief.

Herod sat on a stool and studied the drawings that Cornelius had presented. After a while, he looked at the engineer who was trembling.

"Congratulations Cornelius. It is an excellent solution. Do you see how a small incentive does wonders to inspire the mind?" said the king with a smile.

"Yes, Your Majesty," replied the engineer.

"I want the Temple to be ready in less than two years. How many people do you need to build it?" Herod asked.

"At least a thousand workers, Your Majesty," replied Cornelius.

"There is a problem. The only people allowed to enter certain enclosures of the Temple are the priests. This means that masons, carpenters, and other craftsmen are forbidden to enter", said the king.

"How can we build the Temple without craftsmen?" Cornelius asked the king, nervously wiping his forehead with his handkerchief again.

"This time, I will give you the solution. As we cannot turn the artisans into priests because they have that status from birth, we will turn the priests into artisans. Choose a thousand priests that may seem to you appropriate for the task, and teach them bricklaying, carpentry, marble works, and all the other jobs that are needed to build the Temple," ordered the king.

That night Herod showed me the plans for the new Temple.

"Here," he said, pointing to a location on the map, "we will expand the surface area of the summit of the Mount to more than twice its natural size. It will be the largest acropolis in the world, twice the size of the Acropolis of Athens, and of course, incomparably more beautiful."

"These two open courts surrounded by four rows of columns. What is their purpose?" I asked the king.

"The first one is the Court of the Gentiles where everybody, Jews and non-Jews, will be allowed to enter. In the second court, only Jews will be allowed. We will place signs in Greek and Latin warning the non-Jews that, if they enter, they will receive the death penalty. Next to the courts is the Temple itself, where only priests may enter. Inside is the Holy Sanctuary, and that is limited to the High Priest."

"How are you going to finance this ambitious project? Are you planning to impose more taxes"? I asked the king.

"The people will not pay for it," he replied. "I will pay for the construction with my own money."

Today, as I write these lines, the Temple of Jerusalem is a reality. Just as Herod had envisioned it, the Temple is the largest and most beautiful building in the world. It has no equal in the entire Roman Empire. And the most impressive thing is that this wonderful result was achieved without interrupting the religious rituals and priestly sacrifices, not even for one day, thanks to Herod's organizational talent.

Model of the Temple built by Herod

Chapter 38
Alexander and Aristobulus go to Rome

Herod decided that Alexander and Aristobulus, the sons he had with his late wife Mariamne, should study in Rome where they would receive a cosmopolitan education and have the opportunity to meet and be friends with the most important people of the Empire. Their political and social connections would greatly benefit the princes when they eventually became the rulers of Judea.

The king asked me to accompany his sons on their trip to Rome. I accepted gladly because I liked them, and they treated me with respectful friendliness. They had inherited their mother's beauty and their father's intelligence.

Our ship sailed from Caesarea, a city that Herod had built and named in honor of Octavius Caesar, who was now called Augustus, a title given to him by the Senate.

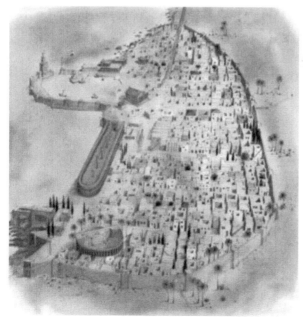

Caesarea in the days of Herod

175

In Rome, the Emperor greeted us warmly and thanked me for the dates that I had brought him. My workers cultivated these dates on land that I bought near Jericho. The Emperor was kind enough to tell me that they were the most delicious dates that he had ever eaten in his life.

Augustus was pleased to see the two young princes and told them that they would live with him in his house and be educated with the nobility's sons.

I stayed in Rome for a few weeks, during which I renewed my friendship with the butcher Lucius and spent delightful evenings with him visiting the brothels in the Suburra neighborhood.

When I boarded the ship that would take me back to Caesarea, I had a most pleasant surprise. The captain was Licinius (the reader may remember him as the ship captain that took me from Alexandria to Ostia when, years before, I delivered letters from Mark Antony to Octavius). It was a providential meeting because Herod urgently needed a commander for the naval fleet that carpenters were building for him on the island of Rhodes.

Upon our arrival in Caesarea, I asked Licinius to come with me to Herod's palace, where I presented him to the king. Licinius made such an excellent impression that, on the spot, Herod offered him the post of commander of the Judea fleet. Persuaded by the great honor and the high salary that the king offered him, Licinius accepted.

The city of Caesarea had been built by Herod. It was a beautiful and modern city, with magnificent mansions. Herod's summer palace was built on a promontory by the sea. Close by, the king built a hippodrome, a theater, and an amphitheater. In the center of the city, the king built a large Temple dedicated to Rome and Augustus. Aqueducts from springs in distant mountains brought water to the city.

The port of Caesarea, the largest on the Mediterranean coast, was the city's most impressive feature. Its importance was not only commercial but also military. It was designed to be the naval base for the future fleet of Judea. Massive warehouses for imported merchandise were located on a wide pier built with enormous rocks.

A beautiful boardwalk, lined with palm trees, surrounded the harbor. People walked there in the evenings enjoying the sea breeze and savoring the delicious snacks offered by street vendors.

I stayed two weeks in Caesarea, a delightful city where I enjoyed a great vacation. I spent my days swimming in the pool of Herod's palace, eating in the excellent fish restaurants in the harbor, watching plays in the theater, and betting in the hippodrome. It is not in my character to enjoy leisure for too long. The day came when I felt that I had to return to my home in Jerusalem. I missed my library with its hundreds of scrolls that I had started collecting as far back as my sojourn in Alexandria. Even more, pressing was my longing to renew my writing of the History of the World. One day before my intended return to Jerusalem, Herod asked me to come to his palace. I found him swimming naked in the pool. He got out of the water and wrapped himself in a towel handed to him by a female slave.

"Augustus is currently in Syria. The town of Gadara has sent a delegation with serious complaints against me. They accuse me of being a tyrant and imposing exorbitant taxes. They demand that Gadara be transferred from my jurisdiction to the authority of the Governor of Syria. What should I do?" he asked me while the girl dried him with the towel.

"I think that we should travel to Syria and speak to Augustus as soon as possible," I replied.

Augustus felt a sincere affection for Herod. He was always glad to see him and enjoyed his company and conversation. He received the king with a hug and invited him to dine that night with him. The after-dinner discussion was lively and witty. Augustus told Herod how satisfied he was with Alexander and Aristobulus' progress in their education and the excellent impression they made on every person they met. "Any Roman father would be proud to have such sons," he said.

Once they concluded the small talk, the two leaders discussed important topics, such as politics, wars, and taxes. I noticed the glaring absence of any mention of the complaints of the delegation of Gadara.

After a long night of feasting, praising, and toasting each other, Herod said goodbye to Augustus and returned to Judea.

The members of the delegation of Gadara realized that they had made a fatal mistake. Fearing that Augustus would accuse them of rebellion and have them tortured, two of them committed suicide, and the others fled to avoid arrest.

Chapter 39
Alexander and Aristobulus return from Rome

One day Herod said to me, "It's time that my sons Alexander and Aristobulus assume their responsibilities in the kingdom. Three years of spending my money in Rome is more than enough. I have decided that next week we will travel to Rome and bring them back to Judea."

We sailed from Caesarea on the *Mariamne*, the flagship of Judea that Herod had named in honor of his late wife. The captain of the ship was my friend Licinius, the commander of our brand new national fleet.

Augustus, advised of our arrival, sent a cavalry escort that accompanied us from Ostia to Rome. Herod's two sons, dressed in Roman togas, were waiting at Augustus' house door.

Herod ran to them, hugged, and kissed them, but they treated him coldly. I attributed this to them being unable to forgive their father for killing their mother, grandmother Alexandra, and great grandfather Hyrcanus.

On our return to Caesarea, a crowd was waiting for us, eager to see the young princes. When Alexander and Aristobulus came off the boat, tall and handsome, dressed as Romans, the people cheered them.

I noticed that the king's sister, Salome, who had come to welcome her brother Herod, seemed worried, possibly remembering that she had contributed to the death of the mother of the two young men with her slander and gossip.

Herod had already chosen brides for his two sons, and celebrated the weddings with a great feast as soon we arrived in Jerusalem. Aristobulus bride was Berenice, the daughter of his aunt Salome, and Alexander's was Glaphyra, the daughter of Archelaus, the king of Cappadocia.

Wherever the two princes went, people cheered and chanted their names. Herod noticed that the popularity of his sons

179

increased continuously, while his own decreased. That was understandable because, due to his paranoia, he was fearful of rebellions and had imposed a regime of terror on the nation.

The king had banned meetings of more than three people and had forced every citizen to swear loyalty to the crown.

No one was above suspicion. Herod's special guard watched the rich and the poor, as well as the nobles and the common people. Herod had a habit, common also to other kings, of going out at night in disguise to ask people on the street what they thought about him. Most of the people who were naïve enough to express an honest, frank, and sincere opinion about the king were taken from their homes in the middle of the night and disappeared forever. Others, more fortunate, were taken to the Antonia Fortress, which was located next to the Temple. There they were interrogated under torture. Those who gave satisfactory answers were allowed to return to their homes. The others were executed without trial.

On one of Herod's secret night tours, I accompanied him to the Essene neighborhood. There were posters in the streets demanding that women cover their shoulders, arms, and ankles and behave modestly when entering the area.

"Do you see that old man praying in the corner? I know him. His name is Menachem. When I was a kid, he prophesied to me that one day I would be king. I want to talk to him," said Herod.

The old man wore the Essene sect's traditional clothing: a black robe and a black turban. I went to where he was standing and told him that someone wanted to talk with him. Wordlessly, he accompanied me to where Herod was waiting. He looked at Herod, and I realized that he had recognized the king.

"Menachem, how many more years will I reign?" asked Herod.

Menachem did not answer. He walked away and resumed his prayers.

Chapter 40
Herod's friendship with Agrippa

Marcus Vipsanius Agrippa, the second most powerful man in the Roman Empire, was a close friend and son-in-law of Emperor Augustus. Herod informed that Agrippa had arrived in Syria on an inspection tour, met him, and invited him and his wife Julia to visit Judea.

The couple accepted the invitation and came to Judea. The people of Jerusalem, dressed in festive clothes, received the visitors with cheers, which became deafening when Agrippa offered a sacrifice in the Temple.

Herod put aside all his obligations and devoted his entire time, day and night, to traveling around the country with the distinguished couple. He took them to Caesarea and showed them the port that he had built. Afterward, he entertained them in his palaces of Jericho, Herodion, and Masada.

After remaining in Judea for two months, Agrippa decided to return to Rome before winter. He said goodbye to Herod, swore eternal friendship, and promised to see him again as soon as possible.

The following spring Herod heard that Agrippa was in the Bosporus fighting against tribes that rebelled against the Empire. He immediately ordered Licinius, the commander of his navy, to take him and the army to Byzantium. There, he and his soldiers joined the Roman army and together defeated the rebellious tribes. The Roman general could not stop thanKing Herod for coming from so far to fight by his side.

Agrippa appreciated Herod's advice regarding the conduct of the military campaign and the management of the civil affairs in the region. Herod sent his army back to Caesarea in the ships, and he and I accompanied Agrippa by land.

On the way, we stopped in the city of Ephesus. The Jews of the city, aware of our presence, sent a delegation to Herod with a list of grievances against the local authorities. Herod asked me to speak to Agrippa and advocate for the Jews.

181

Agrippa summoned all the local officials to the hearing and invited me to speak.

"The Jews of Ephesus have traditionally enjoyed rights and privileges that only Rome has the power to grant or deny. Recently, the local rulers, acting on their own, without authorization from higher authorities, have forbidden the Jews to celebrate their religious festivals. They have forced the Jews to work on Saturday, the Jewish day of rest when they pray and study their sacred books. They have prevented the Jews from sending donations to their Temple in Jerusalem. I ask Your Excellency, on behalf of the Ephesus Jews, who are loyal citizens, to order the authorities to respect their religion and customs," I said.

Agrippa stood and announced his decision.

"What the Jews, represented by Nicholas, demand is fair, and if they would ask for more, I would also grant it in honor of my friend Herod. The Jews have the right to exercise their religion freely, to keep the Sabbath, and to send donations to their Temple in Jerusalem," declared Agrippa.

Herod was thrilled to hear Agrippa's words. He thanked him, and Agrippa reciprocated with a hug.

The people in Jerusalem heard of our successful intercession on behalf of the Jews of Ephesus. Herod was applauded on our return when he rode through the streets of the city. Herod, touched by their enthusiasm, rewarded the people by announcing that he would reduce that year's taxes.

Chapter 41
Antipater returns to the palace

The family situation in the palace continued to deteriorate. Salome openly expressed her hate towards Alexander and Aristobulus, sons of the unfortunate Queen Mariamne, even though Aristobulus was her son-in-law. The two young men reciprocated her antipathy.

Salome was a subtle woman, sly and experienced in the art of provoking jealousy and suspicions. Afraid that the princes would attempt to avenge their mother's death, she began a slander campaign and gossip against them. She circulated the rumor that the sons of Mariamne wanted to write to Augustus accusing Herod of being guilty of the wrongful death of their mother. The story reached Herod through several people and caused him much concern.

Because of their naivety and inexperience in palatial intrigues, the two young men acted insolently towards their father, an attitude that did not favor their cause.

The king realized that he had to do something to counter Alexander and Aristobulus' popularity and make them know that their succession to the throne was not guaranteed. Herod remembered Antipater, the son he had with Doris, the woman he had divorced twenty years before, and brought him back to the palace.

Doris and Antipater, since being banished from the palace, had lived in a hut in the Lower City. Herod had minimal contact with them during all those years except for sending, from time to time, small sums of money for their subsistence.

One day, Herod called me to the Throne Room. I found him there with a young man about twenty-five years old, who looked remarkably like a younger version of the king.

"Nicholas, I want you to meet Antipater, my firstborn son. For various reasons, we have been separated for many years, but today I have brought him to live in the palace."

Addressing Antipater, he said to him, "Meet Nicholas, my best counselor. I have already spoken to you about him."

"Sir," said Antipater to me, "my father has told me all about you. It will be a privilege to work at your side."

My first impression, later confirmed by the facts, was not favorable. From the first moment I saw Antipater, he gave me the impression of being a smart, ambitious, and unscrupulous individual. He was a dangerous man who would search for the best way to take advantage of the unexpected opportunity that fate had given him.

Physically, he bore a striking resemblance to his father. Like Herod, his height was less than average. His skin was dark, and his hair was black. He looked very different from his half-brothers, the sons of Mariamne, who were tall and blond.

Shortly after arriving at court, Antipater heard the rumors that Salome was circulating about the sons of Mariamne and made sure that they reached the ears of Herod. He did his best to ingratiate himself with his father and convinced him to allow his mother, Doris, to live in the palace.

Herod wrote to Augustus asking for permission to send his son Antipater to Rome so that the Emperor could meet him and take him into account as the possible successor to the throne of Judea.

Antipater was received in Rome with great honors. Thanks to the letters of recommendation that Herod had sent, the city's most prominent families opened their doors to him. Despite the warm reception and his social success in Rome, Antipater stayed only for a few weeks. He felt that his presence in Jerusalem was essential to prevent Mariamne's children from improving their relationship with their father.

On his return to Jerusalem, Antipater continued his covert campaign against his half-brothers, Alexander and Aristobulus. His success was greater than what he hoped. Herod's anger against the two young men became so intense that he forced them to travel with him to Rome and have Augustus judge them. Antipater and I traveled with them.

"These two young men, my own sons, have become my worst enemies. They constantly show their hatred to me. I have heard that they want to kill me and usurp the throne. To kill the father who has given them everything and has married them to women from the most illustrious families! As their father, I feel that they lack filial love. As their king, I consider their behavior to be treasonable," complained Herod to Augustus.

I saw that the faces of the two young men showed confusion. They could not proclaim their innocence because refuting their father meant disrespect. And they could not keep silent because this was the equivalent of recognizing their guilt.

Augustus felt compassion for them because of their youth and inexperience and asked Alexander, the elder brother, to speak up in their defense.

"Father," said Alexander addressing Herod, "we know that you have the right as our father and as our king to punish us if we have offended you. The fact that you brought us here, to be in the presence of Augustus, means that you want to save us because you could have punished us in Jerusalem. My brother and I are innocent, but we would rather die than continue to live under the suspicion of having offended our father and our king. That suspicion is based on lies and false rumors. Can anyone prove that we have conspired against you? Can anyone think that if we had committed the heinous crime of patricide, Emperor Augustus would have allowed us to assume the throne?"

The words of the young man moved Augustus. The Emperor rose and spoke to Herod.

"I have not heard any evidence that proves that they are guilty. I am convinced that all the charges against your sons are based on slander. My friend, hug your children. They are your flesh and blood!"

Herod wept and embraced his two sons. Antipater approached his father and his two half-brothers and congratulated them for their reconciliation.

Augustus, happy to have solved his friend's family quarrel, gave Herod a magnificent gift: the copper mines that had recently been discovered on the island of Cyprus. He also confirmed the king's right to name as his successor, whichever son he might choose.

"Augustus, I am willing to abdicate right now in favor of the person that you prefer," said Herod.

"I will not allow you to abdicate," answered Augustus. "While you live, you will be king of Judea."

Back in Jerusalem, Herod called a meeting in the Throne Room of his advisors and principal officers.

"I have called you here to announce that my successor will be Antipater. After his death, Alexander and Aristobulus will occupy the throne. Of course, all this will happen after I am gone, hopefully, many years from now."

Chapter 42
Salome makes trouble

In the twenty-eighth year of his reign, Herod inaugurated a new city in Samaria named Sebaste, the Greek translation of Augustus' name. The king celebrated the event with sports contests, gladiatorial combats, fights with wild animals, and horse racing.

Ambassadors from all the neighboring countries attended the inauguration of the city. Thousands came to enjoy the entertainment and the banquets, all of them paid by Herod. Never before had something so grandiose been done in Judea.

Herod's reputation grew immensely, and rumors circulated, probably initiated by the king's men, that Agrippa had proposed to Augustus that Syria and Egypt be annexed to Judea and thus become part of Herod's kingdom.

Herod's generosity also extended to other countries. On the island of Rhodes, he financed the construction of a Temple to the god Apollo and paid for repairing the island's fleet. He paid for the construction of several public buildings in Nicopolis, a Greek city. In Antioch, Syria, the king paid for the paving of the main road and the building of porches on both sides of the main avenue. He built theaters and amphitheaters in Asia Minor, in several Greek islands, and in Athens.

During the last decades, the Olympic Games had lost much of their importance because no one was willing to assume its high cost. Herod assigned a large annual sum to the Games, and, in gratitude, the organizers named him Honorary President of the Olympic Games for Life.

I never met a person with more contradictions than Herod. His generosity went hand-to-hand with his cruel vanity. If any of his courtiers did not address him with enough respect, Herod would punish him as if the unfortunate man was his enemy even if he was a devoted friend.

187

Herod would have liked to erect his statues in Jerusalem and other cities and have temples dedicated to him. None of this was possible because the Jewish religion forbids it.

He financed many of his generous acts from his personal fortune, not from tax money, which he used only for the people's benefit. He used to say, "What comes from the people goes to the people." He had several sources of income, among them: the copper mines of Cyprus which Augustus had given him, dates plantations in Jericho, the export of balsam, and other commercial and shipping activities.

Once, when his expenses had exceeded his income, and he needed money urgently, he secretly opened king David's tomb. Although he did not find any money in the grave, he took the gold furniture he found there. Although I find it hard to believe, witnesses say that when Herod's guards touched David's corpse, a flame came out of the body and consumed them. The fact is that soon after entering the tomb, Herod built a wall around it and sealed the entrance.

The conflict within Herod's family got worse and worse, to the point that I was tempted to call it "a civil war," where falsehoods and calumnies were mortal weapons. Some called it divine punishment for the violation of king David's grave.

Antipater secretly circulated lies about his half-brothers, while in public and his father's presence, he tried to give the impression of defending them.

The two women who were married to Alexander and Aristobulus, the sons of Mariamne, hated each other. Alexander's wife, Glaphyra, the king of Cappadocia's daughter, despised Berenice, Aristobulus' wife. Berenice reciprocated the feeling and detested Glaphyra.

Herod's sister, Salome, Berenice's mother, hated Alexander and Glaphyra and even her own son-in-law Aristobulus. She forced her daughter Berenice to inform her about everything that her husband said and did. Then she would run to Herod and tell him exaggerated or fabricated stories. On more than one occasion, I was present when Salome slandered her son-in-law, but prudently, I refrained from intervening in the family feuds.

"Herod," Salome would say, "I must tell you something my daughter Berenice mentioned to me. Her husband, Aristobulus, told her that he and his brother Alexander are proud of the excellent education they received in Rome and despise their half-brothers for being uneducated, ignorant, and stupid. He and Alexander have decided that, after your death, they will force your other children to work in the stables cleaning manure because they lack the intelligence and ability to perform other tasks."

Pheroras, Herod's only surviving brother, was considered the second most important man in the kingdom. Unfortunately, he also caused problems for the king.

Herod had offered Pheroras the hand of one of his own daughters in marriage, but Pheroras rejected the offer because he had fallen in love with a servant woman. Herod was offended and stopped speaking to his brother. Pheroras resented Herod's reaction and tried to find a way to get revenge.

Pheroras spoke to Prince Alexander and told him that Herod was trying to seduce Glaphyra, Alexander's wife. The young prince, tormented with jealousy, confronted Herod, who indignantly denied the accusation and sent for Pheroras.

"Only a wicked person can invent such slander! Your intention is clear. You want to turn my son against me. You want him to conspire against me. You want him to poison me!" Herod reproached Pheroras.

"I don't think that this is slander. I only repeated what. I heard from Salome," Pheroras defended himself.

Herod sent for Salome and told her what Pheroras had said. Knowing that her life was in danger, she burst into tears.

"It's a vile falsehood! I never said such a horrible lie. Pheroras hates me because I insisted that he get rid of the servant woman and, instead, marry your daughter," Salome sobbed, beating her chest and tearing her hair.

"Out, you two," screamed Herod. "I can't stand either of you."

As a result of Pheroras and Salome's intrigues, Herod's relationship with his sons Alexander and Aristobulus became warmer, while his affection for his sister Salome diminished.

It did not help Salome that she had fallen in love with Sileus, an Arab who held a high position in the kingdom of Petra and was currently visiting Jerusalem. The Arab asked Herod for permission to marry Salome.

"I will agree to let you marry my sister if you first convert to Judaism," answered Herod.

"I cannot do that. If I convert, the Arabs will stone me to death," Sileus answered. Addressing Salome, he said, "Goodbye Salome. It was wonderful while it lasted."

Chapter 43
The visit of Archelaus,
king of Cappadocia

The prevailing atmosphere of distrust and mutual hate in the palace continued to poison all of us. The situation became tense and threatening following the incident of the eunuchs. Herod had a dozen eunuchs for his personal service. They were black men from Africa, whose loyalty he valued highly. One of them was in charge of bringing him drinks, another brought him food, and a third eunuch helped him get dressed in the mornings. One fateful day, someone told the king that his son Alexander had bribed the eunuchs with a large sum of money to murder him. We never knew who told Herod this preposterous story, but I was convinced, and still am, that it was Antipater who invented the false rumor that caused the eunuchs to be tortured and killed.

Herod's paranoia had always been offset by common sense and pragmatism, but this time, hearing that his faithful eunuchs were plotting against him, the king lost his temper. He ordered his officers to torture the eunuchs until they confessed that Alexander hated his father and wanted to see him dead. The eunuchs also said, and this is what offended Herod's vanity the most, that Alexander had told them that his father dyed his hair black to hide his advanced age.

Herod became suspicious of everybody around him. The higher the position of the person, the greater the king's suspicion. To protect themselves, his officers denounced each other. Herod ordered the execution of some of them, but when he found that they were innocent, he felt remorse. He eased his conscience by condemning the accusers to death.

One day, Prince Alexander came to my house to speak to me about the fear and terror we all felt.

"My friends have been tortured, and several of them have been executed. None of them accused me of wrongdoings

191

because I have never done anything wrong," Alexander told me.

"Do you have any idea why your father hates you?" I asked him.

"No, I do not. I try my best not to offend him. Although I am taller than he is, I hunch myself to look smaller when I walk by his side. When I hunt with him, I always take care that my arrow does not hit the target. Perhaps the only way to convince my father not to kill my friends is if I make up a confession, however absurd it may be. For example, I could say that I conspired with Pheroras against him and that I slept with his sister Salome," he said with a bitter smile.

"Alexander, this is no joke. You can easily lose your life. But I have an idea. Your father-in-law, Archelaus, king of Cappadocia, is an intelligent man and a good friend of your father, Herod. I will send him a letter telling him all that is happening and ask him to come to Jerusalem to help end this terrible situation," I said.

That same day I sent a messenger to Cappadocia. Three weeks later, king Archelaus came on an official visit to Jerusalem.

Seeing Herod's fury and anger, Archelaus decided that his best tactic would be to agree with the king and direct his reproaches to his daughter Glaphyra and his son-in-law Alexander.

"Herod, my friend, I am truly sorry to see you so angry, you who usually are such a calm and peaceful person. I am ashamed that my daughter and my son-in-law are causing you problems and pain. If you wish, I am willing to annul the marriage, take back my daughter and punish her as she deserves," said Archelaus.

Upon hearing these sympathetic words from Archelaus, Herod started to cry.

"I don't want you to annul the marriage of our children. I am sure that everything is a lie and that my brother Pheroras is to blame," said Herod.

Pheroras, pale and trembling, threw himself at the feet of Herod and asked for forgiveness.

A few days later, Archelaus, happy to have reconciled his son-in-law with the king, returned to Cappadocia, carrying with him the gifts that Herod had given him to show his gratitude.

The visit of Archelaus, king of Cappadocia

Chapter 44
The two brothers are sent to prison

A Greek named Eurykles had arrived in Judea with king Archelaus and decided to stay in Jerusalem when the king of Cappadocia returned to his land. Glaphyra and Alexander, under the false impression that Eurykles was a close friend of Glaphyra's father, Archelaus, invited him to stay with them at their home as long as he liked.

Eurykles wormed his way into Alexander's friendship and won his confidence. The naïve young prince told Eurykles that he remembered his mother Mariamne with deep love and sorrow and that her death had been a shameful injustice.

Eurykles requested an audience with Herod and told him what Alexander had told him in confidence. The anger that the king felt toward his son increased even more.

Alexander liked to go horseback riding with two friends from his childhood that he esteemed and loved. Eurykles went to Herod again and denounced that the two men were conspiring with Alexander against the king.

Herod gave Eurykles a reward of fifty talents for having revealed the alleged conspiracy. As soon as he received the money, the Greek went back to Cappadocia, where he lied to king Archelaus, saying that he had succeeded in reconciling Herod and Alexander again.

Archelaus, glad to hear the good news, gave a valuable gift to Eurykles, who fled to Greece before his lies were discovered.

Herod imprisoned and tortured Alexander's two friends until they confessed that Alexander was conspiring with them to kill Herod. A letter was found among the two suspects' belongings, apparently written by Alexander, in which the prince instructed them to kill the king.

Alexander denied having written the letter, but the king did not believe him and sent him to prison.

Aristobulus, Alexander's brother, asked Salome, his mother-in-law, to intercede with the king, but made the mistake of warning her that she too was in danger because she could be accused of revealing the secrets of the kingdom to the Arab Sileus, her ex-lover.

Salome interpreted this warning as a threat. To protect herself, she told Herod that Aristobulus was also plotting against the king. Herod ordered Aristobulus to be sent to the same prison where his brother was being held.

It happened at that time that a band of rebels who had committed crimes in Judea escaped and took refuge in Petra, the neighboring kingdom where Sileus, Salome's suitor, had recently assumed power.

Herod demanded that Sileus hand over the rebels, but the Arab denied that they were in his kingdom. Herod asked the Roman Governor of Syria to order Sileus to give up the bandits and repay sixty talents of silver that Herod had loaned to Petra's previous king.

The Roman Governor of Syria gave Sileus thirty days to deliver the rebels to Herod and pay the debt.

The deadline passed without Sileus delivering the rebels or paying back the loan. Herod went to Petra with a detachment of soldiers, arrived at the village where the band had taken refuge, and captured the bandits. The Arab soldiers that guarded the town attacked the Judean forces, but the king easily defeated them. Twenty Arabs died in the skirmish, including the captain of the garrison.

When Sileus, who was visiting Rome, heard the news, he dressed in black and went to Augustus' house to complain about Herod.

"Herod invaded my country, killed two thousand soldiers of my army, and took with him valuable loot," accused Sileus.

Augustus was furious. He immediately sent a letter to Herod saying that he did not consider him a friend and would treat him like any other vassal from now on.

Herod was shocked when he read the letter. That same day he sent me to Rome to tell Augustus the truth of what had happened. I took a personal note from the king to the Emperor, where he denounced his sons' patricidal intentions and asked the Emperor for permission to prosecute and punish them.

As soon as I arrived in Rome, I went straight to Augustus' house to refute Sileus' false accusations. The Arab was there when I arrived.

"My Lord," I said, "Sileus has invented falsehoods with the wicked intent of causing enmity between you and Herod. He is a despicable murderer who poisoned the former king of Petra to usurp the throne. He is a scoundrel who has committed adultery, not just with the women in his country but also with Roman ladies."

"Nicholas, you are here to explain the actions of Herod, not to accuse Sileus," said Augustus.

"Yes, My Lord. The truth is that Sileus owes a large sum of money to Herod and refuses to pay. As a result of the Governor of Syria's intervention, Sileus promised that he would pay the debt within thirty days but did not keep his promise. Herod indeed crossed the border, but he went in with a small detachment of soldiers, not with an army. He did it to capture a band of outlaws who had committed robberies, assaults, and murders in Judea, dangerous criminals to whom Sileus, instead of putting them in prison, had given shelter. Herod asked the local garrison soldiers not to hinder him in his efforts to capture the fugitives. The soldiers ignored his plea and attacked the detachment. I will not deny that in the skirmish, started by the Arab soldiers, some of them were killed, but the number of the dead was only twenty and not the two thousand that Sileus falsely claims. I have brought as evidence a letter from the Governor of Syria which confirms my words."

Augustus read the letter and addressed Sileus.

"Sileus, tell me how many Arab soldiers died trying to protect the criminals? Twenty or two thousand?" Augustus asked him.

"I was misinformed, My Lord," Sileus stammered.

"I hate lies and, even more, I hate liars who lie to my face. You will pay for your lie with your death," said Augustus.

After Sileus was taken away, I gave Augustus Herod's letter concerning his sons. Augustus was dismayed when he read it.

The next day Augustus handed me a letter to Herod. He gave him ample powers to punish his sons Alexander and Aristobulus if the young men were convicted of attempted patricide.

"Nicholas, I will tell you frankly, it is better to be Herod's pig than Herod's son," Augustus said to me with a sad smile.

Chapter 45
The execution of the two brothers

The trial of Alexander and Aristobulus was held in Beirut. Augustus had asked Herod in his letter to include the Governor of Syria and king Archelaus of Cappadocia among the judges. Herod agreed to include the Governor but not Archelaus because the king of Cappadocia was Alexander's father-in-law.

Herod accused his sons with a voice full of hatred. He declared that he would not admit any evidence or argument in their favor if it contradicted his word as king. He read a letter aloud from his sons where they had written that they wanted to flee Judea for fear of their father. Herod said it was painful to read those phrases that dishonored him as a father and as king. He concluded by saying that he had the Emperor's approval and sufficient authority as a father and as king to punish them as he would see fit.

Without allowing Alexander and Aristobulus to defend themselves, the judges decided to vote. Two important Roman officials, who were present in the audience, asked to speak before the vote took place.

"I agree that Herod's sons are guilty, but they should not be sentenced to death. I am also a father, and I find Herod's indignation completely justified, but killing a son is to go against human nature," said one of them.

"I disagree with what my colleague has said. A son who is disloyal to his father deserves death," declared the other Roman.

The judges voted in favor of the death penalty. Later, when we were alone, Herod asked me what his friends in Rome thought about this matter.

"They all agree that your sons deserve severe punishment, but prison, not death," I answered.

Herod's two sons were taken in chains from Beirut to Caesarea, guarded by an armed escort. Herod, who rode at the head of the troops, was silent and thoughtful during the entire trip.

The two young men had always been acclaimed in Caesarea, but this time the population, fearful of expressing its feelings, watched the prisoners go by in complete silence.

"Herod, do not commit such a terrible injustice!" we heard a loud voice from somebody in the crowd.

Herod stopped his horse and asked, "Who is he who dares to judge my actions?"

"It's me, Tero, a loyal soldier who fought beside you in countless battles. I want to talk to you, Herod, father to father."

"Let him approach!" Herod ordered his soldiers.

An old man, wearing a tattered military uniform, limped forward, leaning on a crutch. The king saw him and smiled.

"Now I remember you. You saved my life on more than one occasion," Herod said to the old soldier.

"Herod, excuse my boldness. Where is your extraordinary wisdom? Do you realize what you are doing? Will you kill these two young men who are the victims of slander and lies?" asked the old man.

I noticed that the king was moved. I gestured to Tero to stop speaking, but the old man, not understanding that there are limits that it is not wise to cross, continued speaking in a loud voice.

"Your officers and the entire army sympathize with your sons. They will condemn you if you kill them," added Tero.

This last sentence was Tero's bane. The king did not tolerate the slightest disloyalty in the army. Herod's face hardened, and in a harsh voice, he ordered his men to arrest Tero and the old man's son who was with him and put them in prison.

That night, the royal barber, to curry favor with the king, told him that Tero had asked him to cut the king's throat while shaving him and had promised that Alexander would give him a generous reward for that deed.

The king immediately ordered his guards to torture Tero, his son, and the barber to determine the truth and to force them to say the names of the army officers who, according to Tero, had condemned the verdict against Alexander and Aristobulus.

I approached Herod and spoke to him in a low voice that only he heard.

"Herod, please remember that a culprit, if he is strong, will proclaim his innocence under torture, but an innocent man, if he cannot stand the pain, will confess that he is guilty," I whispered in his ear.

Herod did not bother to answer me, and the executioner continued to torture Tero.

Tero's son could not bear to see his father's terrible pain and suffering and offered to confess if King Herod agreed to kill them without prolonging the torture. The king agreed.

"It's true. All that the barber has said is true. And now kill us," pleaded Tero's son.

"Kill the old man, his son, and also the barber," ordered the king.

Any doubt that Herod could have had about his sons' guilt vanished. That same night he ordered the executioner to strangle them.

The army officers named by Tero were taken to a field where a crowd stoned them to death.

Herod sent Glaphyra, the widow of his son Alexander, back to Cappadocia, her native country, and returned her dowry because he did not want it to be a cause for a disagreement with king Archelaus, Glaphyra's father.

The small children of Alexander and Aristobulus were brought to the palace. There, they were educated under Herod's direct tutelage. The king lavished on them the love that he had never given his own children.

The execution of the two brothers

Chapter 46
The death of Pheroras

His half-brothers' death meant that Antipater was now officially recognized as the sole heir and successor to the throne. Herod trusted him and did nothing without his advice. The young man's power was so great that many said that Antipater, not Herod, was the real king.

An intimate and influential circle of people surrounded Antipater. They included Pheroras and his wife (the woman who had been his servant in the past), the wife's mother and sister, and Doris, Antipater's mother, who had been Herod's first wife. The group met in secret because Herod despised and detested Pheroras' wife.

To conceal their friendship, Pheroras and Antipater behaved in public as if they hated each other, especially when Herod was present.

Salome, a master of intrigues, was not fooled. She had her servants follow Pheroras and Antipater and informed Herod that the two men met secretly to conspire against him.

Herod had ruled that all the citizens swear allegiance to the Emperor of Rome. A group of Pharisees refused to take the oath. Herod imposed a hefty fine on them that was paid by Pheroras' wife. Her shrewd move won the Pharisees' support, who, in gratitude, prophesied to the woman that Pheroras and her would soon become king and Queen.

Salome wasted no time telling Herod about the Pharisees' prediction. The king ordered his officers to kill the leaders of the sect. The next day he convened an assembly to judge Pheroras' wife, accusing her of causing enmity between him and his brother.

Pheroras was brought before Herod. I suggested to Herod that everybody should leave the room to allow the brothers to speak alone, without witnesses.

"Nicholas, tell the others to leave, but I want you to stay! I want you to hear what I am going to say to Pheroras." When the three of us were left alone in the room, Herod said to his brother, "Pheroras, I want you to divorce that woman who is causing enmity between us. You will do that if you want me to keep considering you, my brother. You must do from your own free will, without me forcing you."

"Herod, I cannot do what you are asking. I will never divorce my wife. She is the person I love most in the world. I would rather die than be separated from her," answered Pheroras.

"If that is the case, you and that woman will leave Jerusalem immediately. You will stay in your land in the north and will not return unless I allow you to do so," Herod ordered.

"That's fine with me. I will not return to Jerusalem while you are alive," answered Pheroras, his face flushed with anger.

Herod gave his son Antipater one hundred talents to refrain from contacting or communicating with Pheroras. He also asked him not to mention this gift to anyone. It would be a secret between them.

Antipater, wishing to distance himself from Pheroras and his wife, decided that it would be best for him to leave Judea for a while. He wrote to his friends in Rome and asked them to invite him to the imperial city. Herod approved the trip and gave him a letter in which he informed Emperor Augustus that he had appointed Antipater as his successor.

A short time later, Pheroras died unexpectedly. Herod gave instructions to bring the body of his brother to Jerusalem and gave him a State funeral.

A few days after the funeral, two servants of the late Pheroras asked Herod to grant them an audience.

"Your Majesty, the death of your brother, should be investigated. Minutes before he died, Pheroras drank a potion given to him by his wife and by his mother-in-law."

Herod gave orders to put the two women in prison. The women were tortured until they confessed that Antipater had told them that the king had given him a hundred talents to stop him from seeing Pheroras. This revelation convinced Herod that the women were telling the truth. They blamed Doris, Antipater's mother, accusing her of wanting the king to die so that her son could occupy the throne without further delay.

Herod summoned Doris, stripped her of her luxurious clothes and jewels, and threw her out of the palace.

"I never want to see you again. I made a mistake when I allowed you to come back to the palace. Go and starve in the same squalid hut where you lived before. And thank God that I do not kill you right now", Herod shouted at her.

Herod ordered his guards to go to the prison and bring Pheroras' widow to the palace. The king questioned her personally. The woman confessed that Antipater had bought the poison that he intended to give to Herod, but Pheroras, not wanting to commit the terrible sin of fratricide, drank the potion voluntarily.

The woman, noticing that her guards were shocked and distracted by what she was saying, ran to the balcony and jumped. She fell on a rock, hit her head, and died.

Herod discovered that one of his wives, Mariamne, the High Priest's daughter, had been aware of the conspiracy but had chosen not to betray the conspirators.

Herod, in a magnanimous gesture, spared her life. He divorced her, dismissed her father from his position as High Priest, and sent him to exile.

The death of Pheroras

Chapter 47
Antipater is sent to prison

The servant who had accompanied Antipater to Rome returned to Jerusalem. The guards searched him thoroughly and found a vial of poison hidden in his clothing.

Herod wrote a letter to Antipater ordering him to return to Judea. He mentioned that he had a minor problem with Doris, Antipater's mother, but it was not important, and the details about it could wait until they would see each other. To avoid arousing Antipater's suspicions, Herod wrote the letter in a very affectionate tone.

When Antipater's ship arrived at Caesarea, he was surprised that the usual official welcoming committee was not waiting for him. Alarmed, he went immediately to Jerusalem, accompanied by friends who had come with him on the ship. The guards at the gate allowed him to enter the palace but told the other men to wait outside. Minutes later, soldiers came out, arrested Antipater's friends, and took them away. Nobody ever saw them again.

Antipater entered the Throne Room, where Herod and the Roman Governor of Syria were waiting for him.

"Father, how good to see you." Antipater greeted the king and approached the throne to embrace and kiss him.

"Do not touch me! Stay away, murderer of your brothers! Tomorrow you will be tried, and I will make sure that you shall receive the punishment that you deserve!" shouted Herod.

Antipater was sent in chains to the palace dungeon. The next day the guards brought him to the Throne Room.

Herod, the Governor of Syria, Salome, and many palace officials were present.

Antipater threw himself to the ground and begged his father to allow him to defend himself. Instead of answering, Herod rose and began to speak, his voice quivering with sobs.

"Antipater has brought me only misfortune. I gave him money with open hands, and I named him my heir. Despite that, he conspired against me and planned to kill me. If the allegations against his dead brothers were true, he has followed suit. And if they were false, he is guilty of their deaths." Herod burst into tears and could not continue. Seeing that, I stood up and spoke to the Governor.

"Governor, the king is too distraught to speak. Let me list all the charges against Antipater and provide undeniable evidence of his guilt," I said.

"Father, I beg you, let me talk," sobbed Antipater.

"'Speak." said Herod.

"Father, these allegations are not only false, but they lack logic. It is absurd to think that I would try to kill you when you have elevated me to a position almost as high as yours, and you have named me your heir. You know how many times I have denounced conspiracies against you. Besides, all the confessions involving me in a plot against you were extracted under torture, a procedure that makes the person say anything to stop the unbearable pain," Antipater said in a broken voice with tears in his eyes.

I noticed expressions of sympathy on the faces of the people in the audience and saw that even Herod was moved.

I went to the king and asked permission to present the allegations and evidence against Antipater. The king nodded with a gesture of resignation.

"One cannot help but be horrified and repelled by the actions of Antipater, by his ingratitude, and by his patricidal intentions. His father gave him the greatest honors and even named him successor to the throne. Antipater's reaction was that of a venomous snake that one mistakenly feeds and tries to tame. Antipater indeed denounced conspiracies, but many of them were deliberate calumnies, invented by him with the intention not to save his father but to destroy his brothers. He hated the two princes because they were his rivals for the throne. Regarding Pheroras, he manipulated him to plot against the king, betrayed him, seduced his wife, and slept with her."

I finished talking and sat down. I made a discrete signal to others to rise and corroborate my accusations. The Roman Governor of Syria listened in silence and then spoke to Antipater.

"Do you have something to say in your defense?" he asked him.

"I pray to God to let me prove my innocence," Antipater replied.

Hearing that impudence, Herod stood indignantly.

"Have you no shame?" he shouted. "You are a scoundrel. People like you commit crimes as if God did not exist, but you appeal to God when your evil acts are discovered. God will not help you. God will not forgive your transgressions. God demands that you be punished!" Herod's anger did not allow him to continue.

Seeing that Antipater remained silent and had no arguments left to defend himself, the Governor of Syria rose.

"I understand that Antipater's servant had a bottle of poison hidden in his clothing. I want to see it. I also want you to bring me a criminal who has been sentenced to death," said the Governor.

Three guards left the room and returned after a few minutes. One brought a small bottle filled with a green liquid. The other two carried a man who had his hands and feet tied.

"Make him drink the liquid!" ordered the Governor.

A guard forced the man to open his mouth; the other poured in the contents of the bottle. The man tried to spit it out, but seconds later, he shook with violent convulsions. He could not breathe, and yellowish foam came out of his mouth. He lost consciousness and died. We looked at him, horrified.

The Governor left the room without a word, and the next day, after meeting with Herod, returned to Syria.

Antipater was taken to a prison cell in the Jericho palace basement, and Herod wrote to Augustus telling him everything that had happened.

Antipater is sent to prison

Chapter 48
Herod's death

Three days later, it was Herod's birthday. As he had done in previous years, the king decided to celebrate the event in his Jericho palace with feasts and festivities. This time it was different. When his family and close friends arrived in Jericho, the palace servants informed us that Herod was in his quarters, seriously ill and confined to his bed.

The king sent for me and dictated his will, in which he left the throne to one of his sons, named Antipas. He bequeathed a thousand talents to Emperor Augustus and left his extensive properties in the valley of Jericho to his sister Salome.

Religious fanatics in Jerusalem heard rumors that the king was dead. They armed themselves with axes and went to the Temple. Their purpose was to destroy the golden eagle that Herod had placed above the Temple's main gate in Augustus' honor. The fanatics believed that this image transgressed their god's commandments. They climbed on a ladder and destroyed the eagle with the axes that they had brought with them.

The Temple guards heard the disturbance. They ran to see what was happening and managed to capture the rebels. Herod, informed of the incident, gave orders to bring them to Jericho.

When he was told that the prisoners had arrived and were under guard in the palace's courtyard, the king had his servants carry him on a litter to dictate their sentence.

Herod said to them, "I built the Temple! I paid for its construction with my own money, and I have adorned it to be my memorial. You have insulted me publicly and will pay with your lives." He ordered his officers to burn alive the leaders and cut off the heads of the others.

Herod's looked terrible. He was covered with sores, and his breath had a foul stench. He complained that he felt fire in his belly and could not breathe. When he realized that he no longer had many days to live, he called for his sister Salome.

"I will die soon. I want the people to be sad and not to celebrate my death. To give them a good reason to mourn, I have given orders to bring the most important people of every Judean town and put them under guard in the amphitheater of Jericho. As soon as my death is announced, the soldiers will kill those people, and the whole nation will mourn and lament. Promise me you will make sure that this happens," Herod requested in a weak voice.

"I promise you, dear brother," answered Salome sobbing.

"Salome, please give me an apple and a knife to peel it" said Herod. She gave him what he had asked for. Herod grabbed the knife and tried to stab himself with it, but I was at his side and stopped his hand in time.

Antipater heard that his father was dying and tried to bribe his jailer to let him go free. The jailer refused and informed the king.

"Guards. go immediately to Antipater's cell and kill him!" Herod shouted with all the strength that he had left. The guards complied.

Five days after Antipater's death, Salome informed me that the king wanted to change his will. I went to his room carrying a scroll, pen, and ink to write his final instructions.

"I have changed my mind. My successor will be my son Arquelaus33. His brother Antipas will be the tetrarch of Galilee, and my son Philip will receive the Golan Heights. To my sister Salome, I leave the city of Ashdod." Those were the last words of Herod that I wrote down. He died a few minutes later. When I saw that Herod was no longer alive, I spoke to his sister.

"Salome," I said to her, "You cannot keep the promise that you made to Herod to kill the hostages. It would be inhumane and cruel. You have to release these men immediately."

Salome hesitated for a moment, then she ran to the amphitheater and ordered the soldiers to release the hostages and allow them to return to their towns.

Archelaus, the son that Herod had named his heir, decided that his father's funeral would be held with unprecedented pomp and luxury. Herod would be buried in the tomb that he had prepared for himself at Herodion, near Bethlehem. His body, covered with a purple cloth, was placed on a litter adorned with precious stones. On Herod's head, they set a golden crown. In his hand, they put a silver scepter.

Herod's sons, wives, family, and friends walked behind the coffin. They were followed by detachments of mercenaries from different countries, dressed in their distinctive uniforms. The soldiers of the army marched in ordered rows after them. Five hundred slaves and servants of Herod followed. The procession took five days to make the journey between Jericho and Herodion37.

We buried the king in the mausoleum that he had built on the hillside and returned to Jerusalem.

Reconstruction of Herod's mausoleum

Herod's Mausoleum and the palace at Herodion

Chapter 49
The massacre in the Temple

Archelaus mourned seven days for his father, as demanded by the Jewish ritual. On the eighth day, he went to the Temple, where people hailed him as their king. Archelaus raised his arms to indicate that he wanted to speak to them, and the people became silent.

"Thank you for proclaiming me king, but that title is not mine until Augustus confirms me as ruler of Judea. In the meantime, I will do my best to rule with justice and respect for the law," declared Archelaus.

"If you want to treat us with justice, punish the murderers of the martyrs who destroyed the blasphemous golden eagle," a voice was heard in the crowd.

"Dismiss the corrupt High Priest appointed by your father! We want a pious and honest High Priest!" cried another voice.

"Free the prisoners! Stop the torture!" people began to shout in chorus.

Archelaus, afraid of being stoned, hurriedly left the Temple surrounded by his guards.

A month later, the festival of Passover was celebrated in Jerusalem. Thousands of people attended the ceremonies in the Temple. To keep order and prevent riots, Archelaus sent a thousand armed soldiers to the Temple. The people saw the presence of soldiers in the holy place as a desecration and stoned them. The soldiers reacted by attacking the crowd with their swords. The result was a slaughter. Over three thousand people died.

The next day I went to talk to Archelaus.

"Archelaus, what has happened is a most tragic and unfortunate incident. Augustus may hold you responsible. I suggest that you travel to Rome to explain to Augustus what happened and ask him to recognize you as king of Judea officially. If you wish, I will go with you."

Archelaus appointed his half-brother Philip as regent and ordered Licinius, the royal fleet commander, to prepare a ship to take us to Rome.

Antipas, the younger brother of Archelaus, Salome, her sons, and family friends, traveled with us on the same ship. She told me that she came to support Archelaus, but in reality, as we later learned, her purpose was to ask Augustus to name Antipas king of Judea.

I did not know it at the time, but the day we set sail from Caesarea to Ostia put an end to the twenty-five years I lived in Judea.

I never returned.

Chapter 50
Archelaus and Antipas
dispute the throne of Judea

The day after we arrived in Rome, all of us, including Salome and her sons, went to Augustus' house to meet with the Emperor. Without wasting time on preliminaries, Archelaus presented to Augustus the last will of Herod, in which his father had named him his successor. Antipas, seeing this, showed the Emperor the former will, in which Herod had appointed him king.

Augustus said that to recognize one of the two as king of Judea, he needed to hear their arguments.

Salome's son, who never hid his intense dislike of Archelaus, rose and asked for permission to speak.

"Proceed," Augustus told him.

"With all due respect to the Emperor, I must say that Archelaus has a lot of nerve asking to be given the throne of Judea. In Jerusalem, he has appointed new army commanders and has sat on the throne, and called himself king. He has usurped the Emperor's authority, who is the only one who can confer that title. He showed no respect for the memory of his father. Just a week after the death of Herod, he held a banquet with music and dancing. Worse of all, he is guilty of the slaughter of three thousand innocent people in the courts of the Temple of God in Jerusalem."

"What about the will where Herod named Archelaus as his successor?" interrupted Augustus.

"That will is worthless. It was made minutes before Herod died when the king was delirious and did not know what he was saying or signing. Herod's true testament is the document that he signed five days before his death when the disease had not yet affected his judgment. In that testament, he named Antipas as his successor."

There was no doubt that Salome's son was an excellent debater. I waited patiently, without interrupting him until he finished his speech. Then, I stood up and asked Augustus if I could be allowed to say a word in favor of Archelaus. The Emperor nodded his agreement, and this is what I said:

"I personally wrote the will that Herod dictated and signed shortly before his death, in which he appointed Archelaus as his successor. I can attest that the king was not delirious, and, although his body was weak, his mind retained the power and clarity that it always had. Regarding the incident in the Temple, Archelaus is completely innocent. The men responsible for that tragedy are those who incited the violence and disorder which, I want to emphasize, were not directed against Archelaus, but against the Emperor of Rome."

I finished talking and sat down. We waited in silence for Augustus' decision. At that moment, the guards allowed a delegation of Jews from Jerusalem to enter the room.

"Your Excellency," said the man who seemed to be the head of the delegation, "we have not come to speak in favor of Archelaus or Antipas. We represent the people of Judea, a country that has suffered too much under Herod, a usurper who received a prosperous nation and left in squalor. That man adorned the cities of neighboring countries and left ours in ruins. He corrupted our virgin daughters' chastity and did not respect the loyalty of our wives. His son, Archelaus, by slaughtering three thousand of our brothers, has already shown how he would govern us. We do not want to be ruled by a cruel and tyrannical king. We ask you to appoint a Roman Governor to rule Judea."

I would not let these words go unchallenged. I stood up and asked again for permission to speak.

"While Herod was alive, no one expressed these complaints. It is not appropriate to do it now that he is no longer with us. These absurd and false accusations do not make sense because, even in the unlikely event that Herod was guilty as charged, he can no longer be punished. Regarding the tragedy in the Temple, I repeat that the mob leaders, not Archelaus, deserve the blame."

"I have listened to all the parties, and in a few days, I will let you know my decision," Augustus said.

Three days later, Augustus ordered us to come back to his house.

"I have a surprise for you," Augustus informed us slyly. "Let him in," he ordered his guards.

The door opened, and a man entered the room.

He was Alexander, Herod's son, who we all knew had been killed by his father!

Archelaus and Antipas dispute the throne of Judea

Chapter 51
Augustus' decision

We were astonished! There, standing before our eyes, was Alexander! He indeed looked older than I remembered, but three years had passed since he had supposedly been executed. He lacked the dignity and grace that had always characterized him, but I attributed it to the hardships he had undoubtedly suffered.

"Please sit down, Alexander," said Augustus kindly. Tell your friends and family what you have told me."

"As you all know, my father Herod ordered the executioner to kill me and my brother Aristobulus, but the soldiers took pity on us and allowed us to escape,'" said Alexander.

"But, what about the bodies that were buried?" I asked, interrupting him

"They belonged to two common criminals that the soldiers killed to make it seem that they were burying my body and the body of my brother Aristobulus. During the following years, we hid in Sidon, living under false names. Only now, when I learned that our father died, did I come to Rome to claim what rightly belongs to me," said Alexander.

"Tell us, please, where is your brother Aristobulus? Why is he not here with you?" asked Augustus with a sympathetic smile.

"Aristobulus remains in Sidon because we did not want both of us to risk our lives traveling. If something happened to me along the way, my mother Mariamne would still have posterity," explained Alexander.

"Most commendable, most commendable," said Augustus. "But, enough of these fantasies. Tell the truth, and I will spare your life."

The man, who called himself Alexander, seeing that his lies were now known, threw himself at Augustus' feet and confessed to the deception.

"I am a Jew of Sidon, born and raised in that city. My friends always told me that I have a strong resemblance to Prince Alexander. In a visit that I made to the island of Crete, I decided, purely as a joke, to present myself to the Jewish community as Alexander. Everyone believed me and gave me so much money and so many gifts that I decided to come to Rome and do the same in this city, where the Jewish community is the most prosperous in the Empire. I apologize, My Lord."

"I promised to spare your life, and I always keep my promises. I see that you are healthy and strong, so you will row, chained in one of my galleys, until the day you die. You must thank me for allowing you to enjoy the ocean breeze instead of letting you rot in a cell with no windows. Take him to Ostia and deliver him to the strictest captain of our fleet." ordered Augustus.

The soldiers took the impostor away, while Augustus couldn't stop laughing. As soon as he regained his composure, he spoke to us.

"Let's deal with more important matters. I have decided that there will be no king in Judea. You, Archelaus, will rule half the country under the title of ethnarch. The other half will be divided between your brothers Antipas and Philip. Salome will receive the city of Ashdod and a palace in Ashkelon.

It was a solution worth of King Solomon that pleased none of the brothers, but, having no choice, they accepted it with apparent satisfaction and gratitude.

"Concerning you, Nicholas, I want you to stay here in Rome. Herod sent me a few chapters of his biography that you had written. I want you to bring me a copy when you finish it, and then I would like you to write my biography."

Salome and Herod's sons returned to Judea with all the other relatives who had come to Rome.

I stayed in Rome, complying with Augustus' order. I still live in the house that Emperor Augustus gave me, in the District XIV of Rome, across the Tiber River.

Except for Archelaus on one brief occasion, I never saw the sons of Herod again. This one encounter happened about ten years later when Augustus dismissed Archelaus from office, ordered him to come to Rome to give account, and then exiled him to Vienna.

During his short stay in Rome, Archelaus found my house's address and visited me with his wife. I opened the door, and there, in front of me, was Archelaus, accompanied by a beautiful woman, who seemed to be older than him.

"Nicholas, I want you to meet my wife," said Archelaus.

I bowed to the lady. Looking at her more closely, I realized to my surprise that she was Glaphyra, the widow of the slain prince Alexander, son of Herod and Mariamne.

"Yes, my dear Nicholas," said Archelaus, amused by my confusion. "She is Glaphyra. I have been in love with her since I was a young boy, but while my brother Alexander lived, I would never have dreamed of declaring my love. After Alexander died, my father, Herod, sent her back to Cappadocia, to her father's palace. A few years ago, we renewed contact, and she agreed to become my wife."

"It's my fault that he has been deposed and sent into exile," lamented Glaphyra. "It is forbidden for a Jew to marry his brother's widow if she had children with the deceased. I had three children with Alexander. Archelaus, by marrying me, violated the precepts of his religion. I told him that I am willing to divorce him so that he can remain at his post. I begged him to let me return to my father's palace in Cappadocia, but Archelaus refuses and assures me that any place in the world is heaven if I am at his side."

223

Statue of Augustus

Chapter 52
A visit to Augustus' house

During the months that followed, I kept busy writing Herod's biography. Once I finished that book, I arranged to have several copies made and took one of them to Augustus' house. I also brought with me a basket of dates that came from my farm in Jericho.

Octavius, despite being the Emperor of Rome and reigning with the title of Augustus, was still living in the same house on Palatine Hill, where, thirty years before, I had delivered the letters of Mark Antony to him. The Emperor, the most famous man in the world, the demigod who had temples dedicated to him in all the Empire's provinces, continued to live simply. His summer home outside Rome, which later I visited many times, although surrounded by terraces and a beautiful garden, was also modest and did not have any frescoes on the walls.

The only addition that Augustus had made to his house was a Temple dedicated to Apollo, the god with whom the Emperor identified himself. It was located behind the garden and was joined to the house by colonnades. Its main feature was an enclosure in which the Senate held its sessions when Augustus, in his old age, was not feeling well and was unable to leave his house.

One of the Emperor's personal servants, a man I had befriended because we frequented the same brothel in the Suburra neighborhood, told me that the house's furniture was plain and simple. The Emperor slept in a bed made of wooden planks. Except for special occasions, the clothes he wore at home were made by the women of his family, his sister, wife, or daughter. His only vanity was wearing sandals with thick soles added by the shoemaker to give him the appearance of being taller than he really was. Augustus always wore a toga when he went out and considered it so essential for the Roman citizen's dignity that he issued a decree obligating all who

225

came to the Forum or entered a Temple to dress in that garment.

I told the commander of the soldiers that guarded Augustus' house entrance that Nicholas of Damascus wanted to see the Emperor. The procedure hadn't changed since the first time I visited the house, thirty years before. The officer ordered me to wait outside and returned after a few minutes. After frisking me carefully to see if I was carrying a hidden knife, he told me to follow him.

I found Augustus chatting with a child and four adolescents, two boys, seventeen and fifteen years old, and two girls, one of them appeared to be sixteen and the other perhaps thirteen or fourteen. The little boy was about eight years old.

"Nicholas, what a pleasure to see you!" Augustus greeted me, cordial as always.

"My Lord!" I greeted him with a bow.

"I want you to meet my grandchildren, the children of Agrippa and my daughter Julia. These two handsome boys, future soldiers of our Roman army, are Gaius and Lucius. This pretty girl, who is already causing me problems, is called Julia, like her mother. Her younger sister is Agrippina, and the child is Agrippa. We call him Posthumous because he was born after the death of his father, Agrippa, my dear friend and son-in-law.

"It's a pleasure to meet your grandchildren, My Lord. I have brought you a basket of Jericho dates that just arrived from my farm in Judea," I said.

"Thank you. I am sure that I will enjoy them."

"I also brought you the biography of King Herod, which I have finished," I said, handing him the scroll.

The Emperor motioned me to sit on the stool next to him while he opened the scroll.

"I see that you have written it in Greek," he commented.

"It is my native language, My Lord."

"Never mind. Although I do not speak Greek fluently, I have no trouble reading it. But, if you want to have many readers in

Rome, I suggest that you should translate your books into Latin," said Augustus.

While August browsed the parchment, sometimes smiling, sometimes frowning, I watched him, comparing in my mind the Augustus of today with the Octavius that I had known thirty years before.

He was still a handsome man. His eyes, clear and bright, expressed an almost supernatural calm. His hair was still curly, but its brown color had changed to gray.

It was evident that the winter cold bothered him because he was wearing a heavy woolen coat.

Augustus looked at me and smiled.

"I am glad that you brought me Herod's biography. I hope you remember that I asked you to write mine."

"I have not forgotten My Lord. It will be an honor," I replied.

"I invited a few friends to dine with me tonight. Afterward, we will play dice. Do you play dice?" Augustus asked me.

"Not well, My Lord," I replied.

"Ah, that's good news for me," joked Augustus. "Come this afternoon at five. We dine early."

A visit to Augustus' house

Chapter 53
An evening in Augustus' house

I returned to Augustus' house at the appointed hour. This time, when I informed the commander of the guards that I had been invited for dinner, he ushered me in and led me to the dining room.

The guests had not yet arrived, but Augustus was there. I greeted him with the usual bow, and he, to my surprise, gave me a bag of silver coins.

"Nicholas, use these coins to bet in the dice games that we will play after dinner," he said.

The guests arrived shortly after I did. I had seen two of them often at the Forum and in the basilicas. One was a Senator and the other an army general. Augustus welcomed them and invited us to sit at the dining table, and then he withdrew from the room. One of the guests noticed my confusion and explained that Augustus' habit was to sit at the table only when the guests had already finished eating.

Indeed, it was so. We had already eaten three or four plates of delicious dishes when Augustus returned and sat with us. The servants brought him a plate with bread, sardines, cheese, and figs, which was all he ate.

The table conversation was lively, and the topic, as could be expected, was politics. At the end of the meal, Egyptian musicians and dancers entertained us.

Augustus noted that I was looking at the agate cup from which he was drinking wine.

"Do you recognize it, Nicholas? This cup belonged to Cleopatra. That's the only item that I took from her palace. I melted her golden utensils and turned them into coins."

The servants took away the dishes and cleared the table. After receiving a few silver coins, the musicians and the dancers left the room. A servant entered, bringing the dice and leather cups.

"The time has come," said Augustus. "Let's start."

It must have been beginner's luck because that night I won almost all the games. In the beginning, Augustus lost heavily, then recovered gradually and eventually ended up even. One of the Senators lost about three hundred silver coins but assured us with good humor that he was sure that he would recover it all and then some next time.

"Nicholas," Augustus said to me with a grin, "if you call your performance tonight 'not knowing how to play dice,' the day that you will acknowledge your true ability, you will bankrupt us all."

Besides his passion for dice, Augustus was also addicted to sports. He often organized gladiatorial combats and fights against savage beasts. Once, he built an artificial lake near the Tiber River, where mock naval battles took place. So many people came to see the spectacle that guards and soldiers had to be stationed in different parts of Rome to prevent thieves from taking advantage of the absence of the home-owners.

He loved horse races because they allowed him to bet with his friends. He generally attended them with his wife, family members, and close friends, with all of them sitting in the imperial box. He donated generous sums of money as prizes to the winners.

I heard that rumors circulated about his sexuality during his youth. Pompey accused him of being effeminate. Mark Antony pretended to be convinced that Julius Caesar had adopted Augustus because they had engaged in unnatural relations. Lucius, Mark Antony's brother, said that Augustus had sold himself to a certain Hircius for one hundred thousand silver coins and that he burned his legs with hot nut shells to make them hairless.

In my opinion, all these rumors were completely false. On the contrary, the main vice that I noticed in Augustus was his fondness for deflowering virgins. The young women were brought to him by various people, including his wife, Livia. Augustus examined them thoroughly, as if they were slaves for sale in the market, to verify if they had all the characteristics he liked.

It was public knowledge that he committed adultery. However, I believe that he was motivated, not by lust or passion, but by his wish to discover his opponents' secrets, confided to him by their wives during intimate moments.

I can testify that on one occasion when I was present, Augustus invited the wife of one of his guests to go with him to another room. After an hour, he brought her back, disheveled, with her clothes in disarray. All the guests, including her husband, pretended not to notice, and nobody commented.

Days later, Augustus sent the woman's husband into exile, explaining that he had received confidential information that the man had accepted bribes.

An evening in Augustus' house

Chapter 54
In Antioch

The revision and editing of my' History of the World' prevented me from immediately starting Augustus' biography. Then, during the next several years, I was busy traveling through the Empire in missions that the Emperor entrusted to me. I postponed the start of his biography from year to year, and now I regret that Augustus never got to read the final version, which I finished after his death.

My diplomatic missions were intended to review the effectiveness of the governors of the Roman provinces and the kings of the vassal countries and then report back to the Emperor.

One of my trips, which began as routine, turned into an unforgettable experience. The Emperor had sent me to Syria to investigate complaints from prominent citizens in Damascus against the Governor of the province. They accused him of being corrupt and abusive. Three weeks in Damascus were enough for me to confirm the truth of the complaints. I sent a report to the Emperor advising him to dismiss the Governor and jail him for corruption and misrule.

Instead of returning by sea as I had come, I decided to return by land and take the opportunity to enjoy a restful holiday in Antioch, the Syrian city that I liked the most.

I always said that Antioch is one of the most beautiful cities in the Roman Empire. It has two main streets that cross at the center of the city and divide it into four neighborhoods. That is why the city was also called Tetrapolis. Most of its six hundred thousand inhabitants were Greek. Actually, there were almost as many Greeks in Antioch as they were in Rome or Alexandria. The rest of the population was Jewish. The dominant language was Aramaic. The main Temple of the city, located in the Forum, in the center of Antioch, was dedicated to Jupiter.

I stayed at the Governor's palace in an area called Dafne, a paradise of lakes and forests, near a small temple dedicated to the goddess Venus.

Two weeks later, when I was getting ready to return to Rome, a caravan of elephants arrived in Antioch. The enormous animals carried people on their backs dressed in exotic costumes. Their gowns were made of silk in iridescent colors that shined. On their heads, they wore turbans. The color of their skin was not white like ours or black like the Ethiopians, but brown. The caravan stopped in a meadow a short distance from the city, where the foreigners raised their tents. They hoisted flags and lit a bonfire in the center of their camp.

The commander of the city's guardians sent a messenger to the Governor to inform him of the mysterious visitors' arrival.

The Governor asked me to go with him to verify if these strange people came in peace so that he would welcome them. If their intentions were not friendly, the troops that came with us would intervene. The foreigners greeted us with bows. One of them approached and spoke to us in a language that I did not recognize at first, but then I realized that it was Greek. His strange accent made it difficult to understand what he said.

"I am Prince Pandion," he said, unrolling a scroll. "I will read you this letter signed by my master, Porus, king of a hundred kings. It says, 'Rome's fame has crossed the Himalayan Mountains and reached my kingdom. I have sent my ambassadors to sign a treaty of friendship with the glorious Roman Empire. Let the gods grant eternal friendship and peace to our two nations.'" The prince finished reading, handed the scroll to the Governor, and clapped his hands.

At the sound of his applause, eight naked slave girls came out of the tents. They brought silver trays on which there was a profusion of gold bangles, ruby rings, pearl necklaces, and diamond earrings.

"Please accept our humble gifts. These slaves and these gems are a modest token of the friendship that we offer."

The Governor, who, until then, had been awestruck, answered in Greek.

"Prince Pandion, to receive such distinguished ambassadors is an honor Antioch will never forget. Our gods bless your arrival, and our citizens receive you with open arms."

"When we arrive at a new country, it is our custom to make a sacrifice to the local gods. May we make our sacrifice?" Pandion asked.

"We would be honored," answered the Governor.

The visiting prince clapped his hands again, and this time a bald man wearing an orange robe appeared. He approached the bonfire and jumped into the flames.

The Governor and I, horrified, ran to pull him out, but the prince stopped us.

"Do not touch him!" he cried. "Do not commit this sacrilege! The monk is immolating himself to honor your gods."

I had never seen such a sight, and I hope the gods will never let me see it again.

In Antioch

236

Chapter 55
The death of Augustus' grandsons

It is a law of nature that children outlive their parents, but that law, like all divine and human laws, has exceptions. It is sad when a son buries his father, but it is tragic when a father buries his child, or, as in the case of Augustus, a grandfather buries his grandchildren.

Augustus loved his grandchildren, especially the two oldest, Gaius and Lucius. He hoped that someday they would succeed him. Fate did not allow Augustus' dream to become a reality. Lucius died at the age of nineteen, and his older brother, Gaius, died two years later when he had just turned twenty-four.

I was not present at Lucius' funeral because, at that time, I was in Egypt on a diplomatic mission, but when Gaius died, I took part in the funeral procession. It was one of the saddest experiences of my life.

Gaius, a brave officer, was wounded in a battle in Armenia. The wound became infected and caused a high fever. He was brought to Rome, to his mother Julia's house. Initially, he showed an improvement, but then despite the doctors' efforts, his situation worsened, and he died a week after his arrival.

I was at the Forum when I heard that Augustus' grandson had died. I immediately went to Palatine Hill, to Julia's house, where all Gaius' friends and relatives had gathered around his deathbed. I arrived when Julia closed her dead son's eyes and gave him one last kiss. Everybody cried, lamented, and called out the name of Gaius. Then, we put the body on the ground, washed it, and anointed it with perfumed oil.

Augustus placed a coin in Gaius' mouth. The deceased's soul had to pay the coin to Charon, the ferryman who carries the recently deceased souls across the Stix River in his boat, from the land of the living to the land of the dead.

Two days later, when the vigil ended, we carried Gaius' coffin in a funeral procession from Julia's house to the cemetery outside the city, where the body would be cremated. Musicians playing their drums followed us slowly.

We stopped at the Forum, and it was Augustus himself, his voice broken by sobs, who gave the eulogy.

At the cemetery, we sacrificed a pig to the gods, and then all the participants shared the meat. The portion designed for Gaius was burned on the altar. Then the body of the young man was cremated and his ashes deposited in an amphora. The ceremony ended when Julia placed the amphora in the family mausoleum of Agrippa, Gaius' father.

According to Roman custom, Julia held a banquet in memory of her son after the nine days of mourning.

The death of his grandson affected Augustus for the rest of his life. I never saw him laugh or smile again.

Chapter 56
Augustus' Testimony

When I write a biography, it is my custom to start by interviewing the protagonist, if he is still alive, of course, and, afterward, people who meet two criteria.

The first criterion is that they must have personally known the protagonist in one of his four life stages: childhood, youth, maturity, or old age. The second criterion is that they must be willing to answer my questions with objectivity and impartiality.

Augustus told me the facts about his birth, childhood, and youth. His wife Livia and his daughter Julia allowed me to interview them. Tiberius, the recently appointed heir of Augustus, initially refused to answer my questions, but, after much prodding, he agreed to talk to me.

In the following pages, I include notes of the testimonies given to me by Augustus, Livia, Julia, and Tiberius.

My father was Gaius Octavius. Although he had an excellent economic position and outstanding reputation, he did not belong to a prominent family. On the other hand, my mother Atia, daughter of Julia, was Julius Caesar's niece, a member of the prestigious Julian family. My sister was Octavia. I also had a half-sister, a daughter from my father's previous marriage.

I do not remember much about my father since I was only four years old when he suddenly died.

When I was twelve years old, I gave the eulogy at my grandmother Julia's funeral. She was Julius Caesar's sister. At the age of sixteen, I fought in Hispania under my great uncle Julius Caesar. When the campaign ended, he sent me to Greece so that I could finish my studies there.

I had turned eighteen when a group of conspirators assassinated Julius Caesar, my grand uncle. As soon as I received notice of his murder, I traveled to Rome. There I

---

learned that my uncle had adopted me as his son and had named me his heir. I immediately claimed my inheritance and officially added the name Caesar to my name Octavius.

I formed a triumvirate with Mark Antony and Lepidus, the Pontiff Maximus of Rome. We defeated my great uncle's murderers and governed Rome for five years.

Lepidus tried to expel me from the triumvirate but failed. I forced him to give up his position as triumvir but allowed him to remain Pontiff Maximus.

To strengthen our alliance, I convinced Mark Antony to marry my sister Octavia. They had two daughters, but he abandoned them and settled in Egypt after he met Cleopatra.

Mark Antony illegally distributed important Roman provinces to the children he had with Cleopatra. This caused the Senate to declare war on the Queen of Egypt.

My fleet defeated Antony and Cleopatra's fleet at Actium. Months later, they committed suicide when I invaded Egypt.

In Rome, I established a system of government that allowed me to have complete control over the Empire. I built a vast network of roads, all of which lead to Rome, according to a phrase that has become popular.

The Senate officially changed my name to Augustus and years later gave me the title, "Father of the Nation." I was elected Pontiff Maximus when Lepidus died. I annexed Judea, a country that previously had been a vassal kingdom. I organized fire and police forces in the main cities of the Empire. I created a powerful naval fleet that justifies the name 'Mare Nostrum' by which we now call the Mediterranean Sea.

I want my tombstone to say, "He received a Rome of bricks and left us a Rome of marble."

Chapter 57
Livia's Testimony

I saw Octavius for the first time when I was nineteen years old. It was at a reception in Rome in honor of a foreign ambassador. I was there with my husband, Tiberius Claudius Nero, whom I had married three years earlier.

There was a commotion near the door, and I heard people mutter, "He has arrived; he is here." A couple entered the room. The man was young, about twenty-four years old. The woman was several years older, probably around thirty. People moved aside so they could pass.

"Who are they?" I asked a man who was standing next to me.

"He is the triumvir Octavius, and she is his wife Scribonia," he replied.

I stared at Octavius, fascinated that such a young man could have that much power. He must have felt my gaze because he turned, looked at me, approached, greeted my husband, and asked him who I was.

"Triumvir, let me introduce my wife, Livia," replied my husband.

"Madam, it is a pleasure to meet you," said Octavius. "Allow me to introduce my wife, Scribonia."

I noticed that the woman was in an advanced state of pregnancy. Coincidentally, I was also four months pregnant with my second child.

For the rest of the evening, Octavius did not leave my side. Once, when my husband was speaking with someone else, he whispered to me that he had fallen in love with my beauty.

I did not see him again for the next two months, but I heard that he had divorced Scribonia39 on the same day that she had given birth to their daughter Julia.

Scribonia was Octavius' second wife. His first wife had been Claudia, whose mother, Fulvia, was at that time the wife of Mark Antony. For some reason that I never bothered to find out,

241

Octavius divorced Claudia almost immediately. He sent her back to her mother with a message that said, "I am returning her untouched", a statement that anyone who knows Octavius would find difficult to believe. Shortly afterward, he married Scribonia, but it was not a happy marriage because, according to Octavius, she was an unbearable, nagging woman with a bad temper.

Others described her differently, saying that she was a dignified and serene woman, an ideal example of a Roman matron.

The day after he divorced Scribonia, Octavius came to my home. A servant ushered him into the room where I was playing with Tiberius, my three-year-old son.

"What's your name, little boy?" asked Octavius. Tiberius, who was shy and timid, did not answer.

"His name is Tiberius, the same as his father's," I told Octavius.

My husband, Tiberius Claudius Nero, entered the room and was surprised to see Octavius.

"Welcome, triumvir. To what do we owe the honor of your visit?"

"I came to speak with you about a very delicate matter, and I think it would be preferable to talk in private."

My husband invited Octavius to go with him to another room and shut the door behind them. They never told me what they talked about, and, to this day, I do not know if Octavius convinced my husband by arguments, bribes, or threats. The fact is that, when they came back to the room where I was, Octavius smiled, and my husband had a grim expression on his face. Octavius came to me, and to my surprise, he kissed me on the mouth in front of my husband.

"Congratulations, my love! Tiberius Claudius Nero has agreed to give me your hand in marriage. He will divorce you today, and we will get married as soon as your baby is born," Octavius told me and kissed me again.

My husband divorced me that same day. Three months later, I gave birth to my second son, Drusus, and two days after that, I

242

married Octavius. My former husband, Tiberius Claudius Nero, was present at the wedding, and at the request of Octavius, he brought me to the altar.

Several years later, I became pregnant, but unfortunately, I lost the baby, and Octavius and I never had children.

It's been nearly five decades since our wedding, and Octavius and I are still married. People now call him Augustus, but to me, he is still Octavius.

I guess we are as happy as a couple can be. I know that Octavius, like all Roman husbands, has little 'adventures' occasionally, but I do not give them undue importance, and they don't affect our marriage. Octavius appreciates my advice more than anybody else's, and he knows that I am loyal to him.

Despite our high position, we have always lived simply. I do not wear much jewelry or expensive clothes.

Tiberius and Drusus, the two sons that I had with my first husband, are today brilliant generals and have given me much cause to be proud of them. I hope that Tiberius will be Octavius' successor.

The problem is that Octavius doesn't like Tiberius and prefers others. As a successor, his first choice was Marcellus, his sister Octavia's son, who was married to Julia, Octavius' daughter. The young man was nineteen years old when I invited him to dine at my house during Octavius' absence. Something he ate must have disagreed with him because he died the next day.

Octavius next appointed Agrippa, who had married Julia, right after Marcellus' death, as his successor. Agrippa died during a military campaign. Gaius and Lucius, the sons that he had with Julia, were then adopted by Octavius.

One day I heard that Lucius was sick in bed with a slight fever. I sent my personal physician to take care of him, but instead of getting better, his malady got worse, and Lucius, who had recently celebrated his nineteenth birthday, died.

His older brother, Gaius, died two years later, at the age of twenty-four. He had been wounded in battle. I was informed that the wound was superficial. I sent him an ointment to apply over the injury, but unfortunately, it did not work. The wound somehow became infected, and Gaius died.

These tragic deaths left the way open for Tiberius. I convinced Octavius to adopt him and name him as his successor. Although he did adopt Tiberius, I was disappointed that Octavius named two successors. Tiberius was one, and the other was Posthumous, Agrippa's youngest son.

Fortunately for Tiberius and me, Posthumous proved to be a rude and insolent teenager. Octavius was so upset with him that he exiled the youth to an island with stern warnings that this was his last opportunity to change his behavior.

I heard rumors that Octavius and one of his trusted friends named Maximus had visited Posthumous on the island. During that visit, Octavius had forgiven the boy for his insolence and promised him that he would be allowed to return to Rome soon.

I asked Maximus if the rumor was true. He refused to answer and was found dead a few days later in an alley in the Aventine neighborhood.

For the time being, Octavius' joint successors are Tiberius and Posthumous. We will wait and see what will happen in the future.

Chapter 58
Julia's Testimony

I have the distinction, if it can be called that, of being the only person born on the same day that her father divorced her mother.

According to Roman law, Octavius, my father, had absolute and exclusive control over me after the divorce. My stepmother Livia took care of my education. I learned to read and write and also studied history, literature, and mathematics. The servants in our home taught me to cook, spin and weave. Livia, a strict, old-fashioned woman, would not let me talk to anyone if my father did not approve in advance.

When I was two years old, my father signed an agreement with Mark Antony. In it, he pledged to marry me to Antilus, the ten-year-old son of Mark Antony, when we would be old enough. The wedding never took place because after my father defeated Mark Antony in Egypt, he killed Antilus.

At the age of fourteen, I married my cousin Marcellus, son of my aunt Octavia. He was also very young, only three years older than I. My father was then in Hispania, and Agrippa, his best friend, gave me away. Marcellus died two years later. I did not have children with him.

Agrippa himself was my next husband. I was eighteen, and Agrippa was already forty-two years old when we got married. He was a good husband, but the difference in our ages was so significant that it gave me a reason to have an affectionate and discreet friendship with a young man named Sempronious.

I had three children with Agrippa, Gaius, Lucius, Posthumous, and two daughters, Julia and Agrippina.

Noticing that my children were faithful copies of my husband, someone asked me how I avoided having children with my lovers. I replied. "My boat accepts passengers only when it is already full." By this, I meant that I only slept with lovers when I knew that I was already pregnant by Agrippa.

245

My father frequently sent Agrippa in diplomatic missions to all corners of the Empire, and I usually went with him. On one of those trips, I almost drowned while crossing a river on a damaged bridge near Troy. My husband was so angry that he imposed a fine of one hundred thousand drachmas on the locals, which really was exorbitant and unaffordable. King Herod, who was visiting us, convinced Agrippa to cancel the fine and invited us to visit his country, which we accepted with pleasure.

My husband Agrippa died suddenly when he was fifty-one years old. My father, who loved him more than anybody else in the world, buried him in the Emperor's mausoleum that he had prepared for himself. I was pregnant at the time, and a few months later, I gave birth to my youngest son, Agrippa, whom we call Posthumous.

Because he had no children, my father adopted my sons and took personal charge of their education.

I was still grieving about my husband's death when my father forced me to marry Tiberius, my adopted brother. We had one child who died in infancy. I was never happy with Tiberius, and he hated me. From the start of our marriage, we led separate lives.

I tried to console myself with Sempronious and other friends. Unfortunately, gossip reached my father's ears, and he had me arrested for adultery and treason. Tiberius was away, but my father acted in his name and sent me a letter annulling my marriage. He sent Sempronious into exile and forced another of my friends to commit suicide.

My father said that he did not know whether to exile me or execute me for bringing shame to the family. Finally, he decided to be merciful and banished me to an island where there were no men.

After five years of living on the island, accompanied only by my mother, Scribonia, my father allowed me to live on the peninsula, in Reggio, near Sicily.

I fear what will happen to me after my father's death. Tiberius will be the next Emperor. He is spiteful and will never forgive me.

Chapter 59
Tiberius' Testimony

I was two years old when Augustus forced my father to divorce my mother. My father never recovered from the humiliation and grief. When he died seven years later, I gave the eulogy at his funeral, although I was only nine years old at the time.

My brother Drusus and I accompanied Octavius on his chariot in the triumphal procession held when Octavius defeated Antony and Cleopatra in the naval battle of Actium. I was thirteen, and my brother was eleven.

When I was twenty years old, I accompanied Agrippa, Octavius' best friend, in his military campaign against the Parthians on the eastern border of the Empire. A year later, I returned to Rome and married the love of my life, Vipsania, Agrippa's daughter. Six years later, we had a son, whom we called, Drusus Julius Caesar.

In the following years, I fought the Germanic tribes, conquered large territories, and discovered the source of the Danube River.

I was thirty years old when Agrippa's death brought great changes to my life. Augustus told me that he was thinking of naming me as his successor. This honor was accompanied by the most humiliating and painful experience of my life. Augustus forced me to divorce Vipsania and marry his daughter Julia, Agrippa's widow. Thus, he did to me exactly what he had done to my father.

Like my mother thirty years ago, Vipsania was pregnant when Augustus forced me to divorce her. The baby was stillborn.

Months later, I saw Vipsania on the street. I couldn't help following her crying all the time. I begged her to forgive me. Augustus heard about this incident and forbade me to see her again.

Vipsania married a Senator named Saloninus and had six children with him. Saloninus had the nerve to say that my son

Drusus was his. I will never forget that, and the day will come when he will pay for it.

The only child that I had with Julia died shortly after his birth. I hated her because she was a promiscuous woman. Rumors circulated that she competed with prostitutes in the Forum selling her favors. Augustus sent her a letter in my name informing her that she and I were now divorced and exiled her to a small island.

In my opinion, this punishment was not enough, and when I take office, Julia will receive what she deserves.

After the death of Gaius and Lucius, the sons that Julia had with Agrippa, Augustus officially adopted me. He appointed me as his successor jointly with Posthumous, the youngest son of Julia and Agrippa.

The truth is that I have no desire to be Emperor. If it would be up to me, the Senate could choose Posthumous, or anyone else they might want, as Emperor after Augustus dies.

Chapter 60
The death of Augustus

Based on the testimonies that I had gathered so far, I wrote Augustus' biography and took the scroll to the Emperor's house for his review. He thanked me but regretted that at that moment, he did not have time to read what I had written. He had to go with his entourage to the Field of Mars to celebrate the conclusion of the census that the Romans conduct every five years.

"Join us, Nicholas," he invited me. "I am sure that as a historian, you will find the ceremony fascinating."

Today's Field of Mars is one of Rome's most prestigious and beautiful neighborhoods, but thirty years ago, it was just a marsh outside the city walls. Agrippa converted the swamps into decorative ponds surrounded by parks and temples, Pantheon the most impressive of all. On its north side stood the immense mausoleum that Augustus had built for himself.

The ceremony that celebrated the end of the census consisted of sacrificing a bull to the gods as public atonement and purification of the Roman people. After seeing so many animal sacrifices in the Serapeum of Alexandria and Jerusalem's Temple, I was not interested in witnessing a ritual slaughter again. My attention was caught by an eagle that had perched atop the statue of the Emperor. A moment after the bird flew away, lightning struck the inscription at the base of the sculpture and melted the first letter of the word 'CAESAR.'

"What does this mean?" Augustus asked a seer who was standing next to him.

The seer hesitated to answer.

"Do not be afraid. Tell me the meaning of what we have seen," insisted Augustus.

"It's a harbinger of your death, My Lord. The letter C, whose numerical value is one hundred, has melted away. That means that you only have one hundred days of life left. The remaining letters form the word AESAR, which means god in the Etruscan language. This means, My Lord, that you will be counted among the gods," explained the seer.

"Thank you for your frankness. I will try to spend my last days wisely. First, I must make some decisions about the future government of the Empire. Then, I will go to Capri."

I felt honored when Augustus invited me to go to Capri with him and a group of his close friends and relatives.

Three months later, we left Rome by land and reached the village of Astura. There, we boarded a ship that took us to the island of Capri.

We stayed in the villa that Augustus had in Capri, resting, having fun, and walking around the nearby town of Puteoli. The passengers on a ship that had just arrived from Alexandria applauded and cheered when they saw Augustus. One of the passengers thanked Augustus on behalf of his companions for the peace and prosperity that he had brought to the Empire. These praises put Augustus in an excellent mood.

Livia, accompanied by Tibcrius, arrived in Capri bringing a basket of figs, which she said she had grown in her garden.

That afternoon we visited the tomb of Masgabas, a person who years earlier had been the Governor of Capri. Judging by the number of visitors that lit candles and torches in his honor, Masgabas must have been a very popular Governor.

At night after dinner, Augustus, while eating the figs brought by Livia, spoke with one of his friends, Trasilus, who boasted of being an expert on the subject of poets and poetry.

"A thousand candles shined over the tomb," recited Augustus. Addressing Trasilus, he asked him,

"Who is the poet who wrote that verse?"

Trasilus thought for a while and did not answer.

"A thousand torches vanquished the gloom," Augustus recited again.

"I am not sure of the identity of the poet, although I think that I have heard that poem before," Trasilus said.

"I am the author of those lines," said Augustus. He laughed and laughed and did not stop joking that night.

The next day Augustus wished to visit Nola, his father's hometown, near Mount Vesuvius.

The inhabitants of Nola greeted him with songs and dances. The Governor of the town gave a welcome speech in which he invited us to see a gymnastic exhibition that had been hastily organized in honor of the Emperor. Augustus apologized, saying that he felt a little tired.

"Please take me someplace where I can rest," he said to us. "My stomach hurts."

The Governor rushed to show us the way to his house, which, thank the gods, was around the corner. We laid Augustus gently on the bed and gathered around him.

"Friends," he said, "let me speak alone with Tiberius."

We left the room. Tiberius stayed and closed the door. An hour later, he came out with tears in his eyes.

"Augustus wishes to say goodbye to all of you," announced Tiberius.

We went into the room. The Emperor saw us and sat up with a great effort.

"Tell me, have I played the comedy of life properly?" he asked and added, "If I have done my part well, clap your hands and applaud when I leave the stage."

Augustus kissed Livia and said, "I loved you from the first moment I saw you. Goodbye, my love."

The death of Augustus

Epilogue

A funeral procession of thousands of mourners carried the body of Augustus to Rome. All public offices were closed on the day of his funeral. Tiberius pronounced the funeral oration in the Forum. Livia, standing by his side, glowed with maternal pride. Then, several Senators carried the emperor's body on their shoulders to the Field of Mars. Thousands followed, crying and tearing their clothes. The priests cremated Augustus' body on a funeral pyre and deposited his ashes in the mausoleum that Augustus had built for himself years before.

The Senate appointed Tiberius as emperor, honoring Augustus' decision. His first action as leader of Rome was to deify Augustus.

Posthumous, the son of Julia and Agrippa, who Augustus had exiled because of his brutal and depraved behavior, was killed by his guards when they learned that the Emperor had died.

Augustus bequeathed two-thirds of his property to Tiberius and a third to Livia. For a time, mother and son gave the impression that they got along. Tiberius even published a law declaring that any criticism of Livia would be considered treason.

Tiberius gradually resented his mother's political power and the constant reminder that he owed her his exalted position. He soon came to abhor his mother. When Livia died, Tiberius, who was in Capri, announced that he was too busy to attend the funeral and forbid the Senate to deify her despite her expressed desire to be proclaimed a goddess after her death.

My age and my health do not allow me to leave my house. My only companions are my memories of the three great men whom I had the privilege to know. My pride is that they bestowed upon me the greatest possible honor that they could give, their friendship.

Agrippa the Great:
adventurer, libertine, and loved by his people

The events related in this book took place between 11 BCE and 44 CE

Chapter 1
I am Agrippa, Herod's grandson

"Agrippa the Scoundrel," "Agrippa the Scammer," "Agrippa the Wasteful"...

Those were some of the titles that people gave me in the past. They also called me by other titles, but good manners prevent me from mentioning them. Those phrases did not offend me because I always recognized, at least to myself, that they were justified and well-founded.

What does offend me is the title they give me today, "Agrippa the Great." Only history can grant a king the title of "Great."

My full name is Marcus Julius Agrippa. Marcus is in honor of Mark Antony, the great Roman general, a friend of my grandfather Herod. Julius is in honor of Julius Caesar. And Agrippa, which is the name by which I prefer to be called, is in honor of Marcus Agrippa, the son-in-law of Emperor Augustus. My names are Roman, but I am a proud Jew.

I was born in Jerusalem a little over fifty years ago, in a unique family, which, I might add, was the most dysfunctional family that you could find anywhere.

Few families have had so many of their members executed. The list includes my father, my grandmother, my great-great-grandfather, my great-grandmother, and two uncles.

Although nowadays, none of these violent deaths could be considered exceptional, what makes my family truly special is that the person who ordered these executions was not a stranger but my paternal grandfather, King Herod.

"Agrippa, you were lucky that your grandfather died when you were still a child. Chances are, if he had lived a few more years, he would have killed you, too", my mother told me when I turned fifteen and asked her to tell me about our family.

"Why did my grandfather kill so many members of our family?" I asked her.

257

"It is difficult to control a habit, and even more so when the murderer is a king with absolute powers. Your grandfather always had a good excuse for killing his relatives. For instance, take your grandmother Mariamne, my mother-in-law. Herod had her killed because somebody told him that she had been unfaithful. I have always thought that your grandfather's reaction to this gossip, which was not supported by any evidence, was exaggerated, especially if we compare it to the reaction of the great Julius Caesar to a similar circumstance."

"I don't know that story. Tell it to me, please", I said to my mother.

"Cesar married Pompeya, a young woman of a good family. She was beautiful and charming but not very intelligent. Pompeya organized a festival in her house for the Bona Dea (Good Goddess), an ancient Roman goddess. Only women were allowed to attend. A young man named Publius Clodio Pulcro managed to enter the house, disguised as a woman, intending to seduce Pompeya. He was discovered, arrested, and tried. Although his guilt would have been easy to prove, he was acquitted because Caesar, for some unexplained reason, did not bother to provide any evidence against him. However, Caesar divorced Pompeya, saying: 'My wife must be above suspicion.' Caesar was satisfied with just divorcing Pompeya, but Herod, more drastic, had Mariamne condemned to death.

"Why did Herod kill three of his sons?" I asked my mother.

"His children, his presumed heirs, were executed because Herod believed that they were impatient to succeed him and were willing to kill him.

"I heard rumors that Herod had all the little children of Bethlehem killed. Is that true?"

"That is not true. Why would Herod kill the children of Bethlehem if no one in that town was his relative?" My mother said and laughed bitterly.

I mentioned above that my family is unique because of the large number of executed relatives, but that is not the only

258

characteristic that distinguishes us. Our motto is "Keep it in the family." Uncles marry nieces; cousins marry cousins. My father, Aristobulus, and my mother, Berenice, were cousins. My uncle Antipas married, to my horror and anger, my sister Herodias, who, a short time before, had divorced Philip, another one of my uncles. Cypros, my wife, is my cousin. My daughter Berenice's current husband is my brother Herod of Chalcis, to whom she has born two children.

My mother was widowed when she was still young, and she never remarried. My father died, leaving her with five children: my elder brother Herod, ten years old at the time, my sister Herodias, nine years old, my brother Aristobulus, four years old, Mariamne, only 8 months old, and I, who was five years old.

I am Agrippa, Herod's grandson

Chapter 2
We move to Rome

A few months after the executioner complied with my grandfather Herod's order and cut off my father's head, my mother decided that it would be prudent for us to move to Rome. Her decision was due to several reasons. She was afraid that her father-in-law, King Herod, would send her to paradise to join my father, her late husband, Aristobulus. Being in Jerusalem brought back too many sad memories. Perhaps more to the point, she was convinced that the education that her children would receive in Rome, the Empire's capital, would be far superior to what they could obtain in Jerusalem.

I don't remember how we traveled from Jerusalem to Caesarea. I assume that we did it on mules or donkeys since there are no paved roads between the two cities. It must have taken us three or four days.

We were exhausted when we arrived at an inn in Caesarea, located a short distance from the Temple that Herod had dedicated to Augustus. That night, as soon as we finished eating dinner, we retired to the rooms they had given us. The next morning, after having the breakfast that the innkeeper's wife brought to our rooms, my mother instructed her two slaves to take care of my brothers and sisters, who, still tired from the long journey, wanted to rest at the inn. She took me by the hand, and we walked to the port where we saw a great many anchored ships since the commercial navigation, suspended by Roman law during the four months of winter, had not yet resumed.

"Can you tell me where I can buy tickets on a ship that goes to Italy?" my mother asked a man who was giving orders to the stevedores.

"Do you see that man who is there talking to two sailors? He is Alcibiades, the captain of the ship Salamis. I understand

261

that in a few days, he will set sail for Puteoli. He might accept passengers. Talk to him," suggested the man.

We approached the captain and the two sailors. My mother waited patiently for the two sailors to say goodbye before speaking to the captain.

"Captain Alcibiades, I need to travel to Italy. I want to buy tickets on your ship for my five children, my two slaves, and me. When will you sail?"

"The ban on sailing during the winter months ends the day after tomorrow. I estimate that it will take us a few days to load the amphorae of oil, dates, and balsam that we will take to Puteoli. Therefore, we will leave within a week. This will give you time to buy the supplies and food your family will need during the three or four weeks that it will take us to get to our destination. I will give you and your children a cabin, but, for your two slaves, you must buy a tent that we will place on the deck", replied the captain.

"How much would the tickets cost us?"

"Let's see. You, five children, and two slaves are eight passengers. At eight hundred denarii per person, the total is six thousand four hundred denarii.

"Captain Alcibiades, what you are asking is too much. I know that the price per passenger from Caesarea to Puteoli is six hundred denarii, and I am not willing to give you even one additional denarius."

My mother and the captain bargained for a while and finally agreed that the eight people's total payment would be five thousand denarii.

During the following days, my mother, accompanied by the two slaves, bought the food and supplies we would need during the trip and a tent for her slaves to sleep on the deck.

One week later, we boarded the vessel. Salamis was a medium-sized ship, about forty feet long. Two or three dozen passengers were already on the deck, surrounded by their scattered belongings, lying on mattresses that they had brought with them.

After taking our suitcases and baskets to the cabin the captain had reserved for us, the sailors showed our slaves the place on the deck where they should put up their tent.

During the trip, the children played on the deck hide-and-seek and other games. Our slaves cleaned our cabin and cooked our meals in the ship's kitchen. My mother did not mingle or talk with the other passengers. Most of the time, she rested in the cabin and read the scrolls she had brought with her. The other passengers, almost all of them men, spent their time gambling with dice.

The ship made two stops before reaching Puteoli. The first was in Ephesus and the second in Corinth. In Ephesus, we took the opportunity to visit the city to see the imposing Temple to Diana, the goddess of the town. We just stood on the great square in front of the Temple but did not enter because we Jews avoid places with idols.

Finally, we arrived at the great port of Puteoli, where we disembarked. Many ships that brought Egyptian wheat were now being loaded with glass, mosaics, iron, and marble destined for other places in the Empire.

We were struck by the fact that the air smelled strongly of sulfur. People explained to us that this was due to the numerous springs of sulfurous water in the area. The unpleasant odor's compensation was the abundance of pozzolan, volcanic sand that, mixed with water, is used to prepare concrete.

We stayed in the city's best inn for a few days while my mother arranged for our transport to Rome. My brothers and I took the opportunity to walk around the city. What impressed us most was the immense amphitheater, which, we were told, accommodates twenty-five thousand spectators.

My mother hired a driver and a four-wheeled carriage to take us to Rome. It was pulled by ten horses and had comfortable seats and an arched wooden roof. Our slaves traveled separately in a simpler carriage, which had wooden benches, lacked a roof, and was pulled by four mules.

On the road to Rome, we stopped every twenty-five or thirty miles in rest areas, where there were restaurants and inns. In one of those rest areas, we entered a restaurant, but our mother made us leave immediately before ordering the food, although we were famished.

"Why, Mom?" My brother Herod asked.

"This place is full of thieves and prostitutes," my mother answered.

"What is a prostitute, mom?" I asked with the innocence of my five years.

"I will not explain it to you now, Agrippa, but don't worry. Ten or fifteen years from now, you will not ask me anymore", she replied, laughing.

I didn't understand what caused her laughter, but I was glad that, for a few moments, my mother had forgotten her sadness and melancholy.

It took us three days to travel the two hundred miles that separate Puteoli from Rome. Our luggage, which we had sent in a cart driven by two oxen, arrived in Rome a week after us.

We arrived in Rome by way of the Via Apia road, which ends at Porta Capena, one of the gates of the thick wall that surrounds the city.

An officer, accompanied by two soldiers, signaled us to stop.

"What's wrong, officer?" my mother asked him.

"You have to wait until nightfall to enter the city," the officer replied.

"Why do we have to wait, officer?

"Ma'am, it's a city regulation. The authorities have forbidden carriages and wagons from entering the city during the day. They say there is already too much traffic and the iron wheels make too much noise. As soon as night falls, I'll let you in," the officer replied.

"This prohibition seems absurd to me," protested my mother. "The iron wheels make as much noise at night as they do during the day, but at night it is worse because it bothers people's rest."

"You are right, ma'am, but that is the regulation, and I must enforce it. But, it will not be long before it gets dark, so tell the driver to place your carriage next to the wall so that pedestrians can pass through the gate. I'll let you know when you can enter the city."

The driver moved the carriage to the side of the gate, and we went down to stretch our legs, numb from the long hours we had spent traveling since our last stop.

As soon as we descended, we were surrounded by some beggars.

"These beggars are Jews," our mother said in a low voice.

"How do you know, mother?" asked my brother Herod, also in a low voice.

"I know because of their clothes. Foreigners, slaves, women, and all those who are not Roman citizens, are prohibited from wearing the toga. If these men were Roman citizens, they would wear the toga, but instead, they are clothed in robes.

"I understand that you know by their robes that they are not Roman citizens, but how do you know that they are Jews and not Greeks or Parthians or Arabs?" asked Herod.

"Because they cover their heads with a cap, which is our Jewish custom," answered my mother.

An hour later, when the sun went down, the officer allowed our carriage to enter the city. The vehicle took us directly to our mansion on Palatine Hill, near Emperor Augustus' residence. There, the servants and the slaves that looked after our property were waiting for us.

We move to Rome

Chapter 3
A walk in Rome

In previous pages, I mentioned that I was five years old when I arrived with my mother, brothers, and sisters in Rome. There I stayed for the next thirty years.

Rome, an enormous city with more than one million inhabitants, made a tremendous impression on my siblings and me, especially when we compared it to Jerusalem. Our native city had a population of 60,000 people (except during the Religious Festivals when thousands of Jews come on pilgrimage from all corners of the earth).

Rome has wide avenues while Jerusalem only has winding streets that in Rome would be considered alleys. Jerusalem has only one Temple, while Rome has many.

Our house on Palatine Hill was close to Emperor Augustus' residence and the mansions of the families related to the Emperor. Unlike our home in Jerusalem, which had two floors, this one had only one floor, but it was more extensive. The floor was covered with mosaics of geometric designs. Curtains and paintings of landscapes decorated the walls. In contrast to those in other houses, our paintings were devoid of human beings because our religion forbids those images.

Our house had two details which made us proud (and caused envy to our less affluent friends). The first was that the house had running water, and the second, it had a private latrine. It was a seat with a hole, located in a room next to the kitchen. The water used to scrub and wash the kitchen floor went to the latrine and carried our bodily products to the street.

The day after our arrival, I went for a walk in the city with my brothers Herod and Aristobulus, accompanied by our two slaves, Emilio and Felix.

I saw people urinating in barrels in the streets. In a corner, we came across two men bringing an empty barrel that they left in the street and then went away, taking with them the barrel full of urine.

267

"Emilio, why are those men taking that stinking urine pot?" I asked one of the slaves.

"They sell the urine to a laundry. Urine has an ingredient that whitens clothes," Emilio replied.

"Beware!" yelled Felix, our other slave, and pushed Herod aside.

Herod intended to reproach Felix for his insolence when he saw that human excrement had fallen in the place where he had been standing. A resident of the building had thrown it from one of the upper floors.

"Those people must be too lazy to lower the trough of the excrement and pour it into the sewer," Felix commented with a smile. "Generally, they throw away the contents at night and not during the day as they have done right now."

The two slaves became nervous when it began to get dark.

"Felix, you look worried. What's wrong?" asked my brother Herod.

"It will soon be night, and it is not wise to walk the streets in places where there are no lights, and everything is dark. The streets of Rome are full of scoundrels, drunks, and irresponsible people. There are night patrols, but they are not enough to deal with all the criminals. The thugs take advantage of the darkness to steal and assault," explained Felix.

"Also, there are gangs of young men roaming in the streets. Some of them, I'm ashamed to say, belong to the best families in the city. They go out in the night and have fun scandalizing, bothering, and vandalizing. One of my friends, last week, was thrown by them into a sewer," Emilio added.

"And do not forget that, as soon as it gets dark, hundreds of carts that were waiting at the gates of the city during the day enter Rome carrying food and merchandise and go through the streets at full speed trying to avoid the traffic jams. Almost every night, they run over a passerby," said Felix

"If Lady Berenice ever gives you permission to go out at night and request us to go with you, we would only do so if we are accompanied by an escort of four or five burly men, armed with clubs and carrying torches," Emilio warned.

When we got back to the house, our mother greeted us with a joyful smile, an expression so different from her usual melancholy.

"Children, I have great news!. Lady Livia, the wife of Emperor Augustus, has invited me to dinner at her house tomorrow. Herod and Agrippa will come with me."

A walk in Rome

Chapter 4
A visit to Lady Livia

In the afternoon of the next day, my mother came to the room that Herod and I shared. She was accompanied by two slave girls bringing, each one of them, a fine white wool fabric, several feet long, adorned with a purple border. The women helped us put on our linen tunics, over which they wrapped on us the clothing they brought.

"Children, what you are wearing is called toga praetexta. These clothes are reserved for boys who are sons of Roman citizens, but you have the right to use them because you are grandchildren of a king," explained our mother.

(From then on, I never left the house without wearing the toga praetexta. I used it until I was fifteen years old when I had the right to wear the toga virilis, entirely white, without ornaments or dyes).

My mother was also dressed in the Roman style. Over her tunic, she wore a pleated linen garment, which reached down to her ankles. The attire was adorned with strips embroidered in various colors, adorned with gold, silver, and pearls.

Thus, dressed as Romans, the three of us walked the short distance from our home to the house of Augustus and Livia.

The impressions that I will describe in the next paragraphs are not any that I could have noticed at the age of five years, but those I formed during the following years.

Before building their palace, Augustus and Livia lived in a simple and small house. Its corridors were narrow and made of ordinary stone. Unlike most residences on Palatine Hill, including ours, the rooms didn't have marble floors or mosaic floors. The beds and tables were hardly worthy of being in the residence of a well-to-do individual, let alone the Emperor of Rome.

Augustus, when we first met him, was about sixty years old. His countenance was serene and imperturbable, his eyes alive and bright, even though he had problems with the sight of the

271

left eye at that time. His teeth were small, clean, and uneven. His hair was slightly curly and blond, his ears medium size, his nose sharp and pointed, and his complexion dark. He was short but wore high shoes to seem taller.

Livia, Augustus' wife, was a stunning woman, although she was also approaching sixty. She was dressed in a simple dress but looked very elegant. Her gaze revealed great intelligence, which confirmed the rumors that she was her husband's chief counselor.

Livia had been married and was pregnant with her second child when Augustus met her and persuaded her husband to divorce her and give her to him.

Livia and Augustus did not have any children, although I understand that they desired to have a baby. Since her marriage to Augustus, she had been pregnant once but gave birth prematurely to a baby who died at birth.

"Welcome, dear Berenice, children!" Livia greeted us when we entered her house. She kissed my mother on the cheek and looked at her with a dazzling smile. "It is incredible how much you resemble your mother Salome, who, as you know, is one of my best friends!"

"As a matter of fact, Lady Livia, I bring you my mother's regards. She asked me to tell you that she misses you so much that she plans to visit Rome soon," my mother replied.

"Come in, Berenice, please. Come in, children. Do not stand in the entrance," Livia said.

Livia led us to a dressing room where we changed our clothes for others hung from hooks, lighter and more comfortable, white, without ornaments or folds. We changed our shoes for sandals, and we took off our bracelets and rings. Livia returned, saw that we had already changed our clothes, and invited us to go to the triclinium, which is how the Romans call their dining room.

Four people were sitting in the triclinium. One of them (my mother told me later, was Lady Antonia, Mark Antony's daughter), was sitting in a divan with two boys and a girl. The three children wore wreaths on their heads. One boy was my age, five years old, the other about four years older. The girl was perhaps seven years old.

Livia gave wreaths to Herod and me. She told us to sit on the divan on her right, and she sat next to my mother.

"Antonia, children, I want to introduce you to our guests, who have just arrived from Judea. Berenice is the widow of the unfortunate prince Aristobulus, son of King Herod.

"Welcome to Rome!" exclaimed Lady Antonia. "What are the names of your children?" she asked my mother.

"The eldest is Herod, like his grandfather, and the other is called Agrippa, in honor of the Emperor's friend," my mother answered.

"The lady next to me is my daughter-in-law Antonia, widow of my dear departed son Drusus. These boys and the girl are her children. The handsome one is Germanicus (she pointed to the older boy), and the other is Claudius. The girl's name is Livilla," said Livia. She gestured to the maids to bring the food and added, "We can start. We will not wait for Augustus. He is resting, as is his custom after lunch. He will come later."

Before proceeding with my story, I must clarify that my mother's parents were Idumeans, like my grandfather Herod. One hundred years before I was born, king Johanan Hyrcanus conquered Idumea and forced its people to convert to Judaism. The Jewish religion forbids us from eating certain foods. In Judea, I have always respected those prohibitions, but during my years in Rome, I allowed myself to eat whatever was on the table, based on the popular phrase: "when you are in Rome, do as the Romans do."

Livia's slaves brought plates filled with eggs, oysters, and vegetables. The main courses were legumes, meat seasoned with herbs and spices, and fish in a sauce called "garum," made of fish macerated in brine. To drink, we were served "mulsum," which is a mixture of wine and honey. For dessert, the slaves brought grapes, raisins, nuts, and a cake made of wheat and dipped in honey.

"The food is delicious, Livia," said my mother.

273

"Thank you, Berenice. My cooks follow the recipes that Marcus Gavius Apicius wrote in his book "De re coquinaria.""

"His name is not familiar to me. Who is he?" my mother asked.

"He's a very wealthy man but very eccentric," Antonia replied. "He is obsessed with creating refined dishes with the most expensive ingredients. At the rate that he is going, I would not be surprised if he loses all his fortune and ends up committing suicide."

The conversation was interrupted when Augustus entered the room, greeted us, and sat next to Livia, his wife.

"Augustus, Meet our guest Berenice and her sons Herod and Agrippa," Livia said to him.

"Your name is Herod, like the king of Judea?" Augustus asked my brother.

"He was my grandfather, sir.

"Then, your father was Aristobulus, whom your grandfather executed?

"Yes, sir.

"I knew your father well when he and his brother Alexander were boys and studied in Rome. It made me very sad to learn that they died. The truth is that it did not surprise me since I have always said that I prefer to be one of Herod's pigs than to be one of his children. But, let's leave the subject. Bring me something to eat," he ordered one of the slaves.

The slaves brought him bread, small fish, cheeses, dates, and fresh figs. I noticed that he ate very little.

The dinner ended when Augustus stood up, placed portions of food, salt, and a glass of wine on a tray, and took it to a small altar in the corner of the room. He placed the tray on the altar next to several small idols and kneeled.

"Gods, please accept this offering and protect this house," prayed Augustus. He got up and smiled at us.

"Excuse me for leaving such a charming company, but duty calls me. I must deal with some boring city problems", he said and left the room.

We also stood. My mother thanked Livia and Antonia and said goodbye. Antonia accompanied us to the door.

"Our children are of the same age. I would like them to be friends," said Antonia to my mother.

"I would like that very much," replied my mother.

A visit to Lady Livia

Chapter 5
My friends in Rome

Two days later, my mother received a new invitation. It was from Antonia. She invited us to have lunch the next day at her house, located on Palatine Hill, close to ours.

This time we all went, including my baby sister Mariamne. Antonia received us with great kindness. After lunch, Antonia told my brothers, sisters, and me to go to the other room and play with her children because she wanted to talk alone with our mother.

That day started the warm friendship between Antonia and my mother that lasted until the end of their lives. Both had much in common; they were of the same age, were widows, did not intend to remarry, and had young children. Because of her friendship with my mother, Antonia loved me like a son, and I considered her my second mother.

I became very close friends with Antonia's youngest son, Claudius, a boy my age, and with Drusus, Antonia's nephew, son of her brother-in-law Tiberius, who was three years older than me.

Germanicus, Claudius' older brother, was several years older than us. I cannot say that we became friends, probably because of the difference in our ages, but I always admired him for his intelligence, courage, and virtues. He was tall, thin, vigorous, and very handsome. He was eloquent and spoke Greek as well as he spoke Latin. He had a great desire to be popular and knew how to achieve popularity. Since childhood, he had no rival with the bow and arrows. He was also adept at handling the spear and the sword. People, when they met him, said that he reminded them of a teenager Alexander the Great.

Augustus never disguised that Germanicus was his favorite among all the young generation of his family, and many were convinced that he would be his heir.

Livilla, a couple of years older than Claudius, was never nice to me. She was a beautiful girl but had a selfish and manipulative character. I could not understand how her cousin Drusus, son of her uncle Tiberius, looked at her in awe and followed her everywhere. She treated him with disdain and took advantage of him to get all kinds of gifts and favors.

Claudius was a particular case. Although he was tall, slender, and almost as handsome as Germanicus, he had suffered, during his early years, various illnesses that left him with a lame leg and a stutter. His insecure legs caused him to stagger when he walked. His laughter was sharp and unpleasant. Her head and hands shook, his nose ran continuously, and sometimes, when he spoke, froth came out of his mouth.

It was not surprising that a family with handsome men and beautiful women was ashamed of him and mistreated him. His mother, Antonia, never liked him. She referred to Claudius as "a monster," and when she wanted to talk about some imbecile, she would say: "He's even more stupid than my son Claudius."

The only one of the family that was kind to Claudius was Germanicus, who, with the nobility that characterized him, protected Claudius and treated him with great affection. Claudius worshipped his older brothers.

Unable to withstand his sight, Antonia sent Claudius to live with her mother-in-law Livia, who hated and despised the boy. She never spoke to him, except to criticize him through laconic letters written with cruel frankness.

Augustus, on one occasion, took me aside, saying that he wanted to talk to me.

"Agrippa, I want you to know that the whole family has noticed the friendship that you show to poor Claudius. I hope that your attitude, actions, and composure will serve as an example to that unfortunate boy," he said to me in a low voice.

Whenever Claudius would arrive for dinner, the family watched, some with disgust, others with pity, while he limped around the table, looking, usually without success, for a place to sit. If, after dinner, he fell asleep at the table, which happened often, one or two of the other children would wake him up by throwing olives and dates at him.

I remember that, on one occasion, Drusus put sandals on Claudius' hands. Everybody laughed, including me—I confess to my shame—when he woke up abruptly and rubbed his face with the sandals.

Upon hearing that a seer had predicted that Claudius would one day be Emperor, his sister Livilla pretended to cry.

"What's the matter, Livilla?" asked her cousin Drusus, always aware of the slightest act or gesture of Livilla.

"I'm sorry for the Roman people. What a horrible fate awaits them!" said Livilla, and everybody laughed.

When Claudius turned fourteen years old, Augustus decided that the boy, having reached the end of his childhood, had to comply with the ceremony of changing the toga praetexta, used by children by the toga virilis, a white and plain toga, worn by the adult citizens of Rome.

I had been present at the public ceremony that Augustus organized when Germanicus turned fourteen and changed his toga praetexta for the toga virilis. Relatives and friends formed a cortege that accompanied the honored boy to the Forum. Because Germanicus' father had died, it was Augustus who took off the boy the gold amulet against the evil that had hung on his neck since his birth. In the Capitol, Germanicus was officially registered as a Roman citizen. Then, he offered a coin to the goddess Juventas and a sacrifice to the god Liber in the Temple of Capitoline Jupiter. We returned to the house of Augustus, where we all enjoyed a wonderful banquet.

In Claudius' case, the shame he caused his family was the reason why, after dressing him in his toga virilis, he was taken n a closed carriage at midnight, without a cortege, to the Capitol. I, his only friend, only found out about it the next day. Of course, there was no banquet.

Augustus chose one of his best friends, famous for his culture, to teach Germanicus how to function in Roman society. However, the tutor that he selected for Claudius was a former mules' driver. That man, crude and cruel, kept Claudius under iron discipline because he was convinced, like almost everybody else, that the boy not only lacked intelligence but was also an innate idler.

I did not understand why Claudius' family had such a low opinion of him. I, on the contrary, always considered him very intelligent and cultured. He knew a lot about Rome's history, which he demonstrated several years later when he wrote erudite books, which many admired. He spoke Greek fluently and could, as he did when he was an adult and had conquered his stammer, give eloquent speeches both in that language and in Latin.

Regarding his stuttering, this defect never manifested itself when he spoke with me, and, during his adolescence, it gradually disappeared. To their great surprise, his family discovered that Claudius was brilliant, far from being an idiot. His mother hired the famous historian Titus Livius and the philosopher Atenodorus to be his teachers. It turned out that Claudius had a great talent for mathematics, grammar, geometry, and history.

I had two other good friends in Rome. One of them was Silas, a boy two years younger than me. His father, a Jew born in Babylon, had accumulated a great fortune importing and selling silk fabrics. Silas followed me everywhere and lost no opportunity to express his loyalty and devotion to me.

My other friend was Lucius Pomponius Flaccus, whom, years later, I visited in Damascus when he was Governor of Syria. But, of that, I will write later.

Chapter 6
My school education in Rome

My brothers and I studied together with Claudius and Drusus. We had the same two tutors, and we shared the same lessons. These took place in the triclinium of Antonia's house.

One of our tutors was a Greek brought to Rome as a slave whose masters had freed him. He taught us to read and write using a wooden tablet covered with wax. We used the pointed end of a stiletto to mark the letters. We smoothed the wax with a spatula in the other end of the stiletto to write again on it. As soon as our tutor felt that we already knew how to write, he allowed us to do it on papyrus and parchment, using feathers and ink made from soot or, sometimes, extracted from the octopus. We learned mathematics using the abacus.

The other tutor, an ex-soldier, taught us to throw the javelin, fight with the sword, ride a horse, box and swim.

The girls—Livilla, my sister Herodias, and about three or four other girls from aristocratic families—studied separately. A patrician woman, who had fallen in hard times, taught them music, sewing, cooking, and, most important, how to be good wives in another room of Antonia's house.

My friend Lucius Flaccus, whose family, although well-off, was far from being as rich as ours, did not have a private tutor. He went in the morning to a school located in the Forum's porches, where the teaching was mixed, boys and girls together, up to twelve years old. He was accompanied to school by a slave with whom, back at this home, he went over the lessons.

My friend Flaccus told me that his teacher was always in a bad mood, perhaps because he was poorly paid. He hit the students for the slightest offense, convinced by the old refrain that says "the letter with blood enters." If the student's answer was wrong, he ordered his slaves to hold the child while lashing him with a leather whip.

When Claudius and I turned twelve, his mother Antonia hired a "grammarian" for her son, other Palatine Hill children, and me. His duties included perfecting our command of the Greek language, improving our writing, analyzing poems, and teaching us to speak in public. He also taught us geography, history, and religion. He also taught us geography, history, and religion. His name was Marcus Verrius. He was a freedman who had become famous for his novel teaching method, motivating students to compete against each other and reward the winner with an old book or another valuable gift.

For our third stage of studies, at fourteen or fifteen, we had to choose between enlisting in the army (which Germanicus had chosen) or continuing our studies of rhetoric, geography, history, philosophy, and literature. Claudius decided to continue with his studies based on his desire to be a historian.

I followed the example of Claudius, but for a different reason. Because I was the grandson of a king, my dream, as a child, was to follow in my grandfather's footsteps and assume the throne of Judea. Being realistic, I knew that possibility to be unlikely since Rome had annulled the independence of Judea and converted it into a province governed by a Roman prefect. But, if I would remain in Rome, the knowledge of rhetoric, philosophy, and literature would be essential for me to succeed in Roman high society.

Chapter 7
The Jewish community of Rome

Once a week, a member of the Jewish community in Rome, hired by my mother, came to our house and taught Torah, Hebrew, and Jewish history to my brothers and me. That was the only contact I had with the Jews of Rome during my childhood and youth.

A few months after our arrival in Rome, eight thousand Roman Jews accompanied a delegation of Jews from Judea requested the Roman Senate to annul the monarchy in Judea and declare it a Roman province. They expressed their profound dissatisfaction with Archelaus, son, and heir of King Herod. The Senate approved their request. This lack of national pride disappointed and angered my mother and further distanced us from Rome's Jewish community. The result is that we rarely set foot in any of the Rome synagogues.

I have never known exactly how many Jews lived in Rome, a city with a million inhabitants. Someone told me there were ten thousand Jews in the town. Others believed that there were forty thousand, which I think is close to the right number. Because the Jews were so prominent in the commercial, industrial, and theatrical life of the city, some people swore that at least 500,000 Jews lived in Rome.

I know that the first contact between the Jews of Judea and the Romans took place during the Judean independence war led by my ancestor, Simon Maccabee, who sent a delegation to Rome to sign a treaty. During the following years, many Jews from Alexandria arrived in Rome and settled on the Tiber River's right bank.

The Roman Jewish community multiplied, due, first, to the invasion of Judea by General Pompey and, later, to the civil war that Herod, supported by the Romans, fought to seize the crown. The captured Jews were taken as slaves to Rome, and there the Jewish community paid large sums to rescue them.

There were also cases of Jewish slaves released by their masters because they could not abide by the obstinacy of their slaves, who insisted on resting one day of the week and refused to eat certain foods.

Julius Caesar allowed the Jews to practice their traditional religious rituals and gave Judaism the status of a legal religion throughout the Empire. The Jews of Rome loved and respected Caesar, and when he was murdered, the Jewish community declared a week of mourning.

Most Jews in Rome speak Greek. Although most are well off, some are very wealthy, many are poor, and the number of Jewish beggars is large.

The Jews of Rome are active proselytizers and have succeeded in converting many people. Although not yet formally converted, numerous Romans have adopted some Jewish customs and believe in the Jewish God.

I have always been amazed at how little the Romans, even the educated and cultured, know about the Jews and Judaism, believing instead in myths and misconceptions. Augustus, for example, was convinced that the Jews fast every Saturday. We do not. We only fast during specific religious festivals.

An example of the ignorance that predominated in Rome about the Jews was the lecture that our grammarian gave us one day during history class. His teachings about the Jews and Judaism were a classic example of the nonsense that many Romans believe about Jews. I will summarize his lecture in the following pages.

Chapter 8
A lecture about the Jews

In Egypt, [our teacher told us in his lecture], centuries ago, there was an epidemic of leprosy, a terrible disease that disfigures people. The king went to consult the oracle of his god and asked him how to solve the problem.

"You must expel all the people who have that disease to another country because Heaven hates them," the oracle replied.

The king ordered the army to gather all the sick people, take them to the desert and leave them there.

The exiles began to walk aimlessly, suffering from a lack of water. One of the expelled, named Moses, when he saw that his companions were lamenting that they would die of thirst in the desert, spoke to them.

"Brothers, we must not seek help from men or the gods. Both have abandoned us. We will trust and accept as a divine guide the first being that can save us.

Suddenly, they saw a herd of wild donkeys heading towards a low hill covered with trees. Moses followed the animals and discovered an oasis with lots of water. The exiles drank and were saved. Afterward, they marched for six days and reached another country. On the seventh day, they fought against the natives of the country, defeated them, and seized their territory. There, they built their city and their Temple.

To ensure his continued dominance over his people, Moses introduced a new cult, which was the opposite of every other religion in the world. All that we consider sacred, the Jews consider profane. They have practices that we abhor. In their sanctuary, the Jews have placed an image of an ass, the animal that guided them to the water that saved them from dying of thirst.

Because pigs are susceptible to leprosy, Jews abstain from eating pork in memory of the plague suffered by their ancestors.

The Jews frequently fast to remember the famine and thirst suffered by their ancestors in the desert. They dedicate the seventh day to rest because it was on the seventh day that they seized the country where they live. They stop working every seventh year because they are idlers.

They have impious and abominable customs. The Jews do not comply with the cults of the countries where they live, but they send money to their Temple in Judea, thus contributing to its wealth and prosperity.

They are stubbornly loyal and compassionate to one another, but they feel hatred and enmity towards all the other nations of the world.

They refuse to eat with other people. Although they are sexually immoderate, they abstain from having sexual relationships with foreign women out of contempt. They prefer to bury their dead rather than burn them.

The Jews circumcise their male children to distinguish themselves from other peoples. They consider it a crime to kill children who are born defective and believe that the souls of those who die in battle or because of persecution are immortal. That is why they are not afraid to face death.

They acknowledge a single god, whom they consider all-powerful, without beginning or end. Absurdly, they say that their god is invisible and that it is sacrilege to make images of their god in human form. That's why they do not have statues in their Temple or their cities.

I listened to that entire absurd, false, exaggerated, and distorted lecture without interrupting the teacher. When he finished talking, I stood up and told him clearly what I thought about his lecture and him.

"Sir, almost all the information you just gave us is so wrong, so distorted, and so exaggerated that it has very little, if any, similarity to reality. I suggest that you should read the Torah, the sacred scroll of the Jews, so that you can verify that most of the information you have given us is false. Worse yet, it's absurd, ridiculous, and, without due respect, it shows your ignorance and your stupidity.

The professor turned pale, and then his face flushed with anger. He did not say anything for a moment, trying to control himself. He knew that if he answered me inappropriately, he would lose Claudius and me as students, and his small income would be reduced to nothing.

"Thanks for the suggestion, Agrippa. It is an excellent idea, but I regret that it will be impossible for me to comply with it since I do not speak or read Hebrew," he said in a tone of voice that did not hide his anger.

"It is not necessary to know Hebrew to read the Torah. There is a Greek translation called 'Septuagint,' which is the text used by all the Jewish communities worldwide, except for Judea that uses the original text. Two centuries ago, in Alexandria, seventy-two Jewish sages, sent by the High Priest of Jerusalem, worked separately to translate the sacred scrolls. When they finished translating, they compared the texts. They were all identical and did not have one single letter of difference between them," I replied.

My confrontation with our teacher had an unexpected consequence, which I found out many years later.

I went to the largest synagogue in Rome during the Festival of Unleavened Bread, and. A man with a long white beard, wearing a head covering and a tallit, the fringed garment worn as a prayer shawl by religious Jews, approached with a big smile on his face.

"Shalom, Agrippa," he greeted me. "Don't you recognize me? I was your teacher many years ago. I gave an explanation about the Jews to you and your companions which made you angry. You suggested that I should get a copy of the Septuagint, which I did. I read it, came to the synagogue, took lessons with the rabbi, and ended up converting to Judaism, *Baruch ha Shem!*" [Blessed be God].

287

A lecture about the Jews

Chapter 9
Germanicus' triumphs

Germanicus had a brilliant military career. The Senate appointed him commander of eight legions, a third of the entire Roman army. He fought against the Germanic tribes, defeated them, and recovered two of the three eagle shields that the Roman legions had lost in a previous defeat. On his return to Rome, he was honored with a triumph, a ceremony the Romans hold to honor the military commander who has returned victorious from his campaign in foreign lands.

It was the most glorious day of Germanicus' life. His army formed rows in the Field of Mars, outside the walls of the city. A military parade entered through the gate called Porta Triumphalis, passed through the Circus Maximus and crossed the Via Sacra to reach Capitoline Hill.

Germanicus rode on a chariot accompanied by a slave who, while holding the laurels of victory over the head of the general, admonished him: 'Look back and remember that you are only a man.' The crowd in the streets shouted his name and cheered him.

The procession stopped at the foot of the steps of the Temple of Jupiter Maximus. Germanicus, surrounded by his officers, entered the Temple and offered his victory laurels to the god.

That afternoon he held a banquet in his house, with the door open for anyone who wanted to come in. It was a day I will never forget. Germanicus was resplendent in his uniform, with his wife Agrippina, Augustus' granddaughter, and their small children by his side.

Germanicus' triumphs

Chapter 10
A visit to my friend Claudius

Claudius was a very cautious person and was careful not to comment on political issues, but one day, when we were in a brothel in Suburra, Rome's worst neighborhood, half-drunk both of us, he sat next to me and spoke in my ear.

"My uncle Tiberius is jealous of the popularity of Germanicus. That is the real reason why he has convinced Augustus to send Germanicus to a military campaign far away from Rome," Claudius told me. "Actually, just between us, I am happy that my brother is leaving Rome. If his popularity continues to grow, his chances of dying young will also increase."

"Sorry, Claudius, I don't understand you. What are you trying to tell me?" I babbled, the result of drinking too much wine.

"Agrippa, a good listener doesn't need more than a few words to understand," he answered.

"I still don't understand you, Claudius. What are you trying to tell me?"

"Don't worry about it, Agrippa. Wine affects different people in different ways. In your case, it dulls your understanding. In my case, it makes me say things that I shouldn't say. Forget what I said, and have some fun. Look at that blonde. She is exactly how you like them, big breasts, great ass. Go to her. She is smiling at you".

Claudius had repeatedly asked Augustus to give him a position where he could start his public career. Augustus always refused and, instead, appointed him to a minor function in the priesthood. Claudius gave up any political aspiration he might have had. Instead, he kept busy during the day drinking wine and playing dice and carousing in brothels at night. I was his constant companion in these activities since I also had nothing better to do. Because I was a foreigner, I couldn't become a soldier or a politician. It was below my dignity and my royal ancestry to become a merchant.

Claudius' life changed the day we went for a walk along the Via Sacra and met the historian Titus Livius, his former teacher. Claudius embraced him affectionately.

"It's been so long since I've seen you! I imagine that you have already finished the history of the Etruscans that you were writing. I would love to receive a copy," Livius told Claudius.

"I have not finished it yet. To tell you the truth, I have not written a single page since the last time we saw each other," answered Claudius.

"You must be very busy! How do you spend your time?" asked Livius.

Claudius blushed and did not answer. I answered for him.

"Wine, dice, and women are to be thanked for keeping us busy," I said and laughed.

Livius' face clearly showed that he didn't find my joke to be funny.

"What a terrible waste of your time and talent, Claudius! Frankly, I'm disappointed. I always thought you were a born historian. I was wrong. Good morning, gentlemen," he told us, turned around, and left without saying another word.

"Agrippa, please excuse me, but I must return to my house now. What Livius has told me is something that I have been saying to myself for a long time. I have to think about it and make a decision," Claudius said. He hugged me and left.

I visited him three days later, but his servants told me that he was no longer in Rome. He had moved to his country house in Tivoli, about thirty miles away, and was not receiving any visitors.

Several months later, one of Claudius' servants brought me an invitation to spend a few days with him in his country house in Tivoli.

I sent back the servant with a note saying that I gladly accepted his invitation and would arrive in a few days.

I had never been before in Tivoli. Seeing that beautiful town for the first time was a wonderful surprise. It is located on the left bank of the Aniene River, surrounded by forests, springs, and waterfalls. On the road from Rome to Tivoli, I saw several quarries where they extracted a stone called Travertine, used in Rome to adorn the most beautiful buildings.

Claudius was waiting for me in his garden, sitting on a bench enjoying the shade of pine trees. I got off my carriage, and we hugged. I stared at him with surprise. He was no longer the thin, almost skeletal young man I had last seen months ago. He now looked robust and tanned by the sun; his head and hands were no longer trembling, and, when he walked with me to his house, I had the impression that even his limp had disappeared.

"You look great! I almost did not recognize you. Are you sure you're Claudius?" I asked jokingly.

"Agrippa, I feel like a new man. I owe it to living in the countryside and breathing this pure air. It is wonderful to relax in my garden and enjoy the silence and tranquility that reigns here," he replied.

"Don't you miss Rome, Claudius?" I asked him.

"Are you asking me if I miss filthy streets, hellish noise, unbearable people, and foul air? I assure you that I do not," he replied, laughing. "But, come. I'll show you my garden."

He showed me his vegetable gardens, the fruit trees, the vineyard, and the olive grove during the next two hours. He had an aquarium with colorful fish and cages with some wild animals in one corner of the garden, including a lion, a bear, and a huge animal that I had never seen before, with a horn on its nose.

"Pardon me," he said when he noticed that I was yawning. "I have been thoughtless. I was so happy to see you that I did not consider that you must be exhausted after spending hours traveling from Rome to Tivoli. Take a nap, and then I'll show you the rest."

He instructed a slave to take me to the room he had given me. I stretched out on the soft bed and fell asleep immediately.

293

A couple of hours later, I woke up refreshed. I left the room and saw the slave waiting in the corridor.

"Where is your master?" I asked.

"He's in the stables. He told me that, as soon as you wake up, I should take you there," he replied.

I walked behind him to a separate building that was a short distance away. We entered through a gate into a courtyard. In its center was a pond where several horses were drinking.

"The rooms you see around the courtyard are the servants'. In that corner is the kitchen," the slave told me, pointing with his finger.

"I do not see your master. Where is he?" I asked.

"He is in the other courtyard, at the end of this corridor," the slave replied.

We arrived at a large patio bordered by a cow barn, a chicken coop, and wheat warehouses. A window with bars caught my attention. I looked through it and saw a chained man inside the room.

"Why is that man chained?" I asked the slave.

"The master has punished him because he is lazy and insolent," he replied.

Claudius came out of the barn, saw me, and approached smiling.

"I see you've already rested. Come, I'll show you my villa," he told me.

We returned to the house where I had napped. Claudius showed me the dining room, the bedrooms, and the bathrooms. Finally, we came to a room with shelves on the walls with hundreds of parchment scrolls. A table with half-written parchments, pens, and an inkwell was in the center of the room.

"This is my favorite room, the library. This is where I write. I already have two completed works. One is the history of the Etruscans. The second is a treatise on the game of dice. I want to give you a copy of each of them, but you have to promise me that you will give me your objective and impartial opinion," Claudius told me.

I promised. Two days later, when I returned to Rome, I had with me the two works that Claudius gave me.

I found the "The History of the Etruscans" to be fascinating and written on a professional historian's level, so I informed Claudius. But, what I really loved was his other work, "How to Win in the Game of Dice", which, to this day, I consider a masterpiece. I have read it and reread it many times and always learn something new.

I am not exaggerating when I say that I have won thousands of denarii playing dice by following the tactics and advice that Claudius gives in his magnificent treatise. I have also lost thousands of denarii playing dice, but that is only because, on those occasions, I made the mistake of trusting my own skill and did not take into account the advice given by Claudius in his masterful work.

A visit to my friend Claudius

Chapter 11
Tiberius and his son Drusus

Tiberius was a dour, sullen man who didn't speak much. I never saw him smile. The only person he got along with was Antonia, her brother's widow. He respected and appreciated her, but I don't think he felt affection for her since he did not have feelings for anyone, including his son, Drusus.

The only person he ever loved was his first wife, Vipsania, his son Drusus' mother. Augustus forced him to divorce her and marry his daughter Julia, whom Tiberius hated.

Once I heard Antonia telling my mother about an incident that happened a few days before, which had caused a distancing between Tiberius and Augustus.

"Tiberius saw his ex-wife Vipsania on the street and followed her crying and begging forgiveness. People who saw this embarrassing spectacle told it to others and, by that evening, all of Rome had learned of the incident. That same night Augustus sent the commander of his guards to Tiberius' house with orders to bring him back with him," Antonia told my mother without noticing that I was sitting in a chair, next to them, listening to every word.

"What did Augustus tell your brother-in-law?" asked my mother, eager to hear the details. My mother was an intelligent and virtuous lady, but she had the same weakness that all women have. She loved to listen to gossip, especially about Augustus and the imperial family.

"He forbid Tiberius to speak with Vipsania. He warned him that if he did it again, not only would Tiberius become the laughingstock of Rome, but he, Augustus, would choose as a successor someone who didn't publicly humiliate himself for a woman," answered Antonia.

Antonia noticed that I was listening to their conversation. She lowered her voice and spoke into my mother's ear. I did not hear what she said, but my mother could not stop laughing.

I was interested to hear more about Tiberius, not only because he was Augustus' presumptive successor, but because he was the father of Drusus, my best friend since Claudius moved to Tivoli.

Drusus was not an intellectual like Claudius, but he did have a talent for politics and the army. He was reckless and violent. In our frequent visits to the brothels of Suburra, Drusus enjoyed getting into fights with other customers, sometimes even pulling out his knife, on the pretext that his opponent wanted for himself the woman that he, Drusus, had chosen that night. He usually ended the night getting drunk.

On one occasion, I went with him to the gladiator fights (Drusus was an enthusiast of that spectacle). We arrived a little late and saw that a person was sitting in the place that Drusus usually occupied.

Drusus went to the man and touched his shoulder.

"Excuse me, but you are sitting in my seat," said Drusus politely.

"I'm very comfortable here, so don't bother me! There are empty seats in the top rows. Sit there and leave me alone," the man replied without turning to look who was talking to him.

Drusus grabbed him by his ears and forced him down to the arena.

"Bring me two swords!" Drusus yelled to his bodyguards.

The man turned pale when he recognized who he had offended and tried to apologize. Drusus ignored him. The bodyguards brought two swords, gave one to Drusus and the other to his opponent.

The man threw the sword to the ground and ran away. Drusus stayed in the arena, laughing loudly. The audience stood up, applauded, and cheered his name. Drusus returned to his seat and made a gesture with his hand for the spectacle to resume.

In the evenings, we usually played dice with a group of friends in a tavern in Suburra. Drusus won most of the time, which was not due to his ability as a player or to his good luck but his dice. He had they made especially for him. Some of his dice had small irregularities in their shape, and others had lead weights on one side. Everyone who played with him knew this, but we never mentioned it, partly because it would have been imprudent to look for a fight with the son of the heir to the Empire, and partly because Drusus was very generous and paid for our consumption in the taverns and brothels of Suburra.

Drusus liked to go frequently to the Circus Maximus to watch horse racing. He said he did to bet, but I always suspected that the real reason for his love of this spectacle was his wish to witness a crash whose impact, if it were strong enough, would destroy the chariots and leave the charioteers and the horses dead or badly wounded.

At the age of twenty, Drusus married his cousin Livilla, whom he loved since childhood. Livilla, Antonia's daughter and sister to Germanicus and Claudius, did not feel affection for him, but the family (Augustus, Antonia, Tiberius) forced her to marry Drusus.

Drusus, from the moment he got married, changed completely. He loved Livilla, stopped playing dice and betting on horses, and, of course, he never went again to a brothel.

He was appointed a permanent member of the Senate and subsequently served as consul and tribune. In all these positions, he performed efficiently and honorably.

One year after the marriage, Livilla gave birth to a daughter whom they called Julia. Fifteen years later, the twins Tiberius Gemelus and Germanicus Gemelus (who died when he was still very young) were born.

I noticed something strange when I went to the house of Drusus to congratulate him on the twins' birth. I couldn't help noticing that the babies didn't look at all like Drusus!

A tragedy, years later, revealed me the cause, as I will tell further on.

Tiberius and his son Drusus

Chapter 12
Germanicus' tragic end

Years passed, Augustus died and was buried with the greatest honors. His successor was his adopted son Tiberius, one of the two children Livia had with her first husband.

Augustus had forced Tiberius to adopt Germanicus, the brother of my friend Claudius. The Emperor's intention was that, when the time came, Germanicus and Drusus, the son of Tiberius, would rule the Empire together.

One of Tiberius' first acts as Emperor was to send Germanicus to Asia Minor to reorganize the province of Cappadocia and incorporate it into the Roman Empire.

The Governor of the Roman province of Syria was Gnaeus Calpurnius Piso, a man known for his cruelty and greed. On one occasion, Tiberius was asked why didn't he fire Piso and send another Governor. His answer was surprising.

"Piso has already stolen and extorted so much that I hope he is satisfied. If I fire him and send another in his place, the new one will steal and extort from the beginning. Better a known thief than a thief that you don't know yet," said Tiberius.

Tiberius' policy was not to send governors or procurators to the provinces while the incumbent was still alive.

"It is natural and expected for a Governor to squeeze his province as much as possible, to satiate his greed," he used to say.

"If I replace him too quickly, the newly appointed will squeeze the province before the population has recovered from the extortion of the previous one," explained Tiberius and added an example: "A large number of flies covered a man's wounds. The people around him, compassionate, wanted to scare the flies away, but the wounded man asked them, 'please, do not bother the flies, they are already full of my blood; if they are frightened, others will come hungry. So please leave them'."

Germanicus, a virtuous and honest man, did not share Tiberius' cynicism. It was inevitable that Germanicus, upon arriving in Syria, would disapprove of Piso's acts and threaten to send him back to Rome to be tried.

Soon after, Germanicus died poisoned. Agrippina accused Piso and his wife Plancina of murdering Germanicus. The couple, accused of extortion, betrayal, and murder, was forced to return to Rome to be tried.

Agrippina returned to Rome, accompanied by her children, bringing an urn with her husband's ashes.

That was the sad end of Germanicus, murdered by a criminal couple. He was the man I have admired the most in my life. I am convinced that, had he lived, he would have been the greatest Emperor of all.

Plancina, at first, remained loyal to her husband but distanced herself from him when she saw that Piso's conviction was inevitable. She got the support of her friend Livia, the mother of Tiberius, and was exonerated.

Piso committed suicide before the end of his trial and left a letter in which he did not mention Plancina.

Years later, when Livia's death left Plancina without her protector, the judges reopened her trial, and she committed suicide.

Chapter 13
Marriages

My friends and I reached the age at which we were expected to get married. As I have told before, the first of us who took that step was Drusus, who married his cousin Livilla.

Claudius, when he turned twenty-five, married a girl of Etruscan descent called Plaucia Urgulanila. Her father had been a general, and her mother was a close friend of Livia. They had two children. The first one was Claudius Drusus, who died shortly after birth, and the second one, a girl, Claudia, who Claudius doubted if she was his daughter. After nine years of marriage, Claudius concluded that the girl was not his and divorced Plaucia.

Four years later, Claudius was forced by Tiberius to marry Elia Petina, the adopted sister of Lucius Aelius Sejanus, the most powerful man in the Empire, prefect of the Praetorian Guard, the military corps that guards the Emperor.

Claudius' second marriage lasted three years until Sejanus fell from grace and was executed. After Sejanus' death, Claudius felt no need or desire to stay married to Elia Petina and divorced her.

One of my cousins came to Rome on a visit. Her name was Cypros. My mother invited her to have dinner at our home so she could meet the family. The moment I saw her I fell in love with her. We married and had five children, Drusus, who died when he was very young, Agrippa, Berenice, Mariamne, and Drusilla.

Marrying Cypros was the smartest decision I've made in my entire life. She is a wonderful, self-sacrificing wife whose wise advice, unfortunately for me, I do not always follow.

Due to my marriage, I abandoned my partying friends and stopped drinking wine in excess. The only habit I kept was playing dice, where I continued to lose more than I won.

At that time, we had a scandal in our family. My sister Herodias, a very obstinate woman, had married my uncle

Philip against my mother's will. The couple had a daughter, Salome, who, since childhood, showed a great talent for dancing.

My uncle Philip was a good man who never hurt anyone. Despite being the son of King Herod, he was happy and content living a quiet, anonymous life. Herodias continually reproached him for his lack of ambition, but Philip didn't change. He continued to be his old easy-going self.

One day, my uncle Antipas came to visit us in Rome. He was the most successful of all my grandfather Herod's children. The Romans had named him Governor, with the title of "Tetrarch", of Chalcis, a tiny territory that included the Galilee and Mount Hermon's slopes.

Herodias realized that this was her chance. She divorced her husband/uncle Philip, convinced her uncle Antipas to abandon his wife, and married him. Although Antipas was not a king, she persuaded him to build a luxurious royal palace in Tiberias, his capital, where she acted like a Queen.

Antipas' first wife was the daughter of the king of the Nabataeans. Her father, enraged by the way Antipas had discarded his daughter, went to Calcis with his army to kill his former son-in-law. The Roman Governor of Syria persuaded the Nabateans to retreat, and my sister, Herodias, did not become a widow.

What my uncle Antipas and my sister Herodias did to my poor uncle Philip made me so angry that I wished my grandfather Herod had added one more relative to the list of those he sent prematurely to the kingdom of Heaven.

After a long and painful illness, my mother died in Rome a few days before my thirtieth birthday. We buried her in the catacombs where the Jews bury their dead.

I used the money that I inherited from my mother, plus loans that I received from the Empire's treasury, to buy gifts for Emperor Tiberius' freedmen to be welcome in the imperial court.

Unfortunately, the moment came when I had to face the harsh reality: not only had I squandered all my fortune, but I owed large sums that I was unable to pay back.

Marriages

Chapter 14
My friend Drusus' death

I do not wish on my worst enemy what happened to my friend Drusus.

I mentioned earlier that Drusus, from his childhood, was in love with his cousin Livilla. She did not reciprocate the feeling, but the family forced them to marry.

Everything went more or less well in the marriage until Livilla met a certain man and fell in love with him. Lucius Aelius Sejanus, the Praetorian Guard's Prefect, was the most powerful man in the Empire after the Emperor. Even more powerful, some would say.

Sejanus, a capable and unscrupulous man, had transformed the Praetorian Guard from a simple group of bodyguards into a powerful institution that practically governed the country. Tiberius, unaware of what was going on, stayed on Capri and seldom visited Rome.

Sejanus was extremely ambitious. Thanks to his influence over Tiberius, he became the most powerful and feared man in the Empire. This was not enough for him. He wanted to be Emperor, and for that, he needed to eliminate Drusus, who, being Tiberius' son, was the natural heir.

The first thing he did was make Livilla, Drusus' wife, fall in love with him. This was not difficult because, during Livilla's marriage, the antipathy that she felt toward her husband had turned into hatred.

Livilla became Sejanus' mistress, got pregnant by him, and gave birth to Tiberius Gemelus and Germanicus Gemelus.

Sejanus' next step was to convince Livilla to kill Drusus by poisoning him gradually so as not to arouse suspicions.

After Drusus' death, Sejanus asked Tiberius for permission to marry Livilla. This marriage would make a suitable candidate for the succession.

To the surprise and disappointment of Sejanus, Tiberius refused his petition and warned him that his excessive ambition could be dangerous. However, the Emperor, at that time, did not take any action against Sejanus and deliberately didn't pay attention to the rumors that Sejanus had murdered Drusus.

Sejanus, who was in Rome, took advantage of Tiberius being on Capri to eliminate his political enemies and, simultaneously, to increase his fortune. He banished Agrippina, the widow of Germanicus, and her two older children. Shortly afterward, Agrippina and her children died in suspicious circumstances. The only son of Germanicus who managed to survive Sejanus' plot was Caligula, who saved himself by going to Capri, where he became part of Tiberius' court.

Sejanus married Livilla and became the true ruler of the Empire.

Antonia, Livilla's mother, discovered incontrovertible proof that her daughter and Sejanus had murdered Drusus and sent a letter to Tiberius accusing the couple.

Tibcrius, knowing that Sejanus had enormous power, acted subtly. He sent him a letter to appear in the Senate to be invested with more powers. At the same time, he notified Nevius Sutorius Macron, the police force's Prefect, to go to the Senate and arrest Sejanus.

Macron complied with Tiberius' order. He arrested Sejanus and strangled him. Sejanus' body was torn into pieces by the crowd and thrown into the Tiber River. His son and his eleven-year-old daughter were also arrested. The boy was executed immediately. Tiberius ordered the executioner to rape the girl before strangling her to comply with the law that forbids a virgin woman's execution.

Upon learning of her children's death, Sejanus' ex-wife committed suicide and left a letter accusing Livila of complicity in the death of Drusus.

Antonia locked her daughter Livilla in a room and starved her to death.

I wanted to express my condolences to Tiberius, but he refused to receive me. His servant told me that the Emperor felt that seeing me, a close friend of his murdered son Drusus would bring back sad memories.

My financial situation at the moment was catastrophic. I owed too much money, and my creditors got into the habit of coming to my house day and night, knocked loudly on my door, screamed, and shouted. My only alternative to escape their siege was to flee from Rome with my wife and children and settle in Judea.

My friend Drusus' death

Chapter 15
Antipas celebrates his birthday

The little money that I had left was barely enough to buy passage for myself, my wife Cypros, and the children, on a ship that took us from the port of Ostia to Caesarea. We continued to Malatha, a town located in the desert between Beersheba and the Sea of Salt. I had a house there that had once belonged to my father, but now, having been abandoned for many years, it was a ruin.

I felt tremendous shame for having fallen, through my fault and my waste, to such a miserable situation. Seeing the crumbling walls, the few rooms that still had a roof, full of the dirt of the animals that had occupied them, depressed me terribly. I started to cry and ran up to the second floor to throw myself through a window and end a life that was no longer worth living.

Cypros ran after me, hugged me, and prevented him from jumping to the rocks below. I hugged her, sobbing. She, a wonderful, kind woman, tried to comfort me and give me the strength to continue living.

"Do not despair, Agrippa. I love you so much. Think of your children. Please do not leave them as fatherless as you were. You will see, we will get out of this situation, and, someday, it will only be a bad memory," Cypros told me.

"I do not see how we can improve our situation, Cypros. We have no money left, and soon we will not have anything to eat."

"Your sister Herodias is the wife of your uncle Antipas, the tetrarch of Chalcis. I will write Antipas a letter telling him about our situation and ask him to help us somehow.

"I forbid you, Cypros! I'd rather die before begging that miserable bastard," I shouted in despair.

"Agrippa, take into account that, if you die, your children and I will also die. Do not let your pride cause a tragedy. We have no other alternative. Today I will write to him," Cypros answered firmly.

My wife was right. We had no other possibility. That same day, Cypros sent a letter to Herodias and Antipas, mentioning our situation. Since we did not have anyone else to turn to, she asked them to help us.

I did not hope that Antipas would help us because the antipathy I felt towards him was nothing compared to his hate for me. So, you can imagine my surprise when, a few days later, a group of soldiers arrived. Antipas had sent them to serve us as our escort and take us to the tetrarch's palace in Tiberias.

The palace that Antipas had built for Herodias was on the shores of the lake. The soldiers took us to a large room, which, we learned later, Herodias called "the throne room", although her husband was not entitled to call himself king. It was adorned with draperies on the walls and carpets on the floor. Antipas and Herodias awaited us, sitting on thrones in the middle of the room.

I will not say that my uncle and my sister welcomed us with open arms because that's not what happened, but they did extend to us a courtesy that I did not expect.

"Welcome, Agrippa, Cypros, children. You have arrived in time to celebrate with us Antipas' birthday tomorrow. You, of course, will be our guests," my sister greeted us.

Herodias stood up from her throne, embraced me, and kissed Cypros and the children. Antipas also saluted us, laughing that obnoxious laugh that characterizes him.

I noticed that he wore kingly garments and had a crown on his head. He had no right to the royal dress or the crown since he was only a tetrarch and not a sovereign, but I kept that thought to myself. He was

"Agrippa, good to see you. Herodias didn't mention it, but we have another guest in the palace. He is staying downstairs, in the room that I considered the most adequate for such an honored person. I want you to see him. Come with me," said Antipas. He grabbed my arm, forcing me to walk with him.

312

We went down several flights of stairs until we reached the palace dungeons. All the cells were empty, except one. Inside was a man with disheveled hair, a long unkempt beard, dressed in rags made of camel hair, stained with blood. It was evident that he had suffered cruel torture.

"Agrippa, I want you to meet my guest of honor, John, son of Zachariah. People call him 'the Baptist' because he likes to dip people into the river, saying that it washes away their sins. Can you imagine that there are people who believe that nonsense? He is not easy to satisfy since he refuses to eat the food we give him, insisting that he only eats locusts and wild honey."

"Thus says God: 'You shall not uncover the nakedness of your brother's wife; it's your brother's nudity'," the prisoner suddenly shouted with a tremendous voice that almost made the walls shake. It certainly made me tremble.

Antipas, frightened, jumped back. He grabbed my arm again and led me to the upper floor. While we climbed the steep stairs, I wanted to satisfy my curiosity about the prisoner.

"Why is that man imprisoned? What is his crime?" I asked Antipas.

"You heard him. He dares to publicly criticize my marriage with your sister saying that it is a sinful incestuous union. Herodias is very much offended by John's accusations. She is furious. She considers his words to be intolerable insults that deserve appropriate punishment. This man will stay in his cell until I decide what to do with him," my uncle-brother-in-law replied.

I understood why Antipas had insisted that I should see the prisoner. It was a subtle warning to me against making a negative comment about his marriage to my sister, his niece. It was an unnecessary threat because I was not such an idiot as to offend someone from whom I hoped to receive help.

The next day the servants lighted the throne room with candles and lamps and adorned it with hundreds of bouquets. They placed the tables for the banquet along the walls, leaving a large space in the center for the dancers' performance and the singers.

The guests began to arrive at nightfall. Herodias told us to sit at the main table next to her. A pretty young woman came and greeted us.

"Uncle Agrippa, Aunt Cypros, I'm so glad to see you again," she said with a warm smile.

At first, I did not recognize her. I stared at her until I realized that she was Salome, the daughter that Herodias had had with my uncle Philip, her first husband.

"Salomé, the last time I saw you, you were just a child. You have become a beautiful young woman! Do you still like to dance?" Cypros asked her.

"Yes, aunt. It's what I like the most," answered Salome.

I can criticize Antipas and Herodias for many things, but not about knowing how to treat their guests. The food was delicious and plentiful. The dancers and the singers were better than those I saw in Rome. I lack words to praise the wine. The guests repeatedly stood up to toast Antipas' health and to wish him a long life, and he drank with each of them.

The effects of alcohol became evident when Antipas, staggering, stood up and asked for silence.

"Ladies and gentlemen, your presence honors me. To end this unforgettable night with a golden touch, I ask my stepdaughter Salome to dance for us the dance of the seven veils." Antipas stammered these phrases, looked around disoriented, and sat down.

"Uncle, excuse me, but I do not feel like dancing," said Salome.

"Salome, if you dance, I'll give you anything you want," Antipas promised, trying to convince her.

Herodias signed to her daughter to come to her and spoke in her ear. Salome listened and made a gesture of surprise. Herodias spoke to her again, and the young woman inclined her head in agreement.

Salome left the room and returned, after a while semi-naked, wrapped in translucent veils.

How I wish I could be a poet and describe Salome's dance! Her eroticism was sublime! Her veils fell, one by one, softly to the ground like snowflakes until she was completely naked, covered only by her long black hair. She continued to dance, her breasts trembling at the rhythm of her feet, and finally, in ecstasy, she fell to the ground. She remained motionless on the floor for a moment, then stood up, gathered her veils, and ran out of the room.

The guests stood up and applauded enthusiastically for a long time until Salome came back dressed and went straight to the table where Antipas and Herodias were.

"I want you to keep your promise and give me whatever I want," Salome told Antipas.

"What do you want me to give you, Salome?" Antipas asked.

"The head of John the Baptist on a tray" Salome replied, without altering the expression on her face. I looked at Herodias and saw her smile.

I heard murmurs of shock and horror in the room. Salome, undeterred, stood in front of Antipas, waiting for his response.

"Salome, if this is a joke, I must tell you that it is in a deplorable taste," Antipas told her.

"It is not a joke. You promised to give me what I wanted, and John's head is what I want," insisted Salomé.

At Salome's insistence, Antipas agreed and ordered the soldiers to comply with Salome's request. The soldiers left and returned minutes later, bringing a silver tray, on top of which was the decapitated head of John, still bleeding.

The banquet ended in chaos. The guests, horrified, left hurriedly without saying goodbye. Some of them, overcome by horror and nausea, could not control themselves and threw up on the floor carpets.

Amid the chaos, Herodias, with a triumphant smile on her face, continued to stare at the head of the unfortunate John.

Chapter 16
Antipas gives me a job

I was awake almost the whole night. Whenever I closed my eyes, I would see John's bloody head. Only at dawn, I managed to fall asleep, and then I slept until noon.

I got dressed and went to look for Antipas. I found him in the throne room.

"Antipas, can we talk?" I asked.

"Of course, that's what you came for," he replied in the same condescending tone with which he usually spoke to me.

"I'll be frank. I am in a desperate situation. I have lost all my money. You are the only person who can help me."

"Agrippa, I'll also be frank. You were always irresponsible, and it's no wonder you've reached this situation. If it depended only on me, I would not mind if you die of hunger, but I'm married to your sister, and she has asked me to help you. Herodias feels affection for your wife Cypros and loves your children. So, good news! I will help you. I have decided to give you a position with a modest salary. It will not allow you to live as you did with your high born friends in Rome, but you will be able to give your family a roof over their heads and food on the table if you do not waste your money.

"I thank you very much, Antipas. What position is that?

"Inspector of the Tiberias market. It is a position of great responsibility," he said in a mocking tone. "You have to go to the market in the early morning, stay there all day, solve the daily disputes between sellers and buyers, and examine the weights and measures of the merchants."

"Don't you have anything else more appropriate to my social standing? Remember that I grew up with the imperial princes," I said.

"To what social standing do you refer?" Antipas laughed. "You are a beggar, and beggars have no right to choose. If you accept my offer, you can start tomorrow. If you do not accept it, you can leave today with your wife and your children and starve in any hole you might find."

I still don't know how I resisted the temptation to punch his ugly face. I had no choice but to accept his offer, clearly intended to humiliate me.

Chapter 17
The carpenter's son

A few months after the death of John the Baptist, I visited Antipas to give him my periodic report about the market.

Usually, he would read the report, try unsuccessfully to find mistakes, make some mocking remarks, and then dismiss me. This time, to my surprise, he told me to stay. He wanted my opinion about an incident that occurred in his latest visit to Jerusalem.

"Agrippa, as you know, from time to time I go to Jerusalem…"

"To pray in the Temple," I said.

"Don't interrupt me, Agrippa, show some respect. Of course I go to the Temple, but the main purpose of my visits is to stay in the good graces of the governor, Pontius Pilate. If he wanted, he could write terrible things to the Emperor, and I would no longer be the tetrarch. Anyway, his guards arrested a preacher who once was one of John the Baptist's disciples. He was suspected of wanting to be king. Days before, when he entered Jerusalem, crowds acclaimed him enthusiastically. Pilate interrogated him, and found out that this man, Yoshua ben Yosef, the son of a Nazareth carpenter, was a Galilean, so he sent him to me because Galilee is part of my territories. He also sent me a note. Here it is."

To Antipas Herod, the Tetrarch of Galilee
from Pontius Pilate, Governor of Judea
We have been informed that this prisoner proclaims himself to be king of the Jews. I interrogated him but he didn't give me a straight answer. Didn't say yes but also did not deny it. It seems that the kingdom he is talking about is not Judea but a fantasy in some other world.
As he is a Galilean, it is for you to decide what to do with him."

I read it and gave it back to him. He continued with his story.

"I was curious about this man because John the Baptist, when he was in my prison, told me that somebody would come soon much greater than himself. It seems that he was talking about this carpenter's son who, people say, performs miracles. When the man was brought to my presence, I asked him to amuse us by doing some miracles for my dinner guests. He just stood silently looking at us. I realized that Pilate was trying to trick me by getting me to condemn an innocent man. I wasn't going to fall into his trap. I ordered the guards to take the man back to the governor. To make a long story short, the Romans crucified him and put a mocking sign, 'King of the Jews,' on his cross. But the story does not end there. His disciples took the body and buried it in a cave, which, after a couple of days, was found to be empty. People are now saying that he resurrected and someday he will return. What do you think?"

"I think the logical explanation is that the disciples took the body away from the burial cave, and hid it somewhere else," I replied to Antipas.

"Yes, you might be right. Who knows? And now, go back to work. Enough with this chit-chat."

Chapter 18
I am a market inspector

I worked a full year as an inspector in the market of Tiberias, a city founded a few years before by Antipas to be the capital for what he called his "kingdom." He named it Tiberias to ingratiate himself with the Emperor. If he had asked me, I would have told him that the Emperor was utterly indifferent to the fact that in some distant province of his enormous Empire, an insignificant functionary had named a small town in his honor.

My work did not require much effort since the market, which was outside the city walls, was open only two days a week, on Mondays and Thursdays. The stalls sold food, clothing, perfumery, jewelry, and all kind of trinkets. The merchants arrived one hour before opening their stalls and met in an adjacent building used as a synagogue, where they listened to the reading of the Torah and an explanation by a rabbi.

The first time I went to the synagogue, I did it only out of curiosity. To my surprise, the Torah reading was so inspiring, and the rabbi's commentaries were so exciting that I continued attending afterward. I even studied the Torah on my own at home in the days when the market was closed.

When the religious services were over, the merchants opened their cubicles. I spent the day going from one to the other, speaking with each merchant. From time to time, without prior notice, I checked their weights and measures, and, on some occasions, not many, I found irregularities. If these were of small importance, I limited myself to giving the merchant a warning to correct the error. But, if I had the impression that it was intentional fraud, I sent the guilty man to prison. More than once, unscrupulous merchants offered me bribes to turn a blind eye. I always refused them, not because I am an incorruptible saint, but because I suspected they were traps prepared by Antipas, my brother-in-law, to get rid of me and, probably to have an excuse to send me to jail.

Cypros and I rented a small house (that was all we could afford with the small salary that Antipas paid me) on the lake's shore, in a neighborhood where there were more Greeks than Jews. The children seemed to be happy; they adapted quickly to their new conditions, and, in a short time, they spoke more Greek and Hebrew than Latin.

We saw Antipas and Herodias rarely, except during the religious festivities when they invited us to dine in the palace. Antipas took those opportunities to treat me with scorn and contempt.

Back at my house, furious, I would swear never again to accept his invitation, but Cypros advised me not to pay attention to my brother-in-law.

"Calm down, Agrippa, please. Your screams will wake the children. Ignore what Antipas says to you. Also, please remember that you have no other alternative."

One night, Antipas, having drunk more wine than usual, began to insult me.

"Hail, great Agrippa, the intimate friend of the imperial family! You think you're better than me because you were educated in Rome, but the truth is that if it were not for me, you would not have anything to eat. You are now are in your rightful place, alternating with shopkeepers. And believe me, that's more than you deserve."

This time I could not take it anymore. I went to Antipas and slapped him with all my strength. Antipas put his hand to his cheek, reddened by my blow, his face congested with fury, and screamed at me.

"If you were not Herodias' brother, right now, you would end exactly like John the Baptist did! You are fired! Get out of my palace, you and your miserable family! I don't want to see any of you again!" Antipas shouted.

That night, after the children went to sleep, Cypros and I talked about our future.

"What will we do now? We don't have anyone who can help us," Cypros, who until then had been a pillar of strength to me, said, crying.

"That's not true, Cypros. Today, I received a letter from my childhood friend, Flaccus. He is now the Governor of Syria and has invited us to visit him in Antioch, his province's capital. Tomorrow, we will travel. I assure you that my childhood friend will be happy to help us."

I am a market inspector

Chapter 19
In Antioch

I had never been to Antioch before, and seeing it for the first time impressed me. Its population is half a million people, the third most populous city of the Empire, after Rome and Alexandria. Many of Antioch's inhabitants are Jews, and all of them have Roman citizenship, a privilege they do not enjoy in other cities.

The Governor's palace was on an island in the middle of the river. We crossed a bridge at the end of a large avenue lined with 3,200 columns to reach it.

I remembered Lucius from my childhood as a slender boy who kept fit by practicing sports. I was surprised to see that he had become enormously obese. He received me with an affectionate hug, greeted Cypros with respect, and kissed our children.

"Agrippa, I have prepared a furnished house for you, including slaves, in the best Jewish quarter. Tonight you and your family will dine with me, sleep in the palace, and tomorrow I will send you in my carriage to your new home."

During dinner, with the courage that I received drinking the excellent Syrian wine that our host served us, I allowed myself to ask him an indiscreet question.

"Lucius, excuse my frankness, but I never saw you as a politician or diplomat. How did you get the Emperor to name you Governor of Syria?

"Because of my great capacity, of course," he replied, laughing.

"What do you mean by great capacity?" I asked, laughing, too.

"The only one I have, Agrippa. I spent two days and one night, without interruption, eating and drinking with Tiberius. When he saw that he could no longer compete with me, he told me: "Lucius, few men have the capacity that you have shown me. As a reward, I'll name you Governor of Syria.""

325

The house that Lucius had reserved for us was a luxurious mansion, surrounded by gardens of palm trees and ponds where colorful fish swam. We had five slaves at our disposal.

I was delighted to find that the city's largest synagogue was very near. I continued with the habit that I had acquired in Tiberias, to go to the synagogue on Monday and Friday, early in the morning, to listen to the Torah's reading. I started to go also on Saturdays.

I was surprised by the number of Greeks who attended the synagogue. Some of them were proselytes, and others just sympathizers. A group of them proclaimed that a preacher, originally from Nazareth in Judea, was a son of God who had resurrected three days after being crucified and had ascended to heaven.

The Roman Governor, Pontius Pilate, had crucified him because, when he asked the preacher if he considered himself the king of the Jews, the man gave an ambiguous answer and did not deny it.

The belief that gods can have sons and daughters with mortal women is widely held in the Greek and Roman populations of the Empire, but it is unaccepted in the Jewish religion. These discussions in the synagogue should have been peaceful theological debates, but they usually ended with verbal insults and sometimes even physical violence.

I was disgusted by this antagonism and stopped going to the synagogue.

Our stay in Antioch was one of the most peaceful and pleasant times of my life. I did not lack money (Lucius gave me a generous monthly allowance). I had plenty of free time that I generally put to good use reading books, enjoying the company of my wife and children, walking around the city, and having frequent dinners with Lucius, who enjoyed speaking with me about our youthful pranks in Rome.

One day, when I arrived at the palace, Lucius greeted me effusively.

"I have a surprise for you!" he told me. He clapped his hands twice. The servants opened the door, and my brother Aristobulus entered!

We had not seen each other for years. We hugged for a long time. Aristobulus told me that he was living in Judea, but when he heard that I was in Antioch, he decided to visit me. I invited him to stay at our house. That same night, as soon as we finished dinner at the Governor's palace, he came to our home with us.

"Welcome, dear Aristobulus! What a wonderful surprise!" Cypros greeted him when she saw my brother.

"Dear, please prepare a room for Aristobulus. He will stay with us," I told Cypros.

Aristobulus was only one year younger than me, but we never had the same friends during our childhood and youth despite the closeness of our ages. I always had a feeling that he was jealous of me and envious of my popularity in Rome, but I did not care. The affection with which he greeted me made me think that he had changed.

I was, to put it mildly, mistaken!

My error was to place my trust in him. We had long conversations. Perhaps it would be more accurate to say monologues because I told him everything about me without hiding anything while he just listened.

I told him in confidence that some people from Damascus, knowing of my great friendship with Flaccus, the Governor of Syria, Flaccus, had given me a certain amount of money to convince my friend to approve a request they had made.

Aristobulus listened with great interest, but, as usual, he did not say anything. The next day, he told me that he was going out to run some errands but that he would see me that night in the Governor's palace, Lucius having invited both of us for dinner.

I arrived at the palace with the same good humor I always had during my stay in Antioch. At the door, the soldiers, instead of greeting me with the usual respect, grabbed me by my arms and dragged me to a room where Lucius and Aristobulus were waiting for me.

"What happened, Lucius? Why are the soldiers treating me like this?" I asked, bewildered.

"Leave us alone!" The Governor ordered the soldiers and waited for them to go out before speaking to me.

"Aristobulus has informed me that you have received a bribe in exchange for trying to convince me to approve the petition that some people from Damascus have submitted. I appreciate my good name more than anything else in the world, and I will not tolerate the slightest suspicion that I accept bribes. If you were not a childhood friend, I would send you to prison right now, and you would rot there for the rest of your life. Instead, for the sake of our old friendship, I will expel you from the province of Syria. Tomorrow, you and your family will leave Antioch. I never want to see you again."

I did not know what to answer, so I said nothing. I went back to my house and told Cypros that Flaccus had ordered us to leave the next day. The only thing that I took with me from Antioch was the memory of my brother Aristobulus smiling when Lucius threw me out of his palace.

Chapter 20
An overnight stay in prison

I had exhausted all my resources. Antipas would never give me a job again. Lucius Flaccus had told me that our friendship was over. I had no future in Judea or Antioch.

I talked about it with Cypros, who, with her clear thinking, was always my best counselor.

"Agrippa, as I see it, the only possibility you have is to return to Rome and try to ingratiate yourself again with the Emperor and his family. My aunt in Jerusalem loves me. I am sure that she will be happy to receive the children and me in her home. As soon as your situation improves, you can return to Judea or send us a letter to join you in Rome."

Cypros was right. My only hope to survive was to go to Rome and renew my friendship with members of the imperial family.

By lucky coincidence, I received news that an ex-slave of mine, called Marsias, to whom I had given his freedom and who had made a fortune trading with dates from Judea, was in the port of Ptolemais (the Jews call it Acre) for business. I always felt affection for him because of his love and gratitude to me for having given him his freedom.

The next day I said goodbye to my wife and my children with tears in my eyes and traveled to Ptolemais to ask my freedman for a loan.

I met Marsias at the inn where he was staying. We were both pleased to see each other. That night, during dinner, I informed him of my harsh situation.

"I am very sorry for what happened to you, Lord Agrippa. How can I help you?" Marsias asked me.

"I need a loan to buy a ticket in a ship to Rome," I replied.

"Unfortunately, I do not have liquidity at this time. I have invested all my money in merchandise."

I felt a great disappointment. Marsias had been my last chance to solve my situation. If he could not help me, I was lost.

Marsias noticed my disappointment and hastened to reassure me.

"Perhaps there is a solution. Do you know a man called Protos?" he asked me.

I am sure that my face became pale when I heard that name, and I prayed in my mind that Marsias did not notice my discomfort.

"Yes, I know him. He is a freedman of my late mother, Berenice," I replied, pretending calm that I did not feel. I hoped that Proto wouldn't remember that I had never returned a loan he had once given me in Rome. Then, I smiled to myself, remembering all I did to avoid meeting him and my efforts to hide when I saw him on the street.

"He's here in Ptolemais. He just sold for a good profit a marble cargo he brought from Puteoli and has a lot of money with him. If you permit me, I can talk to him and ask him to give you a loan.

Based on my previous experience with Protos, I thought it unlikely that he would be willing to lend me money, but I had no choice.

"If you can convince Proto to lend me money, I would appreciate it," I said.

"I'll bring him to dinner tonight, and you can talk directly to him," Marsias replied.

That night I was waiting in the dining room of the inn when Marsias and Protos entered. I got up from the table to shake his hand. Protos ignored my outstretched hand and sat heavily on a chair.

"I have known many scoundrels in my life, but none like you, Lord Agrippa. You dare to ask me for a loan after you escaped from Rome without paying me what you owed me!" growled Proto.

"It has all been an unfortunate misunderstanding, Proto. Before I left Rome, I looked for you everywhere to repay the loan, but I could not find you. I traveled to Judea with the firm intention of paying you back the money at the very first opportunity. I have a proposal for you.

"A proposal? You want me to give you another loan so that you can disappear again?" Proto mocked.

"I've always enjoyed your sense of humor, Proto," I said, forcing a laugh. "Lend me twenty-five thousand drachmas. I will repay you the loan I owe you with part of that money, and when I see you in Rome, I will reimburse you thirty thousand drachmas. How about it?"

Proto looked at me doubtfully and did not answer.

"Proto, the proposal that Lord Agrippa has made to you is excellent. Accept it," Marsias said.

"Lord Agrippa, I will lend you twenty-five thousand drachmas with two conditions. The first is that Marsias should guarantee the payment, and the second is that you should repay thirty-five thousand drachmas. Less than that, it is not worth the risk," said Proto.

"I accept, Proto, and I thank you," I replied.

Proto gave me the twenty-five thousand drachmas, and, from that money, I gave him the ten thousand drachmas that I owed him from the previous loan. I calculated that the remaining fifteen thousand drachmas would be enough to reach the port of Antedon in Gaza and from there to take a ship to Alexandria. In that city, I would ask for a loan from an acquaintance of mine, a wealthy Jew, a friend of Antonia, my late mother's best friend. In one way or another, I had to return to Rome.

I arrived in Antedon and booked passage on a ship that would sail for Alexandria the next day.

That night, while I was sleeping in an inn, soldiers burst into my room. They allowed me one minute to get dressed, and then they took me, with my hands tied, to the residence of the Roman procurator of Gaza.

"I am Herenius Capito, the procurator of Gaza. Are you Agrippa?" the official asked me.

331

"Yes, sir. Please tell me what is happening. Why have the soldiers brought me to you?"

"There is an arrest warrant for you. It's about an unpaid debt of three hundred thousand drachmas which you borrowed from the imperial treasury and never paid back. Tonight, you will stay in the cell, and tomorrow we will put you on a ship to Rome where you will face justice. Take him to the cell!" the procurator ordered the soldiers.

The soldiers pushed me down to the basement of the procurator's house and threw me into a cell. A soldier stood outside my cell, and the others went back upstairs.

The procurator had made a mistake. He had forgotten to frisk me and take the money that I had hidden in my clothes.

I smiled at the soldier, and he smiled back. Thus encouraged, I talked to him.

"Do you have a family?" I asked him

"Yes, Sir. I have a wife and three children," he answered.

"How much does the procurator pay you?" I asked.

"Ten Drachmas a month," he answered.

"I will give you two hundred and forty drachmas, equivalent to two years of your salary, if you let me escape," I offered.

"Give me three hundred and sixty drachmas, and I'll let you go," he replied.

"All right," I said and handed him the money.

"Now, give me one hundred and forty drachmas more, and I will open the door for you."

"But, I just gave you the three hundred and sixty drachmas that we agreed. Why do you want more money?"

"When the procurator finds out tomorrow that you have escaped, he will lock me in the cell. I must also escape tonight with my family. I will use the additional one hundred and forty drachmas to buy a farm in my native country Idumea. The Romans will never find me."

I gave him the additional one hundred and forty drachmas and looked at him with admiration. This man knew how to plan his life much better than I did!

The soldier opened the cell door. We climbed silently up the stairs, he opened the front door, and we escaped. I went straight to the port. He ran in the opposite direction.

At the port, I boarded the ship where I had contracted the passage. I awoke the captain and offered him 500 drachmas if he sailed at that moment.

Two days later, I arrived in Alexandria, the largest city of Egypt and its most important port.

An overnight stay in prison

Chapter 21
In Alexandria

The purpose of my visit to Alexandria was to request a loan from Alexander, the Alabarch, which is the title of the official in charge of customs at the port.

I had met Alexander many years before when my mother was still alive. Lady Antonia, my mother's best friend, invited my wife Cypros and me to a reception at her house in Rome. She saw us and made us a sign to go to her. Next to Antonia was a young man about my age (at that time, I was thirty years old). He was tall, good-looking, and elegantly dressed in the fashion of Egypt.

"Agrippa, Cypros, I want you to meet my guest of honor, Alexander, who manages the properties I have in Egypt. He is Jewish like you. Alexander, this young man is Prince Agrippa, and the beautiful lady at his side is his wife Cypros," said Antonia,

That evening I talked at length with Alexander. Later encounters confirmed my first impression that he was frank, honest, and intelligent. He told me that Julius Caesar had granted Roman citizenship to his grandfather for services rendered to the general. He also spoke about his family, his two sons, and his brother Philo, a philosopher whose fame had extended throughout the Empire.

Alexander was a modest person. He did not mention it to me, but later I learned that he was the leader of Alexandria's great Jewish community. Not only was Alexander enormously rich but also generous and pious. He donated the silver and gold plates that line the doors of the Temple in Jerusalem. Their beauty cause admiration and amazement to all visitors.

Alexander and I became good friends during his stay in Rome, but I must admit that Cypros made a better impression on him than I did. After Alexander returned to Egypt, Antonia told us Alexander's comment: "Agrippa is a nice man, but Cypros is a true lady".

Although I had never been before in Alexandria, it was easy to find Alexander's house. It was the largest and most imposing mansion in the Jewish quarter of Alexandria. He was delighted to see me and invited me to come to dinner that night.

I was flattered when I arrived at Alexander's residence and found that, besides the family members, I was the only guest. Drora, Alexander's wife, invited us to sit on the couches. We were seven in all, Alexander, Drora, their two teenage sons, Philo, Alexander's older brother, Philo's wife, and me.

What a privilege it was for me to sit next to Philo! I had read several of his works where he argued a common ground between Jewish philosophy (the Torah) and Greek philosophy.

"Master, what are you writing these days?" I asked him.

"I'm writing a biography of Moses," he replied.

"How do you present Moses? As a legislator, preacher, or prophet?"

Philo laughed, and, instead of answering me, he drank a glass of wine and held up three fingers of his right hand to give me to understand that he was presenting Moses in his three facets.

It was evident that Philo did not want to pursue that conversation line, so I turned my attention to Alexander's two sons. The eldest was named Tiberius Julius, and the youngest was Marcus Julius. They were very different, one from the other. Tiberius Julius was tall for his age, beefy, his attitude was aggressive, and his gaze hard. Marcus Julius was of thin build, very handsome, although not a big talker, he followed our conversations with great attention.

"I imagine that when you are older, you will help your father in his administrative functions," I said to Tiberius Julius, who sat to my left.

"You are wrong, sir. As soon as I finish my studies, I will begin my military career. My ambition is to become a general and command an army," he replied.

"Do you want to command the Jewish army?" I said with a smile because Judea was a simple province, and the Jews had no army.

"No, sir. I will enroll in the Roman army," he replied.

I asked him a hypothetical question.

"Let's assume, although we know that it will never happen, that the Jews rebel against the Romans. Would you join the Jewish army?"

"I do not differentiate between rebels, sir. If a province rebels, even if it were Judea, the army must end the rebellion and hang the leaders," he replied.

The look on the boy's face sent chills down my spine. May God protect any rebel if this boy becomes a commander in the Roman army!

I turned away from him and joined the general conversation. Alexander and Philo expressed their concern about the constant tension in Alexandria between Jews and Greeks.

"They hate us for no reason, simply because we are Jews," said Philo.

"If the situation deteriorates, Philo and I must go to Rome to present our complaints to the Emperor," said Alexander.

I praised the delights of the dinner, thanked my hostess for her invitation, and said goodbye to all. Alexander called me aside.

"Come tomorrow at noon, and we will talk about your affairs," he told me.

I arrived the next day more punctual than I have ever been. Alexander received me in the room where he conducted his business. I told him everything that had happened to me since his visit to Rome several years ago.

"To sum up, dear Alexander, I have concluded that my only chance of getting ahead and improving my position is to regain the favor and friendship of the imperial family, especially Tiberius," I said.

"I understand you clearly. Agrippa. How can I help you?" he asked me.

"You can help me by lending me money. I need to buy suitable clothes and give gifts, especially to the freedmen of Tiberius. The freedmen are the ones who are in the best position to help me, but they would not do it for purely altruistic reasons."

"How much money do you need?"

"Two hundred thousand drachmas, maybe more," I replied.

"Agrippa, I am going to speak to you with complete frankness, and I ask you not to be offended. You are irresponsible and wasteful. I would be equally irresponsible if I would lend you money.

"Alexander, please," I interrupted him desperately.

"Let me finish. I will not lend you the money, but I will lend it to your wife, Cypros. She is a virtuous and prudent woman. I know that she will repay on time any loan she receives. As soon as she signs the loan document, I will put the 200,000 drachmas at your disposal.

"But, Cypros is in Judea," I protested.

"Send her a note to come to Alexandria."

That same day, I sent a messenger to Jerusalem with a note to Cypros explaining the situation and asking her to immediately come with the children to Alexandria.

During the weeks that elapsed until the arrival of Cypros, I visited the Library of Alexandria daily. I enjoyed reading the scrolls and listening to the philosophers' lectures.

Cypros and the children finally arrived in Alexandria, and that same day, in the afternoon, we all went to Alexander's house.

"Cypros," Alexander told my wife, "Agrippa has asked me to lend him two hundred thousand drachmas. For obvious reasons that you know better than me, it would not be smart for me to lend your husband any money. However, I know that this loan might help Agrippa recover the position he deserves as a king's grandson if he handles the money wisely. Therefore, dear Cypros, I am willing to make the loan, not to him but to you. I know that I can fully trust that one day when circumstances permit, you will return the money."

"I thank you with all my heart, Alexander, for the trust you place in me, and I promise that I will repay the loan. I cannot tell you when, but you will receive the full amount plus the interest that you think it is fair to charge," answered Cypros.

"This loan is interest-free, Cypros. Members of the same family do not charge interest to each other," Alexander said, smiling.

"What do you mean by 'members of the same family'?" I asked him.

"It means that I have the honor of asking you for the hand of your daughter Berenice for my son Marcus Julius. Both are still children, so, for now, we would only celebrate the engagement. Do you agree?"

I was bewildered. It is a tradition in our family to marry only sons or daughters of kings or our relatives. Alexander was not a king, and he was not a relative either. In my wife's expression, I saw that she understood the same thing I did: Berenice's marriage to Marcus Julius was the condition that Alexander demanded to lend us the money.

I looked at Cypros, she nodded slightly, and I turned to Alexander.

"Dear friend, your unexpected proposal honors us and fills us with happiness. We accept in the name of Berenice."

Alexander and his wife Drora organized a big party to celebrate their son's engagement with our daughter. We agreed that the marriage would take place five years later when Berenice would be twelve years old.

The next day, Cypros and I went to Alexander's house to sign the loan document and receive the money.

I counted the money that Alexander gave me and was surprised to see that it was only fifty thousand drachmas.

"Alexander, there's an error. Cypros has just signed a document for a loan of two hundred thousand drachmas, but you have given me only fifty thousand," I said.

"No, my son's future father-in-law. It is not an error. I want to spare you the temptation to spend everything immediately. Take this letter and give it to my representative in Puteoli. He will give you one hundred and fifty thousand drachmas that will complete the amount of the loan."

Cypros and I returned to our inn. I gave her forty thousand drachmas that I hoped would be enough for her and the children until the day when I would be able to bring them to Rome.

The next day I boarded a ship that took me to Puteoli.

Chapter 22
My new best friend: Caligula

The first thing I did in Puteoli was to go to the house of Alexander's representative and give him the letter from his employer that I had brought with me. The man read it and gave me the one hundred fifty thousand drachmas that completed the loan that Alexander granted us.

With that money, I could afford to stay in the best inn in Puteoli and buy clothes that corresponded to a person of my rank.

For the next two days, I did not leave the inn. I spent all my time writing a letter to Tiberius, who, I had been informed, was on the island of Capri. I wrote, read what I had written, corrected it, read it again, wrote again. It had to be perfect. My future depended on my writing skills.

I have not kept a copy of my correspondence, but I clearly remember that in the letter, I offered Tiberius my services and asked permission to visit him in Capri.

A week later, I received the answer from Tiberius. The kindness and affection he expressed surpassed my most optimistic hopes. He wrote that he was happy to hear about my return and invited me to come to Capri, "I want to have the pleasure of seeing you again".

Immediately, I hired a boat that took me from Puteoli to the island, a trip of only a few hours.

Tiberius received me with warm friendliness. He asked me about my wife Cypros and wanted to know how Flaccus had treated me during my stay in Antioquia. I did not want to damage the reputation of a person who had been my friend during my youth, so I did not mention to Tiberius that Flaccus had expelled me from the city with a flimsy pretext. I only said that Flaccus could not have treated me better.

"You must be tired, dear Agrippa. Sleep in one of the palace rooms tonight, and tomorrow, we will have lunch together and will talk more in detail," Tiberius said.

The boat trip had indeed tired me. Again I thanked Tiberius for receiving me, and I said goodnight. One of the palace slaves took me to the room that the Emperor had reserved for me.

I slept until almost lunchtime. I bathed, got dressed, and went to the palace dining room. Tiberius was already there, sitting on one of the couches.

"Good morning, Caesar," I greeted him.

To my surprise, the kindness with which Tiberius had treated me the night before was gone. He grabbed a piece of paper from the table in front of him and waved it in the air.

"Today, I received this letter sent by Herenius Capito. Do you know who he is?" he asked me.

"I know him. He is the Gaza Procurator," I answered.

"Capito has written me that you owe three hundred thousand drachmas that you borrowed from the imperial treasury. He says that when he demanded that you pay the debt, you fled like a fugitive. Don't come back until you pay your debt! And now, get out!" he shouted at me.

I hurried out of the room, congratulating myself on my good luck for not having been sent to prison. I packed my things and took a boat to Puteoli, and from there, I traveled by carriage to Rome.

The only person who could help me was Lady Antonia, who not only had been my mother's best friend but was also the widow of the Emperor's late brother.

Antonia received me with great affection, hugged me, and kissed my cheek. She listened sympathetically to the account of all that had happened to me in Judea and the monetary misunderstanding that had provoked Tiberius' anger. When I finished telling her about my adventures, she expressed her opinion.

"Tiberius is very strict about the imperial treasure. If you do not return the money, he will never allow you to see him again. The only solution is for you to return that loan," she said.

"In that case, I'm lost because I cannot return the loan. I don't have any money," I said.

"Agrippa, I clearly understand that Tiberius' goodwill is the key to your future. I want to tell you that my friendship with your dear late mother Berenice and your disinterested friendship with my poor son Claudius give me enough reason to help you. I will lend you the three hundred thousand drachmas, you will pay the debt, and Tiberius will have nothing against you," Antonia told me.

I could not contain my emotion. Tears ran down my cheeks as I expressed my gratitude. Antonia called the freedman who administered her accounts and asked him to bring her three hundred thousand drachmas.

I traveled back to Capri immediately. I handed over the money to the imperial treasurer and asked him to report the payment to Tiberius.

The Emperor called me the next day.

"I'm glad that you have solved that little problem. I'll explain why I invited you to come to Capri. You were the best friend of my son Drusus; may he rest in peace. He left a son, my grandson Tiberius Gemelus. I want you to be his friend and to be with him all the time. I have made him and his cousin Caligula, the son of my late nephew Germanicus, my heirs. Tonight, during dinner, I'll introduce you to the two boys.

During the dinner, I observed the two young people. Caligula was twenty-five years old. Tiberius Gemelus was seven or eight years younger than his cousin. Apart from the gap in their ages, they differed from one another in their physique, intelligence, and character.

Tiberius Gemelus, supposedly the son of my friend Drusus, was, according to persistent rumors that I found credible, the son of Sejanus, the lover of Livilla, the wife of the late Drusus.

Both Sejanus, strangled by Tiberius' order, and Livilla, whose mother Antonia locked her in a room and starved to death, had a tragic end. It was not surprising that Tiberius Gemelus suffered from a melancholy that made it difficult for him to have friends. Physically, he was unattractive. He was short, fat, with uneven, prominent teeth and long, untidy hair. Regarding his intelligence, I am sorry to say, I always had the impression that Tiberius Gemelus was not normal. It was difficult to understand him because he babbled instead of speaking clearly. When I did understand him, I never heard him talk about anything that was not food. Without going into details, he was not meticulous, to put it mildly, when it came to personal body hygiene.

Caligula, on the other hand, was a handsome young man. He was intelligent, cultured, friendly, easy-going, and energetic. Talking with him about any subject was a pleasure. Tiberius had banished his mother and brothers, and they died in exile. Caligula saved himself by moving to Capri five years before I met him.

To the surprise of many, Caligula never expressed resentment against the Emperor for his mother and his brothers' death. His calmness did not stop some people from circulating rumors that the young man was a great actor who, understanding that he could end up dead like his mother and brothers, secretly hid his hurt.

During the following months, I spent time with Tiberius Gemelus to ingratiate myself with Tiberius, but even more time with Caligula. I formed a deep friendship with him, despite our age difference.

A freedman named Talus, seeing my great friendship with Caligula, whom everyone believed would be the next Emperor, asked me to allow him to make me a loan of one million drachmas.

I allowed him.

I used this nice sum of money to repay the loan that Lady Antonia had given me, buy a house in Palatine Hill, and bring my wife and children back from Judea.

Everything was going great for me until I made a grave mistake that could have cost me my life. I was with Caligula in my carriage when I said something that people might misinterpret. Eutychus, one of my freedmen, was our driver. I had known him for many years and considered him to be decent and loyal and therefore did not mind that he was listening to our conversation.

"Do you have any idea what I ask of God in my daily prayers?" I asked Caligula.

"I don't have the slightest idea. I did not even know that you pray to your god daily," Caligula answered, laughing.

"Well, I'll tell you. I pray that Tiberius will hasten to leave this world and that you will be named Emperor in his place."

Caligula noticed that Eutychus had heard what I had said and was watching us. He turned pale and immediately criticized me.

"Agrippa, I am going to consider that what you have said was a joke, since otherwise, I would have to denounce you. I never want to hear you say something like that again!"

I thought the incident was over without consequences. A month later, I realized that Eutychus had stolen my best clothes and fled to Pompeya. I filed a complaint against him; he was captured and brought before the Prefect of the city.

"I have something vital to inform the Emperor. It has to do with his security," Eutychus told the Prefect.

The Prefect sent him chained to Capri. Luckily for me, Tiberius believed in not doing today what you can do tomorrow and not doing tomorrow what you can do the day after tomorrow.

Tiberius used to say that he did not immediately judge the prisoners whose crimes deserved the death penalty. He preferred to keep them imprisoned since the lack of freedom and uncertainty was a punishment worse than immediate death.

Eutychus would stay in prison until a day far in the future when the Emperor would be willing to listen to him. He would have continued to rot in jail indefinitely if I had not made a second mistake.

Eager that Eutychus should receive punishment for stealing my clothes, I persuaded Lady Antonia to ask Tiberius to judge the thief without waiting any longer.

Tiberius, who respected his brother's widow (he admired her for her virtues, appreciated her intelligence and common sense, and was deeply grateful to her for informing him of Sejanus' conspiracy), listened to her request but warned her.

"I will judge Eutychus because you asked me to do so, but, take into account that, if Eutychus has falsely accused Agrippa, the time he has spent in prison is enough punishment. However, if the accusation is true, the person I will punish will be Agrippa," Tiberius said to Antonia.

Tiberius ordered Macron, the Prefect of the Praetorian Guard who had succeeded Sejanus in the post, to bring Eutychus to his presence.

"What accusations do you have against a man who has given you your freedom?" Tiberius asked Eutychus.

Eutychus, demonstrating an impressive memory, quoted word for word what I had said to Caligula. I denied it, of course, but Tiberius believed Eutychus' version, not mine, probably because he knew that I had not fulfilled his request to befriend his grandson Tiberius Gemelus and, to the contrary, I preferred to spend most of my time with Caligula.

"Arrest that man!" Tiberius ordered Macron and left the room.

Macrón, who knew of my friendship with Caligula, Tiberius' heir, assumed that Tiberius had meant Eutychus and took him back to prison.

That afternoon, while I was taking a stroll through Palatine Hill, I came across Tiberius and Macron.

"Why is that man free? I ordered you to arrest him!" exclaimed Tiberius.

"Who?" Macron asked and looked around.

"Agrippa, imbecile!" Tiberius shouted in exasperation.

I knelt before the Emperor and pleaded with him.

"Caesar, please pardon me for the sake of my friendship with Drusus, your late son, and with your grandson Tiberius Gemelus, whom I have educated to be your worthy successor."

My arguments did not succeed in changing his mind.

Macron ordered the guards to grab me. They tied me up, took me to the prison, chained my legs, and put me in the same cell where Eutychus was.

The guards told Eutychus that he was free to go. The scoundrel looked at me with an expression of hate mixed with mockery. I never saw him again. Did Caligula have him killed? I don't know. I wasn't interested enough to ask Caligula.

One day, when it was scorching, and I was dying of thirst, I saw one of Caligula's slaves, named Taumastus, carrying water in a jar. I called him to come closer to my cell.

"I beg you; please give me a drink of water."

He gave me the jar, despite the guard's threatening looks, and I drank until I was satiated.

"Taumastus, I will never forget what you just did. If I ever get out of this prison, I'll ask Caligula to give you your freedom.

(I am happy to say that I kept my promise. Caligula freed him when he became Emperor. Years later, when I was the king of Judea, I asked Taumastus to come to Jerusalem and appointed him administrator of all my properties. In my will, I have asked my children to keep him in that job).

Sometimes, depending on their mood, the guards allowed the prisoners to leave the cells and spend some time in the prison yard. On one of those occasions, I stood under a tree, on one of whose branches an owl had perched. I heard a German prisoner jabbering to a guard standing nearby, about me, or so I assumed because he was pointing with his finger and making gestures.

The guard must have understood him because I heard his answer. "He is a Jewish prince".

The German approached and started talking to me in his language.

"Excuse me, but I do not speak German," I told him.

Another German joined us.

347

"I can be your interpreter," he offered.

The first German spoke to me in his incomprehensible language, and the second translated his words to Latin.

"I regret that you are now in prison. I have had a vision which I will reveal to you. I had a dream where I saw an owl placing a crown on a man's head. Now that I see you, I recognize you as the man I saw in my dream. You will be freed soon, you will ascend to the highest dignity, you will be envied by all those who pity you today, and you will be loved by your people. But, remember, when you see this owl again, you will die. The only thing I ask in return for what I have just told you is that, when you are released, please do everything to get me released as well."

I liked the German's predictions. Who wouldn't? But I could not stop laughing.

"Thank you for your words. I don't believe in predictions or owls, but you've put me in a good mood, and I'm happy to promise that, if I am released, I'll do everything I can to set you free as well."

Suddenly, the treatment that I received in prison changed for the better. I found out that this was because Lady Antonia had told Macron, the Prefect of the Praetorian guard, to treat me well. The soldiers treated me with courtesy, allowed me to bathe daily, and authorized my friends' visits. The centurion, who previously had seemed to feel a personal antipathy against me, treated me now as a friend. Silas, my childhood friend, loyal and devoted as always, and my freedman Marsias brought me food I liked and clothes to change frequently. This went on for six months.

I would still be in prison, or worse if Tiberius had not died. The doctors initially said that his illness was not serious, but his condition worsened day by day to the point that he realized that he didn't have many days left to live. He decided that he would let the gods choose who would be his main heir, Tiberius Gemelus or Caligula, depending on which of the two would be the first to come and greet him the next day. He preferred

Tiberius Gemelus because he thought that his late son Drusus had been the boy's father. He did not give any credit to the rumors that attributed the young man's paternity to Sejanus, the former chief of the Praetorian Guard, who had been the lover of Drusus' wife.

Tiberius spoke that evening with Tiberius Gemelus' tutor and told him to bring him his pupil the next day very early in the morning. Upon awakening, he ordered his servant to bring in the young man he would find outside the room. The servant went out, saw Caligula, told him "the Emperor calls you", and opened the Emperor's room's door for him.

Seeing Caligula, Tiberius realized that his grandson would lose the Empire and, probably, also his life.

"Caligula, in your hands, I will leave the Empire. I ask you to protect your cousin Tiberius Gemelus, who can be of great help to you in the administration of the State. If he dies, the entire burden would be on your shoulders, a situation that would be very dangerous," Tiberius begged the young man.

"I promise you that I will always protect Tiberius Gemelus, and he will be my right hand in everything I do," Caligula replied.

Unexpectedly, Tiberius began to improve, but five days later, he died. Rumors circulated that Macron, the Prefect of the praetorian guard, had suffocated him with a pillow, instigated by Caligula.

Marsias, my freedman, came running to the prison to inform me of the news.

"The lion is dead," he told me in the Hebrew language so that those who were close would not understand him.

I embraced him with great joy. The centurion, who was in charge of watching me, and with whom I had become friends, saw my reaction and asked me why I was in such good humor.

I answered vaguely, but he insisted on knowing the cause of my joy, and I told him that Tiberius had died. The centurion immediately brought a bottle of wine and two glasses to toast with me and celebrate the news.

While we were drinking, a soldier arrived and informed the centurion that Tiberius was alive and recovering from his disease.

The centurion, fearful for his life, hit me and yelled at me.

"Do you think you can lie to me by saying that our beloved Emperor has died and not receive a punishment? You will pay for this slander with your head," he told me and ordered the soldier to chain me to the wall and to increase the number of guards outside my cell.

The next day it was confirmed that Tiberius had died. Caligula ordered his guards to unchain me and take me to my house. There, I remained under custody because, as Caligula explained to me later, granting me immediate freedom would have given the impression that he disrespected the memory of the late Emperor.

Caligula brought the body of Tiberius to Rome, where a sumptuous funeral took place. After fulfilling that obligation, Caligula went to the Senate, where the Senators applauded him and proclaimed him Emperor.

Two weeks later, Caligula sent for me. I bathed, shaved, changed my clothes, and went to his palace. He hugged me when he saw me, put a diadem on my head, and gave me a gold chain of the same weight as the iron chain that had restrained me in my cell.

"Agrippa, I have good news for you. Your uncle Philip, the tetrarch of Iturea, Traconitis, and the Golan, has passed away. I name you the king of those territories," Caligula told me.

"Caesar, I'm very grateful! I beg you to let me stay in Rome for a few months, to help you as much as possible. Then, I will travel to my new domains." He agreed to my request.

The first thing that Caligula did as Emperor was to declare null the testament of Tiberius due to the clause where the deceased had named Tiberius Gemelus as co-heir to the Empire. His argument, accepted unanimously by the Senate, was that Tiberius was already senile when he wrote the will.

350

A few months later, Caligula sentenced Tiberius Gemelus to death for allegedly conspiring against him.

Caligula, initially, was a wise and popular Emperor who won the respect of Romans and foreigners. Wherever he went, people cheered him and expressed their love and admiration. Not even Augustus was as beloved as Caligula was during the first year of his rule.

The list of the numerous acts he did in favor of the people during his first year could fill up a book. He reduced the taxes that Tiberius had imposed, banished sexual offenders, and held public shows, such as gladiatorial battles; brought the corpses of his mother and his brothers to Rome and gave them an honorable burial; allowed the publication of the history books that the Senate had prohibited; published the accounts of the Empire, a custom introduced by Augustus that Tiberius had not followed; appointed additional judges to do justice faster; established contests of eloquence; finished the construction of monuments and buildings that Tiberius had left incomplete; started the construction of an aqueduct; rebuilt the temples of the gods that were in ruins.

Caligula was generous with the people and with the army. He granted large sums of money to the Praetorian Guard and thus won its support.

He destroyed the documents where the names of those accused of treason were registered, declared that treason trials were a thing of the past, and allowed the exiles to return to Rome.

I stayed with him one year as his counselor until I considered that the time had come to go to Judea and assume the throne of Iturea, Traconitis, and the Golan.

I said goodbye to Caligula, promising to return as soon as I could leave my kingdom's administration in good hands.

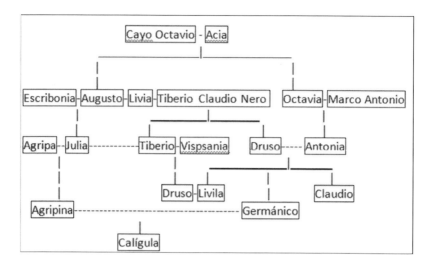

Caligula's genealogy

Chapter 23
A stopover in Alexandria

Caligula placed one of the Roman army ships at my disposal and recommended that I not travel directly to Caesarea but to make a stopover in Alexandria, advice that coincided with what I had already decided. My daughter Berenice had turned twelve, and it was time to celebrate her wedding with Marcus Julius, Alexander's son.

Cypros and the children sailed ahead of me and waited in the port for my arrival.

When I disembarked, there she was, as beautiful as ever. With Cypros at my side, followed by an escort of bodyguards who wore shining armor of silver and gold, we rode white horses down the broad avenue that runs from the harbor to Alexander's mansion. Thousands of Jews, standing on the sides of the route, applauded and cheered me.

The next day, the Greek population of Alexandria, to show their hatred of Jews, mocked my parade by marching on the same avenue behind a mentally disabled man who wore on his head a paper crown,

Alexander, his wife, and his two sons welcomed us outside the gate of their house. I dismounted my horse and hugged him.

"Dear friend, we have come to celebrate the wedding of our children," I said to him.

Alexander answered that he was delighted to see us, but his face showed sadness. I asked him what was wrong. He told me that the Governor of Egypt, Aulus Avilius Flaccus (a distant relative of my ex-friend, the Governor of Syria), hated Jews obsessively. The Governor had destroyed the synagogues, arrested and humiliated the community leaders, and allowed, even worse, incited the populace to attack Jewish neighborhoods, vandalize, steal, rape and murder innocent people for the "crime" of being Jewish.

"Dear Alexander, forget about that man. Tiberius named him Governor, but he is dead. Today I will send a note to Emperor Caligula denouncing the actions of Flaccus and, you may rest assured, his days are numbered," I said to Alexander.

A few weeks later, I am pleased to say that soldiers, sent by Caligula, arrested Flaccus and brought him to Rome. He was tried, sentenced, and executed.

We celebrated Berenice's wedding with Marcus Julius with a party whose splendor had never before been seen in Alexandria. I am told that still today they talk in the city about my daughter's wedding.

Two weeks later, with Cypros and the children (excepting, of course, Berenice, who stayed in Alexandria with her husband), I boarded our ship and continued our trip to Caesarea. From there, we traveled to Jerusalem, where the people gave me a tremendous welcome.

Chapter 24
Herodias pays for her envy

I went straight to the Temple and donated the gold chain that Caligula had given me when he released me from prison.

People, who had known me in unfortunate times, were amazed at how my circumstances had improved so radically.

I stayed with Cypros and the children in the palace that my grandfather, King Herod, built. I appointed a new High Priest to the Temple and traveled with my friend Silas (the childhood friend who had so loyally served me during the months I was in prison) throughout the northern territories that Caligula had granted me.

Back in Jerusalem, I offered daily sacrifices in the Temple, a pious behavior that the people highly praised.

My sister Herodias and her husband Antipas came to Jerusalem, and Cypros invited them to dine with us in the palace. It was an ideal opportunity for me to show them that their poor relative, whom they had treated as a beggar, had returned as a monarch. I received them wearing a splendid purple royal robe, a gold crown on my head, and all the other paraphernalia that kings wear.

That day was one of the happiest of my life. I enjoyed immensely seeing how Herodias and Antipas' faces showed the envy and jealousy they felt and couldn't hide.

At the end of the dinner, I put at their disposal my royal carriage to take them to the place where they were staying. I called the coachman aside and ordered him to listen carefully to the couple's conversation and inform me in detail everything they said.

"Your Majesty," the coachman informed me the next day, "at first, they did not speak to each other. Then, the lady began shouting at her husband. She said, 'That miserable adventurer, who could not even be an inspector in a market, is now a king, and you, the son of a great king, are only the tetrarch of a minuscule territory."

355

"What did the husband answer?" I asked the coachman.

"The gentleman said to his wife, 'What shall I do!'

The lady was furious and screamed at him: 'That has always been your problem! You never know what to do! Well, I'll tell you what to do. We will go from here directly to Caesarea, and we will hire a ship to take us to Rome, and there you will talk to the Emperor, you will give him as much money as necessary, and you will tell him that you deserve to be the king of Judea, not Agrippa, that scoundrel!"

I wrote a letter to Caligula where I denounced Antipas for allying himself with the Parthians against Rome (that accusation, true or false, always gets a result). I also informed that Antipas had armament for more than seventy thousand men in his Tiberias palace. I handed the letter to Fortunato, one of my freedmen, and gave him gifts for the Emperor.

Fortunato traveled immediately to Caesarea, and, by ironic coincidence, he, Antipas, and Herodias took the same ship to Puteoli.

Herodias and Antipas, upon their arrival, were informed that Caligula was in his summer palace in Baiae, a nearby resort. They hired a carriage, and Fortunato followed them in another vehicle.

That day Caligula was in an excellent mood. Being in Baiae had brought back to his mind the memory of what an astrologer had said to him many years before, "Your chances, young man, of becoming Emperor are no bigger than your chances of crossing the waters of the Gulf of Baiae on a horse,"

Caligula, an ingenious man, had given orders to join together many boats and place platforms on them, forming a floating bridge between Puteoli and Baiae. That morning, mounted on his magnificently harnessed horse, he had crossed the Gulf of Baiae over the bridge, from one end to the other.

In the palace, everyone congratulated the Emperor. The astrologer was fortunate to have died years before because he would have become the entire Empire's laughingstock if he had still been alive.

Caligula received Antipas with all due courtesy and invited him to sit down. Antipas mentioned that he wished to give the Emperor a sum of money. It was at that moment that my freedman Fortunato, who had followed Antipas to the palace, entered the room and handed the Emperor my letter.

Caligula read my letter carefully and looked calmly at Antipas, who, confused, did not know what was happening.

"Is it true that you have a huge amount of weapons in your palace?" Caligula asked Antipas. Antipas could not deny it since everyone in Tiberias knew about it.

"That proves that you intend to rebel. From this moment, you are no longer a tetrarch, and your territory will be part of the kingdom of Agrippa. Give Agrippa the money you wanted to give me. You and your wife will go into exile in Lyon, a city in the province of Gaul."

"My wife Herodias is Agrippa's sister," Antipas told him, hoping that the mention of kinship would convince Caligula to cancel the sanctions he had imposed on him.

"Because of the affection I have for Agrippa, his sister Herodias does not need to go with you into exile," Caligula replied.

"Sir, I am very grateful to you for your generous gesture, but I want to be with my husband," Herodias told him.

"That is fine with me. You will go with Antipas to Lyon, and your properties will belong to Agrippa."

Fortunato returned to Judea and told me that Caligula had sent Antipas and Herodias to exile. I had mixed feelings. On the one hand, I was happy that my dominions had increased, but, at the same time, I felt sorry for my sister. However, I believed that God, acting through Caligula, had imposed a justified punishment on her and her husband for the sin of envy and for the way they treated me when I was down in my luck.

A few months later, I received a report that worried me very much. Caligula had been seriously ill, and, although he had recovered, he was no longer the same person he had been

357

before. He had become unstable, unpredictable, and murderous.

I decided that it was better to be in Rome, next to Caligula, rather than in Jerusalem, too far from him.

I appointed Silas to be the Governor of my territories during my absence and chose capable people to assist him.

I went to Rome with Cypros and the children.

Chapter 25
Caligula's madness

It was a shock to see Caligula after almost a year. His physical deterioration was horrific. He was almost entirely bald, with only a few hairs remaining on the sides of his head. He was thin as a skeleton. He walked, stooped, and dragged his feet. He looked much older than his age. But the worst change was in his personality. It was impossible to recognize in him the young handsome, intelligent, friendly, and good-humored man who had been my friend. His gaze was evil, and a constant grimace had replaced his previous smile. I saw him once practicing gestures in front of a mirror that, he explained to me, would cause terror.

I am not a medical doctor or a priest, so I could not diagnose if Caligula had become crazy or was possessed by a demon.

When I went to visit Caligula, the first thing I saw was a statue of Jupiter in the anteroom of the Emperor's private room. I noticed with surprise that Caligula had replaced the god's head with a replica of his own I was staring at the statue when Caligula came out of his room. Instead of greeting me, he went to the statue and spoke to it in a threatening tone.

"Prove your power or fear mine!"

Seeing that the statue did not answer him, Caligula laughed out loud with a laugh that I could only call devilish. He saw me and hugged me.

"Agrippa, my dear friend, welcome!" he shouted/ He put his mouth next to my ear and whispered, "I am now a god, and the moon shares my bed."

"I've heard that, Caesar," I replied, fearing what his reaction would be if I disagreed.

"I had a wonderful dream. Do you want me to tell you what I dreamed?"

"Yes Caesar, please."

"I dreamed that all Rome had one single neck and that I cut it off with my sword!"

"A very interesting dream, Caesar, but now I beg your pardon. I must go and settle some issues."

"Tonight, we will have a banquet to celebrate my great victory over the god Neptune. I want you to come," he invited me.

"Of course, Caesar! I cannot miss this wonderful event," I said.

The "great victory," I was told, had taken place a few days before. Caligula had gathered the army and had marched to the seashore. There, he ordered the soldiers to collect all the shells they found in the sand, bring them to Rome and deposit them in the Capitol. That was his triumph over Neptune.

I went to the palace that night without my wife because I had been informed about Caligula's new habit. He would choose the wife of a Senator, consul, or another guest of importance during dinner and take her to another room. He would comment on the woman's sexual performance after returning with her, either praising or criticizing.

All the guests were sitting on the couches when, at the sound of trumpets, Caligula entered. We all stood up. He was dressed bizarrely. He wore a silk tunic with short sleeves, covered with embroidery and precious stones. He wore numerous bracelets on his arms. Over his tunic, he wore Alexander the Great's armor that he had taken out of the conqueror's tomb in Alexandria. On one foot, he had a military boot and, on the other, a woman's sandal. A beard of gold threads hung from his face, and, in his hand, he carried a trident, symbol of his triumph over Neptune.

It struck me that Lady Antonia, Caligula's grandmother, was not at the banquet. I asked the man who sat next to me about her, and he answered in a low voice that Caligula had had her killed.

My friend Claudius, whom I had not seen in years, was sitting near Caligula, a place of honor that was rightly his because he was the younger brother of Germanicus, Caligula's father. I noticed that Caligula did not treat him with the honor and courtesy that one should treat one's uncle (although not in my case, as all my uncles were rascals). On the contrary, Caligula treated him cruelly. He mocked him and imitated the stuttering that had returned to Claudius.

I approached my old friend and greeted him. We agreed to see each other the next day, and we did so. After a few weeks, our renewed friendship became as close as it had been years before.

Regarding Caligula, I avoided going to the palace. Whenever I was invited to dinner, I would sit in a corner and tried not to be noticed by Caligula, which could be dangerous, even fatal. On one occasion, during a splendid feast, Caligula suddenly began to laugh out loud; two Senators who were sitting next to him asked him why he was laughing.

"I find it very funny to think that with just a signal, I can have you both strangled right now," Caligula answered. Tears ran down his cheeks from so much laughing.

I was invited to a wedding, which Caligula also attended. When the dinner was over, he ordered the guards to bring the bride to the palace. He kept her in his bedroom for a couple of days and then threw her out.

One time, he ordered three Senators to come to the palace at midnight. They arrived overwhelmed with terror; the guards made them sit in the palace theater. Suddenly, to the sound of flutes and tambourines, dressed in the tunic worn by actors, Caligula entered, danced, and then left without saying a word. The Senators were then allowed to return to their homes.

The greatest scandal was his incestuous relationship with his sister, Drusilla, who he openly presented as his wife.

The other great love of his life was a horse called Incitatus. Caligula built a marble stable for him, dressed him in purple robes, adorned him with pearl necklaces, and had slaves serving the animal. One of the palace servants told me that Caligula intended to appoint the horse as consul of Rome.

The people began to hate him when he imposed new taxes and appropriated the homes and properties of individuals who had been killed by his order for no reason at all.

Caligulas's madness

Chapter 26
Apion incites hatred
against the Jews of Alexandria

Two delegations arrived from Alexandria and asked to speak with Caligula. Philo, the brother of my in-law Alexander, presided over the Jewish delegation sent to complain against the persecutions suffered by the Jews of that city.

Apion, a Hellenized Egyptian famous for his knowledge of Homer and his obsession with the Jews, presided over the other delegation. The purpose of their trip to Rome was to ask the Emperor to annul all the rights and privileges granted to the Jews of Alexandria by Augustus.

Apion, whose enormous vanity exceeded his great oratory talent (he proclaimed himself superior to Plato and Aristotle, the greatest philosophers of ancient Greece), wanted to incite Caligula against the Jews. He denounced to Caligula that the Jews not only refused to erect statues of the Emperor but that they were unwilling to swear by the Emperor's sacred name.

After Apion expressed his hate against the Jews, I convinced Caligula that the Jews were loyal to the Empire and him personally. Apion returned to Alexandria, defeated.

Before the illness that changed him so radically, Caligula never expressed hatred for the Jews. But, afterward, he was not the same Caligula I had befriended. He had convinced himself that he was a god. That was not a problem for the Romans, who have numerous gods, and they do not care if an Emperor declares himself to be a god. However, that is not the case for the Jews, who believe in God, invisible and all-powerful, and will never accept a human being as a divine being. I feared that Caligula's obsession could bring dire consequences to the Jews of the Empire.

Caligula received a report sent by Publius Petronius, the Roman Governor of Syria, accusing the Jews of having destroyed an altar for the imperial cult built by the Greek population of Jamnia in Judea.

Caligula considered the destruction of the altar to be a personal insult. He immediately wrote to Petronius, ordering him to build a monumental statue of the Emperor, dressed as Jupiter, and place it in the Temple of Jerusalem. And, if the Jews objected, he authorized him to use his legions to enforce the decree.

Petronius had made a study of the Jewish religion and knew that the attempt to desecrate the Temple with a statue would cause a rebellion. He instructed the sculptors, who were in Sidon, not to rush to finish the sculpture. He marched with his legions to Ptolemais, where he confronted a massive demonstration of Jews protesting Caligula's decree.

Petronius left his army at Ptolemais and went to Tiberias, the capital of Galilee. The Jews of the city told him that they would never accept the presence of a statue in the Temple and would cease to cultivate their land if he did not cancel the decree.

Petronius withdrew his legions from Ptolemais and, to gain time, wrote to Caligula asking him to change his mind because the situation in Judea could become dangerous.

I found out what was happening and went to talk with Caligula. It was fortunate for me that I found him lucid.

"Caesar, I understand that the Jews in Judea object to the placing of your statue in the Jerusalem Temple. May I suggest a possible solution? The Jews could promise not to interfere with the cult of the Emperor in other cities in exchange for not having a statue in their Temple."

Caligula accepted my proposal and sent a letter to Petronius canceling his previous instructions.

I breathed a sigh of relief, believing that the danger had passed, but a few weeks later,

Caligula wrote a letter to Petronius, the Roman Governor of Syria, ordering him to commit suicide for not complying with the Emperor's order to place his statue in the Temple of Jerusalem.

That same day, in the afternoon, Caligula was assassinated by a group of conspirators of the Praetorian Guard. (I will tell more about this in the next pages),

When I learned of Caligula's death, the first thing I did was write a letter to Petronius informing him that Caligula had died and that he no longer had to commit suicide.

A year later, when I met Petronius in Judea, he told me that he had received the two letters together, Caligula's letter ordering him to commit suicide, and mine, informing him that the Emperor had died. Fortunately, he had read mine first.

Apion incites hatred against the Jews in Alexandria

Chapter 27
The assassination of Caligula

Macron, the prefect of the Praetorian Guard, whom rumors accused of having suffocated the old and sick Tiberius at Caligula's request, became one of the private confidants of the Emperor as a reward for his services. Some said that Macron secured the imperial favor by allowing his wife to be Caligula's mistress.

Caligula was aware of the potential threat that Macron represented for him. The man knew too much and was very ambitious. The Emperor appointed him Governor of Egypt. When Macron and his wife arrived at the port of Ostia, soldiers arrested them while preparing to embark. The commander of the detachment informed Macron that he had been dismissed from his post. The couple committed suicide that same day, and Caligula appointed a man named Casio Querea to be the new prefect of the Praetorian Guard.

The Emperor had appointed Querea for considering him docile, weak of character, and having homosexual tendencies.

Fatal error! Querea did not possess any of those characteristics. On the contrary! Querea was a brave man. Years before, he had fought in the Battle of the Teutoburg Forest, in which the Germanic tribes defeated and massacred the Roman army. Querea managed to lead a small group of survivors to a nearby fortress, where they defended themselves heroically until the reinforcements arrived. The exploits of Querea were the reason why many called him "the bravest man in Rome."

Caligula, since his illness, prided himself in having what he called "my great sense of humor." He expressed his so-called humor with cruel pranks, but the only one who ever laughed at his antics was he.

He mocked Querea and made him the main target of his ill-conceived jokes. In the mornings, when Querea came to ask him for the Praetorian Guard's password of the day, Caligula

367

gave him suggestive words, such as "lover boy," "give me a little kiss," or "let's go to bed." When Querea transmitted the ridiculous passwords to his officers, it was inevitable that they would laugh, and Querea, outraged, blamed Caligula for having made him appear foolish.

An old popular phrase applies to this case: "the pitcher goes so often to the well that it breaks at last." That's what happened with Querea. The moment came when he and others could no longer bear the insults of Caligula, his corruption, his perversions, and his crimes, and decided to assassinate him and restore the Republic.

Querea took advantage of the opportunity offered by the Palatine games, for which a temporary theater was built, annexed to the palace.

On the last day of the games, Caligula entered the theater, followed by a group of Senators and friends, me among them. He solemnly offered a sacrifice to Augustus, in whose memory he celebrated the games. Then, he sat down and talked with us in such a friendly, lucid, and open manner that everyone who was nearby was surprised because we had become accustomed to his usual bad mood and his incoherence.

He turned (I was sitting behind him) and spoke to me.

"Agrippa, today is the last day of the games. What do you think? Shall I stay until the end, or shall I go first to the baths and have dinner before returning? He asked me.

"Caesar, today's games will end at a late hour. You have enough time to go to the baths and have dinner and return to see the closing ceremony," a Senator named Asprenas answered before I could speak. Later that day, I found out he was one of the conspirators.

Caligula got up and went to the narrow passage that led from the theater to the palace. Querea and the other conspirators awaited him there.

Querea asked him for the password for the day. Caligula answered him with one of his ridiculous phrases. Querea insulted him, drew his sword, and thrust it into the Emperor's chest while the other conspirators also stabbed Caligula. Having heard his cries for help, Caligula's guard of foreign mercenaries came running and killed several conspirators, but Querea and others managed to escape.

Caligula's guards blocked the exits from the theater and threatened to kill all the spectators. I spoke with the guard's commander and told him that the spectators were horrified and moved by their beloved Emperor's death.

"Please," I pleaded, "let them go to their homes to mourn and pray for Caligula."

The guards allowed the spectators to leave, but they cut off the heads of the dead conspirators and placed them on pikes over the theater's gate.

I carried Caligula's body to his room in the palace and deposited it with great care and kindness in his bed. Caligula's wife came crying and screaming and hugged her husband's body. I retired from the room to leave her alone with the deceased and thus be able to express her pain freely. Meanwhile, Querea had arrived at the Senate building, where the Senators had gathered when they heard the news. They all spoke at the same time. Querea asked for the floor, and everybody became silent.

"Senators of Rome! Since Julius Caesar destroyed our democracy, we have lived under dictatorships. None worse than that of Caligula, who inflicted terrible injustices and miseries on the nation. The fear and cowardice of those who accepted this situation contributed to his tyranny. Today we have shown that Rome does not suffer despots. We're free! Long live the Republic!", proclaimed Querea.

"We must decree the greatest honors to Querea because he, with his brave action, has freed us from a tyrant," proposed one of the Senators with a loud voice.

"Long live Querea!" exclaimed the Senators.

"Gentlemen, Caligula is no longer alive to give us the password of the day. I will give it to you. It is Freedom!" Querea shouted.

The Senators got up and shouted, "Freedom! Freedom!" again and again,

Querea called aside one of the conspirators and told him in a low voice to find and kill Caligula's wife and daughter. The man went to the palace and entered Caligula's room. He found the Emperor's wife crying beside the bloody body of her murdered husband. The murderer cut her throat, then went to the next room and killed Caligula's little daughter.

Chapter 28
Claudius is proclaimed Emperor

Not everyone in Rome shared the wish of the conspirators that Rome should become a republic. The army commanders and the soldiers felt gratitude to Caligula for always being generous and considered a strong government more appropriate than a republic.

One of the commanders proposed to appoint Caligula's uncle as Emperor, my friend Claudius, a man dedicated to learning and culture, who had never offended anyone. People respected him because he was the younger brother of the national hero, Germanicus.

The soldiers entered Claudius' house and searched for him in every room. Finally, a centurion found him hiding behind some curtains, afraid that the armed men who had entered his house would assassinate him.

"I found the brother of Germanicus!" a centurion shouted to his companions.

"Do not kill me, please, do not kill me. I have never hurt anyone. I ask you, for the sake of all the gods, pity me," Claudius begged on his knees.

"We have no intention of killing you. On the contrary! We want you to be our new Emperor," the centurion replied.

The soldiers placed Claudius in a palanquin, as he was unable to walk due to feeling weakness in his legs. He also trembled with chills, caused by the fear he felt. I followed them, walking behind the covered litter, which six soldiers carried on two horizontal poles.

The people who stood along the streets wondered what was happening. Some looked with compassion at Claudius, believing that they were taking him to the military camp to be executed. The reality was completely different. The soldiers were bringing Claudius to their camp to protect him against any possible attempt against his life.

"Make way for Emperor Claudius!" shouted the soldiers.

The Senators informed that the soldiers had proclaimed Claudius emperor, sent a delegation to the military camp to speak with him.

The soldiers allowed two of the delegates to enter the tent where Claudius was.

"Claudius, the Senate has sent us to talk with you. Please ask the soldiers not to use violence to impose you as Emperor. The result would be a civil war since a large part of the army is on our side," one of the delegates told him.

The soldiers surrounding Claudius, hearing the delegate's words, could not suppress their laughter and mockery, knowing quite well (as the Senators also knew) that no one in the army supported the Senate.

"If you want to be the Emperor, the Senate should name you and not the army," said the other delegate.

Claudius did not answer, and the delegates withdrew. I noticed that Claudius was still trembling. He made a gesture for me to come close. I sat next to him, and he spoke to my ear.

"Agrippa, it seems to me that it would be best to leave this matter in the hands of the Senate. It is proper that the Senators should decide what must be done," Claudius whispered.

"No, Claudius! Do not let this opportunity slip away. The soldiers are giving you the Empire on a silver platter! Rome needs you. I am convinced that you will be a great Emperor. Meanwhile, don't do anything and don't say anything. I will go to the Senate and speak to them in your name," I told him.

I left immediately, went to the Senate, and asked permission to speak. The Senators granted it to me, knowing that I had been with Claudius a short time before.

"Roman Senators! Events in this building have changed the course of the history of Rome. What is happening today is one of those events, perhaps the most important of all. I am excited to share this historical moment with you, illustrious patriots, and I want you to know that I am willing to give my life to defend the honor of the Senate, the pride of our democracy."

They interrupted me with applause, and one of the Senators exclaimed:

"We are also willing to die defending our honor and our freedom."

"Gentlemen, let's face reality and put aside illusions. We are not strong enough to face the army and the populace that supports Claudius," I said to them.

The same Senator who had spoken before interrupted me again.

"We have enough money to acquire as many weapons as we would need, and if we free the slaves, we will have an army more numerous than the Roman army," he declared.

"Senators! Allow me to speak to you frankly, even at the risk of causing you offense, which, God forbid, is not my intention. The Roman army that you want to face is brave, expert, and professional. No multitude of slaves, people without experience in wars and military knowledge, can fight against it. These slaves do not even know which end of the sword wounds an enemy!"

The Senators decided to send me as the head of a delegation of five people to talk to Claudius.

We arrived at the military camp, and the soldiers allowed us to enter the tent of Claudius.

"Gentlemen, let me enter the tent before you. I will try to convince Claudius to receive you. Otherwise, he will refuse to see you because of the resentment he now feels against the Senate. I will convince him to listen to our proposition," I told the delegation.

"Claudius," I said as soon as I entered the tent, "the Senators do not know what to do. Their delegation is waiting outside. They want to know if you will receive them. Speak to them with authority, dignity, and determination, and the Empire will be yours."

"I will do so, Agrippa. Tell them to come in," Claudius replied.

What a difference between the Claudius of a few hours before, who trembled with fear, and this one now, full of confidence in himself!

"Gentlemen, welcome. I am not surprised that the Senate is not enthusiastic about the idea of proclaiming me as the new Emperor. I'm not excited about it either, but the army demands it. The previous emperors have been cruel and abusive tyrants, but I will be a fair and just Emperor, and I will share my authority with the Senate. Please go back to the Senate and inform your colleagues what I have told you. We must avoid blood-shedding," he said.

I inwardly smiled at his subtle threat, which, I was sure, the Senators understood clearly. "My friend Claudius will turn out to be an Emperor, after all", I thought.

The Senators returned to the Senate, and I stayed in the tent since I had something of great importance to tell my friend.

"Claudius, the officers, and the soldiers have sworn loyalty to you but do not rely on their oaths. They can change their mind at any time. I suggest you win the gratitude of the army by giving money to the officers right now and promising to give them more in the future," I advised.

Claudius followed my advice. He gave each of the captains ten thousand drachmas and promised them that he would provide a sum of money to each soldier in the army, wherever he was serving.

The consuls convened a Senate session for that same night. Only 100 Senators, from the total of 600, attended. Soldiers and a large number of armed gladiators surrounded the Senate.

Most of the Senators, not being sure how things would turn up, avoided the risk of choosing the losing side with possibly fatal consequences by hiding in the city or going to their country homes. At dawn, Querea left the Senate building with the intention of talking to the soldiers, but the soldiers shouted and threatened him and would not allow him to speak.

"We want the Senate to proclaim Claudius as Emperor!" the soldiers shouted.

"It's incredible that, after you've had a lunatic as Emperor, you now want an idiot," Querea bellowed.

Querea looked at the soldiers with contempt and returned to the Senate, where the debate was still going on. Several of the Senators were afraid of what might happen to them and regretted attending the session.

"I prefer to kill myself before accepting Claudius as Emperor," said one of the conspirators.

"I would not hesitate to kill myself either, but first, I want to hear Claudius' intentions," answered Querea.

Some of the Senators slipped out of the Senate and went to the military camp to pay homage to Claudius. The soldiers saw them, beat them, and kicked them. Claudius looked impassively at the beatings the Senators were receiving and did nothing to stop the soldiers. This is a mistake, I thought. I called Claudius aside and talked to him in a whisper.

"Claudius, tell the soldiers to stop hitting those men. Please treat them with kindness. They are the ones who will support you in the Senate."

Claudius immediately ordered the soldiers to release the Senators.

"I am very sorry for the mistreatment that you have just suffered. The cause is the great affection that the soldiers feel for me, but I assure you that it will not happen again. I want you to go back to the Senate and tell the Senators that I expect them to come to the palace right now," Claudius told them.

The soldiers took Claudius in his palanquin to the palace. On the way, the crowd cheered him. An hour later, the Senators arrived, walking behind Querea.

Claudius saw Querea enter the palace and asked me what he should do with him.

"The action of Querea, killing an Emperor who had become a cruel tyrant, is worthy of praise, but you cannot allow him to stay alive. It would be a terrible example. Future potential killers must know the price they will pay. You have no alternative but to condemn him to death," I advised him.

I must admit that Querea showed dignity and courage until the last moment. When the soldiers took him to the place of execution, he asked his executioner if he had used the sword for that purpose in the past. When the soldier answered that it was the first time, Querea instructed him how to do it properly.

Claudius did not punish the other conspirators, but they all committed suicide.

Chapter 29
I am the king of Judea

One of Claudius' first acts as Emperor was to confirm me as king of the territories that Caligula had granted me: Iturea, Traconitis, and the Golan. His gratitude to me for having helped him to become Emperor went much further. He gave me all the territories of Judea, Samaria, Abila, and Mount Lebanon. The kingdom of Judea is more extensive than it was when my grandfather Herod was king. Only David and Solomon had a larger size kingdom than mine.

The tetrarchy of Chalcis was vacant since Caligula had exiled my uncle Antipas and his wife, my sister Herodias. I asked Claudius to name my brother Herod, king of Chalcis, and Claudius agreed to my request.

By the way, my brother Herod two years later, became my son-in-law. My daughter Berenice had become a widow at the age of fifteen. Her husband, Marcus Julius, son of Alexander, had died when he fell off his horse. Herod, a widower, asked me for her hand in marriage upon learning that Berenice was available, and I granted it to him.

Going back to my story, two weeks after Claudius confirmed me as king of Judea, Cypros, our girls and I traveled to Caesarea in an imperial ship that Claudius had placed at my disposal. My son Agrippa, fourteen at the time, stayed in Rome to continue his education.

Thousands of people welcomed us in Caesarea with flowers and palms. We rested there for three days to and then we continued to Jerusalem.

A reception committee of the most important men in the city, included the High Priest, waited for us at the city gate. The prelate had put on the clothes he wore only during religious festivals. A hundred priests surrounded him, each of them carrying a shofar, a musical instrument made of a ram's horn which the priests blow on religious occasions. Silas, whom I had left in charge of the government, was also on the reception committee. We greeted each other with a hug.

When I got off my chariot, the High Priest made a sign, and the priests blew their instruments simultaneously.

"I believe that people can hear this deafening noise as far as Rome," I whispered to my wife. My youngest daughter, Drusilla, scared, cried, and Cypros had to calm her down.

We walked from the city entrance to the palace built by my grandfather Herod. This would be my place of government and our residence in Jerusalem. The people in the streets cheered and sang *MelechAgrippa, baruch aba,* [Bless you, King Agrippa].

I went to the Temple on Saturday. The priests had placed a throne on a platform built in the center of the central courtyard. When I arrived, the High Priest was already there, holding the scroll of the law in his arms. He handed me the scroll, and I prepared to read it out in a loud voice.

"Your Majesty, you are the king, and kings have the right to read the scroll of the Law while sitting down," the High Priest told me.

"I will read the scroll standing up," I replied.

I saw that my attitude impressed him, and, from that moment on, he always showed me great respect.

I read the scroll aloud until I came to Deuteronomy verse that says: "Choose one of your brothers to be your king, not a stranger".

That verse applied to me! My ancestors were converts. Tears ran down my cheeks and prevented me from seeing the letters. I stopped reading and sobbed out aloud.

People on the platform and in the courtyard saw me crying and shouted, "Agrippa! You are our brother! You are our brother! You are our brother!"

I took special care to comply with all the laws of our religion and did not let one day go by without making a sacrifice in the Temple.

At the Feast of Pentecost, I took part in the ceremony by carrying on my shoulder a basket full of the first fruits of the season.

If, when walking the streets of Jerusalem, I would see a wedding procession, which, according to the protocol, must make way for the king, I would step aside to allow the bride and groom to pass first. Thus, my popularity increased with almost all the people, but not among the religious fanatics. One of them, called Simon, a man well versed in the law, denounced me in Jerusalem while I was visiting Caesarea. He dared to accuse me publicly of not leading a life of purity and said that I should not be allowed to enter the Temple, a privilege reserved only for Jews.

Upon returning to Jerusalem, I called him to the palace and invited him to sit next to me.

"Simon, please tell me what I am doing against the law of the Torah. I will regret having done it and will stop doing it," I said.

He lowered his eyes and did not answer. He remained silent for a long time and then asked me to forgive him.

The only problem I've had so far was caused by someone I never expected to give me trouble. I mean Silas, my childhood friend, the one who brought me food and clothes when I was in prison. Silas, whom I had appointed as the Governor of the territories that Caligula had conferred on me several years before.

The fact that he had been Governor of my territories had gone to his head. He treated me with a familiarity that was not appropriate between a subject and his king. He sat in my presence without asking permission. He constantly reminded me of everything he had done for me, how loyal he had been, the risks that he had taken for my cause.

The time came when Silas' attitude and allegations made me sick and tired. I stripped him of his position as commander of my army and sent him to prison.

Sometime later, when I had calmed down, I sent a messenger to Silas' prison, inviting him to be my guest of honor at the celebrations of my birthday.

Silas refused the invitation and said: "Agrippa mistreated me. Why should I shut up? I have the right to remind him of everything I've done for him. Is sending me to prison his reward for my service? I will never forget everything I've done for him, and never, while I live, will I let him forget it. "

I realized that Silas was incorrigible and let him rot in prison.

Chapter 30
My problems with Vibius Marsus

Beirut is one of my favorite cities. I built there a theater that exceeds in luxury and elegance all the others in the region. I also built an amphitheater and restrooms, which I inaugurated with games where seven hundred gladiators fought against the criminals who had been in prison. All the criminals died, which gave them their just punishment, and, at the same time, it allowed us to save the money we would have wasted taking care of them by feeding them in prison.

At the end of the Beirut games, I traveled to Tiberias, the city where, years before, I had been a market inspector. There, I called a conference of the neighboring countries' kings, including my brother Herod, king of Chalcis, and the kings of Commalena, Emesa, Armenia, and Pontus. I knew all of them because they, like me, were educated in the imperial court of Rome.

The purpose of the conference was to promote commercial relations between our different kingdoms.

Vibius Marsus, the Governor of Syria, heard about our meeting and assumed, erroneously, that our real purpose was to coordinate resistance against Rome. He sent messengers to Tiberias who spoke with each of the kings I had invited and ordered them to return immediately to their countries. They did so, thus frustrating my hopes for an economic resurgence of the region.

Back in Jerusalem, I examined the city walls and saw that, during the decades that Judea had been a Roman province, they had deteriorated. They had become indefensible. I gave instructions to strengthen and extend them.

Vibius Marcus heard that I was rebuilding the walls of Jerusalem, and, again, he misinterpreted my intentions. He assumed that I was reinforcing them to rebel against Rome. Immediately, he wrote a report to Claudius, attributing to me intentions that I did not have.

Weeks later, I received a letter from Claudius written in a tone that did not reflect our old friendship. The Emperor ordered me to stop the work I was doing on the walls of Jerusalem. I had no choice but to comply with his order, but I still hope Judea will be completely independent one day.

I decided to take a few days off and traveled to Caesarea, where my grandfather Herod built his wonderful summer palace. I love Caesarea because it reminds me of Rome, the city of my youth.

I invited the Governor of Syria, Vibius Marsus, to a dinner in his honor, a gesture that I hope would dispel his suspicions and the antagonism he has towards me.

Epilogue:
Letter of Vibius Marsus
to Emperor Claudius

From: Vibius Marsus, Governor of Syria
To: Emperor Claudius

Ave, Caesar!

It is my duty to inform you that King Agrippa died yesterday in Caesarea, after four days of terrible agony, during which he vomited blood repeatedly and shouted with an almost inhuman voice when he felt painful pangs that tore his chest and abdomen. His ordeal began while he was addressing the audience in the amphitheater of the city.

I was sitting in the royal box next to Queen Cypros. As usual in Judea, when it is summer, the sky was blue without a single cloud. The king wore a garment made of silver threads, which, illuminated by the sun, shone like lightning.

The public proclaimed in great voices, "You are a god! You are immortal!"

The king looked up and saw an owl. The bird must have had a terrifying meaning for him. He turned pale, stumbled, put his hand to his chest, and made a gesture of intense pain.

"Lord, you are justly punishing me for not having protested when they called me god," he said in a voice so weak that only Cypros and I, who were at his side, could hear.

He began to tremble and asked us to take him to the palace. Rumors quickly spread throughout the city, and a crowd took to the streets, crying and praying for the king to recover his health.

His agony lasted four days, and his death was a mercy. He had celebrated his fifty-fourth birthday a week before.

As Governor of the province of Syria, it is my duty to give you my honest opinion. Although King Agrippa's death is a

383

tragedy for his relatives, friends, subjects, and in general for the entire Jewish nation, it is a blessing for Rome.

The Jews, distributed in all the cities of the Empire, could have been incited to rebel by a capable and popular leader like King Agrippa, first in Judea, then in Alexandria and other places, and, finally, even in Rome itself. I am convinced that, with the death of Agrippa, Rome has managed to avoid an even more dangerous confrontation than our war against Carthage. The Jews, lacking this leader, will no longer think of rebelling. The death of Agrippa assures decades of peace and tranquility for the Roman Empire.

I inform you that, at the dinner to which King Agrippa invited me before he fell ill, I gave him a bottle of wine as a gift, according to the instructions you sent me.

The last words King Agrippa told me when I said goodbye to him were for you.

"Dear Marsus," he said, "thank you for the delicious wine. It was a kind and thoughtful gift. In your next letter to Emperor Claudius, please convey to him my love and friendship. Tell Claudius that I have always been loyal to him."

THE WAR OF THE JEWS AGAINST THE ROMAN EMPIRE

The events related in this book
took place between
66 CE and 73 CE

Preface

Several chroniclers have written books about the recent war between the Jews and the Romans. However , the authors of these books did not participate in the events, and most of them are prejudiced writers who hate Jews.

Their scrolls are full of falsehoods and unfair accusations against me. They accuse me of being a traitor to my people. They call me an apostate, a deserter.

These accusations are absurd and unfair! How can I, a descendant of the kings of Judea from my maternal side, be a traitor? How can I, Joseph ben Matityahu, priest of our sacred religion, be an apostate? How can I, the commander-in-chief of the forces that heroically defended the Galilee, be a deserter?

The truth is that the real traitors were those fanatics who irresponsibly incited the people to rebel against the Roman Empire and continued provoking even when it was already evident that the Jews had already lost the war.

The Romans did not start the conflict. The Jews did. The Roman general Titus Flavius is not to blame for the destruction of our sacred Temple. The responsibility for that catastrophe falls on the Jewish leaders who turned the House of God into a military fortress.

In this book, I will relate with objectivity and frankness the atrocities committed by the fanatics that led us to the greatest tragedy in our history.

Being objective, as every historian must be, I will also mention the cruel acts of the Romans, the crucifixion of thousands of our fighters, the massacres of the elderly, women, and children, and the sale of the survivors in the slave market.

I will tell how our holy Temple was set on fire and destroyed and why Jerusalem, the most beautiful city of the Empire, is today a sad mound of ruins and rubble.

387

Preface

I, Joseph ben Matityahu, called Josephus Flavius by the Romans, swear that this is the true story of the War of the Jews against the Roman Empire.

Chapter 1
A short autobiography

I want to make clear from this first page that I am a modest man. My purpose in mentioning my noble ancestors is not to boast but to tell the real facts.

From my mother's side, I descend from the Hasmonean kings. I have royal blood in my veins.

My father belonged to the principal family of the first division of priests appointed by king David, blessed be his memory. My great-grandfather, Simon, had nine children. One of them, called Matityahu, married a daughter of the High Priest. His son, also called Matityahu, was my father, a priest of excellent reputation and great prestige.

I must emphasize that I have not written this book with the purpose of telling the story of my life but to let the world know the truth about the Great Rebellion of the Jews against the Roman Empire and the critical role that I played in it. However, I understand, dear reader, that it is natural that you should be curious about the author's personal history. Therefore, in the following paragraphs, I will give you brief autobiographical information.

I was born in the first year [37 AD] of Emperor Caligula's reign. Two weeks before my thirtieth birthday, in the twelfth year of Nero's reign, I was appointed commander of Galilee's defenders.

Even when I was still a child, people noticed my intelligence, excellent memory, and in-depth knowledge of our sacred scrolls. My honesty obliges me to recount something that in other people would be considered boasting. From the time I turned fourteen, the most important men of the city, including the High Priest, used to consult with me and ask my opinion about some verses of the Torah that, for them, were difficult to understand.

When I turned sixteen, I made a comparative study of our religion's three main sects: the Pharisees, the Sadducees, and

389

the Essenes. I will describe these sects briefly in the following paragraphs.

The Pharisees were the largest group in our nation (and they still are, since they constitute the only sect that survived the Great Rebellion). Their main characteristic was, and still is, the belief in the Oral Law, which God gave to Moses at Sinai, along with the written Torah. Their other concepts were, and still are, faith in the resurrection of the dead, faith in the coming of the Messiah who will establish universal peace, and the conviction that God will punish the wicked and reward the righteous in the kingdom of Heaven.

The Sadducees were the sect of the aristocrats and the chief priests. They denied the validity of the Oral Law, insisted on the literal interpretation of the Torah, and did not believe in life after death since the Torah does not mention it. They sympathized with the Hellenistic culture. They centered their lives around the rituals and sacrifices of the Temple, and when the

Romans destroyed the Temple, the Sadducees lost their functions and disappeared.

The Essenes were a sect of hermits who despised the other two denominations accusing them of being corrupt. They lived in the desert and imposed on themselves the obligation of celibacy.

Although I belong by birth to the priestly class, my beliefs today coincide with those of the Pharisees. But, when you're young, you're idealistic. I met once a hermit on a trip I took to the desert near the Sea of Salta. The man was dressed in clothes made of bark; he ate only vegetables and bathed several times a day with cold water to control his sexual desires and preserve his chastity. His appearance and his conversation fascinated me, and I asked him to accept me as a disciple. I stayed with him for three years until I returned to my hometown, Jerusalem. My father convinced the High Priest to give me a high-paid position in the Temple and arranged my marriage with a prominent priest's daughter.

Unfortunately, she died young, without giving me any children.

I married a second time during the Great Rebellion, several months after the Romans captured me. The first time I saw the woman, she didn't appeal to me. I would have preferred not to become her husband, but General Vespasian had ordered me to get married. The wife the General chose for me was a young Jewish woman who the Romans had captured. I could not refuse Vespasian's order, but I did not do it willingly since the Torah, in the book of Leviticus, forbids priests from marrying a widowed, divorced, or desecrated woman. I assumed that the Roman soldiers had raped her, most likely, repeatedly. After all, this is their custom when they capture women, especially if these are young and good-looking,

It was a wonderful surprise and a great relief when I discovered, on my wedding night, that my wife had arrived as a virgin to the marriage bed. Inexplicably, the Romans had not desecrated her.

It did not take me long to realize that the only good quality she had (which she lost on our wedding night) had been her virginity. She was a woman of limited intelligence, uneducated, lacking in ancestry for having been born into a family of peasants. She was far from being an appropriate wife for someone like me, a priest of the first division, and a descendant of kings on the maternal side.

As soon as the war ended, I divorced her. Later, when I was residing in Rome, I traveled to Alexandria and met there the daughter of one of the wealthiest Jews in the city. I married her and brought her with me to Rome. We settled in the house that Vespasian had given me, in Palatine Hill, where he had lived before moving to the imperial palace.

My wife gave me three children, two of whom died when they were very young. Shortly after our tenth wedding anniversary, rumors reached my ears that my wife's behavior was not as it should be. I made the proper inquiries and verified that the sordid gossip was true. I decided to divorce her, but before I could start the proceedings, she died giving birth to Hyrcanus, our third child, or, at least, her third child.

I regret to say that for many years already, I have not been in contact with Hyrcanus due to circumstances and disagreements that are not relevant to the events that I will narrate in this book. I do not even know where he lives.

Five years ago, I married a woman born on the island of Crete, the daughter of a wealthy Jewish family. Her character and her behavior are exemplary. She has given me two sons, Justus and Simon, both excellent boys, educated, intelligent, and very pious. The boys regularly attend the neighborhood synagogue without me because the congregation leaders have told me that my presence is not welcome.

When Emperor Vespasian died, his son Titus, my great friend, succeeded him. He treated me with the same affection that his father had always shown me. Titus died after reigning only two years. His brother Domitian, today our Emperor, also treats me with affection and honor, just as his father and brother did during their respective reigns. He has been very generous with me. Lately, he has exempted me from paying taxes for the lands that Vespasian gave me in Judea.

I hope that these personal data have been enough to satisfy your curiosity, dear reader. Now, I will tell the story of the Great Rebellion and my participation in it.

Chapter 2
A description of the Temple

In the eighth year of Emperor Nero's reign, when I was twenty-six years old, the Roman procurator of Judea, an individual named Felix, imprisoned several priests who had given sermons against the Roman occupation and sent them to Rome to be judged for sedition.

Two weeks later, the Great Sanhedrin invited me to appear before its members. The Great Sanhedrin was the Supreme Court of Judea, responsible for dealing with the Jewish population's religious problems, while the Roman authorities were in charge of civil and military issues.

The Sanhedrin met in the Hall of Carved Stones, which owed its name to being the only room in the Temple complex built with stones carved with iron tools. It was located on the north wall of the Temple Mount and had two entrances. You could reach one of the gates by walking through the several courtyards of the Temple. The other entrance could be entered directly from the outside.

Dear reader, I ask for your indulgence. I mentioned earlier that this book's purpose is to relate the events of the Great Rebellion, but, I think, it is essential to include a description of the Temple for the benefit of future generations who will not have the privilege of seeing what the House of God was. The most terrible consequence of the Great Rebellion, besides the death of hundreds of thousands and the slavery of tens of thousands, was the destruction of the Temple, one of the world's architectural wonders. I have been to Athens, and I can attest that the Acropolis does not compare in size or beauty with what was once the spectacular Temple of Jerusalem.

Gold plates, whose brightness dazzled when they reflected the sun's rays, covered the Temple's facade. Those who saw the Temple from a distance had the impression that it was a snow-covered mountain or a gigantic white marble sculpture.

I usually entered the Temple through the Hulda Gate, on the south side of the Mount, because I found it fascinated me to see the hundreds of thousands of pilgrims and visitors, Jews and Gentiles, who crowded there, especially during the three Pilgrimage Festivals, Passover, Pentecost, and Tabernacles. They came from all corners of the Roman Empire and also from Persia and other nations further east. To see them dressed in the exotic clothes of their different countries, hear them speaking in different languages, listening to them argue with the merchants and moneychangers in poorly spoken Hebrew with many different accents was a delightful spectacle that I never tired of watching.

Thousands of priests, Levites, scribes, and lay Jews worked daily in the Temple. The priests were in charge of the rituals and ceremonies. The Levites, many of them musicians and singers, were responsible for cleaning and maintenance.

The Hulda Gate was reached by a large staircase that led to the Gentiles' Courtyard, a place where non-Jews were allowed to enter. It had many commercial establishments where a visitor could buy knickknacks to take back to his country, animals to sacrifice, and food. Numerous moneychangers exchanged Roman money (unacceptable as a donation because their images of Caesar violate Torah's law) for Hebrew or Tyrian money. There was no shortage of guides who offered to accompany the visitor for a few coins and explain what they saw. And, of course, there were priests everywhere, dressed in white robes with turbans on their heads, always ready to advise the pilgrims about the sacrifices they wanted to offer.

On one side of the Gentiles' Courtyard was the so-called "Royal Porch," which contained a market, administrative offices, and a synagogue for studying the Torah. The visitors could go up to the top floor, contemplate the sacrifices from there and listen to the priests' prayers and the Levites' songs.

The Gentiles' Courtyard ended on the north side in a stone wall that separated it from the interior areas where only Jews were allowed to enter. A sign in three languages, Hebrew,

Greek, and Latin, warned that entry to non-Jews was forbidden.

The Courtyard of the Women, the largest courtyard in the Temple, was on the other side of the stone wall. It was so named because women were allowed to enter it. It was my favorite place in the Temple because the people there danced, sang, and played musical instruments.

The priests reserved one corner of the Courtyard of the Women for people considered ritually impure. A barbershop in another corner was patronized mainly by Nazirites, men who let their hair grow wild when they consecrated themselves to God for a specific time. When the period ended, they would come to the Temple barbershop and have their heads shaved.

From the Courtyard of the Women, passing through the Nicanor Gate, so named in honor of its donor, an Egyptian Jew, you would come to the Courtyard of the Israelites, also called Inner Courtyard, where the High Priest performed the sacrifices.

Behind the rostrum was a building with its entrance covered by a curtain. The altar for the incense and the menorah, the seven branches golden candelabra, stood in front of the curtain. On the other side of the curtain was the Holy Sanctuary, a room where only the High Priest was allowed to enter.

The air in the Temple's courtyards was imbued, not only with incense but also, especially during religious festivals, with the smell of the blood of sacrificed animals.

I mentioned on a previous page that my habit was to enter the Temple through the Hulda Gate and, from there, go to the Hall of Carved Stones. This time, having been called urgently to appear before the Sanhedrin, I went in through the door that led directly from the outside to the Hall.

A description of the Temple

Chapter 3
My visit to Rome

I entered the Hall of Carved Stones and saw that all the Sanhedrin members were already there. They were sitting in their usual semi-circle in front of a table, behind which was the president of the Court, Simon ben Gamaliel, son of the famous Rabban Gamaliel ben Simon, blessed be his memory, who merited that title for being an exceptional sage.

"Joseph ben Matityahu, welcome to the Sanhedrin," Simon ben Gamaliel greeted me and beckoned me to sit on a chair next to him.

Seeing Simon ben Gamaliel always made me feel that it was a privilege of my generation to live in an era with people like him. He was a worthy great-grandson of Hillel, undoubtedly the wisest and most learned man our nation has ever produced. Like his great-grandfather, Simon not only knew the Law profoundly but applied it with tolerance and love.

"Thank you, Rabban. It is a great honor to be in this august assembly," I replied.

"I have proposed to the members of the Sanhedrin that we should send you to Rome to carry out a very delicate mission. I have explained to them that you possess all the necessary qualities to make the task a success. You are intelligent, discreet, and know how to deal with people. You get along very well with the Romans, and, most importantly, you speak Latin and Greek fluently. I am pleased to inform you that the Sanhedrin has approved my proposal unanimously.

"I am willing to fulfill any mission that the Sanhedrin entrusts to me. May I ask what it is? "

"Your mission has two parts. The first is to get the Romans to release several priests that they hold prisoners in Rome. The second is to bring them back to Israel," replied the Rabban.

Why are the priests in prison in Rome?" I asked.

"One of the priests, Jonathan ben Amos, a reckless young man, gave a sermon criticizing the taxes that Felix, Judea's

397

Roman Governor, has imposed. He called them 'extortion."
Felix, informed of the priest's harsh words, ordered one of his
men to bring the priest before him. When the centurion arrived
at the priest's house, the young man and his three brothers,
instead of complying with the summons, which, at most,
would have resulted in a warning, insulted the centurion and
refused to go with him. The centurion returned with several
soldiers and arrested the four brothers. Felix sent them
chained to Rome to be tried by the authorities. Your mission,
as I told you before, is to go to Rome, talk to the people in
charge, convince them to release the four priests, and bring
them back to Judea," Simon explained.

"I know Jonathan and his brothers personally. I always
warned them to measure their words. With the Romans, you
have to be careful."

"I agree with you, Joseph, and hope that those hot-headed
young priests have learned their lesson. We want you to travel
as soon as possible. We will give you letters of introduction
for some people who are prominent in the Jewish community
of Rome."

"Rabban, I want to thank you and the members of the
Sanhedrin for honoring me with such an important and
delicate mission. Rest assured that I will bring the four priests
back with me to Jerusalem."

Although my phrases expressed confidence in the success of
my mission, the truth is that I had no idea how to achieve the
liberation of the four priests. The Romans are not known by
their mercy and are inflexible in all matters that have even the
remotest possibility of rebellion or incitement. But, I have
always considered it necessary to pretend to have high
confidence in myself. I find it indispensable to receive respect
and admiration from other people."

A week later, I joined a caravan that went from Jerusalem to
the port of Jaffa. After three days of trekking through
mountains and gorges, we arrived at the port. I went directly
to an inn to rest. My whole body, even the parts of it that

previously did not merit my attention, ached due to the unaccustomed effort of riding on a camel.

I was informed that three ships were preparing to sail during the following days to the Roman port of Ostia. I visited each of them and spoke with the captains. Finally, I bought passage on the boat that I thought was the best built of the three ships. Its captain also gave me the impression of being more capable than the other two captains.

Unfortunately, I was utterly mistaken in my assessment of both the ship and its captain. The greedy and irresponsible captain had loaded his vessel with more than six hundred passengers, twice as many as his ship could hold. When we reached the Adriatic Sea, the captain, probably drunk, could not avoid some rocks that jutted out of the sea. The ship collided with them and broke in two. Crew and passengers fell into the water, and only those of us who knew how to swim were able to keep afloat during the night. Fortunately for me, my father complied with the obligations imposed by our Oral Law, which include the duty of a parent to teach his child to swim.

When dawn arrived, I found myself surrounded by bodies of drowned people floating in the water. One of the survivors saw a ship that was a short distance away. We shouted, they saw us, rowed towards us, and threw down ropes by which we could climb up to their boat. Only eighty of us survived the ordeal. All the others drowned.

I disembarked at the port of Puteoli, and, from there, I proceeded in a carriage by land to Rome. Seeing the capital of the Empire for the first time made me understand its power. It has one million inhabitants, which makes it by far the largest city in the world!

I was wonderstruck, overwhelmed with admiration when I first saw its wide avenues, its temples built with marble, and its parks adorned with water fountains and beautiful statues.

I want to clarify that the previous paragraph's description applies only to the neighborhoods where the wealthy and noble families live, especially Palatine Hill and its surroundings. In the popular areas, people live in apartment buildings, six or seven floors high. The streets are narrow, and without sidewalks, they do not have names, and the houses do not have numbers.

Soon after arriving, I realized that the most prudent thing to do when I found myself in those neighborhoods was to walk in the middle of the street, even if it was noon and the summer sun was burning fiercely. I would have preferred to walk on the side of the road, under the shadow of the buildings, but, the first time I did that, I found, to my chagrin, that people threw garbage and worse things out their windows, not caring if a passerby was walking below.

When the boat sank, I had lost the letters of introduction that Rabban Simon ben Gamaliel had written to a member of the Jewish community in Rome, but I remembered the name of one, Asher ben Yitzhak. He was the leader of the synagogue located on the Field of Mars, near the Ara Pacis, an altar built by Emperor Augustus, blessed be his memory. I asked a passerby how to get to that impressive monument, and thus I avoided getting lost in the alleys and twists and turns of the roads.

Asher received me kindly, and, after reading the letter of Simon ben Gamaliel, in which the Rabbi praised me in terms that my modesty prevents me from mentioning, he invited me to stay at his house during my stay in Rome.

Asher lived in a six-story building that adjoined the synagogue (I later learned that he was the owner of that building and several other buildings). On the ground floor, he had a store where he sold gold and silver jewelry. The apartment where he lived with his wife and his three young children occupied the entire first floor. The upper floors, divided into small flats, were rented to several families, mostly from the Jewish community.

The tenants who lived on the upper floors used a public latrine situated on the building's side. It was a room that contained a long bench with holes, under which the water ran with the excrement.

Asher's apartment, built of concrete walls, consisted of four large bedrooms, a living room, kitchen, bathroom, and a corridor with windows that faced the street. It had central heating and water pipes.

Regarding the upper floors, the higher they were, the smaller the rooms. The tenants suffered from the heat in the summer and from the cold in the winter. They didn't have kitchens in their apartments and, therefore, had to eat in taverns. They used public latrines for their bodily needs.

Miriam, Asher's wife, was a plump, middle-aged woman, very religious, and, as I was able to appreciate during the following weeks, an excellent cook. Their three children were very polite and respectful.

That first night, the children went to sleep after dinner, Miriam retired to the kitchen to wash the dishes, and Asher and I kept talking while we shared a bottle of wine of such excellent quality that it surprised me. I asked Asher about it, and he replied that he imported it from Greece. Our conversation led to the relations between Romans and Jews, both in Judea and in Rome itself. Born in Rome and having visited Jerusalem only once, he was interested to hear about our life in the Jewish country.

"The Roman authorities respect our religion and our traditions," I told Asher. "However, on one occasion, they demanded that we install a statue of the Emperor in the Temple, saying that this was usual in all the sacred buildings in the Empire, and we could not be an exception. We explained to the Roman authorities that our religion forbids us to have statues in the Temple but that, with great pleasure, we would be willing to sacrifice daily in his honor. Fortunately, they were satisfied with our offer and did not insist."

"I understand that Governor Felix is extremely strict," said Asher.

"Like all the governors of the Roman provinces, Felix has two primary objectives: to maintain order and enrich himself. And the truth is that he is succeeding in both endeavors. But, I would like to hear about the Jewish community in Rome. How many Jews live here? How do they get along with the Romans?" I asked.

"I reckon," he answered," that there are some eight thousand Jewish families in the city, equivalent to some forty thousand people. Most of the Jews of Rome have Roman citizenship. We have a dozen synagogues in various parts of the city and underground cemeteries in catacombs. Emperor Augustus, may he rest in peace, recognized Judaism as a legal religion. In other words, a faith that Romans allow throughout the Empire. We are permitted to send donations to the Temple in Jerusalem. Some Romans like to make fun of us because we do not eat pork, which is the Romans' favorite dish. They call us idle because we do not work on Saturdays. They do not understand why we circumcise our children. In truth, none of those criticisms is relevant. Our real problem is the quality of the water we receive in this neighborhood. It reaches us through a poorly maintained aqueduct and is not suitable for drinking. We have to boil it, filter it, and even then, we cannot get rid of the bad taste."

"Dear Asher, I want your advice. The Sanhedrin has sent me to Rome to obtain the release of four priests who insulted a centurion. Do you think that if I talked to the judge, maybe offer him a gift, this might solve the matter?" I asked him.

"Generally, a gift would be the solution, but not in this case. Felix has excellent relations in the imperial court. His friends are influential, and they would make life difficult for the judge if he releases the priests."

"I cannot go back to Judea without them. What can I do? Please advise me," I asked with a desperation that my voice could not hide.

"You need to get help from someone more powerful than Felix's friends," he replied.

Asher closed his eyes to concentrate and was silent for a while. I did not speak either so as not to distract him. After a few moments, he looked at me and smiled.

"I think I've found the solution," he told me. "Emperor Nero must forgive the four priests. There is no one in the whole Empire more powerful than the Emperor."

Asher must be joking, I thought. He could not be serious! To show appreciation for what I considered to be a weak joke, I laughed out of courtesy, but, in my heart, I was disappointed that my host took so lightly a matter of such importance.

"I see that you have an excellent sense of humor, Asher," I told him. "Please, thank Miriam for the delicious dinner. It's already late, and, with your permission, I'm going to sleep."

I got up from my chair. Asher signaled me to sit down again.

"Joseph, I've spoken to you seriously. The only one who can save your priests is Emperor Nero. I know how you can make contact with him. But, for that, you must come with me tomorrow to the theater."

"Please explain what you mean."

"Not tonight, Joseph. You're right. It's already late. I am also tired. Tomorrow we will continue our conversation."

I slept very poorly that night. I was thinking about what Asher had told me and could not imagine how I, an unknown foreigner, could contact the Emperor.

The next day my frustration continued. Asher continued to refuse to explain what I should do to contact the Emperor.

"Be patient, Joseph. I'll explain everything to you when the time comes. But now we must go to the theater," he said smiling.

We walked until we came to a vast garden adorned with statues and fountains, surrounded by columns that supported a roof.

"This is Pompey's theater. They also call it the Marble Theater because it was the first building in Rome adorned with marble. Do you see the building at the back of the garden?" Asher asked me.

I nodded.

"It is the Pompey Curia. The Senate met there many years ago, and that's where the assassins murdered Julius Caesar," Asher explained.

After crossing the theater's portal, we walked through a vaulted corridor that ended in an ample space, about four hundred and fifty feet wide. It had rows of concentric bleachers where hundreds of spectators were already seated. We climbed to one of the higher stands and sat down.

"We're in what's called the cavea," Asher said," The space in front of us is the stage.

"What will we do here?" I asked.

"Besides applauding or whistling, nothing much," Asher said, laughing. "We will see a play, where the actors will present a story, making us believe that they are the characters. Today's play is a very famous comedy. Its name is Miles Gloriosus. A man named Plautus, who lived two hundred years ago, wrote it," Asher explained.

The comedy ended after a couple of hours. The story was complicated. The main character was a military braggart. Other characters were slaves who cheated and mocked their masters. A girl was in love with a young man, and a courtesan helped her meet her lover.

When I realized that both the girl and the courtesan were men disguised as women, I was horrified and stopped paying attention to what was happening on stage. Our sacred Torah, in the book of Deuteronomy, states that God detests the man who dresses as a woman.

At one point, I saw that all the spectators stood up and applauded. I did the same. People started to leave, from which I deduced that the performance was over.

"Now we will go to greet the actor who plays the role of Miles Gloriosus. His name is Aliturius, and he is a co-religionist of ours. He's a good Jew, though he rarely comes to the synagogue," Asher told me.

We went down the steps to the side of the stage and entered a room where we saw the man we had seen on stage. He had removed the military uniform he had worn during the comedy and was wearing the tunic that the Jews wear in Rome.

"Shalom!" He greeted us as he recognized Asher.

404

"Shalom, Aliturius!" Asher replied." Please meet Joseph ben Matityahu. He has just arrived from Judea, sent by the Sanhedrin. He will explain to you why he is here. I hope you can help him."

I looked at Aliturius with a curiosity I didn't try to hide. It was the first time I had seen an actor. The man was tall, muscular, and very handsome. When speaking, he accompanied his words by making gestures with his hands. His voice was loud and, at the same time, musical.

"Welcome to Rome, Joseph! I hope you enjoyed the presentation. Take a seat. Please tell me how I can help you. May I offer you a cup of wine?" Aliturius asked, smiling.

Asher and I sat on a couch. I politely declined the glass of wine and informed him of the mission the Sanhedrin had entrusted to me. The actor listened to me attentively and without interrupting until I finished telling my story.

"I think I can help you, or at least I can try. I have been friends for many years with Poppea, Emperor Nero's wife. Maybe, through her, I can get you to meet Nero so you can ask him in person to pardon your friends," Aliturius told me.

"That would be wonderful! May I ask you for another favor?"

"Gladly!" he replied.

"I would like to visit the captives. They are in prison, but I do not know in which one."

"My best guess is that they are in the Tullianum Prison, on the side of Capitoline Hill, in front of the Senate Curia. It is a temporary prison where prisoners await their trial or execution. I know the officer in charge. When you go, tell him that you are my friend, and he will allow you to go in and meet your friends."

I thanked the actor effusively, and the next day, early in the morning, I went to the prison. The mention of Aliturius' name was enough to convince the officer in charge to let me in. I told him that I wanted to see the four Jewish priests from Judea.

"I know those prisoners well, actually too well. They are the most difficult to please prisoners I have ever encountered. They refuse to eat the food of the prison and feed only on figs and nuts," the officer told me as he accompanied me to the basement of the prison where the cells were.

He showed me the priests' cell and went back upstairs. Through the bars in the cell door, I saw that the four prisoners were chained to the wall.

"Shalom, dear friends," I said.

They looked at me with great surprise until they finally recognized who I was.

"Joseph! What are you doing here?" one of them asked me.

"The Sanhedrin has not forgotten you. They have entrusted me with the mission of releasing you and bringing you back to Judea," I replied.

I talked with them for quite a while, assuring them that I would do everything possible to help them recover their freedom until the officer came down to the basement and told me that I had spoken with them long enough.

After dinner, Asher verified that the doors and windows were closed and that there was no danger of anyone hearing us. He brought his stool close to mine and told me in a low voice about Emperor Nero's family.

"If you meet the Emperor, it is vital that you should know about him and his family. Agrippina, the mother of Nero, was one of Caligula's sisters, with whom the Emperor had an incestuous relationship. Agrippina was married when she was only thirteen years old and gave birth to a son, Nero. Her husband died when she was twenty-five years old, and shortly afterward, Caligula exiled her for conspiring against him.

After the murder of Caligula, Agrippina returned to Rome. She married a Senator who died a short time later. At the age of thirty-four, she married her uncle, Emperor Claudius, who had just become a widower when he had his wife Messalina executed for infidelity.

Agrippina convinced Claudius to marry his daughter Octavia to her son Nero and to name him the heir to the

Empire, instead of Britannicus, the Emperor's son. Soon after Nero's succession was assured, Claudius died. People believe that Agrippina poisoned him. Nero, sixteen years old at the time, was proclaimed Emperor. Shortly after, he gave orders to have Britannicus killed.

Nero met a lady called Poppea when she was still married to Otto, a good friend of the Emperor. Otto invited Nero for dinner at his home and introduced him to his wife. Nero fell in love with Poppea and made her his lover, with the approval of the husband.

Nero divorced his wife Octavia, the daughter of the late Claudius, and, after killing her, he married Poppea, who had by then divorced Otto. Gradually, Poppea acquired more and more influence over the Emperor until she managed to convince Nero that his mother Agrippina intervened too much in his affairs.

Nero decided to kill his mother, Agrippina. He tried several times to poison her but failed. Finally, he ordered the captain of his mother's ship to wreck it, but Agrippina saved herself by swimming to shore. Finally, Nero got tired of his failed attempts to kill her in secret, accused her of conspiracy, and had her executed."

"Asher, I apologize for interrupting you. Everything you've told me is interesting, but it does not explain why Aliturius thinks he can convince Poppea to plead for my friends before the Emperor," I said.

Asher pulled his stool closer to mine, lowered his voice to the point that I could barely hear him, and spoke into my ear.

"Aliturius was one of Poppea's lovers before Nero met her. Of course, he no longer has that kind of relationship with her, it would be too risky, but they are still great friends. Poppea, if Aliturius asks her, will tell Nero to free your priests."

I do not know the details of what happened, and I did not want to ask about it either, but a few weeks later, the guards released the four priests. The next day, without wasting any time, I took them to the port of Ostia and bought passage on a ship that took us to the port of Caesarea, in Judea.

In Caesarea, we joined a caravan, and, three days later, we were in Jerusalem.

Chapter 4
Back in Judea

The Sanhedrin members were glad to see that the four priests who had been taken captive to Rome had returned safely. They asked me for a written report, which I gave to them, and a list of the expenses incurred during my stay in Rome. They approved all the items without objection.

Rabban Simon ben Gamaliel invited me to dinner that night at his house, an honor that he very rarely granted to young priests like me.

My return, after an absence of several months, allowed me to see Jerusalem with different eyes. I could not help but acknowledge that, in certain aspects, my hometown could not compare with Rome. Unlike the capital of the Empire, the capital of Judea lacked aqueducts, did not have the drainage network that makes Rome justly proud, and few of its streets were paved. It lacked the statues, the triumphal arches, and water fountains that adorn and beautify Rome. The lanes that meandered through the hills on which the city stood were so narrow that only pedestrians, donkeys, and mules could pass through them.

I confess that the comparison that I have just made between the two cities is unfair. Rome has a million inhabitants and is a vibrant and prosperous city due to the taxes it receives from the provinces. Although Jerusalem had only sixty thousand inhabitants, the population increased with hundreds of thousands of pilgrims and visitors from all parts of the Empire during the three annual religious pilgrimages.

The beauty of Jerusalem was extraordinary and unique in the world. Built on hills and surrounded by forests, the city had impressive buildings. The main one was the Temple, an architectural marvel whose reputation for beauty had spread throughout the Empire. Another beautiful building was the palace that King Herod had built during his reign. A high wall, adorned with ornamental towers, surrounded it. It contained large banquet halls and bedrooms for one hundred guests. The walls of the rooms were covered with marble and adorned with gold and silver. The palace garden had many shady trees and walking paths. Canals, where colorful fish swam, crisscrossed it.

The Romans, after the death of Herod, lowered the status of Judea from kingdom to province. They built a theater, an amphitheater, and a racecourse for the exclusive use of the Roman garrison and the Roman and Greek communities that resided in Jerusalem.

After my return, I had many conversations with my friends and with my fellow priests, where I noticed that, during the months that I had been absent, there had been a significant change in the people's attitude towards the Romans. They no longer felt proud to be part of the vast Roman Empire. On the contrary, they considered themselves occupied and oppressed. Many spoke openly about a possible rebellion.

I asked myself what was the reason for the people's discontent. Finally, I concluded that the dissatisfaction had three fundamental causes. The first was cultural and spiritual. The second was the economic situation of the population. The third was the disillusionment of the people with the leading priests.

From a spiritual point of view, it was intolerable for Jews, members of a profoundly religious and cultured nation, to be the subjects of a pagan state where the population, from the Emperor to the humblest citizen, prayed to idols made by craftsmen. They could not accept that the Emperor, a human being like any other, was proclaimed a god after his death. The Jews felt a particular disdain for the Romans and the Greeks (whose culture and religion the Romans had appropriated) and found them naive believers in myths and superstitions.

Regarding the economic situation, the excessive taxes that the Roman governors charged, which exceeded what other places in the Empire paid, had impoverished the population of Judea. Many peasants had been forced to go into debt and had no choice but to sell their property. Thousands of workers, who had participated in the now finished Temple building, were currently unemployed and had no means to support their families.

Concerning the priests, those who now occupied high positions were not the descendants of the traditional priestly dynasty but upper-class, pro-Roman members of the Sadducee sect. These individuals, chosen by the Roman Governor, desecrated the Jewish sacred practices by mixing them with sacrilegious pagan rituals.

I had many discussions where I tried to persuade my interlocutors that it was madness and suicide to defy Rome. We had no army, and our youth did not train for war. The result of a rebellion would be a tragedy as terrible as it had been, centuries before, the destruction of the Temple of Solomon and the exile of our population to Babylon.

Unfortunately, very few people agreed with me. Rumors began to circulate that I was sympathetic to the Romans. I decided to keep quiet to prevent people from distrusting and hating me.

I did not mix in politics during the following years, nor did I participate in the armed rebellion preparations. Instead, I concentrated on carrying on with the Temple's administrative tasks to which the Sanhedrin had appointed me. My responsibilities included overseeing the Treasure Room, where we stored the gold utensils donated by foreign dignitaries and the money sent by all the Jewish communities in the Empire.

Back in Judea

Chapter 5
The beginning of the rebellion

Three years after my return from Rome, in the twelfth year of Nero's reign, shortly after my twenty-ninth birthday, the spark that caused the conflagration that, years later, destroyed Jerusalem and the Temple, was lit in Caesarea.

The population of Caesarea was composed of Greeks and Jews who hated each other. The synagogue of the city was located next to a vacant lot that belonged to a Greek. The Jews, on numerous occasions, had asked the owner to sell them his property and offered an amount of money several times greater than its real value. The man refused to sell and, on the contrary, decided to build in his property a building for commercial uses, leaving one passage that led to the entrance to the synagogue. Unfortunately, the path was so narrow that it would be difficult, almost impossible, for the Jews to reach their premises. The Jews sued the owner. The judge, who was Greek, ruled in favor of the defendant.

The Greek owner's sons, annoyed by the trial's cost and the time it had taken, attacked the plaintiffs and then, accompanied by a crowd, went to the Jewish quarter and massacred dozens of men, women, and children. The soldiers of the Roman garrison of Caesarea witnessed the mob's outrages but refused to intervene and did nothing to defend the unarmed Jews.

A few days later, the Roman Procurator Gessius Florus, who was stationed with his troops in Caesarea, came to Jerusalem, went directly to the Temple, entered the Treasure Room, and seized many valuable utensils and gold coins. Later, we learned that he had acted on Nero's orders. The Emperor needed money for the construction of his palace, the Domus Aurea, in Rome.

Some Jews made fun of the Procurator and started a collection for "poor Florus." The Procurator, who was not known to have a sense of humor, sent soldiers to capture the

413

pranksters. The soldiers returned empty-handed and informed him that they had not been able to catch the men. Florus ordered his troops to loot the market neighborhood and kill anyone they found there to "teach those Jews a lesson."

The soldiers complied with the orders but were not satisfied with just looting the market and killing the people they saw on the street. They entered the houses and massacred about three thousand six hundred people, including women and children.

Princess Berenice (sister of Agrippa, son of King Agrippa The Great, the last king of Judea) went to the Antonia fortress, adjacent to the Temple, to speak with Florus. She begged him to order his soldiers to stop killing the inhabitants of Jerusalem. Florus refused to listen to her. When the soldiers saw that the princess was leaving the fortress, they threatened her. Berenice escaped and took refuge in her palace, where her guards protected her.

Florus hated the Jews and continuously sought pretexts to punish them. He ordered two cohorts, which had about one thousand soldiers, to come from Caesarea to Jerusalem. To humiliate the Jews, he demanded that Jerusalem's inhabitants should demonstrate their submission to Rome by going out in a procession from the city to receive them.

The priests, dressed in their ornamental garments, accompanied by musicians and singers and followed by a crowd, complied with Florus' request. They went to meet the Roman soldiers and greeted them with great courtesy.

The Procurator, for further humiliation, had ordered the centurions not to answer the greetings. Some Jews felt offended and insulted the soldiers. Florus immediately seized upon this excuse and gave a signal to attack. The Roman horsemen ran over the people who were nearby. The Jews ran to the city gate, pushing each other. Those who fell to the ground died trampled and suffocated.

A few days later, Florus returned to Caesarea, leaving a garrison of six hundred soldiers in the palace that had belonged to Herod.

Chapter 6
Agrippa tried to appease the people

Agrippa, the son and namesake of King Agrippa the Great was seventeen years old when his father, the last king of Judea, died. Emperor Claudius considered the son to be too young to reign in Judea, a nation that was always on the verge of rebellion due to its religious convictions. His solution was to convert Judea into a province, directly governed by a Roman official, with the title of "Procurator."

As a "consolation prize," Claudius named the young Agrippa king of Chalcis, a small territory north of Judea, and gave him responsibility for the Jerusalem Temple's upkeeping.

Although the young Agrippa had no jurisdiction or authority in Judea, he felt, as a Jew and as a son of King Agrippa the Great, morally responsible for the welfare of the population of Judea. During his frequent visits to Jerusalem, he would stay in the palace built by his ancestor, King Herod.

When he learned that many people wanted to take revenge on the Romans for the outrage committed by Florus, Agrippa came to Jerusalem and invited the members of the Sanhedrin, prominent citizens, and the leading priests of the Temple, I among them, to meet with him to discuss the situation.

I arrived before the other guests to express my concern to Agrippa about the fanatics' intentions that could lead us to an unprecedented calamity.

"Joseph, you don't need to convince me," Agrippa replied. "I consider you an intelligent and moderate man, and I want to assure you that I am also in favor of reaching a peaceful understanding with the Romans. I will do everything I can to prevent the Jews from rebelling against the Empire and bringing a terrible catastrophe upon our people".

The other guests arrived. Agrippa greeted them and waited for everyone to sit down before he spoke to us.

415

"Dear brothers, I have arranged this meeting to try to avoid a great tragedy. It is true that the procurator Gessius Florus has behaved like a criminal by murdering innocent people and stealing gold from the Temple. But, not all Romans act that way. The Emperor, against whom you want to rebel, has never treated you like that. It is absurd to wage war on a large army to protest the actions of an individual. Also, take into account that Florus will not be a procurator forever. His successor will likely be a fair and decent man, as are most Roman officials. People, stronger and more powerful than you, are happy subjects of Rome. The Greeks, who defeated the vast Persian army of Xerxes, are today part of the Roman Empire. The Macedonians, who conquered the world with Alexander the Great, are today subjects of the Romans. The Germans, a warlike people with an immense territory, are controlled by the Roman legions. Only you, of the hundreds of nations that are part of the Roman Empire, believe that being governed by the Romans is a misfortune and a shame. What army do you have that can oppose the Roman army? Where is your navy? The Egyptians, a nation independent under the pharaohs for thousands of years, pay more tribute to the Romans in a month than you pay in a year. You believe that God will help you, but the Roman Empire's power is proof that God is with them. To make war against Rome is suicide. Your children and your women will die. Fire will consume your cities. This misfortune will not only fall on you but also on the Jews who live in all corners of the Empire. Have mercy on your children, pity your beautiful city, and do not endanger the Temple's sacred walls!

Tears ran down Agrippa's cheeks as he spoke. Most of us remained silent, but some shouted, "Traitor! Roman lover! Out of here!" Some even went to the extreme of throwing stones when Agrippa visited the Temple the next day.

Agrippa, seeing that he could not change the people's resolution, left Jerusalem and returned to his kingdom in Chalcis.

The ball started rolling, and nothing could stop it. Eleazar ben Ananias, the son of the High Priest, was a proud and impulsive young man. Using the authority of his official position, "Captain of the Temple," he ordered to cease immediately the sacrifices that the priests performed in the Temple in honor of the Roman Emperor.

That act was the declaration of war of the Jewish people to the powerful and invincible Roman Empire.

Agrippa tried to appease the people

Chapter 7
The rebels massacre
the Roman garrison

The rebels seized the Temple and threw out the High Priest. The priests who opposed the rebellion sent messengers to the Procurator Florus in Caesarea and King Agrippa, who was in Chalcis, asking for urgent help.

Florus ignored the request, but Agrippa sent his kingdom's cavalry, composed of three thousand armed riders, to Jerusalem. The moderates, with the help of the soldiers of Agrippa, seized Mount Zion in the upper part of the city. There were bloody battles and hand-to-hand fighting between the rebels and the moderates during the next seven days.

The rebels set fire to the High Priest house, to the palace that had belonged to King Herod, and to the residences that Agrippa and his sister Berenice maintained in Jerusalem. They went to the city archives and burned all the loan contracts, thus earning the sympathy and support of the debtors, most of whom belonged to the most impoverished class. The next day, the rebels attacked the Antonia fortress, a building next to the Temple. It served as the headquarters of the Roman garrison. The siege lasted two days, and when the fort fell into the hands of the rebels, they killed the entire regiment.

In those days, a man named Menachem arrived in Jerusalem with a group of assassins who called themselves "Sicarii" (Dagger-men). Previously, they had attacked Masada, the fortress on a plateau next to the Sea of Salt. They killed the garrison's soldiers and seized the weapons they found, swords, knives, shields, spears, and bows.

In Jerusalem, Menachem and his people stormed three towers where some Roman soldiers had taken refuge and massacred them. Then, they sought the High Priest Ananias and found him hiding in an aqueduct. They accused him of collaborating with the Romans and killed him.

419

Menachem, dressed in royal robes, went with his men to the Temple. Eleazar, the son of the slain High Priest, waited there with a large crowd. They rushed at the Sicarii, killing as many as they could. A group of the dagger-men managed to escape and fled back to Masada. Menachem tried to escape, but his enemies captured him before he could leave the city. His attackers tortured him cruelly until finally, they killed him.

The Roman soldiers who were still in the city barricaded themselves in Herod's old palace. The rebels besieged the palace for a month until the Romans ran out of supplies. They offered to surrender and give up their weapons to be allowed to leave the city unharmed. Eleazar accepted their request.

As soon as the soldiers surrendered, Eleazar ordered his people to kill them. All the soldiers died except their commander, who saved his life by pleading with the rebels to pity him and promising that he would convert to Judaism and be circumcised.

Chapter 8
The rebels defeat a Roman army

The Roman Governor of Syria, Cestius Gallus, assembled a large army and marched towards Jerusalem, accompanied by Agrippa who served as his guide. The Romans set fire to the towns they found on their way and massacred their inhabitants. When they arrived at Lydda, they saw that only fifty elders remained there since all the rest of the population, men, women, and children, had traveled to Jerusalem to participate in a religious Festival. Gallus ordered them killed and continued on his way.

The rebels ambushed him. The attack, which killed five hundred and fifteen Roman soldiers and only twenty-two rebels, came as a surprise to the Romans, who believed that the Jews would not attack them because it was the Sabbath.

Agrippa, eager to find a peaceful solution, sent two of his friends to talk to the rebels and inform them that Gallus offered them forgiveness and immunity if they surrendered. The insurgents killed one of the messengers and wounded the other. Upon hearing the tragic result of his attempt at mediation, Agrippa returned to his kingdom of Chalcis, north of Judea.

The forces of Governor Gallus came to Jerusalem and camped on Mount Scopus. A group of moderates contacted him and offered to open the doors of the city. Gallus, suspecting that it was a trap, did not accept the offer.

The Romans attacked the city and reached the gates of the Temple. Surprisingly, at this moment of victory, Gallus ordered the withdrawal of his troops. Until now, I am unable to understand what motivated him to act like that. Maybe he received a bribe, or perhaps he thought the rebels had learned the lesson. Whatever the reason for his strange behavior, the fact is that Gallus did not take the opportunity to end at that moment a rebellion that was just in its beginning. This terrible Roman error was paid for by the Jews years later with hundreds of thousands of deaths, exile, slavery, and the Temple's destruction.

Gallus marched with his troops through the narrow gorges that lead from Jerusalem to the coast to return from there to Antioch.

A force of two thousand four hundred Zealots (a name by which the most violent and fanatic anti-Romans called themselves), led by Eleazar ben Simeon, a priest, member of a distinguished family of Jerusalem, ambushed the six thousand soldiers of Gallus. Almost all the Romans died in the battle. Gallus saved himself by jumping into a ravine where he hid until the rebels returned to Jerusalem. He barely managed to reach Antioch, humiliated by having lost his army and an enormous amount of weapons and war material.

The Zealots returned to Jerusalem loaded with booty, weapons, and catapults taken from the Romans. Eleazar ben Simeon proclaimed himself the leader of the rebellion. However, the new High Priest, Ananias ben Ananias (brother of Eleazar ben Ananias), whose desire was to end the conflict and reach an agreement with Rome, deposed him.

The defeat of Cestius Gallus had the important, and, I would even say, the fatal, consequence of convincing people who, until that moment, wanted to make peace with Rome, to join the rebellion. Paradoxically, a Roman triumph would have been preferable because it would have prevented the rebels from fantasizing that the Jews had the force and the ability to defeat the mighty Roman Empire, master of the known world.

Chapter 9
Commander of the Galilee

The most important men of the city and the chief priests met in the Temple to appoint commanders for the army we were raising. Simon Ben Gamaliel, the president of the Sanhedrin, signaled me to sit next to him.

I had two surprises during the meeting. The first was that they rejected my proposal to appoint Eleazar ben Simeon as commander of the rebellion, even though he had defeated Cestius Gallus' army.

"Why has the Sanhedrin rejected my proposal to make Eleazar ben Simeon the commander of our forces?" I asked Simon ben Gamaliel.

"He is fanatic, impulsive, and tyrannical. We have not been spared from the Romans to be under the orders of a man as violent as Eleazar" he replied.

My second surprise was when Simon ben Gamaliel stood up and spoke to the assembly.

"I propose that we appoint Joseph ben Matityahu as commander of our forces in the Galilee," he said, and everybody applauded.

I stood up immediately to reject the proposal.

"It is a great honor for me that Rabban Simon ben Gamaliel considers that I am capable of taking on the great responsibility of defending the Galilee, but, I must tell you with humility and frankness, that this would be a grave mistake. I am adept with the pen, not with the sword. I have never had military training, nor have I taken an active part in conflicts. I appreciate the honor, but I cannot accept," I said and sat down.

Simon ben Gamaliel rose again and spoke.

"It's true, Joseph, that you have no military experience. But you have intelligence, an amazing facility to learn quickly, and great organizational capacity. What you have not learned from experience, you know from your reading and your study

423

of the battles of our ancestors as related in our sacred books. I reiterate my proposal for your appointment, and I ask that the assembly choose you unanimously."

I felt very flattered when everyone present stood up and cheered my name. I had no alternative but to accept the responsibility.

A week later, I traveled to Galilee to organize an army that would defend the Galilee.

Eleazar ben Ananias, the young priest who had started the rebellion by forbidding the sacrifices that the priests had previously made in the Temple in honor of the Roman Emperor, was sent to far away Idumea, probably because he was considered too impetuous and unreliable. I never heard from him again. He probably died fighting the Romans like so many others did.

Eleazar ben Simeon, resentful that the Sanhedrin had not given him official command of the rebellion, seized the Temple and made it his headquarters.

Chapter 10
I organize the defense of the Galilee

When I was commander of the Galilee, the experience I acquired taught me that the most important thing for a general is the population's support and goodwill. My first measure was to choose seventy people, prudent and of excellent reputation, to rule Galilee with me. I also appointed seven judges in each city for minor trials, reserving the most significant judgments for me and the seventy leaders.

I toured all the cities and towns of Galilee to check the condition of their walls. I gave orders to build walls around the towns that still did not have them and repair and reinforce the other cities' walls. The exception was Giscala, where an individual called Yochanan ben Levi, but better known as John of Giscala (who later caused me many problems), took charge of the city with my consent.

One hundred thousand young men volunteered to serve in the army that I was forming. I armed them with the swords, spears, and bows that I had collected or manufactured. Following the example of the Roman army, I appointed officers to command ten soldiers, captains to lead one hundred soldiers, and commanders to be in charge of a thousand soldiers. I taught them to march, to blow signals with the trumpet, and to do maneuvers. Not all of them were fit for military service, and, in the end, I ended up with an army of sixty thousand infantrymen, two hundred and fifty soldiers on horseback, four thousand five hundred mercenaries, and six hundred guards to be my bodyguards.

I organize the defense of the Galilee

Chapter 11
Opposition and revolts

I mentioned in the previous chapter an individual called John of Giscala. I didn't go into details previously, but now I will do so.

I lack adjectives to describe that scoundrel. His "qualities" included being a shrewd, perverse, deceitful, hypocritical, and thieving man. He surrounded himself with people like him, who followed him blindly. When I met him for the first time, he had under his command a band of four hundred outlaws.

I regret to say that my first impression of John was utterly mistaken. I took him for an honest and decent man, a sincere patriot. He asked for my permission to raise funds to repair the walls of his hometown, Giscala, and I, without suspecting anything, immediately gave it to him. I learned later that he extorted money from the rich in the city with threats and used that money for his personal needs and pleasures.

He deliberately gave me the false impression that he was a devout man. He did this by mentioning that he was worried that the Jews living in Syria did not use the oil produced in the land of Israel for their rites. He asked for, and I granted him, the monopoly of selling Galilean oil to the Jews of Syria. This business earned him immense sums of money.

A group of young Galileans convinced themselves that Agrippa was a collaborator of the Romans. They assaulted the king's butler on the road and stole six hundred gold coins, silver utensils, and expensive clothing.

At that time, I was in Tariquea, a town north of Tiberias, spending a few days vacation in a house on the beach. When I heard what had happened, I forced the assailants to come to my house and hand me the stolen goods. I intended to return his belongings to Agrippa at an opportune moment. The assailants spread the rumor that I intended to keep the money for my use.

A noise woke me up at dawn. I looked out the window and saw that an angry crowd, armed with torches, surrounded my house, intending to burn me alive. All the soldiers of my guard, except four, fled in terror. I went outside and faced the crowd.

"I want you to listen to me," I said.

Some of the men in the crowd shouted at me, "Traitor!" Others cried, "Kill him." Luckily for me, a few men told the crowd to allow me to speak. Gradually, people calmed down. I waited for complete silence, and then I spoke.

"Fellow countrymen, I have no intention of sending the gold and silverware to Agrippa. Much less do I intend to keep them. During my stay in Tariquea, I found that the city needs walls for its defense, and I want to use that gold and silver to build them. I did not say it publicly to prevent the people of Tiberias and other cities from demanding that I give them the money, which, as I just said, I want to use for the defense of your city.

The people of Tariquea applauded me enthusiastically, but the men from Tiberias who were there booed me. The result was that the men of Tariquea began to argue with the men of Tiberias, the arguments turned to insults, and finally, they pushed and hit each other. When I saw that the crowd was no longer paying attention, I went back to my house and closed the door.

When they saw that I was no longer with them, most of the people in the mob saw no point in staying and went away, except for about thirty hotheads who remained and shouted threats to come into my home by force.

I went up to the roof of the house and spoke to them.

"You make so much noise that I do not understand what you want from me. Send some of your representatives to talk with me, and I will gladly comply with your demands," I said and went downstairs to speak with my four remaining guards.

"Let three or four of the ringleaders enter and bring them to the farthest room in the house. I will be waiting there," I instructed them.

The guards allowed three men to enter the house and brought them to the room where I was. I ordered the guards to close the door so that the people outside would not hear the men's screams. The guards tied them and proceeded to whip them until they fainted. Meanwhile, the people outside waited patiently, assuming that their representatives were informing me of their demands.

Finally, I told the guards to throw the three men out of the house. Their companions, seeing them come out bloody, with their clothing in rags, threw down their weapons and ran away.

The next day I received a note from John of Giscala. At that moment, I still did not know or even suspect the kind of miserable individual he was.

The note said:

> *From John of Giscala to Commander Joseph ben Matityahu: Shalom Joseph! I hereby inform you that I am ill. My doctors have recommended that I go to the hot baths of Tiberias to recover my health. I ask you to give me sick leave.*

I answered:

> *From the commander Joseph ben Matityahu to John of Giscala: Shalom John! I grant you sick leave. I have instructed the authorities of Tiberias to provide you with all the necessary facilities, including accommodation. I wish you a quick and complete recovery of your health.*

According to the information reliable people sent me a few days later, John tried to incite a revolt against me when he arrived in Tiberias.

Immediately, I went to Tiberias to confront the scoundrel. The individual refused to see me saying that he was in bed, very sick, and that the doctors had forbidden him to leave the house and did not allow him to receive visitors.

I summoned the leaders of Tiberias and informed them of what John had tried to do. That night, a group of armed men sent by John broke into my house, intending to kill me. My two bodyguards and I jumped out the window and ran to the lake. We got into a boat and paddled with all our strength until we were far from the shore, but still close enough to see from there that my troops had caught the would-be murderers.

We rowed back to the shore. My men were waiting for me with the news that John had fled to Giscala, his hometown. I proclaimed that John's supporters had to surrender within five days, or, for those who did not, I would set fire to their homes on the sixth day with their families inside. My threat paid off, and all those known as supporters of John gave up their weapons and surrendered.

John sent messengers to Jerusalem who accused me of being a power-hungry tyrant, who was planning to march with my army to Jerusalem to proclaim myself head of the rebellion.

Some influential people in Jerusalem believed those lies and sent John two thousand five hundred armed men and a sum of money to hire mercenaries. My friends in Jerusalem secretly informed me of what was happening. This knowledge gave me time to prepare my army for any eventuality. John, seeing that I had discovered his plans, took refuge in Giscala.

Seeing that the danger had passed, I sent my army to harvest wheat while I remained in Tariquea. The population of Tiberias took advantage of that opportunity to rebel.

I went to the shore and counted the boats anchored in the lake. Their number was two hundred and thirty. I gave orders to the people of Tariquea to place four men in each vessel.

We sailed towards Tiberias. The men in the boats, following my orders, anchored at a certain distance so that the people on the shore would be unable to notice that the boats were practically empty. The only vessel approaching the coast was the boat where I was, accompanied by seven armed guards.

The crowd that watched us from the shore assumed that all the boats carried armed soldiers. When I disembarked, the leader, a man named Clitus, came to me and begged me to forgive the people for their revolt. I ordered one of my guards to punish Clitus by cutting off his hands. The guard, afraid of so many armed people standing nearby, refused to comply with my order. Clitus, seeing that I was unsheathing my sword, spoke to me.

"Joseph, I beg you to cut off just one of my hands," Clitus pleaded.

"I agree to your request, on condition that you cut off your hand," I replied.

So great was Clitus' fear that he did not hesitate a moment. He drew his sword and cut off his left hand.

A few days later, my soldiers arrived. I permitted them to plunder the city and ordered them to bring me the booty. The next day I returned the looted items to their lawful owners. I obtained a double result: I taught a lesson to the population by allowing looting, and I won their goodwill by giving them back their belongings.

This incident ended the revolts, and I could finally concentrate on the coming battle against the Romans. Meanwhile, in Jerusalem, the population reinforced the walls and manufactured weapons.

Opposition and revolts

Chapter 12
About the Roman army

Emperor Nero, alarmed by the rebellion, sent Vespasian, one of his most experienced and able generals, to Syria with an army to fight against the rebels in Judea.

General Vespasian, a fifty-eight-year-old man, had fought with great success against the German and British tribes. When he arrived in Syria, the first thing he did was order his son Titus, who was twenty-eight years old, to go to Alexandria and bring the two legions based in Egypt.

Vespasian marched with his troops from Antioch, the Syrian province's capital, to Ptolemais, called Acre by the Jews. There, he was joined by the soldiers of Agrippa, under the king's command, and by Jewish volunteers from Sepphoris, a city in the Galilee that remained loyal to Rome.

The Roman army consisted of sixty thousand soldiers, plus an equal number of servants who had also been taught to fight.

I base the following descriptions of the Roman army on observations I made when, sometime later, I became their prisoner.

Roman soldiers train daily, both in times of war and in peacetime, which allows them to maintain an excellent physical condition.

When entering enemy territory, the first thing they do is gather stones and rocks to build a square fence or wall around their camp. In each section of the wall, they construct a tower from which they shoot arrows. The wall has four entrances, one on each side of the wall. Two streets divide the camp, one from north to south and the other from east to west. The commanders' tents are in the center, and in the middle of them stands the general's tent.

The sound of the trumpet marks the time to go to sleep and the time to get up. The trumpet also gives the order to dismantle the tents, place the luggage on the mules and burn what remains in the camp so that it does not fall into the enemies' hands.

Every morning the officers go to the general's tent to receive the password and the day's orders. An officer on the right side of the general asks in a loud voice, "Soldiers! Are you ready?"

"We're ready!" the soldiers shout in one voice before they start marching.

The soldiers wear a helmet on their heads and armor that covers their chests. On their left side, they have a sword, and on the right, a dagger. They carry a spear and shield and also an ax and provisions for three days. The discipline of the soldiers is extraordinary because their rules are stringent. Deserters receive the death penalty.

During the march, a group of soldiers marches ahead to verify that the enemies are not preparing an ambush. The archers follow them. Then come the commanders, surrounded and protected by their guards. Behind them, the general with his cavalry guard, along with the soldiers who carry the imperial eagle's emblem. The mules follow, carrying the luggage, the tents, and the catapults. Finally, the soldiers march, in rows of six, followed by a crowd of servants and mercenaries.

Chapter 13
The siege of Yodfat

Vespasian marched with his army to Galilee. The first city he found, Gadara, had few defenders and the Romans conquered it quickly. The general gave instructions to kill all the men and sell the women in the slave markets. After doing that, the Romans set fire and destroyed the city.

I was in Garis, a village near Sepphoris, when a survivor of Gadara arrived and told me what happened. I knew that my army was not large enough to face Vespasian, and I also realized that many of my combatants had lost their courage and wanted to surrender. I felt strong doubts about our possibilities against the Romans. I determined to get away as far as possible, and, thus, with the men who were still with me, I fled to Tiberias.

That night, sitting on the shore of the lake, I debated with myself what I should do, surrender to the Romans or die fighting. I chose not to betray my nation and not dishonor my name, despite my pessimism about our war chances.

Knowing the strength of the enemy and our weakness, I wrote to Jerusalem asking for reinforcements, or, if they could not send any, to authorize me to negotiate with the Romans.

Without waiting for an answer, I traveled to Yodfat to organize its defense and personally direct it because, being the best-fortified city in the whole of Galilee, it was likely that Vespasian would consider it his first and most important objective. And that is what happened.

Yodfat was built on the top of a hill. Deep abysses surrounded it, except on the north side, where there was only a defensive wall. The only road that led to the city was narrow and rocky. Infantry soldiers could use it but not the cavalry and, still less, the carts that carried the catapults.

The Romans camped on a hill in front of the city. It took four days for the Roman workers to level the hill and pave a road. On the fifth day, a group of soldiers, under the command

435

of a centurion, approached the city's walls. I went out with many of my fighters, attacked them, and forced them to retreat. We killed thirteen Roman soldiers, but seventeen of our warriors died in the skirmish, and six hundred were wounded.

We saw that the Romans were cutting down all the trees that were outside the city. They also brought rocks and stones and used those materials to build a ramp that reached the top of our wall.

We shot arrows at them and threw stones. The Romans responded by firing projectiles with their catapults. My men attacked the Roman workers who were building the ramp and set it on fire.

I thought it necessary to increase the wall's height that surrounded the city, but my men argued that working on the top of the wall would make them easy targets for the Roman archers' arrows. I checked and verified that the enemy archers shot so many arrows that it would be suicidal for anybody to stand on the exposed top of the city wall.

However, I have always said that no problem is impossible to solve if one uses intelligence and ingenuity.

"Prepare stakes," I ordered," Place them at a close distance one from the other and spread skins of cows and oxen between them. Standing behind the skins will allow you to work on the walls behind the hides, and. Roman archers will not be able to shoot you because they will not see you.

Thus, we managed to raise the walls' height, and on top of them, we built towers and parapets.

My combatants recovered their fighting spirit during the following days. They went out of the city several times, taking advantage of the darkness of the night, to attack by surprise the enemy soldiers and set on fire their catapults.

Vespasian, seeing that arrows and catapults were not enough to defeat us, decided to surround the city to prevent us from receiving provisions and thus cause a famine that would force us to surrender. What he did not know was that we had wheat and food in abundance. We lacked water since there were no fountains or wells in Yodfat, and the water used by the inhabitants was what they collected in the rainy season. Unfortunately, it was summer, the time of year when it does not rain in Galilee.

I gave orders to use water as little as possible and limited the amount given daily to each person. So that Vespasian would not suspect our lack of water, I hung soaked clothes on the parapets that dripped down the walls. Seeing how we wasted the water, the Romans, believing that we had an abundance of the liquid element, returned to their previous tactic of trying to defeat us using arrows and catapults. This was also what we wanted since we preferred to die fighting than to die of hunger and thirst.

I saw that our supplies were dwindling. Taking advantage of a section of the wall which abutted on an abyss, I sent a group of my men, skilled in climbing mountains, to bring back what we needed. I instructed them to cover themselves with sheepskins so, in case a Roman soldier would spot them, he would think they were animals.

I concluded that we could not continue resisting much longer and considered the possibility that some warriors and I should leave the city to save our lives and keep fighting. The people of the town learned what I was planning and begged me to stay to defend them.

"We cannot believe that you, our general, want to flee and escape as if we were a sinking ship," they told me.

Of course, I denied those allegations, although I must admit that they expressed the truth of my intentions.

"Friends, if I would ever leave you, it would not be to abandon you but to bring reinforcements. My presence here does not benefit anyone. On the contrary! The Romans, knowing that the commander of all the forces of Galilee is in Yodfat, will continue to besiege us until they capture or kill me. However, if they find out that I am no longer in the city, they will likely withdraw and look for me in other places," I argued.

My argument did not convince the people. All of them, men, women with children in their arms, and the elderly, threw themselves at my feet and begged me to stay. I realized that if I would try to leave the city, it was likely that the defenders would kill me.

"Dear friends, I will never abandon you. I will continue fighting at your side, whatever happens. Honor and glory are more important to me than my own life," I told them.

To show the people that I was not giving up the fight, I went out with a group of my most seasoned fighters. We reached the Roman camp and set fire to several tents. The soldiers pursued us, but they were unable to catch us due to their heavy armor. We managed to return to the city without having suffered a single loss.

Vespasian decided to use the battering ram against our wall. It was a thick log of wood, with iron in the shape of a ram's head on one end. The soldiers who carried it went back a few steps, took impetus, and ran with the battering ram towards the wall to strike and weaken it. From the ramps that the Romans had built, which were as high as our wall, they threw spears and stones that killed several of our defenders while the battering ram continued to pound the wall. Those of us who were standing on the wall's parapet felt it tremble from the blows. It was inevitable that the wall would crumble if we allowed the battering ram to continue ramming in the same place.

I instructed my men to fill bags with straw and hang them from the parapet to cover the place where the battering ram was hitting the wall. The full bags managed to cushion the blows of the battering ram. But, Vespasian was also an ingenious man. He ordered his soldiers to tie hooks and knives at the ends of long poles with which they managed to cut the bags and empty them, which allowed them to continue hitting the wall with the battering ram.

One of my men, a muscular giant, grabbed a rock and threw it to the ram with such force, and with such good aim, it broke the head of the ram-shaped iron. He jumped down, grabbed the ram's head, and climbed up the wall. The Romans were astonished but soon recovered and riddled him with arrows. Our fighter fell to the ground, dead, but even then, he did not let go of the ram's head that he held in his arms.

From the parapet, I saw in the distance a group of men who, judging by their uniforms, seemed to me to be officers. In their middle stood one officer surrounded by all the others.

"I think that man is Vespasian. Do you see him?" I asked my best archer, pointing with my arm.

"I see him," he answered.

"It is our opportunity. Kill him!" I shouted enthusiastically.

The archer shot his arrow. The man, who sI thought was Vespasian, fell to the ground. Numerous Roman soldiers ran towards him. All of us on the parapet shouted jubilantly and hugged each other. We stopped when we saw that the fallen officer managed to stand up with another officer's help and walked away limping.

Sometime later, I learned that, indeed, the officer that my archer had injured was Vespasian himself and that the arrow had wounded his leg superficially.

The Roman soldiers, furious that we had wounded their general, ran towards the city's wall, firing arrows. Their catapults threw rocks that destroyed part of the parapet and killed a large number of my fighters. I saw a rock that was coming in my direction, and I threw myself to the ground. The stone passed over me and split in two the head of the man who was behind me.

The women sobbed and pulled out their hair when they heard the cries of the dying men. The wounded screamed in pain. There were so many dead that it was impossible to move from one side of the wall to the other without stepping on them. Blood covered the parapet.

I ordered the women to go back to their homes so that my combatants would not listen to their tears and become infected with their fear.

The section of the wall, weakened by the battering ram, crumbled. My fighters closed the gap with their bodies and prevented the Romans from entering the city.

The next day, Vespasian ordered his army to surround the city. I told the men who stood in the sections of the wall weakened by the battering ram's impact to cover their ears so as not to hear the Roman cries of war.

"Men," I ordered them. "Use your shields to defend yourselves from the arrows. If you see that the Roman soldiers are placing ladders to climb the wall, do everything you can to prevent their attempt."

The Romans blew their trumpets and shouted at the same time. The noise was immense, but it did not affect my men, who, following my order, had covered their ears. The enemy's arrows darkened the sky, but our victims were few because we protected ourselves with our shields.

"Courage!" I exclaimed to strengthen the resolution of my soldiers. "We must fight so that our old men will not be slaughtered, our women will not be raped, and our loved ones will not be captured and sold into slavery."

The Romans placed their ladders against the wall and began to climb. I gave orders to pour boiling oil over them. The hot liquid ran under their armor on their bodies and caused them terrible burns. They fell from the ladders and wallowed in the earth, trying to get rid of the unbearable pain. The soldiers who had been behind them took their place and continued to climb up.

We poured over them a liquid mixed with fat that caused the ladders to become slippery. The climbing soldiers fell to the ground, one on top of the other. This allowed our archers to shoot them easily. The Romans finally retreated, taking with them their dead. On our side, we only lost six men.

Vespasian ordered to increase the height of the ramps and to build three towers, which, covered with iron, we weren't able to destroy by fire. Their archers and javelin throwers climbed up the towers and shot us from the top, killing many of my men.

440

Meanwhile, an officer of the Roman army, commanding two thousand soldiers and a thousand riders, attacked a nearby town defended by a double wall. The defenders went out of the city to fight against the Romans but, forced to retreat, took refuge in the corridor between the first and second walls. Before they were able to close the outer gate, the Romans pushed their way inside. The fighters tried to enter the town, but the people, fearing that the Romans would also come in, closed the inner wall's gate.

The combatants knocked on the gate and begged the people inside to open it, but their pleas were ignored. The Romans slaughtered all the men who were trapped between the first and second walls.

On the forty-seventh day of the siege of Yodfat, a Jewish deserter went to the Roman camp and informed Vespasian that very few fighters remained in the city. He added that they were exhausted by the constant fighting and lack of sleep and that the best time to attack would be between midnight and early morning, when everyone would probably be asleep.

At the agreed time, a group of Roman soldiers went towards the city in complete silence. The Romans placed ladders against the walls that surrounded Yodfat, climbed up, and jumped inside, led by Tito. The soldiers who followed him surprised the sentries and killed them before they could sound the alarm. Then, they opened the city gates so that the rest of the army could enter. During six hours, my men fought the Romans hand-to-hand, house by house, while the women, from their windows, threw whatever they had to the Roman soldiers. The soldiers broke down the doors, entered the houses, and slaughtered those they found inside.

Many of my men committed suicide; others jumped into the abyss. A group of our fighters climbed to the top of the wall towers and managed to resist for several hours until the Roman soldiers killed them all.

A single Roman soldier died during the fight in the city. The Romans slaughtered all the men that they caught, including the old and the children. Vespasian ordered his soldiers to burn and destroy the town. Later, he sent the captured women to the slave market where brothel owners bought them.

Yodfat had resisted the mighty Roman army for forty-seven days, a resistance that cost us forty thousand dead. This happened in the thirteenth year of Emperor Nero's reign. [67 AD].

Chapter 14
I surrender to the Romans

The Romans, driven by the hatred they felt towards me for having caused the death of so many of their soldiers, and by the enormous impact that the news that the Jewish commander of the Galilee had been captured or killed would have on the morale of the rebels, made them search for me throughout the city.

The truth is that even today, I am unable to explain how I survived the massacre of the city without suffering even a scratch while most of the other defenders died. Undoubtedly, God protected me.

I ran through the alleys, pursued by soldiers. I turned a corner, saw an open door, entered the house, and closed it silently. The soldiers did not see me go in and continued running past the house. A few minutes later, I opened the door cautiously, saw that the street was deserted, and, hiding behind mounds of rubble every time I saw a soldier, I arrived at my house. There, I kept the uniform of a Roman officer I had killed in one of our skirmishes. I put on the uniform, the armor, and the helmet.

I left my house and headed for the city gate. I found a patrol of soldiers on the road, and fear paralyzed me. The soldiers stopped, stood stiffly, and greeted me with the Romans' usual greeting, touching their chest with their right fists closed. I returned the greeting with a calm that I was far from feeling and kept walking.

When I arrived near the city gate, I saw many Roman soldiers standing there. Their centurion talked to every man who was trying to enter or leave the city. It was evident that he asked them for the password. It was impossible for me, from where I was, to hear the questions and answers. I saw that an officer approached the gate, and a centurion stopped him. By the gestures of both men, I got the impression that they were arguing. Suddenly, the centurion tried to grab the officer's arm; the man pushed him aside and started running, pursued by the soldiers.

I recognized him! The "officer" was one of my men, who, like me, had disguised himself as a Roman soldier.

Minutes later, I saw him being dragged back and forced to kneel in front of the centurion, who took out his knife and cut the man's throat.

Obviously, I could not escape through the gate of the city. I turned around to try to reach a breach in the wall where, if God continued to protect me, I might not find any enemy soldiers. On the way, I came across a Roman officer who looked at me with curiosity. I accelerated my step.

"Stop! I want to talk to you," he shouted.

I started to run, followed closely by the officer who had unsheathed his sword. I intended to reach a deep cistern, which, according to what I remembered, was connected to a cave that was not visible from the surface. My desperation made me run faster than I thought I could. The officer who was chasing me fell behind. I reached the cistern and, without hesitation, jumped down. I landed on a mound of earth that cushioned the blow, rolled several feet, saw the cave entrance, stood up, and entered limping.

The cave was full of people! I had the impression that there were at least forty men and a few women. In the corner of the cave, I saw some provisions that would probably be sufficient for all of us for a couple of weeks.

For two days, I hid in the cave. On the third day, I heard voices shouting my name. I went out from the cave to the cistern and looked up. Two officers with a woman stood at the edge of the cistern. The woman was one of the people who had been in the cave, but she had left during the night. I assumed that she denounced me to the Romans to save her skin. I did not blame her. Many, maybe me too, would have done the same, and even worse, to save themselves.

The officers ordered me to surrender. They assured me that they would not kill me. I did not believe them and went back to the cave.

One or two hours later, I heard again my name being called. I went out and, although the man was wearing the uniform of a Roman officer, I recognized him. He was a Jew named Nicanor, with whom I had become friends in Jerusalem. In our conversations, he had always expressed sympathy to the Romans, so I was not surprised that he had joined their ranks.

"Joseph," he said," you have fought heroically. Vespasian admires you. He does not hate you. The general told me that if you surrender, he will not punish you. On the contrary, he will treat you with the honor you deserve. That's why he sent me when I told him that I'm your friend. You know me, and you know I do not lie."

I did not answer. The soldiers who were at Nicanor's side set torches on fire and were ready to throw them at me, but Nicanor forbade them.

At that moment, I remembered a dream I had a few nights before. I dreamed that God spoke to me and warned me that the Jews would suffer a terrible calamity. He also gave me a message about the Roman emperors. I needed to inform the Roman general of the message that God had given me.

"I will go with Nicanor, not as a deserter but as a bearer of a message from God," I said to myself.

"Nicanor!" I shouted," I'll go with you. I will climb up."

The men who were in the cave, when they heard me, came out, grabbed my arms, and forced me back into the cave.

"Joseph, you have persuaded many fighters to die for our freedom. Now you want to surrender to the Romans?" one of the men asked me, his face red with fury.

"Here is my sword," shouted another," Use it and die as a Jewish general should die. And, if you refuse, I will use it, and you will die as a traitor!"

To die before giving the divine message to the Roman general would be to betray God! I could not die! I tried to convince the people in the cave with arguments.

19 "Friends, it is honorable to die in a war at the hands of the enemy, fighting for freedom. But, it is a cowardly act to take your own life when you do not have to. Why do we fear

giving ourselves to the Romans? Is it because they will kill us? Why should we be afraid of that if we are willing to kill ourselves? Are we afraid of being enslaved and losing our freedom? But, do you call freedom being stuck in this cave without being able to leave? Suicide is a crime against God who has given us life. We have no right to offend him by taking away the gift that God has given us. Those who die of natural death will resurrect in the future. Those who commit suicide are condemned to be in Sheol, the dark underground place where all dead people go, the good and the bad, for all eternity. It is preferable to die by the hand of those who have defeated us. I'm not going to the Romans as a traitor; I'm not a deserter who acts to save his life; I'm going to them to get killed."

I could not convince them. Quite the opposite. They insulted me and shouted "coward" and "traitor." One drew his sword and threatened to plunge it into my chest.

I did not give up. I tried again to convince them, and this time I was successful! Never before in my life, and never since have I had such great success with my powers of persuasion as I did that day. I called one of the men by his name and embraced him as a friend. To another, I spoke severely, the way an officer talks to a soldier. I took the hand of a third man and begged him to be serene. To another, I assured him that anything I would do would be for his good. Little by little, they calmed down, and those who had drawn their swords sheathed them. When they all became quiet, I spoke again.

"Dear friends, I see that you have resolved that we must die in this cave. I accept your decision, and I suggest the following so that we do not sin by committing suicide: let's cast lots to determine the order of our deaths. Whoever gets drawn first will be killed by the second, and he, in turn by the third, until, finally, there will be left only one man alive. He will kill himself, and, in consequence, only he will be guilty of the sin of committing suicide.

They accepted my proposal and proceeded, one by one, to kill each other. The man who killed another man was in turn killed by a third man, and so on. Finally, (I cannot tell if it was due to luck, to God's decision, or my ingenuity), only two of us were left alive, myself and another man.

When it was my turn to kill the only companion still alive or be killed by him, it was not difficult to convince him that surrendering to the Romans was our best alternative. We left the cave and climbed to the edge of the cistern, grabbing the ropes that the soldiers threw at us.

I surrender to the Romans

Chapter 15
My prophecy to Vespasian

Nicanor, my Jewish friend who had joined the Roman army, took my surviving companion and me to the Roman camp. The soldiers separated us, and I never saw him again. The Romans likely killed him that same day.

The soldiers came out of their tents and pushed each other to look at me more closely. Some stared in amazement, others with a contemptuous smile, and most of them with hatred. I heard shouts demanding my death.

Nicanor took me to a tent, which was bigger and more luxurious than the others. It had carpets on the floor and elegant furniture. Nicanor chained me to a chair, instructed four soldiers to keep an eye on me, and went out to tell his superior officers that I had been captured.

A while later, Nicanor returned with an officer, a young man, perhaps one or two years younger than me (I had turned thirty a few weeks before).

"Joseph, I have the honor of introducing you to General Titus, son of General Vespasian," Nicanor announced.

Titus and I looked at each other with mutual curiosity. I think he was surprised at my youth, and I was amazed to see in person a man who, despite his young years, had become a legend for his righteousness, his courage, and his intelligence. Neither of us imagined that, with time, we would become best friends.

I had heard many stories about him. There were numerous accounts of his bravery and his prowess. Once, in a battle, when the enemies killed the horse he was riding, he immediately mounted the horse of a soldier who had just fallen dead at his side and continued fighting. In the siege of one of our cities, he shot dead twelve defenders with twelve arrows.

"General," I said," I must speak with General Vespasian. I have to tell him something of immense importance."

449

Titus, accompanied by an escort of ten soldiers, took me to his father's tent. He ordered the soldiers to keep me outside and went in to talk to the general. Months later, I learned that Vespasian had already decided to send me immediately to Rome to be tried by Emperor Nero and executed. However, his son Titus had convinced him that he must first listen to what I had to say.

Titus untied my hands, held me by my arm, and took me inside the tent. I saw three men. One of them, Vespasian, was sitting. The other two stood by his side. The three officers looked at me without saying a word.

"Ave, Vespasian!" I greeted him as the Romans do, striking my chest with my fist. I do not present myself to you as a defeated general but as the messenger of divine news. God has sent me to tell you a prophecy. For many years my nation has believed that a man will come out of Judea to rule the whole world. That man is you, General Vespasian! God has commanded me in a vision to tell you that you will be Emperor."

The reaction of Vespasian, Titus, and the two other officers was not what I expected. Instead of expressing amazement and admiration for my prophecy, they laughed out loud.

"You are as clever with words as you were in defending your city," Vespasian said, laughing, and added," but that will not save you."

"If you are such an excellent prophet, why did you not prophesy the people of Yodfat that their city would fall into our hands and that all resistance was useless?" one of the commanders asked sarcastically.

"Commander, I assure you that I prophesied to my people that the city would hold out for forty-seven days and that I would be taken alive by the Romans," I replied.

"It's easy to verify if you're telling the truth," Vespasian said. Addressing the commander who had spoken to me, he ordered," Bring me one of the Jewish officers we've captured, and we'll ask him if it's true that this man prophesied the fall of the city."

The commander who had mocked me left the tent and returned with one of my soldiers who had his hands tied. I noticed that the man was shocked to see me but did not say a word.

"I want you to tell us if it is true that Joseph prophesied that Yodfat would be captured at the end of forty-seven days of siege," Vespasian ordered him.

I did not dare to make a sign, not even to look at him, but, silently, I prayed to God to inspire the man to give the correct answer. My life depended on what he would say.

The man remained silent for one or two minutes, the longest of my entire life.

"Answer already! We're not going to wait for you all day," Vespasian shouted irritably.

"Sir, it's true. General Joseph ben Matityahu summoned all the officers on the first day of the siege and told us that he had had a vision in which God announced that we would fight with honor for forty-seven days, but, finally, the Roman army would take the city," replied the man.

God had heard my prayer and had dictated to the man the perfect, unbeatable, wonderful answer!

"Joseph, I see that you were sincere in informing me of the prophecy. I will not send you to Rome, but I will not let you free until your vision is fulfilled. In the meantime, you will be part of my son Titus' entourage. It is no longer appropriate in this case to call you by your Hebrew name. We will change it to Latin. From today on, you will no longer be called Joseph, but Josephus."

Months later, people told me about the reaction in Jerusalem when the leaders of the rebellion heard that Yodfat had fallen. At first, they refused to believe it, but later, when survivors of the siege arrived, they had to accept the bitter reality. They heard rumors that I had fallen defending the city, and they mourned for me. However, when they eventually learned that I had surrendered to the Romans and received special treatment, they accused me of being a cowardly deserter and traitor.

My prophecy to Vespasian

Chapter 16
Vespasian

Before continuing with the story of the Great Rebellion, I want to describe Vespasian.

He became emperor after a civil war broke out in Rome. Three generals, when Nero committed suicide, successively proclaimed themselves emperors. Each of them governed for only a few months until the last of the three was defeated and killed by troops loyal to Vespasian.

When I first met Vespasian, he was fifty-nine years old. He came from a family that, generations before, had a humble origin. His predecessors climbed the social ladder that culminated with Vespasian, who acquired fame and reputation when he commanded the army that defeated the savage tribes of Britain. As I mentioned earlier, Emperor Nero considered him the most capable of his generals and sent him to Judea to suppress the rebellion.

Vespasian was an extraordinary general. Despite imposing a rigid military discipline and applying harsh punishments to those who deserved it, his troops adored him. In the battles, he fought in the front line and was wounded more than once. On one occasion, he told me that he had lost count of the numerous arrows he had managed to stop with his shield.

He had great faith in oracles, prophecies, and omens, all of which had announced that he would one day be Emperor, though none of the other predictions was as clear and specific as mine.

Vespasian was a man of medium height, stocky, with the appearance of a boxer. His face had the peculiarity of always being red, with an expression of constant effort, which gave the impression that he was at that moment striving to fulfill a physiological need.

He was, without a doubt, the most intelligent and astute man I have ever met in my life. He had an excellent sense of humor. He once asked his treasurer how much he estimated

453

his funeral would cost when he died. The treasurer replied that it would cost at least several million sesterces. Vespasian replied, "Give me one hundred thousand sesterces now and throw me to the river Tiber when I die."

Perhaps it is not respectful to his memory to say that he was rude, but, to put it frankly, his conversation was not that of a refined man. His vocabulary was more suited to a soldiers' barrack than to a palace.

If he had one defect, it was his hunger for money. On one occasion, his son Titus, who was his right hand, criticized him for imposing so many taxes.

"The only thing you haven't done yet is to impose fines and taxes on those who urinate in the street," Titus told him.

A few weeks later, Vespasian called Titus to his office and gave him some coins to smell.

"Do they smell bad?" Vespasian asked his son.

"No," Titus replied.

"These coins are the payment for the tax I have imposed on urine," Vespasian told him and laughed.

On another occasion, one of his servants, whom the Emperor esteemed, asked Vespasian to give a job to a man who said the servant was his brother. Vespasian did not answer but called the candidate.

"How much did my servant demand for getting you the job?" asked Vespasian.

The candidate mentioned the amount, and Vespasian said, "Give me that money. You have the job."

Then he called the servant and said: "Find another brother, the one you thought yours is now mine."

During a reception, I witnessed a humorous incident. Several citizens approached the Emperor and informed him that they had collected a sum of money to build him a statue. Vespasian opened his palm and told them, "This is the pedestal. Put the money here."

He rose before dawn and read and answered the correspondence that had arrived during the night. Then, he allowed his friends to come into his room and dressed while

454

talking to them. He went out for a while on a litter, then returned to his room to rest, usually (after his wife's death) in the company of a woman. Afterward, he would go to the dining room with excellent humor, which his courtiers took advantage of to present him their requests.

Vespasian was Emperor for ten years until he died shortly after his seventieth birthday [79 AD]. He retained his sense of humor until the end of his life. When he became ill, he said, referring to the Roman custom of proclaiming the divinity of the deceased emperors, "Woe is me; it seems to me that I am becoming a god!"

His son Titus, who succeeded him, died of an illness after reigning for only two years. The current Emperor is Domitian, Titus' younger brother.

Bust of Emperor Vespasian

Vespasian

Chapter 17
The Battle of the Lake

Winter, a time of heavy rains, was approaching. Vespasian, whose tactic was to destroy methodically, one by one, all the cities of Galilee and Judea, decided to give his troops a rest. He took the army to Caesarea, where the population (most of them were Greeks who hated the Jewish minority) cheered him.

A delegation of the city leaders asked Vespasian for an audience and demanded my death, a demand that was disregarded by the general, fortunately.

Vespasian, not wanting to burden Caesarea with the maintenance of the whole army, sent two legions to Scytopolis (called Beith Shean in Hebrew) so that the soldiers could rest there for a few weeks.

Meanwhile, a problem arose in Jaffa, a fishing port south of Caesarea. Having decided that it was more profitable for them to be pirates than fishermen, its inhabitants were ravaging the entire coast from Egypt to Phoenicia.

Vespasian sent a legion to Jaffa. The inhabitants fled in their boats out to sea beyond the reach of the Roman arrows. What happened next clearly proved on whose side was God. Suddenly, a hurricane wind arose that made the boats collide against each other and pushed them against rocks that jutted out of the water. The bodies of hundreds of drowned people covered the sea. Those who swam and managed to reach the shore were killed by the Romans, who then burned down and destroyed the city. That was the end of their piracy.

Agrippa, the king of Chalcis (son of Agrippa the Great, the last king of Judea), invited Vespasian to spend a few days in his palace in Caesarea Phillipi, a city located on the Golan Heights.

Two days after the general's arrival, Agrippa was informed that Tiberias and Tariquea, two cities that belonged to his kingdom, had rebelled.

457

Vespasian ordered the legions in Scythopolis to march on Tiberias. The rebellion's ringleaders fled and took refuge in Tariquea, a city situated on Lake Galilee's shores, north of Tiberias. It was fortified and defended by fanatical rebels who were unwilling to surrender. Vespasian, foreseeing that the siege could last weeks, ordered his soldiers to build a camp halfway between Tiberias and Tariquea.

Vespasian had assigned me the duties of translator and interpreter. In practice, that meant that he called me only when the Romans managed to capture a rebel, which did not happen every day. I spent my time, always guarded by two soldiers, sitting in front of the lake under the cozy shade of palm trees, enjoying the cool breeze and, sometimes swimming, when the day was sweltering. The lake's water was crystal clear and had a sweet taste, more refreshing than any other water I have ever drunk in my life. I enjoyed relaxing on a boat near the shore while fishing fish which I had my people cook for me.

One day, many rebels went out of Tariquea and lined up in front of the city walls. Vespasian ordered his son Titus to go with six hundred riders to disperse them.

Titus, seeing so many rebels, sent a messenger to his father asking for reinforcements. Then, riding his horse, he climbed onto a promontory and addressed the troops intending to rid his soldiers of their nervousness and fear.

"Roman soldiers! The Jews are courageous and despise death, but they are not an army. They are a mob! Their few weapons are primitive, while you are heavily armed. They are on foot, and we are on horseback. They indeed fight for their freedom and their nation, but we fight for the glory of Rome. I will be the first to fight and attack the enemy. Follow me!"

Finishing his speech, he unsheathed his sword and lashed out at the rebellious mob. The soldiers followed his example, drew their swords, and galloped with impetus and fury.

The horsemen ran over the rebels and pierced them with their spears and swords. Many of them died trampled by the legs of the horses. The surviving rebels fled back to the city.

Almost immediately, the soldiers heard shouts of arguments and fights coming from the city. The citizens of Tariquea, most of them peaceful people and Roman sympathizers, tried to prevent the rebels, who were from other towns, from entering through the gate, fearing that their presence would destroy the city.

Titus immediately realized what was happening and shouted at his soldiers.

"They are fighting among themselves! Carpe diem! Seize the day! Let's take the city!"

Titus spurred his horse and was the first to cross the open gate of the city. All the soldiers followed him. The rebels, seeing that both the population and the Romans were attacking them, fled to the lake, climbed on their boats, and rowed away from the shore.

Titus ordered his soldiers to board the Roman ships, larger and faster than the rebels' fishing boats. The Romans approached the insurgents' vessels, who, lacking weapons, threw at them the stones that served as ballast in the boats.

The soldiers responded by shooting arrows. Then, sword in hand, they boarded the boats of the rebels, who, to save themselves, jumped into the water.

The Romans fired arrows at the men who were in the water. They cut the heads and the hands of those trying to save themselves by clinging to the boats. The rebels who managed to reach the shore were stabbed to death by the soldiers.

Hundreds of bodies floated in the lake, and the water, tinged red with blood, was no longer crystalline. Nobody buried the dead, and, for the next few days, the smell of rotting bodies on the shore was atrocious.

Vespasian met with his principal officers to determine the fate of Tariquea and its inhabitants. It was evident that the inhabitants of the town were not rebels. In fact, many of them had expressed sympathy for the Romans. There was also no doubt that the rebels, all of them killed in the struggle, came from other cities and had entered Tariquea against the population's will.

"I accept that the people of Tariquea are not rebels, but taking into account that we have destroyed their houses and their properties in the siege, they probably hate us now," one of the officers argued.

"I am convinced that if we let them go, they will join the rebels of other cities and fight against us," another officer said, agreeing with the first one.

Vespasian meditated for a few minutes and came to a decision.

"I agree with both of you. There is no other alternative. We have to execute them, but we must do it so that it will not cost even one of our soldiers' lives. They would resist if they suspected our intentions. Let's tell them that we will settle them in other cities, but that first we must take them to Tiberias to interview them and hear from each of them in which city he would like to live. They must believe us, so tell them to take all their belongings with them. That way, they will not have a reason to distrust us."

The people of Tariquea, men, women, children, and old men, were taken to the stadium of Tiberias. The soldiers surrounded them and set apart the elderly, the invalids, and those they considered useless. They took them outside the stadium and killed them.

The Romans sent the young men to the Isthmus of Corinth to work in Nero's canal. To show his friendship to Agrippa, Vespasian sent him two hundred teenagers as a gift, telling him that he could decide what to do with them.

Agrippa sold them in the slave market.

Chapter 18
The siege of Gamla

Gamla was the largest city in the Golan Heights. Its name, Gamla, referred to the fact that the inhabitants, most of them immigrants from Babylon, had built their city on the almost vertical slope of a mountain whose hump resembled a camel, ["gamal" in Hebrew].

Gamla was surrounded by deep precipices and fortified with a wall that I had ordered built when I was the Galilee commander. The city, from a distance, appeared to be a gigantic staircase, with rows of houses resembling steps. The pavements of each street were the roofs of the houses that were in the street below.

Vespasian gave orders to dismantle the Roman camp near Tiberias and marched with three legions to Gamla, accompanied by King Agrippa.

After setting up their camp on a high hill from whose heights they looked down on the city, the Romans began to construct ramps. King Agrippa, anxious to prevent further massacres, approached the wall to ask the defenders to lay down their weapons. A stone, shot by a skillful defender with a sling, wounded his right arm.

"These men are savages!" commented a Roman officer to his companions, with a mixture of admiration and contempt. "If they have no qualms about attacking one of their compatriots, who is speaking to them for their own good, imagine what they would do to us if we fall into their hands!"

Once the ramps were finished, the soldiers used battering rams against the wall. A sector of the wall, weakened by the blows, collapsed, and the Romans stormed the city, some of them blowing the trumpets.

The melee was unequal. The Romans were more numerous and better armed. The defenders fled to the upper parts of the city, closely followed by the soldiers. There, the rebels ambushed the Romans and killed several of them, taking

461

advantage of the narrow streets and their knowledge of the twists and turns. The Roman soldiers tried to retreat, but it was impossible because other soldiers huddled behind them in the narrow alley. The Romans managed to escape by jumping on the roofs of the lower row of houses, but the roofs were not strong enough to withstand the weight of so many individuals, and they collapsed. Many soldiers were buried in the rubble or died suffocated by the dust. The rebels killed the soldiers who had been injured or stunned by the fall and seized their weapons.

The surviving soldiers fled without seeing where they were going due to the thick clouds of dust covering the alleyways. They couldn't distinguish who was a Roman soldier and who a rebel, and many ended up fighting each other.

Vespasian, as was his custom, had been among the first Romans to enter the city. He was dismayed when he saw his soldiers buried in the ruins of the houses. Forgetting his own safety and accompanied by only a few soldiers, he kept climbing to the higher streets until, without realizing it, he reached the top of the city. There, a group of defenders ambushed them. Vespasian and his soldiers kept the attackers at bay, defending themselves with their swords and shields. They retreated, going back step by step, without turning their backs on their enemies, until they managed to get out of the city.

Vespasian noticed that his men's morale had fallen due to the defeat they had suffered and the shame they felt for having allowed their general to be in danger of his life.

The general ordered his men to place a table in the center of the camp, climbed on it, and spoke to the troops.

"It is natural in a war to have successes and setbacks, but it is absurd to be overjoyed at a victory or depressed too much by a temporary defeat. What happened today cannot be attributed to our weakness or the courage of the Jews but the difficulty of the place and our tactical errors. Instead of following our enemies when they fled to the city's upper parts, we should have stayed in the lower parts and made them ours.

The impetuosity that you showed is not characteristic of our army, and I am sure it will not happen again. We will remain calm, avenge our fallen comrades and punish those who killed them. I will continue fighting at the head of you against our enemies and will be the last to withdraw."

During the following weeks, the army limited itself to besieging the city and preventing reinforcements and provisions from entering. Many in Gamla, due to the lack of food, became weak and even starved. Some tried to escape by digging tunnels.

One night, three soldiers crept silently towards a tower that was part of the city wall. The soldiers, after loosening and removing the rocks that supported the wall, jumped back. The tower fell with a great rumble, destroying a section of the wall. Although the population, hearing the noise, believed that the Roman army was entering the city, the soldiers, remembering the previous disaster, did not rush in. They waited until Titus, at the head of two hundred horse riders, climbed over the debris. The city guards saw them and raised the alarm. With their children and women, the men ran up the alleys and took refuge in the fortress at the top of the mountain.

Vespasian ordered the army to enter the city and attack the fortress. The Jews defended themselves by throwing rocks and shooting arrows, but due to a great wind that blew against them, the arrows did not reach the Romans. The soldiers arrived at the door of the fortress without encountering any opposition. They knocked the gate down and entered. The defenders, seeing themselves lost, grabbed their children and their wives and jumped into the abyss. The whole population died like that. There were no survivors.

The Roman army remained in the camp for a few more weeks, burning and demolishing the city so that no one would occupy it again.

Vespasian took advantage of those weeks to solve a problem. A group of rebels had seized a fortress on Mount

Tabor's summit, a high mountain located in the central part of Galilee, from which they controlled the valley below.

The general ordered one of his commanders to go with six hundred riders to Tabor to take possession of the fortress. A week later, the commander returned and gave his report.

"When I arrived in Tabor, I saw that it was impossible to climb to the top of the mountain riding our horses. I sent a messenger to the fortress with a note in which I invited the rebels' leaders to come down to talk with me. I offered them safe conduct. My purpose, of course, was to kill them. The rebels accepted my proposal, but, in reality, they intended to kill me. I, anticipating what those men would try to do, gave orders to saddle my horse. The moment the traitors took out the knives they had hidden in their clothes, I mounted my horse and escaped, pursued by them. According to my plan, my soldiers hiding behind a wall pounced on the rebels. Not one of them was left alive. The rebels, who were still in the fortress, hearing that their leaders had died, fled to Jerusalem. And so I managed to take the fortress without risking the life of a single soldier."

Chapter 19
The conquest of Giscala

John, an individual whom I have described in a previous chapter as "a shrewd, perverse, deceitful, hypocritical and thieving man." defended Giscala, the only city in the Galilee that the Romans had not yet taken. He surrounded himself with people of his ilk, who followed him blindly.

Vespasian sent his son Titus with a force of a thousand cavalry soldiers to besiege Giscala, while he went to Caesarea with the rest of the army to allow his men to rest after such a difficult campaign. They needed to regain strength before besieging Jerusalem.

It would not be easy to take the capital of Judea since it was not only defended by massive walls but also by an army of thousands of brave rebels who had fled from Galilee to take refuge in Jerusalem.

Upon his arrival at Giscala, Titus saw that the walls of the city were low and weak. He had no desire to take the city by force, although this would not have been a difficult task. After witnessing so much destruction and death in the previous months, he now preferred a peaceful surrender.

He invited the people in the city to send a delegation to the Roman camp to speak with him. Only one man came, my hated adversary, John of Giscala. Titus received him in his tent.

"John," Titus said," I appreciate your coming. I admire your courage, but it does not make sense that you continue fighting when the whole Galilee, except Giscala, is already in our hands. I could understand it if you had the smallest possibility to resist us, but you do not have it. If you and your companions surrender and lay down your weapons, we will respect your lives and property. We promise that we will not damage the city."

"Commander, I appreciate your words and your proposal. I know that you are an honorable man and will fulfill what you

465

promise me. I will convince my people, with arguments or by force, to surrender, but I ask you to give us one more day. Tomorrow is the Sabbath, the day when we are forbidden, not only to wage war but also to speak of peace. I beg you not to force us to violate God's commandments. On Sunday, we will surrender and deliver you our weapons," John replied.

Titus agreed to wait one more day for the surrender of the city. That night, John and his supporters secretly left Giscala and fled to Jerusalem, forcing numerous children and women to go with them. When they were already some distance from the city, they saw that the women and children did not allow them to advance as fast as they needed and decided to abandon them on the way.

On Sunday, Titus, according to the agreement, entered the city by the open gate. The population received the Romans with applause and cheers.

"Where are John and his companions?" Titus asked the elders of the city. "We had agreed that today they would surrender and hand me their weapons."

Upon learning that John had escaped during the night and was heading to Jerusalem to join the defense of the capital, Titus sent a group of soldiers with orders to pursue and capture him. The soldiers found only the children and the women and brought them back to Giscala.

Titus, although John had deceived him, fulfilled his promise. He forbade his soldiers to plunder the city and ordered them to respect the lives of the inhabitants.

The conquest of Giscala was the end of the Roman campaign in Galilee. The next objective: Jerusalem!

Chapter 20
Anarchy in Jerusalem

A large crowd greeted John of Giscala and his men when they arrived in Jerusalem. People were anxious to know what had happened and if it was true that they had fled to avoid fighting the Romans.

"We are here, not because we have fled from the Romans, but because we want to defend Jerusalem. The Romans found it very difficult to conquer the cities of Galilee. Capturing Jerusalem, now that we are here with you, will be impossible for them," John told them, boasting as was his custom.

In Jerusalem, there was total anarchy. The zealots, as the extremists called themselves, attacked their opponents, ransacked their homes, and murdered those who wanted to negotiate peace with the Romans. They seized the Temple's precincts and named High Priest an unknown individual ignorant of his religious obligations, to whom the Zealots dictated what he should do.

Ananias, the rightful High Priest, summoned an assembly of the population in front of the Temple and spoke to them.

"The Zealots have turned our sacred Temple into a fortress, a refuge for criminals and outlaws. It is preferable to be subjects of an Empire that owns the world and respects our laws and customs than to be the victims of tyrants and murderers who desecrate the House of the Lord. We must defend ourselves, not against the Romans, but against these fanatics who want to lead us to a catastrophe."

The Zealots heard the words of Ananias, came out of the Temple with their swords drawn out, and attacked the supporters of the High Priest. There were many dead and injured on both sides. The fanatics, then, retreated to the Temple and closed the gates.

In the following days, John constantly remained at the side of the legitimate High Priest, pretending great loyalty to him, but, at night, in secret, he informed the Zealots of everything

467

that the High Priest's supporters planned to do. Even though he was not invited to participate in the discussions, his constant presence aroused the suspicions of some people. At a meeting, the Hight Priest Ananias spoke frankly to him.

"I want you to swear that you are on our side and that you will not betray us by revealing our plans to the Zealots," the High Priest told John.

"I swear," John replied, smiling to show that Ananias' doubts and suspicions had not offended him.

"I know that you are a righteous man. I have so much confidence in you that I will ask you to go to the Temple and speak, in my name, with the Zealots to end this mutual butchery that does not make any sense," the High Priest told him.

John went to the Temple and spoke with Eleazar ben Simeon, the chief of the Zealots.

"Eleazar, I want to inform you that Ananias is trying to negotiate with Vespasian. He has proclaimed a fast for tomorrow and will ask you, on that pretext, to allow him and his supporters to enter the Temple. If they succeed, they will try to take revenge and kill you. I tell you with all sincerity that you can't continue resisting the siege any longer if you do not get reinforcements."

Chapter 21
The Idumeans come to Jerusalem

The Zealots, alarmed by John's words, decided to follow his advice and asked for reinforcements. The only ones who could help them were the Idumeans, a nation of brave people, descendants of Esau, the brother of our patriarch Jacob. They had been conquered and forced to convert to Judaism about two hundred years before. King Herod had been one of their descendants.

Eleazar ben Simeon sent them a note.

> *"Idumean brothers, we have rebelled because the High Priest Ananias wants to betray our people by surrendering to the Romans. We are besieged inside the Temple. If you do not come immediately to help us, Ananias and his people will capture us and deliver the city to the Romans."*

The Idumeans read the note and were enraged against Ananias. They quickly organized an army of twenty thousand fighters and marched towards Jerusalem.

The High Priest Ananias ordered the city's gates closed and placed guards on the wall upon learning that the Idumeans were coming to Jerusalem to help the Zealots. The Idumeans, unable to enter the city, camped in front of the gate.

One of the chief priests went to a tower on the wall and, from there, he spoke to the Idumean forces:

"You have come to help evil people who have mocked the sanctity of the Temple and who are celebrating their looting with drunkenness in the Sanctuary. The accusation that we want to surrender to the Romans is vile slander. There is no evidence or proof to support that lie. We would indeed have preferred this war not to begin, but, once initiated, we prefer to die fighting like free men than to live like slaves in captivity. You must assist us in fighting against those criminals who despise our laws, who do not respect our Holy

469

Temple, and who have illegally tortured and executed many prominent men of the city without bringing them to trial. If you don't believe me, we will allow some of you to enter the city without your weapons. You will see for yourself and decide who tells the truth. Your other soldiers will wait outside the wall."

The Idumean commander became offended and enraged that most of his fighters were denied entry to the city and that the few who were allowed to enter had to lay down their arms.

"The traitors are you who want to surrender to the Romans without fighting. You have cornered brave patriots in the Temple and falsely accuse them of illegal actions when it is you who violate the law by denying us entry to our capital. We will fight against our enemies, be they the foreign Romans or the traitors to our people. We will remain here outside the city, with our weapons, until you repent of your actions," shouted the commander of the Idumean army.

That night, a terrible storm broke out. The heavy rain, lightning, thunder, and hurricane winds blew away the Idumean camp's tents.

"Brothers, this storm is a sign that God supports us and fights for us. Go and rest. You deserve a good night's sleep," the High Priest Ananias told the men who were besieging the Temple.

The Zealots, seeing that the men of Ananias were no longer outside the Temple, took advantage of the rain's noise and the thunder to cut with saws the bars of the Temple windows and went out without being heard or noticed. They maintained absolute silence until they reached the city gate. They opened it, and the Idumeans entered Jerusalem.

The Zealots and the Idumeans went to the Temple. They killed the guards who were sleeping. Those who woke up shouted for help. A crowd arrived, thinking that it would face only the Zealots, but they found an armed army against them.

The Idumeans killed the people indiscriminately until they covered the esplanade in front of the Temple with hundreds of bloody bodies. Then, their fury still not satisfied, they scattered through the city, ransacked the houses, stabbed and killed the inhabitants. That night, more than eight thousand people died. One of the men murdered was Ananias, the High Priest.

They forced the young men that they had captured to join their ranks. Those who refused were tortured till they died.

The Zealots installed an illegal court to try one of the wealthiest and most important men in the city, whom they falsely accused of negotiating peace with Vespasian. Seventy people of the populace, people without authority or knowledge of the law, were appointed judges. To everyone's surprise, the judges declared that the accused was innocent and told him that he was free to go. The man left the compound, but the zealots followed him and killed him in the street.

The Idumeans by then had calmed down and realized that the Zealots' accusations had been false. No one was negotiating peace with Vespasian, and the Romans, at that moment, had no interest in attacking Jerusalem. The Idumeans realized that they had taken part in criminal acts. Instead of saving the city, they had massacred thousands of its inhabitants. They repented of their actions, freed their prisoners, and returned to Idumea.

The Idumeans come to Jerusalem

Chapter 22
The Zealots' reign of terror

The Zealots rejoiced at the Idumeans' departure because it meant that no force was left in Jerusalem to oppose them.

They instituted a reign of terror by killing anyone they wanted, especially prominent people and those who, out of recklessness or bravery, openly denounced their murders and abuses. They murdered some men because of envy, others because of fear. If someone did not greet them in the street, they killed him for being proud. If the person spoke to them with too much freedom, they killed him for behaving insolently. If someone did not speak, they killed him, suspecting that he was conspiring.

They left the murdered men unburied, lying in the street, and punished those who, fulfilling what our religion imposes, wanted to bury them.

Many inhabitants of Jerusalem tried to leave the city. The Zealots stopped them at the gate and accused them of being deserters and traitors. If the person paid them the sum of money they demanded, they would let him go, but they killed those who refused to pay.

The Zealots' reign of terror

Chapter 23
Vespasian postpones
the attack on Jerusalem

The Roman soldiers set up camp on the beach outside Caesarea, and Vespasian took advantage of the sun and the sea to relax for a few weeks.

One day, sitting on a stool next to his tent, he was idly peeling an apple with his knife while watching some soldiers who were playing on the shore and diving into the waves.

Vespasian saw three of his officers approaching his tent and, assuming that they wanted to talk with him, stood up and invited them to enter the tent with a wave of his hand.

"Do you want to talk to me?" He asked.

"Yes, general," answered one of them.

"Speak!"

"We have captured several Jews who deserted from Jerusalem. During their interrogation, they informed us that the defenders of the city are killing each other ..."

"I know what is happening in Jerusalem," Vespasian interrupted impatiently." Get to the point!"

"We have talked among ourselves and have come to a conclusion."

"And what is your conclusion?" Vespasian asked.

"We should attack Jerusalem right now. This is the ideal moment while the Jews are fighting against each other," the officer replied.

Vespasian did not respond. He finished eating the apple and looked at them smiling.

"I'm glad to see that you are so eager, but your enthusiasm has made you forget one of the fundamental principles of the military art: when enemies are killing each other, one should not interfere. Their mutual killing decreases our enemies' number, and we must not do anything that may cause them to stop their madness. If we attack them now, they will put aside their quarrels and unite against us. While the Jews are busy killing each other, they do not have time to strengthen their walls or make weapons. As the Jewish Holy Book says, "There is a time to tear and a time to sew, a time to be silent and a time to talk, a time for war and a time for peace." Gentlemen, listen well, there is a time to act and a time to be idle, and, until I give the order, we will be idle. Do not worry. I'll let you know when the time is ripe for attacking Jerusalem. Meanwhile, I suggest you enjoy the sea and the beach."

Chapter 24
The rise of John of Giscala

John of Giscala, a crooked but charismatic man, was admired by many for his determination and courage. After he arrived in Jerusalem, he joined the Zealots, who accepted him as their boss. Eleazar ben Simeon, the previous leader of the Zealots, agreed to be his second in command.

Those who had been supporters of the slain High Priest Ananias resented that John now controlled the city, but they cooperated with him out of fear. However, sometimes there were violent confrontations between John's followers and his opponents.

The Sicarii, a name that means "dagger men," was a violent band that had seized the Masada fortress next to the Sea of Salt. From there, they attacked and robbed the neighboring towns. During the Festival of the Unleavened Bread, when the Jews celebrate their freedom from slavery in Egypt, the Sicarii raided a small village called Ein Gedi. They murdered most of the inhabitants who had not managed to escape, expelled the survivors, and took all the food and supplies they found. They did the same in other towns.

Perea, a region situated east of the Jordan River, between Tiberia and the Sea of Salt, was in the rebels' hands. Vespasian and his army marched against Gadara, the largest city of Perea, where a small group of insurgents had imposed their authority by force on the reluctant population.

The leaders of Gadara sent a message to Vespasian expressing their sympathy for Rome and their desire for peace. The rebels, knowing that the population of the city opposed them, escaped when they saw the Romans encamped in front of the city walls,

The people of Gadara opened the gates of the city and welcomed the Roman soldiers with jubilant acclamations. Without waiting to receive an order from Vespasian, the people demolished the walls to show that they wanted peace.

Vespasian sent one of his commanders with five hundred riders and three thousand infantrymen to pursue the rebels, who had reached the Jordan River but were unable to cross it because it was the rainy season and the river had risen markedly.

The rebels, outnumbered and with few weapons, seeing themselves surrounded and unable to escape, fought hopelessly. Most of them died in the battle, and the rest were captured by the Roman soldiers and killed on the spot. The river carried their bodies to the Sea of Salt.

The other towns of the region surrendered without offering resistance, and thus the Romans completed the capture and pacification of Perea.

Vespasian left a garrison at Gadara and returned to Caesarea with his army.

Chapter 25
Simon bar Giora arrives in Jerusalem

Simon bar Giora, a young man of extraordinary strength and courage, was a native of Gerasa, a city located on the Jordan River's east bank, north of the Sea of Salt. When the Romans captured his town, Simon escaped and took refuge in Masada's fortress. There, he accompanied the Sicarii when they went to attack the neighboring towns. His fighting ability caused many men to admire him and to want to fight under his orders. He gathered an army and took over a town called Nain, which he fortified with a wall. His ex-companions, the Sicarii, attacked him, but Simon and his people drove them back to Masada.

Simon, with twenty-five thousand armed men under his command, decided to take Idumea. The Idumeans tried to resist, but one of their commanders conspired with Simon to deliver Idumea to him without spilling blood. The traitor told the other Idumean commanders that Simon's army was far larger than it was, and they, frightened, surrendered.

Simon, after adding the Idumeans to his army, had forty thousand fighters. He took the city of Hebron and, from there, marched to Jerusalem.

The Zealots, fearful of confronting Simon openly in a battle, ambushed him. They were unable to kill him but succeeded in capturing Simon's wife and brought her to Jerusalem.

From there, they sent a message to Simon that said: "Your wife is in our hands. If you want us to give her back to you alive, surrender,"

Simon's reaction was not what the Zealots expected. Instead of surrendering, he marched with his army to the gates of the city. He killed everyone he met on the way, including women and the elderly, except for a few men, whose hands he cut off and sent back to the city with a note. It said, "I swear to God that if you do not return my wife safe and sound, I will enter the city and punish the entire population, no matter who is guilty or who is innocent,"

The Zealots immediately released Simon's wife. Simon left his army encamped in front of Jerusalem, went to Idumea, and returned with more fighters.

Inside the city, John of Giscala and his men continued their reign of terror. They entered the homes of the rich, robbed, killed the men, and raped the women. Those who managed to escape from the city were killed by Simon's fighters who camped outside the gate.

The people of Jerusalem were afraid that the Zealots would continue to commit atrocities. A priest named Matias convinced the population that Simon bar Giora would protect them from the violence of John of Giscala and his Zealots. The people opened the city's gates and welcomed Simon bar Giora and his army with applause and cheers. They called him "Saviour of Jerusalem," without knowing that the future would show that, as the popular phrase says," the remedy was worse than the disease."

The Zealots, who had been scattered in the city, returned to the Temple and entrenched themselves there.

The first thing that Simon did when he took possession of Jerusalem was to assault the Temple but was forced to abandon the attempt when the Zealots' arrows killed several of his men.

Then, he ordered his men to bring the priest Matias and his three sons to his presence. Not caring that Matias had opened for him the gates of Jerusalem, he accused the four men of being in cahoots with the Romans, refused to listen to their defense, and condemned them to death.

"I beg you to grant me one last favor," Matias begged.

"What do you want?" Simon asked.

"Please, kill me first. I do not want to witness the death of my sons," answered Matias.

Simon ignored Matthias' request and killed the priest's sons before killing him.

Believing the rumors that I had deserted to the enemy, he had my parents thrown in prison.

Chapter 26
My prophecy to Vespasian comes true

It was a coincidence that there was a civil war that year [69 AD] not only in Jerusalem but also in Rome. General Galba, the governor of Hispania, rebelled against Emperor Nero, who fled Rome and committed suicide. Galba reigned for seven months until Otto murdered him. Otto, who had been the husband of Poppea when Nero made her his mistress, reigned for three months until he committed suicide when General Vitellius defeated him.

Vitellius brought his army of mercenaries to Rome and forced the wealthiest citizens to welcome the armed men into their homes. The mercenaries, most of them barbarous Germans, seeing the comforts and the riches of their hosts, could not control their envy. They murdered them and robbed their possessions.

Vespasian, aware of what was happening in the Empire's capital, was furious and wanted to go to Rome and restore order but could not return to Italy because it was the winter season when Roman ships stay in the ports and do not navigate.

The soldiers of the Roman army in Judea heard what was happening in Rome. They decided that Vespasian should be Emperor and save Rome from the tyrannical and corrupt government of Vitellius. They went to Vespasian's tent and hailed him as Emperor. The general came out of his tent and spoke to them.

"Friends, I thank you, but I cannot accept. I prefer private life to that dignity."

The soldiers, hearing his refusal, unsheathed their swords and threatened to kill him if he did not agree to be their Emperor. Vespasian tried again to refuse, but, seeing that the soldiers would not listen to his arguments, he allowed himself to be persuaded and accepted that they should proclaim him Emperor.

As he did in his military campaigns, Vespasian meticulously prepared his campaign to take over the Roman Empire. He decided that his first step would be to control Alexandria, the principal city of Egypt, and the port through which Egypt exported the wheat that fed Rome's population.

He immediately sent a note to the Governor of Alexandria, Tiberius Alexander, who had previously been one of his officers.

From Vespasian to Tiberius Alexander.
Dear friend, the army has proclaimed me Emperor, and I, forced to accept the burden of government, ask for your support.

As soon as he received the letter, Tiberius Alexander summoned his legions and made them swear allegiance to Vespasian, which they did with enthusiasm. All the other Roman legions in the east of the Empire also supported Vespasian with oaths and celebrations.

By the way, Tiberius Alexander, whom I had not yet met but had heard much about him, was born a Jew, although I didn't know if he still considered himself to be one. He was the son of Alexander, who had been the leader of the Jewish community of Alexandria, and the nephew of the famous philosopher Philo.

Vespasian traveled from Caesarea to Beirut, where the delegations that came to see him from Syria and other provinces congratulated him and expressed his support.

Vespasian remembered what I, Josephus, had prophesied to him when Nero was still Emperor. He brought me into his presence, praised my courage in defending Yodfat, and said that he now believed that God had inspired my prophecy.

"It is a shame that this man, a messenger of God, is in chains. Release him immediately," he ordered the soldiers who kept guard over me.

"Father, it's not enough to remove his chains. It is usual when a man has been unjustly chained, to tear apart the links of his chains," said Titus.

Vespasian ordered to bring a saw to cut my chains and decreed that, from that moment on, I should be treated with the honors that corresponded to a messenger of God.

The general considered that he didn't need to travel immediately to Alexandria, a city that supported him unconditionally, thanks to Governor Tiberius Alexander. Instead, he went to Antioch, where he stayed for a few weeks, while his legions, commanded by his officers, went to Rome, confronted the army of Vitellius, defeated him, and killed him.

Vespasian and Titus traveled to Alexandria and took me with them. In the Egyptian capital, he received delegations from all the provinces of the Empire that came to greet and congratulate him. He decided that the time had come to return to Rome and assume the throne. Before traveling, the general ordered his son Titus to march against Jerusalem, conquer it, and destroy it. He instructed Titus to take me with him and ordered me to serve his son as his counselor, translator, and interpreter during the siege of the Jewish capital.

Accompanied by three legions, we left Egypt, crossed the Sinai desert, arrived in Gaza, proceeded to Ashkelon, then to Jaffa. From there to Caesarea, where the legions that Vespasian had left awaited us.

Tiberius Alexander, who had resigned his post as Governor of Alexandria, came to Caesarea and was appointed Titus' second in command.

King Agrippa also sent his army to serve as auxiliary troops to the Roman army.

My prophecy to Vespasian comes true

Chapter 27
Eleazar ben Simeon
forms a third faction

I mentioned in previous pages that Eleazar ben Simeon, the former leader of the Zealots, had agreed to be John of Giscala's second in command when John arrived in Jerusalem accompanied by a group of his Galilean followers,

John's arrogance and tyranny were so overwhelming that Eleazar and his Zealots could no longer bear him. They left John and took possession of the Inner Courtyard of the Temple. From there, Eleazar and his Zealots harassed John and his Galileans.

John and his people stayed in control of the rest of the Temple. With an army composed mainly of Idumeans, Simon bar Giora occupied the Jerusalem neighborhood called Upper City and most of the Lower City (the area situated in a valley between the Upper City and the Temple). His headquarters were in Herod's palace and the three towers next to it.

It was an absurd, tragic truth that the defenders of Judea were divided into three factions, enemies of one another, instead of fighting united against the Romans.

The fighters of the three groups set houses on fire and killed people when they had the slightest suspicion that their victims were supporters of one of the other two groups or intended to escape from the city.

The arrows fired by the factions against each other and the stones they threw often killed people who were sacrificing to God in the Temple, and that innocent blood stained the Altar. The bodies of the dead combatants, priests, and townspeople were left unattended on the pavement outside the Temple. The unburied corpses gave off a stinking smell that permeated the air of Jerusalem.

The noise in the city was incessant day and night. It came from the shouts of the factions fighting each other and from the cries and sobs of people mourning their dead.

Due to the shortage of food in the Temple, John's followers and Eleazar's fighters united temporarily, went out of the Temple unexpectedly, and attacked Simon Bar Giora's forces. They entered houses and warehouses and appropriated all the provisions that they could find. They burned what they were not able to take with them. Thus, they destroyed the wheat reserves that the people had accumulated in the city, preparing for a siege that could last years.

Jerusalem was without food.

Chapter 28
Description of Jerusalem

I am about to arrive at a crucial point in my story, the siege of Jerusalem. Before proceeding, I wish to describe the city as it once was, before it was burned and destroyed, since today only ruins and debris remain.

Jerusalem was situated on two hills, which were surrounded by impassable precipices. Three walls, which included towers at a certain distance, one from the other, were its primary defense. The district called the "Upper City" was on the higher hill. The Temple was on the other hill, and next to it was the fortress Antonia. The valley, which separated the two hills, was called the "Lower City."

A recently built neighborhood named the "New City" was on the northern side of the city. It was surrounded by a wall, called the "Third Wall," built by King Agrippa the Great, the father of Agrippa, king of Chalcis. It made a curve from the royal palace to the northeast corner of the Temple complex.

The other two walls were "the First Wall" and the "Second Wall." The First Wall surrounded the Upper City and the Lower City. It was built by Nehemiah several centuries ago and had been renovated by the Hasmonean kings. The Second Wall, built by King Herod a hundred years before the rebellion, went diagonally from the royal palace to the Antonia fortress.

Three of the towers that were part of the Second Wall had been built by King Herod, who gave them the names of three people he loved. The most beautifully decorated tower was seventy-five feet high and commemorated the memory of his wife, Queen Mariamne, whom Herod, in a fit of jealousy, had ordered executed.

The highest of the three towers (one hundred and forty feet high) was called Fasael, in honor of Herod's older brother. During the rebellion, it was used by Simon bar Giora as the headquarters of his faction.

The third tower, one hundred and thirty feet high, bore the name of Hippicus, a close friend of King Herod.

Next to those three towers was the old palace of King Herod. Although the king had other palaces in Masada, Herodion, and Caesarea, the Jerusalem palace had been his royal residence.

The palace was on a platform whose height was twelve feet, its length nine hundred feet, and its width one hundred and eighty feet. A forty-five feet high wall surrounded the platform. The palace had two wings; the north wing was called "Caesar" and the south wing," Agrippa," in honor of Augustus' friend. The large garden between the two wings had a profusion of plants, trees, canals, cisterns, dovecotes, and decorative statues.

I regret to say that the rebels, not the Romans, burned and destroyed the palace, whose beauty was a source of pride to the people of Jerusalem.

In previous pages, I have described the Temple, a sacred building converted by John of Giscala into a military base.

Another important building was the Antonia fortress: it was built by Herod and named in honor of his friend Mark Antony. It was located next to the northeast corner of the Temple complex. It had thick walls sixty feet high. Inside, it had numerous rooms, bathrooms, armories, and courtyards. It had been the seat of the garrison that was in charge of Jerusalem until the rebels expelled the Romans from the city.

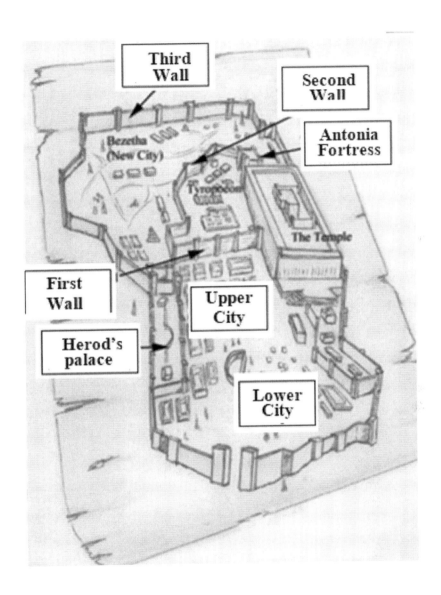

Description of Jerusalem

Chapter 29
The Romans surround Jerusalem

Under Titus's command with Tiberius Alexander as his second, the Roman army left Caesarea and marched towards Jerusalem. The auxiliary troops of King Agrippa marched in the vanguard, followed by the engineers who were in charge of building the roads and putting up the camps. Then came the baggage of the commander and the soldiers of his guard. Titus followed with his detachment of bodyguards. Behind him came the catapults and the men who blew the trumpets, followed by the flag bearers who wore the emblems of the legions' eagles. Next, the soldiers marching in rows of six. Behind were the servants, and, closing the march, the mercenaries.

The Romans set up their camp on a hill near Jerusalem, called Givat Shaul, [February 70 CE]. Titus, accompanied by six hundred horsemen, went to inspect the defenses of the city. Absorbed while looking at the wall, he rode alone, leaving his companions far behind. A large group of rebels suddenly emerged from one of the city gates and rushed at him. Titus couldn't advance because in front of him were ditches built to protect the gardens that the defenders had planted outside the city. He ran over the enemies that stood between him and his soldiers, slashing with his sword those who tried to grab his reins. Although the rebels killed several of the soldiers who came to his aid, Titus managed to escape and arrived safely at the camp.

A rumor circulated among the soldiers that it was a miracle that Titus came back unharmed. I was amazed, when I saw him, that he was as calm as always. If it had been me who had escaped from fighters armed with swords and spears, be sure, dear reader, that I wouldn't have been so serene.

Titus sent two legions to Mount Scopus to set up their camp. It was a strategic place since, from its height, you could see

491

everything that happened in the Temple. Two other legions camped on the Mount of Olives, on the east side of the city.

Seeing that the Roman army had surrounded Jerusalem, the rebel factions agreed to a temporary truce between them. They went out of the city and attacked the camp that the Romans were setting up on the Mount of Olives. The soldiers, taken by surprise, were not carrying their weapons, and the Jews killed several of them. The other soldiers fled to the summit of the Mount. The Jews followed and attacked them with renewed fury and would have succeeded in killing all the soldiers if Titus, who was watching the fight from a distance, had not arrived with reinforcements, compelling the Jews to retreat into the city.

The temporary truce between the three Jewish factions ended during the Festival of Unleavened Bread due to a vile act of deception and betrayal by John of Giscala.

Eleazar ben Simeon, the chief of the Zealots, a profoundly religious man, decided to open the gate of the Inner Courtyard of the Temple, which was under his control, so that any person in the city who wished to fulfill his religious obligations to pray and sacrifice during the Festival could enter.

John disguised his fighters as pilgrims and ordered them to hide their weapons under their clothes. As soon as the Zealots opened the gate for them, John's men stormed into the Inner Courtyard with their swords drawn-out, screaming wildly.

The Zealots, taken by surprise, took refuge in the basement of the Temple. John's supporters unleashed their fury by hitting and slashing the people who had come to pray.

John offered the Zealots to spare their lives if they joined his group. Many of the Zealots accepted, including their leader, Eleazar ben Simeon, whom John named his lieutenant. Other Zealots managed to sneak out of the Temple and joined forces with Simon Bar Giora, who controlled the rest of the city. John now had mastery of the entire Temple.

Titus, meanwhile, decided to dismantle the camp he had set up on the summit of the Mount of Olives and move it to a place closer to the city walls. He ordered his soldiers to cut down all the trees and demolish all the buildings between the camp and the walls.

The Jews devised a stratagem against the Romans. A group of rebels left the city, pretending to have been expelled, while others, from the wall's parapet, shouted in favor of making peace and offered to open the city's gates to the Romans if they would respect their lives. To make their performance more credible, they threw stones at the men who had gone out, who pretended to beg the men on the wall to let them return to the city.

The Roman soldiers saw the pantomime, believed it, and approached the walls, thinking that the crowd would open the gate. Titus, suspecting that the Jews had set a trap, shouted at the soldiers to return. Several soldiers ignored his order, or perhaps they did not hear it. They ran towards the wall, and the rebels riddled them with arrows. Few soldiers were able to escape because the Jews outside the walls cut off their retreat.

The rebels returned to the city, and the people who were on the walls celebrated their successful deception with exclamations of joy.

That evening, Titus, furious, spoke to the soldiers who had managed to return to the camp.

"The Jews are not professional soldiers like you, but they know how to plan before acting, while you act before you plan. The result is that many soldiers have died needlessly today. All the soldiers who disobeyed my order and ran to the wall will be put to death.

Titus' officers asked for clemency for the condemned soldiers.

"General, we agree with you that the just punishment for a disobedient soldier is death, but when the fault has been committed not by one but by many, the punishment should be limited to a warning," the officers told Titus.

Titus accepted their argument and canceled the death penalty to the soldiers who had disobeyed his order.

After the soldiers cut down all the trees outside the city walls and demolished the buildings, Titus ordered to set up the camp as close as possible to Jerusalem's walls. The presence of numerous Roman troops next to the walls made it very difficult for the rebels to leave the city and attack the soldiers by surprise.

Chapter 30
The siege of Jerusalem

The rebels' three factions had been reduced to two. John of Giscala led one of them, Simon bar Giora the other The third faction, that of the Zealots, had been forced by John to join him.

John of Giscala had ten thousand fighters, a quarter of them Zealots. His headquarters were in the Temple.

Simon bar Giora had fifteen thousand men under his command, five thousand of whom were Idumeans. His headquarters were in the Fasael Tower, next to the old palace of Herod. From there, he controlled the entire city, except for the Temple.

The houses in the Lower City, between the Temple and the Upper City, had been burned and destroyed by both factions. It was now an open area where the constant fratricidal struggles between the followers of Simon and the supporters of John took place.

I occupied a tent next to Titus', in the center of the Roman camp, and served him as an interpreter when he interrogated Jewish prisoners. One day he called me.

"I am going to ride around the city walls accompanied by a group of soldiers to determine which would be the best place to use our catapults and battering rams. Meanwhile, I want you, accompanied by one of my officers, to approach the wall and talk to the defenders. Demand them to surrender. Tell them that if they do not resist, we will respect their lives, and we will not harm the city," he ordered me.

I approached the city wall accompanied by an officer. A crowd on top of the wall watched me and waited to hear what I would say.

"Brothers, your heroic resistance does not make sense. The Romans are more numerous than you. They are stronger and more experienced in the art of war. General Titus admires your courage and says that spilling blood uselessly does not

495

make sense. He offers to respect your lives, respect your city and respect the Temple if you lay down your arms, open the gate and surrender," I said in a loud voice that was heard by the crowd.

"Traitor!" they shouted at me. "Apostate! You will die together with your beloved Romans!"

They threw stones at me and shot arrows. Fortunately, I was unharmed, but an arrow severely wounded the officer with me. Several soldiers ran towards him and carried him away from the wall.

The people's aggressive response did not surprise me since I knew well how determined were the Jewish fighters.

That night I gave my report to Titus.

"The defenders of Jerusalem did not accept your offer of peace. They prefer to die fighting than surrender," I told him.

"If so, we will fulfill their wish," Titus replied.

The next day Titus ordered to burn all the fields outside the city and cut down all the remaining trees. He also gave his soldiers an order that seemed contradictory to me.

"Do not stop anyone who wishes to enter the city. But, don't allow the departure of anyone who wants to leave the city," ordered Titus.

Based on the friendship I had forged with him, I dared to ask him a question.

"Excuse me, Titus, but what is the logic of your order? To let the pilgrims enter Jerusalem is to provide reinforcements to the combatants. Preventing them from leaving the city makes it impossible for those who want to defect from the rebellion."

"Josephus," Titus answered, smiling, "the pilgrims we will allow to enter the city include women, children, and the elderly. None of them constitutes a reinforcement for the rebels. On the contrary, they consume food. Not allowing them to leave the city will make the food run out faster. We must force them to surrender. If our weapons do not defeat them, hunger will."

Pilgrims who had come from abroad to celebrate the Festival of Unleavened Bread congested Jerusalem. A city that generally had a population of sixty thousand inhabitants now had hundreds of thousands, perhaps more than a million people.

The rebels used against the Romans the catapults they had captured from Cestius Gallus' army [see Chapter 8]. Unfortunately for them, they lacked experience and skill in using these artifacts, in contrast to the Roman soldiers who were experts in their use.

Initially, the rocks thrown by the Roman catapults to the city were white. The Jews, seeing them coming, would shout "Beware of the rock!" and would throw themselves on the ground, thus avoiding fatalities and injuries. The Romans, when they realized that white rocks were easy to spot, painted them black.

The leaders of the two rebel factions decided on joint action against the Romans and sent fighters with torches to set fire to the catapults.

Titus ordered his horsemen and archers to repel the attack, but the Jews fought furiously and succeeded in destroying one of the catapults. At the head of his horsemen, Titus attacked the rebels, managed to kill a dozen, and forced the rest to flee back to the city.

The Romans captured a rebel and crucified him in a place that was visible from the wall, complying with Titus' order.

The siege of Jerusalem

Chapter 31
The Romans capture the Third Wall

Titus ordered his soldiers to build three towers, each seventy-five feet high, made of wood covered with metal plates, from which the archers could shoot the rebels who were on the wall.

One night, shortly after the towers were finished, one of them collapsed with a deafening noise. The soldiers woke up and, believing that they were being attacked by the rebels, grabbed their weapons and left the tents. Disconcerted at not seeing any enemies, they thought that the rebels had disguised themselves as Roman soldiers and had entered the camp. They looked at each other suspiciously and demanded the password. It took them hours to understand that the tower's collapse was an accident and not a deliberate action by the Jews.

The two remaining towers proved to be extremely effective. The archers, thanks to the height of the towers, could easily shoot the rebels who were on the walls, thus causing deaths and injuries. One night, the rebels came out of the city and tried to push down one of the towers, but it was so heavy that they could not do it. It was also impossible to set them on fire because of their metal coating.

Meanwhile, the soldiers, using hammers, tried to break the Third Wall, which surrounded the New City. Finally, they succeeded in making a breach and entered through it [May 70 AD]. The defenders fled and retreated behind the Second Wall. The soldiers opened the gates of the city, and the entire army entered.

Titus gave orders to demolish the Third Wall and set up camp in the area between the Third Wall and the Second Wall.

John and Simon bar Giora combined their forces. John defended the Second Wall sections near Fortress Antonia, and Simon defended the rest of the wall.

That night nobody slept on the two sides. The Romans feared that the Jews would attack them, while the defenders expected an attack on the Second Wall at any moment.

The Jews were willing to fight until they died. The Romans had the advantage of their discipline and experience in wars.

The next day Titus ordered to pound with the ram a tower in the Second Wall's northern part. Eleven Jewish fighters inside the tower felt it shaking from the ram's thrust and shouted for mercy.

Titus ordered the soldiers to stop hitting the tower with the battering ram and spoke to the men in the tower.

"Will you surrender?" Titus asked them.

He heard bitter discussions in loud voices coming from inside the tower. Some rebels wanted to surrender. Others exclaimed that they preferred to die free rather than to live as slaves of the Romans. Their leader spoke to Titus from the window.

"Please have patience while I try to convince my companions," said the rebel.

In a loud voice so that Titus could hear him clearly, the leader asked the others to trust the Romans and surrender. The Romans saw that some of the rebels on top of the tower drew their daggers and, apparently, stuck themselves in their breasts and fell. Meanwhile, as we learned later, the leader had sent a pigeon with a message to Simon Bar Giora, where he had written: "We are trying to buy time to escape."

"Josephus," said Titus to me, "go inside the tower and convince those who are still alive to surrender. Tell them I admire their courage and that I give them my word that I will respect their lives."

Carrying on Titus' order would have meant committing suicide. I refused as politely as possible, hoping that he would not take my frankness for cowardice.

"Titus, I know the tricks of these people. What we are witnessing is a pretext to delay us until they manage to escape. It is senseless to go to them," I said.

To my relief, the leader of the rebels shouted at that moment.

"Send someone to receive the gold coins that are stored in the tower."

Upon hearing that he would receive gold, one of the rebels who had deserted the city offered to go to the tower. Titus sent him accompanied by a soldier.

The defenders, when they saw the deserter approaching, threw a massive rock at him. The deserter jumped to the side and was unharmed, but the soldier who accompanied him did not have the same agility due to his heavy armor and was hit by the stone in the chest.

Titus was furious when he realized that the defenders had lied to him and ordered the soldiers to use the battering ram against the tower.

The rebels set fire to the tower and escaped through a tunnel.

The Romans capture the Third Wall

Chapter 32
The Romans capture the Second Wall

Five days after capturing the Third Wall, the Roman forces managed to open a breach in the Second Wall, through which Titus and a thousand chosen troops entered.

The area of Jerusalem surrounded by the Second Wall was characterized by its narrow streets where it was easy for people who were unfamiliar with the city to get lost. Numerous merchants had their stores there, especially those who sold wool, cloth, and bronze articles.

Titus, with whom I already had a close friendship, was a man with a great heart and good intentions, which, on occasion, made him act against the tactical interests of the military campaign. In this case, the military doctrine required widening the breach in the wall so that soldiers could escape quickly, if necessary. Titus, whose desire was to suppress the rebellion with the minimum number of victims in the Roman army and the rebel forces and preserve the city's integrity and beauty, ordered not to widen the breach. He also forbid the burning of the houses and the killing of the prisoners.

The rebels attributed his benevolence to an inability to conquer the rest of the city instead of appreciating Titus' kind gesture. They threatened to kill anyone who tried to surrender or talk about peace.

The rebels attacked the Roman soldiers, who retreated and tried to escape through the breach, but it was too narrow to allow more than one soldier to leave at the same time. Many soldiers died or were wounded. Titus instructed the archers to stand by the breach and shoot arrows at the rebels, thus preventing more soldiers' death.

The rebels celebrated their success in expelling the Romans from the Second Wall without considering that the Roman army had many more soldiers than the few who had entered through the breach. Another problem that the city's defenders did not consider was the shortage of food, which was already beginning to cause famine in the population.

For the following three days, the rebels defended the breach with their bodies, preventing the Romans from entering again. On the fourth day, it was no longer possible for them to resist, and the Roman forces broke through the Second Wall, widened the breach, and conquered all that area of the city.

Titus did not make the same mistake he had made days before. He gave orders to completely demolish the Second Wall, burn the houses where the fighters had taken refuge, and kill anyone who resisted.

That night he gathered his commanders to determine the next step: the assault on the First Wall.

Chapter 33
My speech to the defenders of Jerusalem

I mentioned before that Titus had a kind heart. Instead of proceeding immediately to assault the First Wall, he decided to wait a few days to allow the rebels to reconsider and realize that it would be a useless suicide to continue the rebellion.

To impress the people of Jerusalem with his army's might, Titus ordered his commanders to parade with their troops in front of the First Wall. The people of Jerusalem huddled on top of the city wall, and the walls of the Temple saw the impressive spectacle of tens of thousands of Roman fighters marching in front of them, the soldiers in armor and carrying their weapons, the riders on decorated horses, the musicians playing their trumpets and drums. When the commanders gave the order, the soldiers drew their swords and rhythmically beat their shields.

The military parade did not have the result expected by Titus. The stubborn Jews preferred to keep fighting rather than surrender, which, they feared, would mean being tortured and crucified or, in the best of cases, sold as slaves.

The Romans began to build ramps, but the rebels, who had become adept at handling the catapult, were able to slow the work by shooting at it and injuring the soldiers.

Titus called me to his tent to entrust me with an important mission.

"We have not managed to convince the Jews to surrender. I want you to try once more. Use your eloquence, speak to them in their language and convince them that there is no point in continuing their rebellion," he ordered.

This time I was not able to refuse the mission. Titus had spoken to me with his usual kindness, but he was giving me an order. I did not dare say to him that, in my opinion, the chances of convincing the rebels to surrender were nil, but the chances that an arrow or a rock, shot or thrown from the wall, would kill or hurt me were overwhelming.

Accompanied by two soldiers, I approached the wall but stayed a prudent distance from it, in a place from where they could hear me but would find it difficult to hit me with their arrows.

"Brothers! It is a tragic irony that the Romans, who are not of our religion, want to avoid causing damage to the Temple, while you, with your stubbornness, will destroy the House of God. The Romans have demolished two of the three walls that protected the city. The one that remains is the weakest of the three. Most of the city is already in Roman hands. You cannot resist. The Romans, whom God has made masters of the world, are invincible. Who are you to oppose the will of God? Your main enemy is not the Roman army but the famine killing more people than those killed by Titus' soldiers. The Romans are practical people. They know that destroying a city, killing its inhabitants, and turning the country into a desert, does not give them any profits. All they want is that you respect their order and laws and renew the payment of the taxes you always paid in the past during so many years. You know that most of that tax money was invested right here, in Judea, building roads and aqueducts that benefit the population."

While I was speaking to them, they shouted insults and shot arrows that, luckily, did not reach me.

Seeing that what I had said did not convince them, I appealed to their family feelings.

"Have mercy on your families, your children, your wives, your elderly parents. If you continue this useless resistance, your loved ones will die of hunger, or, if they survive, they will be sold as slaves. Many of you know that my parents are inside the city and share your fate. I am not asking you to put down your arms to save my family. If you believe that, kill my loved ones and kill me too, if that is what you need to recover your reason and cease this suicidal war."

The only answers I received were more insults and more arrows. It did not make any sense to continue standing there, risking my life. I returned with the two soldiers to the camp to inform Titus that I had failed in my mission.

My speech to the defenders of Jerusalem

Chapter 34
The famine in Jerusalem

"General," I greeted Titus, "I am sorry to tell you that I failed to convince the Jews to surrender. Instead of listening to me, they insulted me and tried to kill me."

"Do not worry, Josephus. I did not expect that they would surrender just by listening to you, but I thought it was worth trying to make a last attempt to avoid bloodshed, however useless. Forget about it. The die is cast. I have something important for you now. We have captured a Jewish fighter, and I want you to question him about the situation in the city," Titus replied.

I realized that in the shadows, behind Titus, was a man chained to a pole. His clothes were rags, and his face was bleeding.

"Shalom," I said.

"Shalom," he replied.

What he told me was so terrible that I do not want to quote his words. I will limit myself to summarize them.

"Food in the city has run out. If they see a person in apparent good health, the fighters follow him home, suspecting that he is hoarding food there. If they cannot find food, they torture the man to find where he hid it. If they enter a house and see people eating, they tear the food from their mouths even if they are children or old people. If the door of a house is closed, they consider it a sign that there is food inside, and they knock down the door. They go to the houses of the rich and accuse them falsely of treason before they kill them and seize their possessions. They devise terrible methods of torture to discover if the suspect is hiding a piece of bread, including inserting sharp sticks in the different openings of his body,"

In the following days, I questioned other deserters who had managed to escape from the city. They told me that they had sold everything for whatever price they could get and had

509

swallowed the coins so that the thieves would not find them, hoping to recover them when they would come out after following the natural path through the digestive system.

Other deserters did not have the luck to fall into the hands of the Romans. If the rebels caught them, they cut their throats without listening to their explanations or pleas for mercy.

Chapter 35
Titus crucifies thousands of Jews

Many Jews, even those who were not combatants, sneaked out of the city to bring plants and leaves from the neighboring valleys to feed their families.

Titus ordered his soldiers to capture all the Jews they could find, whether armed or not. Those taken prisoners were whipped, tortured, and, finally, crucified in front of the city wall. The soldiers captured an average of five hundred Jews daily, but there were days when they captured more.

Crucifying these people caused great sorrow to Titus, but he had no alternative since he lacked enough guards to care for so many prisoners. He also hoped that the people on the wall, seeing the cruel spectacle, would surrender to avoid the same end.

The reaction of the combatants was the opposite of what Titus had expected. The rows of hundreds of crosses in front of the wall did not scare them or induce them to surrender. On the contrary, the rebels took advantage of the atrocious spectacle to force the crucified men's relatives to go to the wall and witness what happened to those who fell into the hands of the Romans. Despite this, people kept trying to escape from the city, preferring a quick death at the Romans' hands than a slow death from famine if they remained in Jerusalem.

Because all the trees, which previously surrounded the city, had been cut down, there was not enough wood to make new crosses. Titus ordered to cut the hands of the captured Jews, so that they could no longer fight, and sent them back to the city with a message for John of Giscala and Simon bar Giora, that said: "If you do not surrender immediately I will destroy the city and the Temple."

John and Simon went to the wall and shouted their response.

511

"We prefer to die than becoming your slaves! The threats to destroy Jerusalem and the Temple do not scare us because God is the only one who will decide the end of our fight."

Chapter 36
The rebels destroy
the Roman ramps

The Romans constructed four ramps, one of them in front of the Antonia fortress and the other three in front of the wall, at different intervals.

John of Giscala and his men dug a tunnel under the ramp in front of the fortress and propped it up with columns and wooden beams. They brought flammable materials and set the roof beams on fire. The tunnel collapsed, bringing down the ramp and all the soldiers standing there at the time. The noise of the fall was deafening. Many soldiers were buried alive, and others had difficulty breathing due to the thick smoke and dust clouds.

The Romans installed battering rams on the other ramps, which, with their blows, made the wall tremble and crumble.

Simon bar Giora and his men came out of the city, carrying burning torches. The Romans attacked them, but the rebels managed to set the ramps on fire and seized the battering rams. The fire spread over the ramps, and the Romans were forced to retreat to their camp. The Jewish fighters followed them and fought hand-to-hand with the soldiers.

Titus, searching for the appropriate place to build a new ramp against the Antonia fortress, arrived at that moment with soldiers. The rebels, having achieved their purpose of destroying the ramps, escaped and returned to the city.

The rebels destroy the Roman ramps

Chapter 37
The Romans surround Jerusalem with a wall

Titus convened a meeting of his commanders, to which I was invited to participate.

"Gentlemen, I want to hear your suggestions and opinions on what we should do, now that the Jews have destroyed the ramps and we have no materials with which to rebuild them," Titus said to us.

"General, so far, we have only used part of the army in our attacks. I suggest we attack with the whole army. We are many more than them, and they will not be able to resist us," proposed one of the commanders.

"Does anyone have another idea?" Titus asked.

Several commanders raised their hands. Titus pointed to one of them.

"I suggest we build the ramps again. There are indeed no trees in the vicinity, but there are trees in valleys that are not so far away," said the officer.

"Excellent suggestion!" Titus exclaimed, "I'll take it into account at the appropriate time. What do you think?" he asked, pointing to another commander.

"I think we should have patience and expect the famine to do our work for us," the officer replied.

"I do not think it's appropriate for the morale of our soldiers to wait with their arms crossed and do nothing while waiting for the enemies to die of hunger. It is possible that the rebels, who know the secret exits of the city, will stock up on food and so may continue resisting. We have to devise a plan that avoids that possibility. What do you think if we build a wall around the entire city, with garrisons from place to place? This will prevent them from going out and attack us by surprise, and it will make it impossible for them to get food from the outside. It will also give us time to rebuild the ramps and, when the time comes, we will be able to overcome them easily because the famine will have weakened them," said Titus.

The commanders were enthusiastic about Titus' plan, and the next day the entire army began to build the wall. Everybody worked with enthusiasm, the soldiers to impress their decurions, the decurions to their centurions, the centurions to their tribunes, the tribunes to their commanders, and these to Titus. A job that should have taken weeks, maybe months, was finished, incredibly, in three days!

Chapter 38
Jerusalem becomes hell

The famine turned the inhabitants of Jerusalem into walking skeletons. People rummaged the drains for food and checked the animals' dung in the hope of finding among the feces some seed or grass to appease their terrible hunger. The rebels, who were the only ones in the city who still had some food, entered the dead people's houses and stole what they found.

The houses were full of dying women and children. The men who could still walk did so as shadows. The alleyways were covered with corpses because people were too weak to bury the dead. When the stench became unbearable, the rebels took the bodies to the city wall and threw them outside.

The deserters, unable to escape through the city's gates, jumped down from the walls. Several men who saw them drew their swords, told the gatekeepers to let them out to punish the deserters, shouting, "Let's kill them!" Once they were outside, they also surrendered to the Romans.

The soldiers pitied them and gave them food. The deserters, who had been starving, choked on the food and died.

The Arab and Syrian mercenaries, aware that the inhabitants of the city swallowed their gold coins to prevent the thieves from stealing them, went to the mounds where hundreds of corpses were crammed, cut their abdomens, and checked their intestines to see if, among the excrement, they could find coins. Even when they found men lying among the corpses but still alive, they did not hesitate to cut them open.

Titus was horrified to learn of this practice, but he did not punish the evildoers. I am convinced that he would have sentenced them to death if there had not been so many "harvesters" of coins.

On one of my inspection tours along the wall, a rock, thrown with excellent marksmanship, fell on my head and made me lose consciousness. Seeing me fall, the people who were on the wall shouted jubilantly. A group of rebels came out of the city to capture me. Titus saw what was happening and ordered four soldiers to run in my direction. The soldiers arrived before the rebels, picked me up, and brought me back to the Roman camp.

The rumor circulated in Jerusalem that Joseph ben Matityahu had died. It reached the ears of my mother, who was in the prison where Simon Bar Giora had confined her. A survivor, to whom I spoke months later, told me that my mother, hearing that I had died, said: "Ever since the war began, I have always had the feeling that I will never see my son again. My tragedy is that I cannot bury the one who should have buried me,"

Those were the last words my mother said before dying of starvation.

As soon as I regained consciousness, I returned to the place where I had been wounded and shouted at the rebels who watched me from the top of the wall.

"Very soon, you will be punished for hurting me. Allow whoever wants to leave the city. The Romans will respect their lives."

Their response was to throw me more stones that, this time, fortunately, did not hit the target.

Chapter 39
The Romans conquer
the Antonia fortress

Jerusalem, before the war, had been surrounded by forests, gardens, and farms. As one famous phrase says, "Of the ten measures of beauty that God gave to the world, he gave nine of them to Jerusalem." When I was a child, my parents used to take me for a walk around the city. I always felt that I was in the middle of an earthly paradise.

Not anymore.

The Romans had cut all the trees down, the gardens were dry, and the farms were charred ruins. I couldn't help but shed tears as I contemplated the desolation of my beloved city.

Inside the city, the dead were so many that no one bothered to pick them up anymore. The bodies lay in the streets where they had fallen. They were so many corpses that people could not avoid walking on them. The city was impregnated with a horrible, putrid smell that the wind sometimes brought to the Roman camp and induced vomiting.

The Romans felled the trees that remained in the valleys where they had not yet been cut and, working day and night, built new ramps in only three weeks. Soldiers defended the workers, fearing that if the Jews destroyed the ramps again, it would be impossible to build them for the third time due to the lack of materials.

The rebels, seeing the progress of the ramps, felt that the end was approaching. They continued going out sporadically to attack the Romans by surprise. However, although they were the only ones in Jerusalem who still had food, they were malnourished and weak, and the Romans threw them back easily.

The soldiers brought the catapults and the battering rams to the ramp in front of the Antonia fortress under a rain of stones and arrows shot by the defenders. Although the fortress walls gave the impression of not being strong enough to withstand the attacks, they did not fall. Several soldiers, protected by their shields, removed stones from the wall's foundation, but the wall remained standing.

That night, suddenly, the wall collapsed. The Romans were surprised the following morning when they approached the wall's rubble and saw that the combatants had built a temporary wall. Although it wasn't as high as the collapsed wall, none of the soldiers dared to climb it, fearing that it would mean certain death.

Titus arrived at the place, examined the newly built wall, spoke with a commander, and then, climbing on a rock, addressed the soldiers.

"Soldiers! I agree with you that it is difficult and dangerous to climb this wall, but we, Romans, are not inferior in courage to the Jews. Taking possession of this fortress, from which we can attack the Temple, means that we are about to conquer the city and end the war. The first soldier who climbs this wall will be promoted to official and receive all the rewards he merited. Who are the brave men who will volunteer for this action that will fill them with glory?"

For a minute, no one moved until one soldier stepped forward. Everyone, including Titus, looked at him with great surprise. The volunteer was a small, thin man who did not seem to have enough strength or agility to climb stairs, let alone the wall.

"What's your name, soldier?" Titus asked.

"My name is Sabino, my General! I will climb the wall. I hope to do it with good fortune, but if I fail in the attempt, I want everyone to know that I did it of my own volition," exclaimed the soldier.

Titus hugged him. Sabino unsheathed his sword and began climbing the wall. Soon after, eleven soldiers followed him.

The defenders of the wall shot arrows and rolled stones that knocked down several of the soldiers who were following Sabino.

Sabino managed to reach the top of the wall and attacked the rebels who were there. The defendants fled, believing that the

Roman soldier who attacked them was the vanguard of the whole army. Sabino stumbled on a stone and fell to the ground. The rebels heard the noise of his fall, looked back, and saw only one soldier. They ran towards Sabino with daggers in their hands. The Roman tried to defend himself, managed to wound one of his attackers, but there were too many, and the heroic soldier died fighting. Regarding the eleven soldiers who followed him, three died when they fell from the wall and the other eight, wounded by the arrows of the defenders, were carried back to the camp.

Two days later, twelve of the soldiers who had witnessed Sabino's heroism, ashamed for not climbing with him, decided to make an effort during the night and take the wall. Accompanied by a soldier who carried the legion's emblem and a trumpeter, they walked silently over the fallen wall's rubble and climbed the temporary wall. The rebels who were guarding it were sleeping. The soldiers cut their throats and ordered the trumpeter to blow the trumpet. The other insurgents assumed that the whole Roman army had managed to climb up and fled to the Temple.

Titus heard the trumpet's sound and ordered the soldiers to put on their armor, and, leading them, he climbed the wall and pursued the rebels to the very entrance of the Temple. The Romans fought against the Jews hand-to-hand with daggers and swords. The rebels resisted desperately until Titus, having cleared the Antonia fortress of rebels, considered that this was enough for the moment and ordered his soldiers to return to the camp.

One of the Roman soldiers, a stout man of high stature, disobeyed the general's order, ran towards the rebels, cutting them left and right with his sword, killing all those who tried to stop his advance. Like those of all Roman soldiers, his boots had thick nails in the soles, which caused him to slip and fall on the polished stone slabs that covered the pavement. The rebels attacked him with spears and swords. The soldier tried to get up and defend himself with his sword, but his attackers cut him down.

Titus wanted to go to the soldier's aid, but his commanders held him by his arms and did not allow him to go to what would have been his certain death.

Chapter 40
The rebels refuse to surrender

The Romans, methodically and gradually, had conquered almost the entire city. They now needed to take the Temple.

I can't understand what drove the rebels to keep fighting and dying for a cause that was already lost. They lacked food. They were too few. It was impossible to prevent the Romans from taking the Temple. Any reasonable person would have surrendered. To continue fighting was suicide.

Titus ordered the soldiers to demolish part of the Antonia fortress and clear the road of rubble so that the troops could reach the Temple more easily. He again entrusted me with a mission.

"Josephus, I do not want to destroy the city, much less the Temple, but the resistance of the rebels is forcing me to do it. I want you to talk to the rebels again. Tell them, if they want to fight it out, we are willing to do so in the open field, without harming the city or the Temple."

I approached the Temple wall to make it easy for John of Giscala and his men to see and hear me.

"General Titus respects the Temple of God and does not want to commit a sacrilege by destroying it, but you, with your stubbornness, are forcing him to do it," I shouted in Hebrew.

"Joseph," shouted John from the top of the wall. "You should be ashamed to ask us to surrender. Have you forgotten that you were responsible for the defense of the Galilee? You are a traitor! You have betrayed us! We do not fear that Titus will damage the Temple because it is the House of God, and God will defend it."

The tremendous hypocrisy of John's words caused me to answer him with bitter sarcasm.

"It is admirable how you have kept the city pure and virtuous! You deserve praise for the tremendous respect you have shown the House of God by turning it into military barracks! God, I am sure, will help you for having been such a pious man! You are the one who has betrayed our people by inciting them to continue this suicidal resistance. Because of you, the sacrifices in the Temple, our religious duty, are no longer carried out. And you believe that God will defend you!"

Tears ran down my cheeks, my voice was broken, and sobs interrupted my sentences.

"You and your people have caused the destruction of the city and the death of hundreds of thousands. You have desecrated and contaminated the Temple by turning it into a graveyard and, worse still, leaving unburied corpses on that holy ground. God will indeed intervene, but not to save you! He will do it to purify the city and the Temple with fire and death!"

While I was talking to John and his people, a group of priests took advantage of the fact that the rebels were distracted to escape the Temple and surrender to the Romans.

Titus received them with kindness and spoke to them in a tone that expressed his heart's generosity.

"Gentlemen, I welcome you! I know that your religious laws regarding food make it impossible for you to share our food and that your customs prevent you from living in this camp. I have instructed my men to take you to a nearby town, where you will remain until this tragic conflict ends. I promise you, as soon as there is peace, I will allow you to return to Jerusalem, and you will be able to resume your high positions in the Temple," Titus assured them.

To discourage whoever had the intention of deserting, the rebels circulated rumors that the Romans had executed the priests. To disprove this false information, Titus had them brought back from the town he had sent them. The moment they arrived, he ordered me to take them to the Temple's wall so that all would see that the priests were alive and in good health. This convinced many to defect and take refuge in the Roman camp.

Although he did not follow our religion, Titus had a deep sense of respect for all gods and all temples. His anger at the Temple's desecration made him approach the Temple's gates, and, from there, he blamed John and his followers for their actions.

"We Romans, decades ago, authorized the Jews to place a sign prohibiting entry to the Sanctuary to non-Jews, under penalty of death, but you rebels trample corpses in this holy precinct and desecrate it with the blood of Jews and non-Jews. Respect your own Temple, and I will order my soldiers to respect it too," exhorted Titus.

The rebels disregarded the words and good intentions of Titus. On the contrary, they considered that Titus had spoken like that because he feared the Jewish combatants.

Seeing that the rebels refused his offer, Titus ordered a third part of the army to put on their armor and assault the Temple with him in the front line. His commanders spoke to him to convince him not to take a personal part in the attack.

"General, it is not necessary for you to take part in the fight. Please direct it from the top of Antonia Fortress. This way, you will be able to determine who are the soldiers who deserve a reward for their courage and who should be punished for his cowardice."

"I'll do that," Titus replied.

The Roman soldiers attacked at night, expecting to find the Temple guards asleep, but they were alert and heard the Romans coming. The guards sounded the alarm, and all the defenders came running. It was a night in which the moon was absent, and clouds covered the stars. The darkness made it very difficult to see who was fighting with whom. The Romans had the advantage of defending themselves with their shields and recognized each other by saying the password.

The battle lasted all night. At dawn, the rebels could see that many of their men had been wounded. The Romans returned to their camp, and the Jews took refuge behind the doors of the Temple.

Seven days later, the soldiers, after clearing the rubble from the road to the Temple, started to build ramps against the outer wall of our sacred precinct. The work progressed slowly because wood and other materials had to be brought from far away.

The discipline and professionalism of the soldiers were admirable. In all the time that I was with them, I only knew about a single negligence case. Several Roman riders left their horses loose while they collected materials for use on the ramps. The rebels took advantage of this neglect to go out of the Temple and seize the horses, which they later killed and ate.

Titus, furious, had one of the horsemen executed so that his death would serve as a lesson to the others. No one left his horse loose again.

One of the riders, embarrassed by his mistake, cleared his name a few days later. He and three other cavalrymen were on the Mount of Olives when a group of rebels attacked them by surprise. Other soldiers came to their aid, and the rebels escaped. The protagonist of this anecdote chased one of the rebels, and when he reached the man's side, he bent down from his horse and grabbed his ankle. Galloping, he dragged the rebel to the tent of Titus. The general, hearing the noise, left the tent, congratulated the rider on his prowess, gave him a prize, and ordered him to kill the captive.

The rebels, meanwhile, demolished the bridge that linked the Antonia Fortress to the Temple to prevent the Romans from using it.

A tragicomic incident happened that I want to mention. One day, a rebel, a short man, almost a dwarf, dressed in rags, came out of the Temple and began shouting insults to the soldiers.

"I challenge any of you to fight against me, one on one, or, if you cowards prefer, all of you against me," he bellowed in a booming voice, unexpected in a man who seemed to be so weak and inoffensive.

The soldiers, seeing such a ridiculous and insignificant individual, broke into laughter.

"Cowards! Sons of bitches! Let one of you come to me if he is a man, and I will show him how a Jew fights," the rebel shouted.

The response of the soldiers was to laugh even louder.

The rebel turned around, took off his rag, and, pointing to his backside, shouted: "Kiss me here!"

One of the soldiers could no longer endure such insolence. He drew his sword and ran towards the rebel. He stumbled on a rock and fell to the ground. The rebel, with surprising agility, in a second was at his side and plunged the dagger into the fallen soldier's chest. Then he jumped and shouted with joy.

The soldiers stopped laughing and shot arrows at him. The rebel fell dead over the body of the Roman he had just killed.

The rebels refuse to surrender

Chapter 41
The rebels set a trap

The defenders of the city felt hopeless when they saw that the ramps were ready to be used. Inspired by their desperation, they devised a trap for the Roman soldiers. They filled with combustible elements the beams that supported the roof of a pergola in the Gentiles' Courtyard and withdrew, giving the impression that they were retreating.

Several impetuous soldiers placed ladders and climbed the wall surrounding the Gentiles' Courtyard without waiting for an order. Other soldiers, more cautious, did not move, distrusting the intentions of the rebels.

When the pergola roof was full of soldiers standing over it, the rebels set it on fire. Some of the soldiers jumped and fell on the outside of the wall where their companions were. Others fell on the Courtyard, on the rebels' side of the wall, where they were surrounded and killed.

Titus and I were close by and witnessed the incident. One of the soldiers who were on the wall shouted to one of his tent mates.

"I am going to jump. Please try to catch me when I fall to cushion the blow," he asked.

The friend, a tall, muscular man, stood by the wall and shouted back at the soldier above.

"Jump, do not be afraid! I will catch you," he said.

The soldier jumped. The man caught his friend in his arms but stumbled, fell backward, and broke his head on a rock. He had saved his friend at the cost of his own life.

The rebels set a trap

Chapter 42
The horrors of the famine

The inevitable moment arrived when the famine, which had already killed hundreds of thousands in the city, also affected the combatants. If they saw a corpse on the street or a man dying, they would check his clothes, looking for some crust that they might find. Their hunger was so great that they ate their sandals' leather and the leather that covered their shields.

Everybody was willing to fight to the death over a piece of bread, even if the other person was his best friend.

Dear reader, what I am about to write makes me shudder with horror. If you fear that the terrible images will remain engraved in your mind, I suggest you do not read this chapter and turn the pages to the next.

A woman belonging to a wealthy and prominent family who lived in a town on the other side of the Jordan River had arrived months before to Jerusalem with her baby to celebrate the Festival of Unleavened Bread. Due to the siege of the Romans, it became impossible for her to leave the city.

Crazed by hunger, she spoke to her child.

"Poor son of mine! If you manage to survive the war and your hunger, you will be sold as a slave by the Romans. Your life will be a continuous string of miseries. It's better for you and me if you help me to stay alive," the woman told the baby.

She grabbed a knife, killed the baby, roasted it, ate half the body, and hid the rest. The rebels, attracted by the smell of roasted meat, entered the house and threatened to kill the woman if she did not give them the food she had cooked.

"I've saved you a good portion. Here," she said as she lifted a cloth that covered the baby's remains.

The horrified fighters could not say a word.

"Eat! Eat! It's delicious," the woman said to them, and, seeing they were stepping back, she added, "If you're so prissy, I'll eat it all by myself."

531

Titus, when a deserter told us what had happened, trembled with horror.

"The Gods knows how many times I have offered peace and freedom to the rebels. They preferred to choose rebellion instead of coexistence, war instead of peace, famine instead of abundance. They are the only ones responsible for this tragedy," Titus told me and entered his tent.

He did not come out again until the next day, which was the 9th of the month of Av.

Chapter 43
The 9th of Av

The month of Av [generally coincides with August or the beginning of September] is the hottest month of the year in the Land of Israel. I woke up early that morning but, against my habit, did not go to the mess tent where the officers were already having breakfast. It was the 9th of the month of Av, Tisha be Av, as we call it in Hebrew, the anniversary of the destruction of the Temple built by King Solomon [The Babylonians destroyed the Temple the 9th of Av in the year 585 B.C.] and the Jews, commemorate that day fasting and mourning to commemorate our loss,

I recalled vividly the strange dream I had that night. I dreamed that the sky was covered with gray clouds and a light rain was falling. A group of stars shone in the sky, forming the image of a sword. At the altar, the High Priest raised his knife to sacrifice a heifer when, suddenly, the animal gave birth to a sheep. Suddenly, I heard a noise, the High Priest and I looked back and saw that the heavy brass gate of the Inner Courtyard, which usually needed twenty men to open or close it, was opening by itself.

"God has opened the door to our happiness," the High Priest whispered in my ear.

"You're wrong!" I said. "God has opened the door to let our enemies in."

The priest looked up to the sky and started crying.

"You're right. I see carriages of soldiers and armed troops running through the clouds," he said sobbing.

His face gradually lost its color and its flesh until only the skull could be seen. Teeth fell from his mouth, and blood flowed from the sockets of his eyes. I shuddered with dread. At that moment, I woke up.

Titus was in an excellent mood when he saw me that morning.

"Josephus," he greeted me. "Today, my troops will conquer the Temple. We have tried for six days to hit the Temple wall with our battering rams without making a dent. Today, we will try a new tactic. The soldiers will carry ladders with them to climb the wall."

The soldiers placed the ladders against the Temple wall and started to climb. The rebels pushed back the ladders, and the soldiers who were on them fell to the pavement. The swords of the defenders killed the few soldiers who succeeded in reaching the top of the wall.

Seeing that his soldiers had not succeeded with the ladders, Titus gave the order to set fire to the Temple's gate. The fire spread rapidly into the enclosure.

Titus had no intention of destroying the Temple. (I am convinced of that, although many believe otherwise). He hastily assembled his commanders to decide what to do. Titus' lieutenant, Tiberius Alexander, son of the man who had been the leader of the Jewish community of Alexandria, was the first to express his opinion.

"We must demolish the Temple. While this building stands, the Jews will always rebel."

The other commanders agreed, saying that the Jews had turned a sacred place, which deserved reverence and respect, into a citadel that must be destroyed. Titus listened to each of them and, finally, announced his decision.

"Our fight is against the rebels and not against inanimate objects like this Temple, the most beautiful in the Empire. Command the soldiers to put out the fire."

The Jews attacked the soldiers who had managed to enter the Courtyard of the Gentiles. Titus, from the top of the Antonia fortress, saw what was happening and sent reinforcements. During the battle, one of the soldiers grabbed a beam engulfed in flames and threw it inside the Sanctuary. The fire devoured the curtains, and the fire spread so quickly and violently that the rebels couldn't put it out.

Titus and his commanders came running and shouted for the soldiers to put out the fire. The soldiers ignored the orders, perhaps because the noise of the flames and the wooden roofs falling made it impossible for them to hear, or, maybe because they were busy grabbing the gold plates that covered the doors and walls of the Sanctuary and seizing the gold and silver vessels that they found there.

Numerous priests, seeing that the flames consumed the Sanctuary, wrapped themselves with the sacred scrolls and jumped into the fire to die. A few rebels stopped fighting and did not resist the soldiers who stabbed them and cut their throats. Others escaped through secret tunnels and joined those who still struggled in the Upper City.

Thousands of Jews had taken refuge behind the thick walls of the Temple during the previous weeks. The soldiers, driven mad by their feelings of revenge and obsessed by their frenzied desire to seize gold and silver, massacred them, regardless of the sex or age of their victims.

That night, to celebrate the conquest and destruction of the Temple, the Romans hung the emblem of the legions in what had been the Eastern Gate of the Sacred Precinct and offered sacrifices to their gods.

Thus, the Temple built by Herod was destroyed, the most imposing building in the world since the Egyptians built the pyramids thousands of years ago. [The Romans destroyed the Temple in the year 70 C.E.]

Chapter 44
Titus' speech to the crowd

Simon bar Giora and his men barricaded themselves in the Fasael Tower, next to Herod's old palace, the only remaining focus of resistance in Jerusalem in the Upper City.

"Why do these rebels persist in their struggle?" Titus asked me. "We have demolished the three walls that surrounded Jerusalem. The remains of the Antonia Fortress are in our hands, and the Temple is today a smoking ruin. Hundreds of thousands of Jews have died as victims of the war and hunger. We only need to take the Upper City to complete the conquest of Jerusalem. It makes no sense for the rebels to continue fighting.

"Perhaps the explanation is the Roman proverb, *Quos Deus vult perdere, prius dementa* [those whom the gods wish to destroy they first make mad]" I answered.

"I'll try to talk to them to put an end to this madness," Titus told me.

Titus, accompanied by his bodyguards, went to the bridge that linked the Temple with the Upper City. On his way, he met a group of soldiers holding several priests that they had captured.

"Your Excellency, grant us our lives," the priests begged.

"The time for forgiveness has passed. The Temple where you worshipped has been destroyed, and it is proper that you die with it. Crucify them!" Titus commanded the soldiers and continued walking.

On the sides of the bridge, a crowd was waiting to hear what Titus would say. On one side were the Roman soldiers, and on the other side the Jews, including women and children.

"Hundreds of thousands have died!" Titus told them. "The Temple is a ruin! These are the results of your madness. Did you imagine that you were stronger than us? If the ocean that separates Britain from Europe is not an obstacle to our conquest, even less were your weak walls. Not only has

537

madness motivated you, but also ingratitude. We have been generous with you, we have respected your religion, we have allowed you to receive donations from the entire Empire for the Temple, but you have used that money, which the Jews of the world had destined for God, to wage war against us. My father, Vespasian, decided not to attack Jerusalem directly to allow you to repent. Instead of repenting, you built new walls. Many times I have asked you, I have begged you, to lay down your arms. You despised my offers, thinking that they were the product of fear and weakness, when in fact, they were a demonstration of my humanity. I offer you now one last opportunity to lay down your weapons and save your lives."

"General! My commander, Simon bar Giora, has sent me to give you a message," shouted one of the men in the crowd.

"Speak!" Titus ordered him.

"My commander has sworn he will never surrender. He asks you to let him leave the town with his fighters, wives, and children. He intends to settle in the desert," said the man.

Never, since I first meet him, had I seen such fury in Titus' face. He made attempts to speak, but his words choked him. After a few minutes, he regained his composure and spoke again.

"Do you want to impose conditions on us as if you were the victors and we the defeated ones? Listen well! I have now changed my mind. I no longer want you to surrender. You will all die," he said. Turning at the soldiers, he added, "Roman soldiers! I authorize you to burn and loot the city. This is your reward for your heroic campaign."

Chapter 45
The Romans conquer
the Upper City

Simon Bar Giora and the fighters who were still with him left the Fasael Tower and attacked the nearby palace that had belonged to Herod. The Roman garrison fled, but the rebels succeeding in capturing two soldiers. One they killed immediately.

"Do not kill me," the other soldier begged," I have valuable information for your leader.

The rebels took him to the presence of Simon bar Giora.

"What is your information? If it is useful to me, I will spare your life."

The man fell silent, not knowing what to say. Simon realized that the man had no information to give him, and he had said it only to save his life.

"Take him to a place where the Romans can see him and cut off his head there," Simon ordered one of his men.

The combatant tied the soldier's hands, blindfolded him, and took him to a field in front of the Roman camp. There, he took off the soldier's eye bandage. The man pushed the rebel down and began to run with great speed, driven by his despair. The rebel got up, drew his sword, and started to pursue him but could not reach him. The man arrived safely in the Roman ranks and was immediately taken to Titus' tent.

"You allowed our enemies to capture you instead of fighting to the death. You do not deserve to be a Roman soldier. I expel you from your legion," Titus told him.

"My general, I cannot live with that shame. I'd rather die," the man replied.

"I will grant your wish," Titus replied.

539

The Romans conquer the Upper City

Chapter 46
The Romans complete
the conquest of Jerusalem

The Roman soldiers went from house to house in the Lower City, looking for booty and rebels. They did not find either one because the rebels had escaped to the Upper City, taking all their valuables. The soldiers only found putrefying bodies of women and children who had died of hunger.

The rebels still offered resistance in the Upper City. The climb from the Lower City, which was in Romans' hands, to the Upper City, was very steep. Titus decided to build ramps.

The commanders of the Idumeans who had fought under the command of Simon Bar Giora [See Chapter 27] met secretly and decided that there was no point in continuing to fight. They sent a delegation of five people to the Roman camp. Titus received them and agreed to respect their lives if they surrendered.

The five men returned to inform their companions. Simon bar Giora found out what they had done, killed them, and imprisoned all the Idumeans' commanders. This did not stop the Idumean fighters from attempting to desert. Some were killed by Simon bar Giora, but others managed to escape and reach the Roman camp.

The soldiers had stopped killing the prisoners. It was more profitable for them to sell them as slaves. The result was that there were so many slaves offered for sale, including women and children, that their price went down to just a few coins for each.

One of the surviving priests asked to speak with Titus and offered to give him the Temple's hidden treasure that the Romans had not yet found in exchange for his life and freedom. Titus sent him to the Temple accompanied by an escort that returned loaded with gold plates, gold and silver coins, golden candelabra, garments decorated with precious stones, and bags of incense used in the Temple's rituals.

It took the Romans eighteen days to build the ramps that led from the Lower City to the Upper City. The day after they finished, they attacked Herod's palace where Simon bar Giora had fortified himself.

Instead of staying inside the palace and the three towers next to it, [See Chapter 28] where they could have resisted for a few days, perhaps even weeks, the rebels went outside to fight the soldiers. This was a fatal mistake since the Roman soldiers were more numerous, heavily armed, and in excellent physical condition. The unequal struggle ended when the rebels fled and hid in tunnels and underground caves. The Romans occupied the palace and the towers.

To celebrate the fall of the last focus of resistance, the soldiers went through the city's streets with their swords drawn, killing whoever they saw and burning the houses.

Titus arrived at Herod's palace and admired the three towers' beauty, height, and sturdy construction.

"Josephus," he commented, "I am convinced that God helped us by convincing the rebels to go outside these inexpugnable towers. It would have been challenging to capture them."

The three towers made such a deep impression on Titus that, although he ordered his troops to destroy the city and demolish the Temple he gave instructions to leave the Towers intact.

It had taken the Romans six months to conquer Jerusalem.

Chapter 47
The Romans dispose
of the survivors

The population of Jerusalem, before the war, had been about sixty thousand people, but, during the Festivals, especially during the Festival of Unleavened Bread, it increased to more than a million due to the multitude of Jewish pilgrims who came to the city from all corners of the Empire. I calculated that, at the end of the siege of Jerusalem, a maximum of two hundred thousand survivors, between men and women, were still alive. Four out of five persons in the city had been killed by the sword or had perished by hunger.

Titus gave orders to kill the people who still resisted. The soldiers complied with the order but expanded it by also killing the elderly and the sick. The surviving prisoners were taken to one of the Temple's courtyards and kept there standing in the rubble under guard. Titus delegated to one of his commanders the decision of what to do with them.

The commander called the prisoners one by one and interrogated each one personally. Any prisoner who gave the impression that he had been a rebel was killed on the spot.

The officer selected the tallest and best-looking ones to parade in the Triumph that Titus would celebrate in Rome upon his return. Those who were over seventeen years old, he sent in chains to Egypt to work in the mines. The younger boys were sold as slaves.

The Romans dispose of the survivors

Chapter 48
Titus awards prizes to the soldiers

Titus ordered to build a wooden platform in the middle of the camp. He stood on it, accompanied by his second-in-command, Tiberius Alexander, and other commanders, and spoke to the troops.

"Roman soldiers! Our struggle has come to an end. We have triumphed. I want to congratulate you for your courage, your discipline, and your admirable obedience to the orders of your commanders. All of you have fought with courage and determination, but some have done extraordinary heroic and glorious deeds, and we must recognize them. I will read the list of their names and ask them to step forward."

Titus read the list. The soldiers whose names were mentioned took a step forward. A commander called them to the rostrum, one by one. Titus handed each of them a gold spear, a silver badge and placed a golden garland on his head. He also promoted each of them to a higher rank.

After the ceremony, Titus and the officers, acclaimed by the soldiers, came down from the rostrum and went to the camp's altar, where they sacrificed a bull to the gods, thanking them for the victory.

Titus decided to take a vacation and traveled to Caesarea Phillipi, on the Golan Heights. There, he rested and enjoyed spectacles in which the captives fought against wild animals or were forced to kill each other.

Titus awards prizes to the soldiers

Chapter 49
The Romans capture
John of Giscala and Simon bar Giora

The Romans entered the tunnels and caves where several rebels had taken refuge and killed all the people they encountered, except John of Giscala, who was taken prisoner.

Simon bar Giora and a handful of his companions fled to a cavern, carrying with them provisions and tools to dig a tunnel. Their goal was to dig until they would reach a place from which they could climb to the surface and escape. They didn't encounter any obstacles when digging the tunnels until hard rocks they could not move or break stopped them. Seeing that he had no alternative, Simon put on a white robe, covered himself with a purple cloak, and surfaced in what had been one of the Temple's courtyards. The Roman soldiers were stunned to see him emerge from the earth.

"Who are you?" they asked him.

"Bring me your commander. I'll tell him who I am," Simon replied.

One of the soldiers went and returned with an officer.

"I am Simon bar Giora," declared the former rebel leader.

"Take him to prison. Inform General Titus that we have captured the rebel leader. He will determine what to do with him," the commander ordered the soldiers.

After hearing that Simon Bar Giora and John of Giscala had been captured, Titus ordered them to be chained and kept in prison until he would take them to Rome with him.

The Romans capture John of Giscala and Simon bar Giora

Chapter 50
Anti-Jewish riots in Antioch

Jewish communities have existed for many years and continue to exist in every city in the known world. One of the most important Jewish communities was Antioch, the third-largest city of the Empire, after Rome and Alexandria. The Jews lived, prospered, and had the same rights and privileges as the rest of the population.

The Jews of Antioch, like all other Jews throughout the Empire, were moved by the tragic events that happened to their brothers in Judea but remained loyal to the Empire.

I have had the opportunity in my life to notice that those who hate the Jews the most, and do to them as much damage as they can, are men, themselves of Jewish origin, who have ceased to identify with their people. This was the case of Tiberius Alexander, Titus' second-in-command. His late father, a devoted and respected man, leader of the Jewish community of Alexandria, defended the Egyptian Jews in Rome when he was a member of a delegation that met with Emperor Caligula. Tiberius Alexander did not follow in his father's footsteps. On the contrary, he was the one who proposed that Titus should destroy the Temple.

Another Jew-born Jew-hater was Antiochus, son of the leader of the Jewish community of Antioch. This individual appeared before an assembly of the city's dignitaries and falsely accused his father and other leaders of the community of planning to burn and destroy Antioch. He expressed his slander with such passion that the people who heard him believed him. Antiochus, followed by a frenzied crowd, went to the Jewish quarter, where the mob killed dozens of men, women, and children and set their houses on fire.

Antiochus was not content with that. He had the surviving Jews brought to a pagan Temple where he forced them to offer sacrifices to idols. Those who refused to do so were killed right there. He forbid the Jews to rest on Saturday.

549

A gentile, overburdened with debt, decided that the only way out of his predicament was to burn the city's archives where the documents of his loans were kept. Antiochus took advantage of the incident to blame the Jew for the fire and again incited the mob against them.

The Roman Governor investigated the fire. He discovered the real culprit and declared the Jews innocent, but the community continued to live under the threat of terror and persecution.

Chapter 51
Celebrations of triumph

Titus traveled from Caesarea Philippi to Beirut, where he celebrated his victory with spectacles where many captive Jews fought and died. From there, he went to Antioch. The population, informed of their arrival, came out of the city and lined the road's sides to receive him with applause. That afternoon, Titus received the dignitaries of the city, who requested that he expel the Jews.

"I cannot accept your proposal. The country of the Jews has been destroyed. If I expel them from this city, they will have no place to go," Titus replied.

"Your Excellency, in that case, we ask you, at least, to annul all the rights that the Jews have," one of the dignitaries asked.

Titus again refused to grant the request. From Antioch, he traveled to Alexandria. From there, he sailed to Rome, taking with him the prisoners John of Giscala and Simon bar Giora and another seven hundred captives who had been chosen for their height and good looks to take part in the triumphal parade.

People told me that they had never seen a more impressive and beautiful parade in Rome. The entire population was out in the streets, witnessing the parade and cheering the victorious generals and soldiers.

The soldiers opened the parade. They marched led by their commanders, followed by Vespasian, and Titus adorned with laurel wreaths and dressed in purple robes. It is impossible to describe the enormous amount of wealth and articles of gold, silver, and ivory that the captives carried, including the sacred candelabrum with seven branches made of pure gold that had adorned the Temple. Then came the allegorical carriages, some of them four stories high, each representing a walled city, catapults, or destroyed houses. On top of each carriage was the commander who had conquered the city represented by the carriage.

551

The parade arrived at the Temple of Capitoline Jupiter. Simon bar Giora, who walked in chains among the other captives, was forced to climb to a platform. The public shouted with joy when the executioner cut off his head.

John of Giscala was sentenced to life imprisonment.

That night, Vespasian and Titus offered a banquet to their closest friends, I among them.

Vespasian gave a short speech.

"Friends, today we celebrate that peace has returned to the Empire after a long and difficult war. The riches that my son Titus has brought from Judea are countless, and we will make good use of them. We will build a Temple of Peace, where we will keep all the gold and silver items that we have taken from the Jewish Temple. I have decided that part of the immense sums of money that we found in the Temple's Treasure Hall should benefit Rome's entire population. With that money, we will build a large amphitheater that we will call Colosseum."

The Triumph of Titus
A reconstructed relief panel from the Arch of Titus, Rome

Chapter 52
The conquest of Masada

I mentioned, in previous pages, that a group of fanatics, called "Sicarii" (Dagger-men) was expelled from Jerusalem by the Zealots at the beginning of the rebellion and had taken refuge in the fortress of Masada. Their leader, Menachem, was captured and killed when he tried to leave Jerusalem. Eleazar ben Yair succeeded him.

The Masada fortress, located a short distance from the Sea of Salt, is on a plateau surrounded by steep precipices one thousand two hundred feet deep. The plateau is one thousand nine hundred feet long by nine hundred forty-five feet wide. It can be climbed only by a narrow path fifteen thousand feet long that meanders (which is why it is called "the path of the serpent") on the edge of the abyss, thus making it impossible for an army to climb it.

Masada had initially been built as a summer palace by one of the kings of the Hasmonean dynasty. King Herod, fearing that his subjects might rebel against him, fortified it with a high wall and thirty-eight towers. His purpose was to use the fortress as a refuge if it was necessary.

Inside the perimeter wall, he built a luxurious palace whose pavements and walls were covered with marble and beautiful mosaics. He dug canals that carried the rainwater to underground cisterns. He stored wheat, wine, oil, and dates in quantities that could feed thousands of men for many years. He had weapons In his arsenal that would have sufficed to equip an army of ten thousand soldiers, apart from large quantities of metals (iron, lead, and bronze) that would be used to make more weapons.

The Roman Governor of Judea, Lucio Flavius Silva, decided to conquer Masada and end once and for all the last remaining holdout of the rebellion. Nine hundred and sixty-seven Jews, including women and children, that occupied the fortress refused to surrender.

Silva marched towards Masada with an army of nine thousand soldiers, composed of a Roman legion, four auxiliary cohorts, and two cavalry wings, besides numerous Jewish servants and slaves.

The Roman's first action was to build eight camps to house the troops and a wall surrounding the plateau. This made it impossible for the rebels to escape or to receive reinforcements.

Silva also ordered his soldiers to build a ramp on the plateau's western side, on a promontory called "the White Rock," where the plateau was only one hundred and fifty feet high. Knowing that the rebels, being Jews, would refuse to shoot arrows at other Jews, Silva forced hundreds of Jewish slaves to work in the ramp's construction.

The construction, which used thousands of tons of stones and rammed earth, was finished in three months. During the same time, the soldiers built a tower ninety feet high covered with iron plates, from which the Romans fired their arrows.

Once the ramp was completed, the soldiers placed a battering ram on the lower floor of the tower, with which they continuously pounded the wall. They managed to open a breach but were surprised when they found two parallel wooden walls with the space between them filled with earth and stones. The rebels had built the interior parallel walls foreseeing that the stone wall would not resist the battering ram.

The Romans hit the second wall with the ram, but the blows compacted the soil behind it, and the wall, with each strike, became more resistant.

Seeing that the ramming was not effective, Silva sent a group of soldiers with torches to set fire to the wooden wall. A strong wind began to blow unexpectedly and fanned the flames that destroyed the wall entirely.

The soldiers returned jubilantly to the camp where Silva had gathered his officers.

"I want you to put up a strong guard to guard the remains of the burned wall. We must prevent the Jews from escaping through the breach during the night. Tomorrow we will launch the final attack," announced Silva.

Eleazar ben Yair, the Sicarii leader, summoned all the combatants and their families to a meeting in the fortress's largest hall.

"Dear comrades," he said to them. "We, the Sicarii, were the first to rebel against the Roman yoke, and we are the last to be still fighting. God has granted us the honor of dying as free men and not being conquered as so many thousands have been. Tomorrow, the Roman army will enter Masada. We cannot avoid it because the walls that defended us have been destroyed. Our enemies intend to capture us alive and sell us as slaves. The wind that God sent yesterday and that helped destroy our defense is a sign that we must abandon any hope we ever had. God punishes us for our numerous sins, but we must not allow the Romans to apply this punishment to us. We, ourselves, must be the instruments of the divine wrath. I propose that our women die before becoming victims of the Roman soldiers' abuse and that our children die before living as slaves. Once our loved ones are dead, we will kill each other. But, first, we will destroy our possessions. The Romans will be much disappointed at not finding booty. Let us leave our provisions intact so that our enemies will see that our decision to die was an expression of our free will, not because of lack of food.

Eleazar fell silent when he noticed that some of the fighters were looking at their women and children with tears in their eyes. He remained silent for a few minutes and then continued.

"My brothers, you must not fear death. Death frees our immortal souls. The tragedy is life, not death. Regarding those who have died in this war, we must consider them blessed because they died defending their freedom. Those who deserve our compassion are those who were left alive. Men have been tortured and devoured by wild animals for the amusement and rejoicing of the crowds. Women were raped by the soldiers and passed from hand-to-hand. Personally, I regret not having died before seeing our beautiful city and our Holy Temple destroyed by our enemies. Brothers, we must leave this world as free men and express our love to our women and children by taking them with us."

As soon as Eleazar finished speaking, the men embraced their wives and children, kissed them tenderly, and cut their throats. After each man had killed his own family, the men burned their possessions and chose by lot ten of their companions to kill the others. They lay on the ground next to their wives and children and offered their necks to their killers. After killing their companions, the ten men cast lots and chose one who killed the other nine, burned the fortress, and then committed suicide by stabbing himself with his dagger.

The next morning [Masada fell in April 73 AD], the Roman soldiers put on their armor, placed footbridges over the burning wall, and burst into the fortress, prepared to fight the rebels. They were surprised by the silence they encountered. They entered the fortress and saw the lifeless bodies of men, women, and children.

Silva sent one of the soldiers to check another building. He returned with two women and five children, the only survivors. The Romans, impressed by the death of the defenders and their families, spared their lives.

556

The conquest of Masada

Having written these last lines, I have fulfilled the two promises I made at the book's beginning. The first was to narrate with objectivity and frankness the atrocities committed by the fanatics that led us to the greatest tragedy in our history. The second, to tell the cruel acts of the Romans, the crucifixion of thousands of our fighters, the massacres of the elderly, women, and children, and the sale of the survivors in the slave market.

The conquest of Masada

Epilogue

Thirty years have passed since I arrived in Rome, accompanying Titus, shortly after the conquest of Jerusalem.

Emperor Vespasian honored me by giving me his family name. He had the generous gesture of allowing me to live in his house in one of Rome's most elegant neighborhoods after he moved to the palace.

I do not need to work. Vespasian gave me lands in Judea and assigned me a generous monthly sum. All he asked from me in return was to write a book telling the story of my people with objectivity and sincerity and the chronicle of the Great Rebellion of the Jews.

Vespasian died surrounded by the love of his people after reigning for ten years. He was succeeded by his son Titus, the first Roman Emperor who succeeded his father on the throne.

It is a tragedy for Rome that Titus died due to a fever after reigning only two years. He was a just, compassionate, and generous ruler. He is the only Emperor who, during his reign, did not condemn anyone to death.

He was an extraordinary rider and an exceptional athlete. He spoke Greek as if he had been born in Athens; he sang with a beautiful voice and played the harp better than any professional musician.

One day his officers brought to him two conspirators accusing them of wanting to seize the throne. Titus ordered his soldiers to remove the chains of the two men.

"You understand that you can never be emperors. Imperial power is a gift of destiny. But, if you need anything else, ask me," he said and invited them to dinner.

One evening he said something I will never forget.

"Josephus, I just realized that today I haven't helped anyone. What a wasted day!" he lamented.

If Titus had lived more years, I do not doubt that he would have been considered the greatest Emperor who ruled the Empire. His enormous popularity caused the Roman Senate to deify him after his death.

Titus was succeeded by his younger brother, Domitian, who, to honor the memory of Titus' triumph over the Jews, built an arch on the Via Sacra, opposite the Colosseum. The Jews of Rome avoid going under the arch because it shows Titus' triumphal procession with the Temple's booty, including the seven-branched candelabrum, the golden trumpets, and the Holy Bread Table, overlaid with gold. All these images bring back painful memories.

The Jews of Rome do not allow me to enter their synagogues. They refuse to speak to me and, when they see me, they do not greet me.

How can they call me a traitor when I fought and risked my life, first for my nation's freedom and later for its survival?

I fought the Romans and risked my life. When I understood that it was God's will that Judea should be a Roman province, I risked my life again, this time to try to convince the fanatics to lay down their arms and thus save the city, the Temple, and themselves. The great tragedy of my life is that I failed to convince them.

I know in my heart that one day God will allow the Jewish people to live again in freedom in the land of Israel. I do not know when that will happen, maybe in a hundred years or a thousand years, perhaps even two thousand years from today.

I have no doubt that day will come, and when it comes, only ruins will remain of Imperial Rome, but Jerusalem, the capital of our nation, will be what it once was, the most beautiful city in the world.

Titus Arch with the captured Menorah, Rome
The Roman Empire today is remembered in ruins
Israel and Jerusalem are today more vital than ever, while
the Roman Empire lies in ruins.

Menorah in front of the Israeli Parlament

561

A note to the reader

Dear reader:

I thank you for having read these pages. I hope that they have entertained you.

I would appreciate it very much if you could give your comments to Amazon about this book.

Your comments or review would be handy to other readers to help them decide whether to read this book.

The procedure to comment on Amazon is as follows:

a) Visit the page of this book in the Kindle Store at www.amazon.com or www.amazon.com.es.

b) Move the cursor to the bottom of the screen until you get to Write my opinion (or Write a Customer Review on the website in English)

c) Click on that phrase to write your comment.

With thanks and best wishes

David Mandel

Bibliography

Although it is a novel, this book follows closely the histories related by ancient chroniclers, especially Josephus Flavius.

I have consulted the following books:
The War of the Jews by Josephus Flavius
Annals and *Histories* by Publius Cornelius Tacitus
The Lives of the Twelve Caesars by Gaius Suetonius Tranquillus
Rome and Jerusalem by Martin Goodman
Herod, King of the Jews and Friend of the Romans by Peter Richardson
A History of the Jews by Paul Johnson
A History of Judaism by Martin Goodman
Jews, Judaism and the Classical World by Gedalyahu Alon
Ten Caesars by Barry Strauss
Encyclopedia Judaica
Encyclopedia Britannica

I have been inspired by, and have tried to emulate, the three best novels of historical fiction that cover that period:
Augustus by John Williams, winner of the National Book Award in 1973
I, Claudius by Robert Graves, winner of the James Tait Black Prize, the oldest literary award in Britain.
Claudius, the God by Robert Graves

BOOKS BY DAVID MANDEL
**Distributed by Amazon.com
in printed and digital versions**

LONG WAS THE ROAD

DAVID MANDEL

"Long was the road" is a passionate novel based on real events that captivate, thrill, and inspire. It is the story of a Jewish family from the late 19th century to the present day, and, at the same time, it is a microcosm of the history of the Jewish people, told not by a historian, but by its protagonists.

The author's literary device of personal letters between family members gradually reveals the family's story and the historical events that impact it and makes the reader feel that he is also a witness to those events.

In his book "Long was the road," David Mandel achieves a very unusual goal: he masterfully merges the story of an ordinary family with historical events of which these people

565

are witnesses and participants. The literary resource of letters exchanged by family members gradually reveals the family's history and the historical facts that impact it.

The Klausner family, originally from a small town in Poland, escaped from pogroms and emigrated in the early years of the 20th century to Germany and Austria, which they consider liberal and democratic countries.

World War I causes them to enlist in opposing armies. Later, they witness the rise of the Nazi party. Historical circumstances empower Hitler, who blames the Jews for Germany's defeat in the First World War and is obsessed with exterminating them.

Part of the family tried to assimilate in Vienna, but, when the Nazis come, finds refuge in London, and are a victim of the Nazi bombings. Others are sent to death camps, they rebel in Sobibor, and take part in the heroic defense of the Warsaw Ghetto.

A branch of the family immigrated to Peru, where, with determination and initiative, they achieved a comfortable position. Another part of the family arrives in Palestine and takes part in the fight for Israel's independence. Finally, the Peruvian branch immigrates to Israel, where triumphs and tragedies also await them.

The Klausner family's events illuminate and illustrate the age-old struggle of the Jewish people for survival. Both aspects cannot be separated, and thus, in Mandel's book, the story of the Klausner family is, at the same time, the history of the Jewish people during the last two centuries, years that have been the framework of its most significant historical tragedy and, also, of its rebirth in Israel.

The sixty stories included in this book constitute a history—the history of the Jewish people. They are individual mosaics of a panoramic picture that covers 4,000 years.

The first story takes place four millennia ago in Ur, the capital of Sumer, the oldest kingdom in history. The last story is about an entrepreneur in Tel Aviv, one of the leading centers of global high technology, and the event it reports. If it did not happen yesterday, it might happen tomorrow.

Through this book's pages, pass patriarchs and prophets, kings and queens, saints and villains, philosophers and generals, politicians, and scientists.

The stories use various literary formats. Some are anachronistic, such as a radio interview with King Jeroboam or Rabbi Akiva's life in a three-act play. Some, especially those of the biblical age, are presented with humor.

Many of the stories are told in the first person by characters that, in some cases, are from real life and in others imaginary, but, always, the events mentioned are historical.

The theme of this book, actually the underlying theme of Jewish history, is the survival of the Jewish people, who, despite being one of the smallest nations on the planet, have, during their long existence, faced and survived the most powerful Empires.

The pharaohs of Egypt, the emperors of Rome, the fanatical monks of the Spanish Inquisition, the Nazis guilty of the worst genocide in human history have all disappeared. However, the Jewish people are still here, actively contributing to the progress of humanity.

Mark Twain, the distinguished American writer, wrote an essay titled Concerning the Jews: "All things are mortal but the Jew; all other forces pass, but he remains." He finished his essay with a question: "What is the secret of his immortality?"

The author found the answer to Mark Twain's question in a most unexpected place: in a detective novel, Postmortem, by writer Patricia Cornwell, in a phrase that could serve as the national motto of the Jewish people: "Surviving is my only hope, Succeeding is my only revenge."

Books by David Mandel

THE SECRET
OF THE SANTAMARIA FAMILY

By David Mandel

A prominent Spanish doctor discovers in an old trunk in his attic documents that reveal his family's secret, hidden for generations.

The novel tells the story of a Spanish family, from the 11th to the 17TH century, whose members include heroes, martyrs, and passionate defenders of their different convictions.

In "The Secret of the Santamaria Family," David Mandel has written a novel where he reconstructs historical people and events and combines them with the agility of his imagination. The clarity and amenity that characterize his style make us feel that we are contemporaries of his characters.

"The Secret of the Santamaria Family" is a work that must be read to know and understand a tragic chapter in Spanish history. The novel will thrill, illustrate and fascinate its readers.

Books by David Mandel

A novel by David Mandel

The HERODIAN TRILOGY is an epic historical novel that spans the years 35 B.C.E. to 73 C.E., one of the most dramatic periods in the Jewish people's history. The rebellion of the Jews against the powerful Roman Empire and the destruction of Jerusalem and the Temple affected not only the Jews but had and continues to have a great influence on Western civilization to this day. Never, from then until the 20th century, did the Jews experience such traumatic and crucial events.

Each of the three parts of the trilogy is told by its own
protagonist, making us readers feel we are living in their times
and being contemporaries of the characters.
The first part, "At King Herod's Court," tells Herod's story, the
builder of the Temple of Jerusalem.
The second part, "Memoirs of Agrippa," is related by Marcus
Julius Agrippa, one of the most fascinating and charismatic
figures in Jewish history. In his youth. He was an adventurer,
a gambler, a spender, and was even a prisoner of debt, but
when he assumed the throne of Judea, he deserved to be the
only Jewish king who is called "the Great".
The narrator of the third part, is Josephus Flavius historian
and participant in the Jewish war against the powerful Empire
Roman, one of the most traumatic events in the history of the
Jewish peopleThe Jewish rebellion ended with the destruction
of Jerusalem and the Temple and has gone down in history as
one of the greatest tragedies of the Jewish people and the
beginning of an exile that lasted 2,000 years.

THE LYRE AND THE SWORD

A novel about King David
Musician, poet, warrior, seducer and murderer

by David Mandel

"The Lyre and the Sword" tells the life of King David, the most famous king in history or literature, an exceptional man, a superb poet, a talented musician, and a great military leader.

He was also an unscrupulous and ambitious politician who used his intelligence and courage to climb from his humble beginnings as a shepherd to the summit of an Empire. His failure as a father, his reluctance to discipline his children, and his indulgence were the cause of tragic events in his dysfunctional family.

The author presents David as a living character, not the idealized king, but a man whose virtues were matched by his shortcomings.

THE ART AND LIFE OF
Ruth Mandel
יצירתה וחייה של
רות מנדל

By David Mandel

The Art and Life of Ruth Mandel is not just one book, but many books rolled into one magnificent masterpiece. It is a beautiful and colorful tribute to a great artist, painter, sculptor, philanthropist, humanist: Ruth Mandel. It is also a biography of a loving wife, mother, grandmother, a friend to so many, a world traveler, and a keen observer of the human condition (which she translated into her art). It is a heartwarming memorial by her devoted husband, daughters, son, and all those who loved her. By rolling all these aspects into one book, the authors paint a picture of the art and life of Ruth Mandel.

This book should be of interest to art lovers in general and all those who always wondered how a person develops his/her passion for their art. How the whole person (the woman, the descendant of holocaust survivors, the mother, and the wife) turned into what we all aspire to, a complete human being.

The Art and Life of Ruth Mandel is a book to be cherished. Her family history and the life she led are right out of a historical novel, but she lived it, and it is her legacy.

Her husband, David, tenderly tells her story. They both grew up in Lima, Peru and David married her when she was seventeen. Their life together was an adventure, and the narrative lets you ride along with them to many continents spanning many decades.

It is Ruth's artwork that is the real joy that emanates from this book. Her color pallet is as bright and vivid as any you have seen. Her style reflects her joy in life. Turning the pages is to view the visible color spectrum through the prism of her creativity.

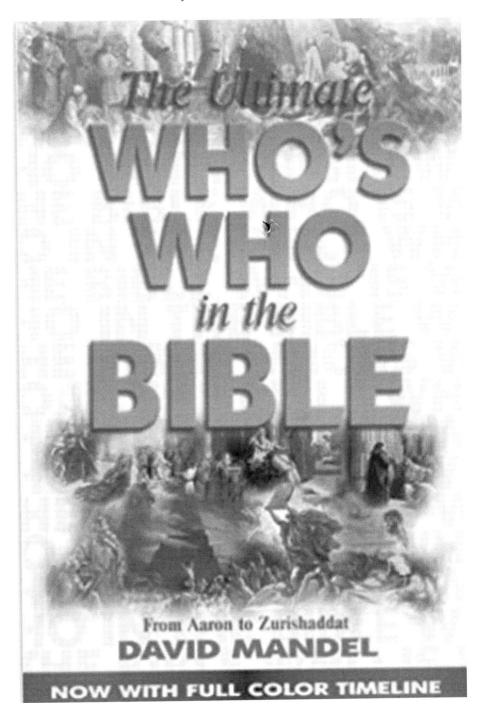

The Ultimate WHO'S WHO in the BIBLE

From Aaron to Zurishaddat

DAVID MANDEL

NOW WITH FULL COLOR TIMELINE

The most extensive who's who book of biblical history! The Ultimate Who's Who in the Bible brings 3000 people in the Bible to life in a narrative format that presents the biography of each person in a coherent and continuous story. Every person in the Bible is included, from Aaron to Zurishaddai, along with information on the meaning of each name. Authoritative and indispensable, *The Ultimate Who's Who in the Bible* is much more than a reference book—it's an essential tool for every Christian's library.

David Mandel has undertaken the enormous task of cataloging every character in the Bible. From Aaron to Zurishaddai, this comprehensive biographical dictionary gives its readers the opportunity to get up close and personal with everyone named in the Bible—its patriarchs, matriarchs, and prophets, warriors and peacemakers, holy men and sinners, heroes and villains.

Arranged in a comprehensive A to Z format, *The Ultimate Who's Who in the Bible* contains detailed biographical information about all the Bible's characters as well as fascinating facts and intriguing stories, written in a contemporary narrative style, Each entry also includes the origin and meaning of the name, the dates he or she lived (if known), and the person's first appearance in the Bible by book, chapter, and verse.

The Ultimate Who's Who in the Bible is the most thorough and comprehensive book of its kind and an invaluable reference for students, teachers, rabbis, and anyone interested in knowing more about the people of the Bible. Those who search for a name in the Bible, whether well-known or obscure, will be rewarded with well-organized information that will add new meaning and enjoyment to their reading.

GOLIATH'S MOTHER

**and other Biblical stories that
you will not find in the Bible**

by David Mandel

It is said that the Bible is the book that everybody has in his/her home, but very few have read it. This motivated David Mandel, the author of Who's Who in the Jewish Bible, to write a version of the Bible stories that everybody can read and enjoy.

Goliath's mother recreates with delightful humor the events, and characters of the Bible, as seen through the eyes of the 21st Century reader. The book, sometimes irreverent, follows the original biblical version faithfully.

The characters and events are presented through a contemporary lens with political, social, ethical, and philosophical overtones.

The Biblical characters are shown as persons that, if we had lived in those times, we would have enjoyed meeting. Includes in these pages are God's monologue explaining why he decided to create the universe. Joseph was the first psychoanalyst. Queen Esther's diaries. Newspaper headlines at the time of Moses. Interviews with Goliath's mother and Samson's parents. A lecture by the prophet Jeremiah, and much more.

577

Family matters

David Mandel

This book tells the stories of four Jewish families, ancestors of the author, from small towns in Poland to faraway Peru, and, in the author's case, from Peru to Israel.

Mandel tells these stories with affection, irony, and delightful humor. His pleasant and clear style gives them his unmistakable personal seal.

The biographical and autobiographical stories that Mandel tells in this book constitute individual mosaics that, as a whole, give a panoramic picture that covers more than one hundred years and includes personal, family, and historical events.

The real issue, the true meaning of these family stories, is the tenacious survival of the Jewish people, as evidenced by the Mandel, Korngold, Braun, and Kerszenberg families.

Through the microcosm of four families, Family Matters illustrates the Jewish history of the last hundred years, including the tragedy of the Holocaust and the rebirth of an independent Jewish state 2,000 years after the Romans destroyed it.

ADVENTURES AND MISADVENTURES OF LUIS CABREJOS

Founder and only member of the Institute of Nameology

by David Mandel

In this delightful novel, the protagonist, Luis Cabrejos, doctor in Spanish grammar, founder and only member of the International Institute of Nameology, recounts in his "autobiography" his adventures and misadventures. These take him from his native Lima, where he studied in a school run by British teachers, to a university in Madrid.

Then, back in Lima, after being sent to prison, he later lives with a tribe of Indians in the Peruvian jungle. Finally, closing the circle of his saga, he returns to the school where he spent his childhood, but this time as a Spanish teacher. Cabrejos remains always, despite his misadventures, optimistic and enthusiastic, although he is plagued by an irrational obsession, similar to that of his former teacher whose place he now occupies.

The background of the story is a satire of the Latin American world of the 20th century, with its corruption and coups d'état.

Three Peruvian Stories
Viceroyalty, Independence, Republic

**The saga of a family of La Mancha that rose
from poverty to the presidency of Peru**

David Mandel

Three Peruvian Stores: Viceroyalty, Independence, and Republic, relate three different periods of Peru's history and constitute the saga of a family, from their humble beginnings in La Mancha, Spain, until the election of one of their descendants as President of Peru. In an amusing and entertaining style, the author mixing historical erudition with humor makes us feel the characters' contemporaries.

Doña Maria and the School Inspector

**A story of love and mushrooms
by David Mandel**

This book tells the story of Pedro Suazo, a school inspector, an ex-member of Lima's police force, and his romance with his landlady, the three times married, Doña Maria. It is a charming story of humor, irony, suspense and deceit told in the style of O. Henry. It is a fast-paced story that keeps your interest to its sudden yet quirky denouement.

The Autobiography of

MOSES

40 years searching for the Promised Land and all I get are complaints!

The Biblical story retold with zest and humor

By David Mandel

Reading the Bible was never so much fun! David Mandel, the autor of Who's Who in the Bible, has written a delightful version of the Biblical story, faithful to the original, but retold with humor and zest. "The Autobiography of Moses is an unparalleled combination of scholarship with humor. The result is wonderful entertainment.

"The Autobiography of Moses combines scholarship with humor. The result is great entertainment.

Operation Balaam's mule

**A satire of the BDS campaign
(Boycott, Divestment, Sanctions)**

by David Mandel

David Mandel's novel "Operation Balaam's mule" is a satire on the current BDS (Boycott, Divestment, Sanctions) anti-Israel campaign of delegitimization and false accusations of apartheid and genocide.

The author uses, with ingenuity and display of humor, the literary technique of the roman à clef presenting under the mantle of fiction situations and people, some with fictitious names and some with their real names.

The character of the financier George Tzures, who hires a group of people to accuse and condemn Israel, is based on the anti-Zionist billionaire George Soros who uses his fortune to support anti-Israeli organizations and campaigns.

Professor Asher Reubeni of the novel, anti-Zionist and pro-Palestinian fanatic, is inspired by Professor Ilan Pappe, self-exiled to a provincial university in England, author of history books that falsify and distort the historical facts.

Simultaneously, "Operation Balaam's mule" is a contemporary version of the biblical account of Balaam, the seer who was hired to curse the Israelite people but ended up blessing him.

A parody, updated and modernized

David Mandel has written a contemporary parody of the biblical book of Job, which is both funny and faithful to the original.

Made in the USA
Middletown, DE
04 July 2021